FINDING LOVE IN MICKLEWICK BAY

ELIZA J SCOTT

Storm

PUBLISHING

Ebook ISBN: 978-1-80508-544-7
Paperback ISBN: 978-1-80508-545-4

Cover design: Rose Cooper
Cover images: Shutterstock

Published by Storm Publishing.
For further information, visit:
www.stormpublishing.co

ALSO BY ELIZA J SCOTT

Welcome to Micklewick Bay Series

The Little Bookshop by the Sea

Summer Days at Clifftop Cottage

Life on the Moors Series

The Letter – Kitty's Story

The Talisman – Molly's Story

The Secret – Violet's Story

A Christmas Kiss

A Christmas Wedding at the Castle

A Cosy Countryside Christmas

Sunny Skies and Summer Kisses

A Cosy Christmas with the Village Vet

Heartshaped Series

Tell That to My Heart

To my family xxx

PROLOGUE

How was it possible to love anyone this much? Eighteen-year-old Alice Hutton gazed down at the bundle cradled in her arms. She'd never set eyes on anything so utterly perfect, the little button nose and rosebud mouth. Gently, she stroked her daughter's doll-sized hand and marvelled at her perfectly formed fingernails, so reminiscent of tiny seashells. In an instant, the small hand grasped her finger, squeezed tightly and sent a tidal wave of joy flooding through her chest. *Oh my days!* Alice felt certain her heart would burst at any moment. The fear that had crept over her in the run-up to this day had been engulfed by the overwhelming feeling of love that was now surging through her, infiltrating every fibre of her body and pushing the exhaustion of a sixteen-hour labour out of the way. Her baby was less than an hour old and yet she'd already managed to generate such powerful, almost primal, feelings it took Alice's breath away.

She rested into the stiff pillows of her bed, too wired for sleep despite the hospital's soporific warmth that belied the frosty January night. All was quiet on the maternity ward except for the background hum of medical equipment, the occasional voice from the corridor or the swift steps of a midwife walking by. It was almost midnight. Alice and her little daughter were the only ones awake in her bay, while the three other newly delivered mothers and their babies apparently slept soundly.

She may not have succeeded at much in her eighteen years, except for being a huge disappointment to her parents – and if what they'd said to her the last time she'd seen them was to be believed, she'd really excelled at that. Her now ex- boyfriend Johan hadn't been too impressed with her either for that matter, not that she cared what he thought now. But, despite the great list of failings and faults that had been hurled at her by both parties, there was one thing she was determined to do well. She knew it wasn't going to be easy, that the road ahead would be rocky, but Alice was going to do all in her power to be the best mum she could possibly be to this gorgeous little cherub, so warm and snug in her arms. She didn't need her parents, and she most certainly didn't need her waste-of-space ex-boyfriend. In fact, Alice decided, she didn't need anyone. She'd make a new life for them both, somewhere where nobody knew them. And she'd prove them all wrong; she'd make a success of herself, make her little daughter proud. Alice felt her determination soar. If there was one thing she had by the bucket-load, it was determination.

Buoyed by her new-found resolve, Alice smiled down at the two navy-blue pools blinking up at her. Speaking softly, she said, 'Hello there, little one, welcome to the world. I'm your mummy.'

She closed her eyes as she leant forward and pressed a gentle kiss to the baby's forehead, breathing in the delicious smell of newborn. Her heart swelled with emotion, triggering a lump in her throat, the burn of tears misting her eyes. Blinking them back, she said, 'I'm afraid it's just you and me, and I know I might not seem like much right now, but I promise you this,

I'm going to take good care of you and make sure you have the best life possible. We don't need anyone else. We're going to take on the world, show them we can do it. Just you see!'

With a sigh, she glanced out of the window. Though the light pollution of the city of York had watered down the Milky Way, it gladdened Alice to see that the stars were still visible, quietly twinkling away in the night sky.

It was while she was gazing up at the stars that a name came to her.

'Stella,' she said quietly, before repeating it as if trying it out for size. 'Stella.' She recalled reading that the name meant star, which sounded appealing and somehow appropriate in this quiet moment. She moved her gaze to her little daughter, as a smile spread across her face. 'That's it! That's the one!' she said softly as excitement tingled through her.

Though she'd drawn up a list in the knowledge she was having a girl, Alice had struggled to settle on a first name. Nothing seemed to appeal or feel right. Unlike her baby's middle name, which had taken no thinking about at all. Alice had already decided it was going to be May in memory of her beloved maternal grandmother to whom she'd been close until her death four years earlier. But as her due date had inched ever closer, a first name had remained impossible to choose.

Until tonight.

'Stella May Hutton. Perfect!' Alice smiled happily, dropping a soft kiss to her baby's brow. 'My little star.'

ONE

THIRTY-THREE YEARS LATER

Stella slid the off-white horsehair barristers' wig from her head and threw it onto the large table that occupied the centre of the oak-panelled robing room of York Crown Court, puffing out her cheeks as she did so. It had been a tough week, one she wasn't sorry to see the back of. Only a handful of fellow advocates remained at court, most heading off as soon as they could, intent on making the most of their Friday evening. And, much as she loved her job as a criminal barrister, today she'd be glad to shed her robes and head back home to Micklewick Bay on the North Yorkshire Coast.

'What's up, Hutton?' asked a plummy voice from the other side of the table, pulling her out of her thoughts. It wasn't unusual for members of the bar to address one another by their surname. 'Thought you'd be happy it's Friday at last.'

She glanced over to where the voice came from and released a noisy sigh. 'Hi, Ferdy, didn't see you sitting there.' She dredged up a smile. 'I can't tell you how happy I am it's Friday, but it's been a right pain of a day, that's all. Actually, make that it's been a right pain of a week.' Her North Yorkshire accent stood in stark contrast to the well-spoken tones of her fellow barrister, but Stella had never felt compelled to modify the way she spoke to "fit in" as some of her contemporaries had, which resulted in some amusing, affected tones. She shrugged off her black gown, dropping it onto the seat before her.

'Ah, yes, I'd heard you were the unlucky so-and-so who's prosecuting one of the notorious Dixon clan opposite Elliott; a dodgy duo if ever there was one.' Aiken Ferdinand KC pulled a sympathetic face, closing his laptop.

Stella nodded, reaching around to the back of her neck and unfastening the starched white collarette with its attached bands, pulling it free from where it was tucked in the jacket of her tailored black suit. 'Hmm. And don't I know about it.' She threw the collarette on top of her wig then smoothed her hands over her blonde hair that was tied back in the usual sleek ponytail she wore for work.

'*Ughh!* You have my sympathies. I've heard the case is a stinker and it won't be helped by the fact your opponent's a devious weasel. Wouldn't trust him as far as I could throw him.'

'Tell me about it. Thanks to Elliott's fannying about, and deliberately dragging his heels, the trial has run into next week which has meant I've had to return a manslaughter trial. The CPS aren't happy about it, but there's nothing I can do.'

Stella rolled her eyes as she headed over to the line of heavily polished, age-worn oak lockers, stopping at the one allocated to her and pulling out her red cloth brief bag that bore her initials embroidered in cream wool. She dumped it heavily on the table beside her laptop and papers, before opening it and fishing out her black metal wig tin, her name printed on it in gold lettering. Ferdy watched as she folded her robes neatly before pushing them into the roomy fabric bag, then grabbed her wig tin and placed it on top. That done, she tugged firmly on the bag's drawstring rope, ensuring it was closed.

'That really is rotten luck, Hutton. And I've heard the defendant's family have been giving you a rough time too, heckling from the public gallery.'

She released another weary sigh. She'd just passed them giving Vaughan Elliott an earbashing on the corridor, with the odd vociferous insult being hurled her way.

'Yeah, they have. There's no doubting where the defendant gets his charming personality. His father was shouting his mouth off about how his son was innocent and that if he's found guilty it'll be a travesty of justice. He conveniently appears to have forgotten his son's string of convictions for assault and aggravated burglary, not to mention drug dealing. All carried out before he'd celebrated his twenty-third birthday too, the little cherub.'

'I dare say the said little cherub will have picked up a few tips from his dear old dad Gav,' Ferdy said wryly. 'That family are trouble, and not one of them seem to be in possession of a conscience, as his father's outburst testifies.'

'Oh, without a doubt. He only quietened down when Judge Hoskinson threatened to hold him in contempt of court and send him to the cells.'

Stella decided not to share that when she'd glanced behind at the public gallery – which was something she rarely ever did – she came eye-to-eye with Gavin Dixon who was directing a menacing glare at her. The ferocity of the look had shocked her for a moment, sending a chill up her spine, but she'd kept her poker-face and quickly regrouped. There was no way she was going to let such an unpleasant bully intimidate her or interfere with her carrying out her job.

Ferdy gave an amused smile. 'Knowing Judge Hoskinson, it wouldn't take much for him to have him sent down to cool off.'

'Shame he didn't carry out his threat today which, I can confirm, really is officially the day from hell. The complainant's only gone hostile on me, refusing to give evidence, saying that it was all her fault and she'd asked for it because she'd provoked her husband.' Stella shook her head in disbelief. 'Not sure how she can blame herself for him giving her such a violent beating he'd ended up breaking her arm and three ribs. He's clearly been working on her, getting into her head. I just wish she could see that it's not her fault and he'll end up hurting her again.'

After what she'd witnessed from Gavin Dixon, she wouldn't have been surprised if he'd paid his daughter-in-law a visit and persuaded her to change her stance, but without proof there was nothing she could do.

'Hmm. Coercive controlling behaviour; it's nasty stuff, especially where the Dixon family is concerned. Seriously don't envy you with that one, Hutton.' Ferdy steepled his fingers as he observed Stella, the look in his eyes betraying his fondness for her.

Stella blew out her cheeks. 'She's now saying she loves him and wants to get back with him as soon as he's released from prison. She's been sending him letters while he's been locked up, signing herself as "wifey for lifey".'

'Oh, good Lord! Prosecutor's nightmare. Don't fancy your chances of winning this one.'

'I know,' she said with a groan.

If that wasn't bad enough, it was made a hundred times worse that counsel for the defence was Vaughan Elliott. He had a reputation for being the slipperiest barrister on the north eastern circuit, who'd try to pull a fast one whenever he could. Such underhand behaviour was viewed as bad form at the bar, but it didn't seem to bother him. It meant you needed your wits about you when you were involved in a case with him, and not because he was a decent lawyer. Stella would have preferred it if he was; she got a kick from a good bout of courtroom sparring. But Elliott had the knack of being disruptive in a trial and was regularly pulled up by the judge for asking leading questions or sneaking evidence in when he shouldn't, ambushing his opponents. He definitely didn't play by the rules.

'On top of that, I've got the case lawyer from the CPS breathing down my neck about it which isn't helping. She knows what Elliott's like.'

'If ever there was proof needed that the bar's no longer a gentleman's profession, it's there in the shape of Vaughan Elliott. How that shyster gets instructions beggars belief. If it wasn't for Brentley and Co briefing him he wouldn't have a practice. Their reputation is as dubious as his,' Ferdy said sagely.

'Very true.' Stella nodded her agreement. 'Actually, I've heard a whisper that Brentley and Co are being investigated by the Law Society.'

She headed back to her locker, pushing her brief bag inside. She turned the key, glancing over at Ferdy when she was done. Their eyes locked for a moment and a dart of attraction shot through her. At forty-eight, he was fifteen years her senior and an experienced barrister with a successful practice whose opinion she respected. She'd been known to run things by him, especially when she was newly out of her pupillage, interested to hear his take on a situation. In his twenty-five years at the bar, he'd developed a skill for sniffing out when things didn't add up, his eagle eye spotting the tiniest of lacunas in a case. Adding to this list of credentials he was good-looking in a tall, broad-shouldered way. His thick, dark hair, shot with the odd thread of silver, had a slight wave and was swept back off his face revealing a strong brow. He had a patrician nose which sat well with his square jaw, and a warm skin tone, thanks to the many trips he took to his villa in Nice. On top of that, he had a way of looking at you with his intense, blue eyes that made you feel you had his full, undivided attention. It was something he used to great effect in the courtroom, as well as on the female members of the bar, Stella included. His good looks combined with his affable, old-school charm and easy confidence meant he was never without a female companion, and also made him a popular member of the bar. However, his even temperament belied his courtroom persona. He possessed the skill to win a defendant round, making them believe he was on their side, before pouncing with a quietly savage line of questioning, knocking the unsuspecting accused individual off balance.

'Yes, I'd heard that little nugget too.' His eyes ran appreciatively over her curves that were clad in a sharply tailored black trouser suit, her three inch heels emphasising her long, slender legs. His gaze didn't go unnoticed by Stella.

'I dare say the rumour-mill will get into full swing soon, and all the sordid little details will become common knowledge. You know what lawyers are like for gossip.' She gave an amused smile as she reached under the table and pulled out the cabin case she used to transport her laptop, papers and, when she was in court out of the area, her brief bag. She lifted it up onto the table and placed her laptop inside along with her notepad and collection of brief papers relating to the Dixon case.

'I don't think I'm aware of a profession where gossip travels faster. Anyway, it's about time Brentley and Co got their comeuppance, they've been fleecing the Legal Aid Board for years. Can't stand them, especially their head honcho, Garfield Brentley. Despicable man.' Ferdy paused a moment, watching as Stella zipped her cabin case and lifted it to the floor. 'Don't suppose I could tempt you to a snifter at the Wig & Pen?' He raised his eyebrows in question. 'Maybe grab a bite to eat there?'

''Fraid not, I'm driving.' She knew the subtext of his words, knew where his invitation was heading.

'You could always leave your car here; head back to my place afterwards. I could drop you off in the morning.' He gave her an inviting smile, his eyes twinkling. 'Come on, Hutton, you know you'd enjoy yourself. If my memory serves me correctly, you certainly did the last time I suggested it.'

She smiled back. Any other night she might have been tempted, he was good company, had a great sense of humour, and he was right, she had enjoyed the last time they'd got together. Very much so. An image of them making their way to his bedroom, their clothes scattered everywhere, filled her mind. If it hadn't been a Friday, she'd have jumped at the chance, especially after the day she'd had, but not tonight. 'As good as your offer sounds, Ferdy, Friday evenings are when I meet my friends for a catch-up and nothing could stop me from joining them, especially tonight.'

'Ah, yes, of course, how could I forget?' he said with an easy-going chuckle. 'Friday evenings are strictly off limits for the rest of us mere mortals.'

'You got it in one.' She flashed him a wide smile. 'I'm outta here. Have a good weekend, Ferdy,' she called over her shoulder, blowing him a kiss before striding out of the robing room, pulling her case behind her.

At over six feet tall in her black patent designer heels, Stella cut a striking figure, with her strong, angular shoulders, athletic figure and sleek blonde hair. "Amazonian" was a term that had been used to describe her on several occasions. She exuded an air of "don't mess with me", her male colleagues in chambers regularly joking she could pack a bigger punch than all of them put together.

'With her sharp brain and already formidable advocacy skills, she'll go far and her rise will be stratospheric, mark my words,' her pupil master had said when asked if she should be offered a tenancy once her pupillage had ended. 'She's destined for the bench and she's exactly the calibre of barrister we need to nurture here.'

As she made her way across the compact city, her heels clicking over the pavement, Stella felt the tension of earlier begin to slip away. It wasn't like her to get rattled by a case, or opponent – or a sinister-looking relation of a defendant for that matter – but today's courtroom drama didn't rest easy with her. After the menacing look she'd received from the defendant's father, she found herself feeling grateful that her wig and gown went some way to disguising her appearance, as well as the dark-framed glasses she reserved for court work.

Her mind segued to the conversation she'd had earlier that morning. It was with Fay Norton, a silk from Newcastle chambers with whom she got on well. Fay had told her how she'd recently purchased a family history DNA test kit, since she was keen to learn her ancestry and find out if there was any truth in the rumours her mother's side hailed from Greece. It had set Stella wondering if she should invest in one. She was fully aware it wouldn't reveal the identity of her father, but it would at least give some clues to her background which was more than her mother had been prepared to do. Each time Stella had asked as to the identity of her father, Alice Hutton had clammed up, the conversation ending before it had even got started. Though it had been a while since Stella had last troubled her about it, her curiosity still swirled around at the back of her mind. One day, she'd find out who he was. Of that Stella was sure.

By the time she arrived in chambers, Stella had already made up her mind she wasn't going to hang around for long. She'd just nip into the clerks' room, have a brief word with Allegra, her clerk, update her on the situation with the Dixon case then head home. She didn't want to linger and run the risk of getting drawn into a conversation with fellow tenant, Simon Fagan, who'd been in court there earlier today. He had a reputation for being long-winded and mind-numbingly boring, going into minute detail whether he was talking about one of his cases or what he'd got planned for the weekend. He'd even managed to make a trip to Paris with his wife sound beyond tedious, which took some doing, Stella had thought at the time.

During the week, she'd hang back in chambers, get a decent amount of prep under her belt on the case in hand – provided

Simon Fagan wasn't holding court, of course – before leaving for home. Once back at her apartment, she'd continue poring over her brief, stopping only when she felt fully prepared for the following day in court. But Friday nights were different, Friday was the only night of the week when work was strictly off limits. It was reserved solely for her to switch off and catch up with her group of friends, which was something she looked forward to enormously. Meeting up with them all at their usual table, tucked away in a corner of The Jolly Sailors down in the old part of Micklewick Bay wouldn't come quickly enough this evening. The thought brought a smile to her face.

TWO

Stella had barely been in chambers for five minutes before she heard the monotone voice of Simon Fagan floating down from the room the junior barristers shared upstairs. It was all the motivation she needed to beat a hasty retreat. She bid the staff a speedy goodbye, wishing them all a good weekend, and made a dash for the door, leaving them all wearing a knowing look; Simon Fagan's reputation was legendary.

In the chambers' car park, she threw her cabin case into the boot of her silver hatchback A-Class Mercedes, climbed behind the wheel and selected her favourite Friday evening playlist, cranking the sound up. Moments later, she was inching out into the line of rush-hour traffic, singing along at the top of her voice, drumming her fingers in time to the beat. The Friday feeling was already kicking in.

The commute from York to the North Yorkshire Coast was one Stella relished. It offered the perfect amount of distance – mileage-wise and mind-wise – for her to put the stresses and niggles of the day behind her, shake-off her barrister persona and gradually unwind. She'd heard plenty of her contemporaries saying how their partners complained that they were still in "barrister-mode" when they got home, still primed for confrontation, some still strutting around as if they were taking part in a courtroom exchange. She couldn't imagine that working in a domestic setting. Only yesterday, she'd heard a colleague complain that her husband had told her she was behaving like a pompous twit – again. Stella was always mindful that she'd slipped out of her "barrister-mode" along with her wig and gown by the time she reached home – not that she was going back to anyone – she'd never been in a long-term relationship, the thought of sharing her home with someone else held no appeal for her – she'd go as far as to say it filled her with fear.

She'd be the first to acknowledge that once she'd donned her "pantomime dame" gear, as her friends jokingly referred to her wig and robes, she felt ready for her day in court. She often compared it to an actor getting into character for a role and was aware it was something a few of her contemporaries struggled to shake off. There was no way she would ever want to run the risk of taking her barrister behaviour home and directing it at her friends or her mum. And, heaven forbid, if she ever did, she knew none of them would be having any of it! They'd pull her back down to earth with a heck of a bang and give her backside a sound verbal kicking. She couldn't help but chuckle at that thought.

The sun was still shining by the time Stella arrived at her home town of Micklewick Bay, its rays glittering on the gentle undulations of the North Sea as she drove along the top promenade. Thanks to the mid-August sunshine, holidaymakers were still ambling along the broad pavement and a lengthy queue had formed at an ice-cream van that had parked up.

Stella felt a flutter of excitement in her chest as she made her way along the road to her new apartment. She'd only collected the keys from the estate agents last Saturday morning and was still settling in. Her mind went to the boxes that were piled up in the hallway. She'd been so busy with her work, unpacking them had proved to be a slow process. Her mum had kindly offered to help, but Stella had told her she'd prefer to do it herself; she knew where she wanted things to go and she didn't relish the prospect of having to hunt around for her stuff and ending up having to call her mum to find out where she'd put them. Thinking about it now, she should have taken the week off to move in, but the thought hadn't crossed her mind. She'd have felt unprofessional if she'd returned the Dixon brief at the last minute, especially with it concerning such a notorious family. And Stella didn't do unprofessional.

Arriving at the line of garages at the rear of the property, she stopped before the one allocated to her apartment and zapped her key in its direction. Seconds later, the electronic door slowly rolled back allowing her to slip her vehicle into the space.

She'd just climbed out of her car when her mobile phone pinged. Stella tapped the screen, smiling as she saw that it was a group message from Jasmine. It was in her friend's usual upbeat tone with a flourish of celebratory emojis.

Hiya lasses. It's Friyay! Woohoo!! Looking forward to seeing you all at the Jolly tonight! Jazz xxx

Stella fired a quick text back, her thumbs flying over the keys.

Hi Jazz, woohoo indeed! Looking forward to seeing you too! Sxx

That done, she slipped her phone into the pocket of her jacket, aimed her key fob at the garage door and watched as it slowly unfurled.

As she was making her way along the side street, her high heels tapping on the York stone flags, her eyes alighted on a man walking towards her. He was tall and broad-shouldered, with close-cropped dark hair. Dressed in jeans and a pale-blue linen shirt, he walked with an easy-going roll. Their eyes locked as they drew closer, and Stella felt the familiar punch of lust in her stomach. Wow! He really was out-of-the-way good-looking.

'Hi,' the man said in a voice that could melt chocolate. He flashed a lopsided smile, his clear blue eyes twinkling, triggering an unexpected flutter in Stella's chest.

Well, hello! Her interest had been well and truly piqued. 'Hi.' Stella returned his smile, her immaculately groomed eyebrow arching ever-so-slightly.

They maintained eye contact until they'd passed one another. Two strides later, Stella couldn't resist the urge to look over her shoulder, only to find him looking back at her. His grin widened and he raised his arm in a wave. Stella's heart gave an unexpected leap. *What the heck was that?*

Reaching the front of the imposing building and feeling slightly discombobulated by the unfamiliar feelings the stranger had stirred inside her, Stella tapped in the keycode for the over-sized front door, pushing it open with a swish. Her nose was instantly assaulted by the smell of fresh paint. A thrill rushed through her as she stepped into the communal entrance area which had been tastefully decorated in neutral shades, the walls adorned with black and white photographs of the former ware-house in its previous incarnation. Large olive trees in oversized terracotta pots stood either side of the door, softening the look.

The vast, former commercial building had stood empty for decades in what had become a less than desirable part of town. Built in 1801 from imperial sized bricks, it stood five storeys high and had originally served as a warehouse, passing through many hands during its lifetime, most notably the wealthy and titled Fitzgilbert family. It had been purchased early last year and work under instruction of a mystery buyer had begun in earnest once plans for its conversion to nine luxury apartments had been given approval. It had generated a great deal of local interest.

Though the building wasn't listed, it had managed to retain many of its original features, including the wood panelling in the entrance area as well as that in the ground floor room that had once served as an office. This space had also managed to cling onto the coving around the ceiling, though the cast iron fireplace had long since gone. The wooden staircase in the centre of the entrance area was simple in its design – as could be expected of such a building. Several treads had been replaced and were now covered with a thick, hardwearing wool carpet. Its original wooden banister, worn smooth from years of hands running up and down it and contributing to its rich patina, was found to be in perfect condition and had been polished to a deep shine. The old lift, to the left of the stairs, had been given a thorough overhaul too, bringing it up to today's safety standards while still retaining its original charm.

To the right of the stairs was a row of metal letter boxes, one for each of the apartments. They sat above a long wooden bench that had been left in the derelict building. It too had been cleaned up and painted in the same shade of dove-grey eggshell to match the walls and was accessorised by plump tweed cushions in complementing shades. Lighting was courtesy of a vast contemporary style pendant light with strategically spaced spotlights in the ceiling. The whole space exuded an air of quiet sophistication juxtaposed against a shadow of its commercial heritage.

The exterior of the building had been given a face-lift too, the bricks cleaned up, its mortar repointed. The old, rotten window frames, once filled with the gaping jaws of grimy smashed glass, had been replaced with metal-framed Crittal windows which sat perfectly with the industrial vibe. The style was echoed in the wide doorway, allowing extra light to flood into the entrance.

To the rear of the old warehouse, the large outside space that had been piled high with rubbish and rubble had also had new life breathed into it. It been skilfully landscaped and divided into eight narrow, but long gardens, one for each apartment.

The building had been transformed from a derelict eyesore into an imposing and desirable property.

When news of the proposed development of the old warehouse had broken and the virtual images of the completed apartments displayed on a noticeboard outside the property, a frenzy of interest broke out. There were to be two, small, one-bedroomed apartments on the ground floor, two, larger apartments on the next three floors, with the grandest of them all occupying the entire top floor. It boasted three vast, arched windows. The central one had a door added that gave out to a large, wraparound balcony. Completing the refurbishment, it had been fitted with a domed roof-light of impressive proportions.

Having been given a tip-off by her contact at the local estate agents, Stella had been quick-off-the-mark in paying a deposit to secure herself an apartment; she'd put her own on the market straight after. That too had been part of an industrial conversion, though on a smaller, less imposing scale.

Since then, the air of neglect that had hung around the area had slowly begun to slip away. Another disused building nearby had gone up for sale, complete with plans for its conversion into more apartments. No one was surprised that it was quickly snapped up. The small run-down row of terraced houses to the rear of Stella's apartment building were also undergoing something of a renaissance. And the rubbish that was usually strewn around the streets in that part of town had disappeared. It had spurred the local council to give the rusting metal railings that formed a barrier to the drop down to the bottom prom a new lick of paint.

The once grotty area, where people avoided straying after dark, had suddenly become rather desirable, and property prices had shot up rapidly. Stella was glad she'd snapped her apartment up when she had.

After retrieving her post from her pigeonhole, she made her way up the stairs to her second-floor apartment, eschewing the lift in favour of taking the healthy option and clocking-up some steps, as she always did. Somewhere up above, she heard the click of a door closing. Though she'd heard activity on the stairs and the whirr of the lift, the building had been relatively quiet and she was yet to meet any of her new neighbours; she guessed not everyone had moved in.

A feeling of calm washed over her as she entered the hallway of her new home. Leaving her cabin case at the door, she kicked off her heels and strode across the thick wool carpet through to the living room. She slipped her jacket off and lay it over the back of the sofa, then headed straight to the glass door that opened out onto the balcony. Pushing it open, she stepped outside, taking a lungful of the warm, salty air, the tiles refreshingly cool underfoot. She closed her eyes for a moment, opening them again and slowly releasing her breath. *Bliss!* Her gaze swept over the panorama, following the broad arc of golden sand, continuing along to the cove that housed Old Micklewick over in the right, and resting on the clutch of higgledy-piggledy fishermen's cottages that were nestled there. It was here where her friend Lark lived in the quaint, but tiny, Seashell Cottage on Smugglers Row. This old part of town was also home to her favourite pub, The Jolly Sailors, and where she'd be venturing to in a couple of hours' time. It was something she was looking forward to enormously. Looming over the cove stood the powerfully majestic Thorncliffe. Its brooding presence signalled the start of the huge line of cliffs that ran along this part of the North Yorkshire Coast, keeping the surging power of the North Sea at bay.

Hearing the sound of her mobile phone ringing, Stella reluctantly pulled herself away from the view and headed back inside, leaving the door open. She reached into her jacket pocket and pulled out her phone to see it was her mum calling.

'Hi, Mum. How's things?' Stella flopped down onto the large L-shaped sofa, stretching her long legs along its generous proportions.

'Hello, lovey, not bad thanks. How about you? Have you had a good day?'

'Put it this way, I'm glad it's Friday.' Stella twirled her ponytail around her fingers, her eyes scanning her new living room.

'Oh dear, that doesn't sound too good, but at least it's the weekend now.'

'Yeah, thank goodness.'

'Anyway, I was just ringing to say that I've spoken to Andrea and let her know you've moved. She'll be cleaning your new place on Monday mornings, same as she did at your other flat, as well as collecting your washing so nothing's changed there. And I've arranged it so she can clean the communal entrance area and the stairs on the same day too; makes sense.' Stella noted her mum had adopted her efficient tone once she'd switched to talk of work.

'Thanks, Mum. Organised as ever I see.'

'I just wanted to keep you up-to-speed with everything.' Her mum hesitated a moment. 'I also wanted to double-check you're still okay to come round for Sunday dinner?' Her voice, usually so sure, suddenly quavered with uncertainty.

'Course I am. I'm looking forward to it.'

'Thanks, lovey.' Another pause. 'I hope you'll like him.'

The sound of traffic floated up from the road through the

open balcony door. It was joined by a burst of laughter and the shrieking cry of a seagull.

'If he's making you happy, Mum, I already do.' Stella desperately wanted to believe her own words but she was still getting her head around the idea of her mum having a man in her life after all these years. It wasn't that she felt threatened or jealous, it was just that it felt *different*.

Her mother's relief was tangible down the phone line.

This new situation that had apparently softened Alice's usually tough persona was a first for them. Stella couldn't imagine how it would pan out, especially when it went against the steely advice her mum had drilled into her for as long as she could remember. 'Be independent, Stella. Don't rely on a man for anything, they only end up letting you down... Think twice about living with a man, you don't want him to have any claims on you... Never get emotionally attached to a man,' were amongst the many words of warning Alice Hutton had regularly espoused. Stella had never thought to question her mum or challenge her about her views. After all, she'd grown up in a single-parent home, with no father figure in sight, and she'd felt nothing less than loved and happy and secure. Why would she doubt the person she trusted most in her life?

'Righty-ho, lovey, I'd best get off. Enjoy yourself with the lasses tonight and I'll see you on Sunday.'

'Thanks, Mum. You have a fab night too.' Stella ended the call and set her phone down on the coffee table. She gnawed on her bottom lip a moment, lost in her thoughts. She knew her mother was seeing Rhys this evening. Would he be staying over? she wondered. Not that she wanted to dwell too much on that, but it was hard to imagine her mum putting up with anyone else in her home, never mind a boyfriend – if that was the correct term for her gentleman friend. The only people who'd ever been allowed to stay over were Stella's friends when they'd have sleepovers, or if she'd brought a friend home from university. It wasn't anything she'd given much thought to, until now.

Pushing herself up, Stella headed to the kitchen, running a glass of water, gulping it down thirstily.

She would await Sunday and meeting Rhys Baker with great interest.

THREE

Alice Hutton was a self-assured, successful businesswoman who'd never allowed herself to fall in love since her heart had been so cruelly broken by Stella's father, the charismatic, and much older, Johan de Groote – someone she'd seen neither hide nor hair of since she'd broken the news of her pregnancy to him. Now in her early fifties, Alice was still an attractive woman who took pride in her appearance, dressed well, and wasn't short of admirers. She'd ventured out on the occasional date since then but had remained resolutely single, refusing to let another man get close, determined never to be foolish enough to allow herself to fall in love again. The only love she'd welcomed into her heart was for her daughter, on whom she'd bestowed her affection generously and unequivocally. Until recently, when Rhys Baker had come into her life and Alice had felt herself warming to the faint stirrings of attraction.

Stella had gradually become aware that her mum had been dropping his name into conversations with increasing regularity. It had coincided with a change in her demeanour and an added sparkle in her eyes. Stella had found herself intrigued at this new version of the hitherto brisk, businesslike woman her mum usually presented to the world.

'So who's this Rhys. Would I know him?' she'd asked a couple of weeks earlier when she'd called round at her mother's house.

'Oh... um... I don't think so, he's a client.' Alice had struggled to meet her daughter's eye, the hint of a blush colouring her cheeks.

'Oh, right.' Stella had observed with interest, leaning against the kitchen worktop, mug of tea in hand. 'And is he a new one?' She'd done her best to rein in the urge to question her mum as if she were a witness in one of her cases, but it hadn't been easy; she'd been dying to find out more.

'Yes, quite new.' Alice had suddenly started busying herself, opening the kitchen cupboards as if looking for something, still avoiding eye contact. 'He's a very nice chap, actually. He's a businessman; he's very busy.'

He's very busy? Curious response. 'That's good.' Stella had taken a sip of tea in an attempt to smother the smile that had been tugging at her mouth. She'd peered over her mug, bemused at the sight of her mum looking flustered; she'd never seen her like this before.

Eventually, Alice had stopped and stood up straight, brushing her hair off her face. She'd taken a deep breath and said, 'Actually, Stella, he's become more than just a client.'

Stella had set her mug down, her interest well-and-truly piqued. 'He has?'

Alice had nodded, swallowing audibly. 'I've been out on a couple of dates with him. Well, more than a couple actually. And the thing is, lovey, I've grown quite fond of him.' She'd clasped her hands to her chest in a most un-Alice-like way. 'And he says he's very fond of me.' She'd risked a glance at her daughter, her face still flushed.

Stella's heart had swelled with love for her mum; she was

glowing. But she'd also felt a little niggle of uncertainty, for which she'd quickly remonstrated herself. After all, didn't her mum deserve to be happy? Didn't she deserve to enjoy being in a relationship? Didn't she deserve to be loved by a man again?

Stella had tried asking a few more questions about Rhys, wondering how long they'd been dating, where he lived, how long he'd lived in the town, but talking about him had made Alice appear uncomfortable, and her answers had become increasingly brief. It had generated an awkward atmosphere between the two of them and, as much as she was keen to know more about Rhys, and where he'd suddenly sprung from, Stella had found herself having to resist the urge to dig further. Her job dealing with criminals and unsavoury characters had made her wary and suspicious of everyone until she'd got to know them. Instead, she'd smiled warmly and said, 'Well, I'm happy for you, Mum, really I am.'

Relief had washed over her mum's face. 'Thanks, lovey. It's all so new, it's taking a bit of getting used to.'

You're not kidding!

Though Stella and her mum were close and their love for one another ran deep, they both shared the same air of independence, with neither of them keen to live out of the others' pockets. Their conversations usually revolved around work and friends, or what was happening in the town or events or parties they'd attended. Alice had never quizzed her daughter about her love life, and Stella had never had any need to ask her mum about hers since it had been non-existent. Which was why it was such a novelty to Stella now.

It was fair to say Stella didn't share the same kind of closeness that her friend Florrie had with her own mother. The pair spoke on the phone several times a day and rarely went a day without seeing one another. And nor would Stella want to. Stella respected what Florrie had with her mum, Paula, but would have found that kind of closeness stifling. It didn't mean what she had with her mum was in any way a lesser or inferior relationship, it was just different. She knew her mother was there for her if ever she needed her, and she was there for her mum in return. Indeed, the bond they shared was invincible. After all, they'd only ever had each other. Until now.

FOUR

Alice had fulfilled the promise she'd made to her newborn daughter thirty-three years earlier. *I'm going to take good care of you and make sure you have the best life possible.* Her words had regularly revisited her over the years, and she'd marvelled at just how far they'd come, the two of them.

Not long after leaving hospital, Alice had packed up the few belongings she had in her bedsit in York and quietly slipped away to the small, cheap flat she'd found in Micklewick Bay. She hadn't bothered to tell her parents where she was going. The hurt had still been too raw from their cold-hearted refusal to meet their little granddaughter, after telling Alice they'd washed their hands of her. Disowned her. As far as they were concerned, she'd thrown her life away by getting herself pregnant and keeping her baby.

Alice had been stunned by their reaction. Despite the fact she'd told herself she didn't need them, she'd talked herself into giving it one last try. She'd clung onto the hope that her parents would soften once their grandchild had been born, that Stella's arrival would override their initial shock of Alice's unplanned pregnancy and their hearts would melt as they'd cradled the baby in their arms. Instead, their cruel rejection had set a mix of hurt and anger swirling around inside her. They'd left Alice in no doubt they weren't going to change their opinion any time soon.

Their words had hurt more than she could ever have imagined, but as she'd made her way back to her bedsit, her sadness morphed into a burning determination to prove them wrong. She hadn't thrown her life away! She hadn't ruined things! Her life was simply following a different plan to the one they'd had so meticulously mapped out for her for as far back as she could remember. And she wasn't sorry about it. Not one little bit.

Her parents had both been doctors – her father a GP, her mother a consultant neurologist – and they'd been so efficient at drumming into Alice that she wanted to follow in their footsteps as she'd grown up she'd actually begun to believe it herself. It was only when she'd taken her GCSEs that doubts had started to creep in, but she'd been too afraid to rock the boat by telling her parents that medicine was the last path she wanted to head down. Instead, she'd had aspirations to work towards a business degree, and had harboured a desire to set up her own company, which, if the passion it inspired within her was anything to go by, she'd felt sure she could make a success. Alice wanted to be her own boss, wanted to be in charge of her own destiny, instead of being told what she should do and having very little say in any decision-making that involved her.

By the time it came to enrolling on a university course, she'd grasped the nettle and told her parents of her wishes. She'd been disappointed – though not at all surprised – to find her ideas met with outrage. Didn't she realise she'd be the fourth-generation medic in her family? Did she want to be the one responsible for breaking that pattern? What would the rest of the family think? Didn't she realise they'd be ridiculed? In the end, after having been thoroughly browbeaten, Alice applied to med school, her hopes and dreams trickling away before they'd even got started. Her parents had been overjoyed when her applications had been accepted and she'd been offered several places. Alice had felt weighed down by their expectations, her heart heavy with dread.

It was halfway through her first year when she'd fallen pregnant, shattering her parents' dreams so spectacularly. They'd gone so far as to accuse her of doing it on purpose, so she didn't have to complete her degree. Even though she'd anticipated an explosive reaction, Alice hadn't expected it to trigger such a cavernous divide between them and her.

At a time when she'd needed them the most, they'd withdrawn their support and turned their back on her.

Once in Micklewick Bay, it hadn't taken Alice long to realise that her parents' cold-hearted rejection of their granddaughter had given her the perfect excuse to follow her heart. So she'd dried her tears and set her plans for a new life in motion. Onwards and upwards! There'd be no looking back, she'd told herself, a new-found determination coursing through her veins. After placing cards advertising her laundry services in the local shops and on the town's noticeboard, her phone was soon ringing with enquiries.

Taking in other people's washing and ironing had proved the perfect solution to her earning some much-needed cash, especially since she hadn't been able afford the childcare she'd need to go out to work. Alice had been thrilled when word of her high standards and efficiency spread so quickly. Before long, she'd gained a regular list of clients, with crisply starched shirts and fresh-smelling bedding being her speciality. It had been hard work, juggling a baby and copious amounts of laundry, ironing into the early hours, but it had been worth it. She'd squirrelled small amounts of money away at the end of each week, feeling a sense of satisfaction as her savings slowly grew.

When Stella started at the local playgroup, Alice had taken on a couple of cleaning jobs – in addition to her laundry services – increasing her days once her daughter had started school. This extra cash had meant they'd been able to move to a small, terraced house with a postage-stamp of a garden where Stella had loved to play.

The day Alice had walked away from her parents' home, her heart aching and their hurtful words ringing in her ears, had seemed a lifetime ago.

By the time Stella had reached the age of eight, Alice had completed an online business degree which had armed her with the skills required to set up Spick 'n' Sparkle Cleaning Services in which she used the eco-friendly, essential oil-based cleaning products she'd developed herself. A year later, her services had been in such demand, the company had expanded and Alice had two members of staff on her payroll.

Fast forward five years, and Spick 'n' Sparkle's glowing reputation had sky-rocketed. It now boasted ten employees – all carefully selected by Alice for their high standards – with its award-winning cleaning products standing proudly on the shelves of all the big supermarkets. Alice soon discovered she no longer had the time to go out and clean houses or take in laundry herself. Instead, she'd found she needed to focus her attention on the business and admin side of things, though it didn't mean she wasn't prepared to roll up her sleeves and help out if they were a member of staff down.

Her early dreams of setting up a business had come to fruition. And she'd proved her parents wrong.

In quiet moments, Alice had often found herself reflecting on how, though she'd become a mum at a young age, it had, hands down, been the best thing that had ever happened to her. Which made it even harder to comprehend how easily her parents had turned their back on her, their only child. She'd made a silent vow to herself that she wasn't going to let history repeat itself. She'd never put her daughter under the pressure she'd faced growing up. Instead, Alice would encourage Stella, give her every opportunity to follow her own dreams, while offering gentle support whenever it was needed. She'd also encourage her daughter to be self-sufficient; after her own experience with Stella's father, she didn't want her daughter to rely on a man. It was fair to say, Alice had been a good role model, instilling a strong work ethic in Stella, without being overbearing. But most importantly, she'd make sure Stella knew she was loved, and that her thoughts and feelings were valued and important.

Which is exactly what Alice had done. Though she'd be the first to admit it hadn't all been plain sailing, and she hadn't got it right all of the time, particularly when Stella had hit the teenage years head-on. To say there'd been fireworks would be an understatement! With their personalities being so similar, it had resulted in some spectacular clashes! But Alice had done her best, and had made sure the pair had never gone to sleep on an argument and that a bad atmosphere hadn't dragged out for days. Talking, and sharing thoughts and feelings had been encouraged – Alice hadn't always appreciated what had come out of these talks, but she'd bitten her tongue as best she could and tried her hardest to see things from her daughter's point of view. As a consequence, the pair enjoyed a close relationship, without it being stifling. Alice had taken great pride in watching her daughter grow into a kind and thoughtful young woman who'd carved out a successful career at the bar, with no pushing at all from her corner.

It wasn't until recently that she'd begun to wonder whether being such a strong proponent of staying single, and advising her daughter to keep romantic relationships at arm's length had been the best idea.

FIVE

After a quick shower, and a spritz of her favourite crisp perfume, Stella threw on a sleek maxi-dress in a shade of ice-blue that emphasised the colour of her eyes – as with her work attire, she favoured unfussy, clean lines. She added a simple silver necklace and fixed her hair in a loose chignon. That done, she pushed her feet into her white leather trainers, hooked her designer cross-body bag over her shoulder and grabbed her cardigan before setting off for The Jolly Sailors pub.

The walk to the Jolly in Old Micklewick, which was the oldest part of town, took a little longer from her new apartment, but tonight she was glad of it after a day spent cooped up in a stuffy courtroom. The air was still balmy and warm, the sky above a clear, bright blue, seagulls cawing in the distance. She crossed the road and made her way along the top promenade, a spring in her step as she savoured the generous vista of the beach. At just gone seven o'clock, it was still busy, folk squeezing every last bit out of the day's sunshine, enjoying a stroll or walking their dogs; this late in the summer, you never knew when autumn was going to come calling. Stella continued along the path, swerving round a loved-up couple who were ambling along at a leisurely pace. Her attention was drawn to a car that was crawling by, its windows down, music bouncing. It appeared to be jam-packed with teenage boys who were in high spirits if the laughter and ebullient conversation was anything to go by. She caught the eye of the youth in the front passenger seat, he turned to his friends and in the next moment a chorus of wolf-whistles and leering calls broke out. 'Really?' Stella shot them her best icy glare, the one she usually reserved for the courtroom. Hadn't they heard that sort of behaviour wasn't acceptable? Her look appeared to have silenced them and a moment later, the driver revved the engine and shot off. She rolled her eyes in disgust.

The annoying interlude aside, Stella was enjoying her walk along the prom, delighting in the light breeze that brushed over her skin, lifting the loose tendrils of her hair, the stresses of her day in court loosening its grip. Her mind went to the handsome stranger she'd seen earlier, wondering if he was a visitor to the town or if he was a local – if the latter were the case, she hadn't seen him before, but then again, though Micklewick Bay wasn't the biggest of towns, new people moved in all the time, especially since the housing estate had been built on the edge of town. She found herself hoping she'd bump into him again, the thought making her heart flip. *What's going on there?* She felt suddenly disconcerted by this unexpected reaction.

Deliberately marshalling her thoughts in a different direction, she glanced up at the tall, five-storey Victorian houses that lined the promenade, affording it an exclusive air. All had well-tended window boxes or oversized pots by their doors, filled with artfully arranged plants. And all were immaculately kept, a sense of neighbours trying to out-do one another pervading the haughty terrace. Stella often wondered what the houses were like behind the perfectly painted, huge front doors. This area, situated high on the cliffs, was considered the "new" part of town, with the grand houses starting life as the holiday homes of the wealthy who'd fallen in love with the beautiful beach and the sea-bathing that was fashionable at the time. All of the properties had since been spliced-up into smaller, more affordable, apartments and sold off. What hadn't changed though, was the glorious view of the beach and the imposing line of cliffs, the mighty Thorncliffe taking centre stage.

Tearing her gaze away from Thorncliffe, Stella's eyes landed on a tall, dark-haired man walking towards her. In his hand was a dog lead attached to a young Labrador with huge paws who was trotting along jauntily. Her heart leapt and butterflies took flight in her stomach. It was the handsome stranger who only moments ago had filled her mind! Their eyes locked as he drew nearer, making her stomach loop-the-loop.

'Hi – again,' he said in that deliciously rich voice, his smile lighting up his bright-blue eyes that momentarily fell to her mouth. The waggy-tailed Labrador pulled towards her but was given a gentle tug of his lead accompanied by a quick, 'Fred! No!'

'Hi again.' Stella's heart was now jumping wildly about her chest, her eyes fixed on the handsome stranger. Using her well-honed courtroom techniques, she did all she could to steady herself as he walked by, a lazy smile tugging at his mouth. *What is wrong with you, woman? Get yourself under control!* She felt utterly wrong-footed by the strength of the emotions rushing around inside her. She'd never experienced such an overwhelming attraction to anyone before and it took every ounce of her strength not to look back, the urge seemingly impossible to resist. It wasn't like her at all, she usually oozed confidence with the opposite sex, kept her cool, especially with those to whom she was attracted, but this felt different. *Way, way* different. And she wasn't completely sure she liked it. But the temptation not to snatch a look behind her was proving to be too great, and before she knew it, she'd turned, her gaze meeting that of the handsome stranger's. He flashed her a cocksure smile and a flick of his eyebrow then continued on his way.

Annoyed at herself, Stella marched on, determined to push him out of her mind. Tonight was all about switching off and having a laugh with her friends. It most certainly was not about letting a man dominate her thoughts, even if he was drop-dead gorgeous in a broad-shouldered, smouldering kind of way and, in fact, just her type.

With that, she switched her mind to her new apartment and the large black and white photo she'd seen in Lark's Vintage Bazaar – a shop in town, owned and run by her friend Lark. It stocked an array of vintage clothing and accessories along with other intriguing finds Lark hadn't been able to resist on her searches and travels. The photo would be perfect for hanging above the state-of-the-art electric faux fire that was set into the chimney breast of the lounge. But it wasn't long before she found her mind wandering again. *If I've seen him twice in a short space of time, Mr Hot is very probably living or staying nearby. Which means, there's a good chance I'll bump into him again...* That thought made her feel inordinately happy.

The narrow steps that led down to the bottom prom and the beach were busy with people making their way back up to town, so Stella continued along to Skitey Bank, instead taking the path that edged the steep, twisty-turny road. She was still doing all she could to keep her thoughts from straying onto Mr Hot, but it was proving easier said than done when his handsome face insisted on appearing in her mind.

Soon her long legs were striding past the higgledy-piggledy stack of lobster pots and small boats that lined the seawall, the smell of seaweed lingering in the air as she drew closer to where the Jolly was nestled below the cliffs. She wasn't surprised to see the pub's sunny terraced area jam-packed with drinkers and diners, their laughter and chatter filling the air.

'All right, Stella,' a voice called from a table in the far

corner. She glanced over to see it belonged to Nate, owner of a local upcycling business, who was keen on her friend Lark. He had a bottle of beer in his hand and was wearing his familiar easy-going smile, his rosy face betraying the fact he'd spent a chunk of the day in the sun.

'Hi, Nate. Had a good day?' She smiled back.

'Aye, not bad, thanks. You?'

'It's better now I'm here.' Stella gave a laugh. 'I'll see you later,' she said as she continued along the age-worn path.

'Righto.'

As she made her way closer to the door, the jaunty sound of folk music joined the gentle lapping of the sea against the shore. She stepped inside the low doorway of the quirky, whitewashed building, that had occupied the spot for several centuries, and was instantly met by the mouth-watering aroma of the pub's signature dish of fish and chips. *Mmm.* The delicious smell jolted her appetite into life with a start, making her realise just how hungry she was, her lunch all but a distant memory.

The heavily beamed bar area was already heaving with the usual locals and a generous dash of holidaymakers. Stella headed in the direction of the polished oak bar, its shiny brass beer pumps gleaming under the soft glow of the repurposed hurricane lamps that were fixed to the walls. 'S'cuse me,' she said, smiling politely as she squeezed by a group of friends who were deep in conversation. Her gaze went to the table by the old inglenook fireplace that was always reserved for her group of friends on a Friday evening. Being so tall meant she could easily peer over the crowd, and she spotted Maggie sitting opposite Lark, the pair chatting away. She caught Maggie's eye and her friend gave her a friendly wave, causing Lark to turn and beam at her. Spotting a bottle of wine already on the table, Stella took a detour from the bar and made her way over to them; she'd grab another one later.

'Hiya, lasses.' Stella smiled as she slipped onto the settle beside Maggie, her thoughts finally drifting away from Mr Hot. 'Been here long?'

'Hiya, Stells,' Lark and Maggie chorused warmly as Stella unhooked her bag and set it down on the settle beside her.

'I've just got here,' said Lark, reaching for the bottle of Pinot Grigio that was propped in the ice bucket. She poured a glass for Stella, her armful of bracelets jangling. Lark was looking ethereal as usual in a boho-style sundress in muted rainbow colours, trimmed with sparkly beads. Her long, wavy blonde hair hung loose around her shoulders, a silk rose fixed above her ear.

'And I wasn't much before,' said Maggie. She was wearing a loose-fitting cotton shirt in a delicious shade of tangerine that hid her small baby bump. Her chestnut curls were scooped up on top of her head and tied in a lime-green scarf, while her glowing complexion was topped off with a sprinkling of freckles that danced across her nose and cheeks.

'Florrie says to tell you she's running late – not like her, I know, something to do with a phone call with an author that overran – she's still stopping off for Jasmine on her way down though,' said Lark. As a rule, Florrie, who was co-owner of the local bookshop, would call for Jasmine on her way to the Jolly of a Friday evening, Jasmine being the one who was usually running late. Maggie, who lived at the other end of town at Clifftop Cottage, always arrived on her own, as did Stella who lived further out, while Lark lived close by in a tiny cottage on one of Old Micklewick's narrow, twisting paths.

'Fair enough.' Stella picked up the glass of wine and sank back in the settle, the easy-going atmosphere of the Jolly washing over her. She gave a contented sigh. 'I can't tell you how happy I am it's finally Friday evening and I'm sitting here with you.'

'Aww, Stells,' Lark said in her familiar soft tone, reaching over and giving Stella's arm a sympathetic rub. 'And we're glad to be sitting here with you too, flower.'

'Had a rough one, Stells?' asked Maggie, before taking a sip from her glass of lemonade, the ice cubes rattling. 'Don't tell me there's problems with the new apartment?'

Stella shook her head. 'No, everything's fine with that; I love it.' She couldn't help but smile as an image of it popped into her mind. 'It's just my oppo at work, he's been really dodgy, constantly trying to pull a fast one.'

'Is he the one you mentioned before? Always trying to sneak things in he shouldn't? asked Lark.

Stella nodded, her top lip curling in disgust. 'Yep, he's the one, Vaughan Elliott. Doesn't help that he's a total slimeball and makes my skin crawl. Honestly, a conversation with him makes you feel like you need to take a shower afterwards.' She shuddered at the mere thought of him.

'Eeuw! I can't bear that sort.' Maggie pulled a face.

'Me neither,' said Lark, her nose wrinkling.

'Bloomin' 'eck! What's up with you lot? From the expressions you're wearing anyone would think there was a horrible stink around here.'

The three turned to see Jasmine smiling at them, her bright green eyes offset by her dyed-red pixie crop. She was wearing a loose, white shirt over her favourite khaki combat trousers. Florrie was standing beside her and, despite the warmth of outside, she was looking surprisingly cool in a Breton-striped T-shirt and cropped navy linen trousers.

'Please tell me it's not cos you've got downwind of my plimsolls,' Jasmine said with a chuckle. 'I have to admit, they're a bit rank; reek like a well-rotted compost heap. I'm going to have to leave them outside tonight when I get home; should keep the vampires away.'

'Hiya,' said Maggie, laughing. 'Thanks for sharing that, Jazz.'

'Now then, lasses. Yeah, you sell yourself well, Jazz.' Stella grinned.

'I do my best.' Jasmine grinned back.

'Hi, all,' said Florrie as she eased in beside Lark who was struggling to contain her giggles.

'Talk about TMI, Jazz,' Lark finally managed to say.

'Hey, I reckon it's only right I warn you.' Jasmine pulled out the chair at the top of the table. 'Anyroad, sorry we're a bit late – for once it wasn't me running round like a loony.' She pointed her thumb in Florrie's direction. 'It's all down to her ladyship here.'

Florrie splayed her palms. 'Jazz's right, and I'll share the reason for it once you lot tell us why you were all pulling a face – I'm sure it's not because of Jazz's pongy plimmies.'

'I wouldn't be so sure,' Jasmine said with faux seriousness.

'We'll let Stells tell you,' said Lark as she busied herself pouring the new arrivals a glass of wine each.

'Ah, that explains things perfectly,' Jasmine said, nodding once Stella had finished her story. 'He sounds like a total creep.' She gave a shudder.

'He so does,' said Florrie. 'But if anyone can handle a bloke like that it's our Stella.'

'Hmm. I'd really rather not have to though, but you're bang on the money, Jazz, he is a total creep,' Stella said. 'Moving swiftly on, and to a much more palatable subject, I gather the reason you were uncharacteristically late was owing to a conversation with an author.' She hitched an enquiring eyebrow at Florrie.

'Yep, come on, Florrie, spill,' said Maggie. 'I'm dying to hear how it went.

Florrie's face lit up, a wide smile spreading across her face. She pushed her glasses up her nose, her dark-brown eyes shining. 'Well–'

'Actually, before you start, flower,' Jasmine said, resting her hand on Florrie's arm, 'seeing as though I know what you're going to tell them, why don't I go and put our food order in before we get stuck behind a great long queue? I could eat a scabby horse between two mattresses, I'm that hungry, and I don't think my stomach would take it well if it had to wait.'

'Best get that order placed, then, Jazz.' Florrie laughed.

'Too right.' Maggie pulled a faux concerned face.

'Usual all round?' Jasmine cast an enquiring glance around the table as everyone answered in the affirmative.

'So,' Florrie continued, tucking a strand of her brunette bob behind her ear. 'I've been trying to build the courage to contact Thea Carlton, with a view to organising a book signing with her, for ages – she's the romance author from Northumberland.' She threw a quick glance between them. 'I knew it was a long shot, but Ed and I thought it was worth a try. I mean, the worst she could do was say no; wouldn't be the end of the world. She doesn't seem to have an agent, so I contacted her directly on social media. Honestly, I got the shock of my life when she replied!'

'Wow! Thea Carlton! Florrie, she's a *big* name!' Lark's pale-green eyes grew wide.

'She so is! And how did it go?' asked Maggie. 'Please tell me you've been successful. I *love* her books.' She clutched her hands to her chest.

Stella couldn't help but smile at Florrie's enthusiasm. The previous year, her friend had inherited half shares in The Happy Hartes Bookshop in the town's Victoria Square and had worked tirelessly to make the once flagging business a success. Florrie and her partner Ed – of both the romantic and business variety – were always thinking up exciting new ideas to bring the bookshop up-to-date and widen its appeal. The window displays, designed and created by artist Ed, had been growing increasingly elaborate and had garnered much local interest. The shop's footfall had also had a helping hand when nationally renowned Yorkshire poet and author Jack Playforth had moved to the area and had as good as become the bookshop's in-house author.

'I have! Oh my goodness! I can hardly believe it!' Florrie's face was wreathed in smiles as she clasped her hands to her face. 'Honestly, I was so nervous when I saw she'd replied, but she was really lovely and friendly. She offered to do a reading too. Can you believe that?' Florrie glanced around at them.

'That's fantastic, Florrie! I'm so pleased for you. Thea Carlton is hugely popular, it's a real coup for the bookshop.' Stella beamed at her.

'It is! It's brilliant news!' Maggie reached across and squeezed Florrie's hand.

'Oh, Florrie, how wonderful.' Lark's eyes shone with happiness. 'Mr and Mrs H would be so proud of you.'

'Right then, that's grub ordered.' Jasmine returned, plonking herself back in her seat, chasing away the shadow of sadness that had momentarily clouded Florrie's eyes at the mention of her old bosses. 'Fab news, isn't it? I mean Florrie's about Thea Carlton, and not that I've ordered our food, though I have to say, that's pretty fabulous news too.' She gave a hearty chuckle.

'It's awesome.' Stella's heart filled with happiness for her friend, glad to see her looking so settled and content. The previous year had been a tricky one for Florrie. Her beloved boss Mr Harte, to whom she'd been close and thought of as a grandfather – or Mr H, as she'd called him – had passed away suddenly and had stunned her by bequeathing fifty per cent of the bookshop to her. The other half he'd willed to his grandson Ed. This had outraged Mr H's estranged son and daughter-in-law, who'd demanded that the shares be handed over to them. On top of that, Florrie's fledgeling relationship with Ed had almost ended before it got started. It had been a stressful time for her in the midst of her grief for the loss of Mr H. Thankfully, after taking legal advice that informed them Mr H's will had been expertly drafted and was as watertight as was possible, Ed's parents' anger appeared to have burnt itself out, and Florrie and Ed had got back on track, their relationship stronger than ever.

'So when's it happening?' asked Maggie, just as a lively tune struck up from the folk band in the corner, accompanied by much foot tapping and clapping.

'Well,' said Florrie, leaning in to make herself heard above the music, four pairs of eyes looking at her expectantly, 'the good news is, owing to Thea Carlton's other commitments, and the fact that she's going to be in the area at the time, it looks like it's going to be on the twelfth of September, which is three-and-a-half weeks' time.' Florrie's smile grew wider. 'And I can't quite believe I'm saying this, but she squeezed us in specially.'

'Go you, Florrie,' said Maggie, beaming.

'That's brilliant! I reckon it'll be tickets all round for us lot,' said Stella, smiling, her friend's happiness infectious. 'Here's to our Florrie!' She held her glass aloft and the others followed suit.

'Here's to our Florrie,' they all chorused enthusiastically.

'Anyroad, enough about me, how's the new apartment, Stells?' Florrie asked, her eyes still sparkling.

Stella took a quick sip of her wine. 'Well, I've still got a few boxes to empty but other than that, I'm loving it. Having a balcony door I can fling open and let the breeze float in is just wonderful, especially in this warm weather – might be a different story when winter sets in and a raging north wind howls in from the sea.' She laughed. 'And I know the views from my old apartment were good, but with the warehouse being at an angle to the prom, they're even better from my new place; I get the most amazing view of the cliffs.'

'Ooh, sounds dreamy, can't wait to see it. Which leads me nicely on to asking when's the housewarming party going to be?' Maggie grinned before taking a generous swig of her lemonade.

'Well, I was actually thinking next Saturday night, if that fits in for everyone. It'll be incentive for me to get the remaining boxes unpacked.' Stella glanced around at her friends. 'How about you, Jazz? Do you think you'll be able to get a babysitter?'

Jasmine nodded enthusiastically. 'Wild horses wouldn't keep me away. Oh, and you've got to let me make you a house-warming cake.'

'You don't need to do that. Haven't you got enough on your plate without giving yourself the extra burden of making a cake for me?'

'Not at all, I insist, and besides, it's never a burden if it's for one of my besties.' Jasmine beamed at her.

'Well, if you're sure, then it sounds lovely. Thank you, Jazz.' Stella smiled warmly at her friend.

'You might not be thanking her if it's anything like the one she did for a hen party a couple of weeks' back,' said Maggie, pulling a mock horrified expression. 'Who knew penises came in lime-green or shocking pink with bright orange stripes?'

'You've clearly led a sheltered life, Maggie Marsay,' said Florrie, through her giggles.

Stella gave a hoot of laughter causing heads to turn at nearby tables. 'Florrie Appleton, you dark horse! And here's us thinking you were Little Miss Prim-Knickers!'

'My thoughts exactly,' Lark said, giggling.

'Come on then, you're going to have to tell us where you've seen such wildly coloured appendages. Are you referring to Ed's, I wonder?' Stella waggled her eyebrows mischievously, making the friends splutter with giggles and further piquing the interest of the other diners.

'And what about Jazz? Where on earth have you seen any like that to model them on?' Lark asked, barely able to speak for laughing.

Jasmine snorted. 'Hah! I wish! I've just been going from a vague and distant memory. It's been that long since I've seen one in the flesh, if you'll excuse the expression. The chief bridesmaid said she wanted something outrageous and colourful with a penis theme, so...' She gave a shrug. 'I followed her brief to the letter. Here, I've got a photo on my phone – of the cake, not vibrant penises, so you can calm your jets, Stells. Here, you can see for yourselves.' Jasmine fished her phone from her bag, the others watching as she selected the photo. 'There, what d'you think?' A wide grin spread over her face as she handed her phone to Florrie beside her. 'Pass it round.'

'Wowzers!' said Florrie, her eyes wide. 'The one in the middle's... um—'

'Would have your eye out if you weren't careful,' said Lark, causing the friends to dissolve into further giggles. 'What do you think of that, Stells?' she asked, handing the phone over to her.

Stella scrutinised the image, pushing her lips into a pout. 'Actually, penis theme aside, I think it's actually very creative and expertly executed,' she said, wrestling with a smile.

'Mmm. Me too,' said Maggie peering over at it. 'Mind, I'll bet you've never seen any willies that colour, Stells, even with your vast bedroom experience.' She shot her a mischievous sideways look. Stella's colourful love life often attracted much teasing from her friends, which she always took in good spirit.

'Can't say I have, nor any covered in glitter, for that matter.' Stella returned an amused smile. 'But there's always a first; maybe this Christmas.'

Just then, a familiar cackling laugh spliced through the chatter of the room courtesy of craggy-faced local fisherman Lobster Harry. He was a permanent fixture at the Jolly when he wasn't out to sea in his ancient trawler, much to his wife's chagrin.

'Well, that thought tickled Lobster Harry, Stells,' Lark said dryly, causing the friends to collapse into a further bout of raucous laughter.

Stella swiped tears of mirth from her cheeks, her face was

aching from laughing so hard. This was just the light-hearted tonic she needed after her stressful week; her friends could always be relied upon to make things better. She glanced over at Jasmine, her heart squeezing with affection for her. Jasmine always seemed to be negotiating stress, albeit for different reasons to her own, yet she always seemed to be upbeat, never let it faze her or get her down. Stella often found herself thinking she'd rather deal with the sort of hassle she was faced with at work, rather than the variety Jasmine had to navigate. To make matters worse, the poor lass had her deceased partner's parents to deal with, and they were a nightmare, always intent on making her life difficult and having nothing to do with their grandchildren. It was another good reason not to get emotionally entangled with a man – not that Stella needed any more convincing.

Jasmine was a single mum of two, whose partner had died six years ago. She held down three jobs and always seemed to be dashing around, whether it be taking Zak and Chloe to their after-school classes and parties, or heading to her next job – she not only worked as a cleaner for Stella's mum, but she did several shifts at Seaside Bakery, the shop two doors down from The Happy Hartes Bookshop. Making celebration cakes had started out as a side-hustle to boost her earnings so Zak and Chloe didn't go without, but over the last year it had really taken off, her skilfully crafted designs speaking for themselves, including cakes decorated with penises apparently.

'What are you lot cackling about?' The friends looked up to see Ando Taylor standing by their table, a half-drunk bottle of Micklewick Mischief in his hand. His familiar back-to-front baseball cap was set at a cock-eyed angle on top of his thinning long, blond hair. His usual teenage-youth-style get-up of slashed jeans, brightly coloured trainers and battered leather jacket belied the fact that he was well into his forties.

'Now then, Ando,' said Maggie, smiling up at him. 'Having a good Friday night?'

Ando was generally regarded locally as something of a beach-bum and a bit of a daft lad. But in recent months, the friends' opinion of him had softened thanks to his quick thinking in calling for an ambulance when Maggie had been involved in a traffic accident a few weeks ago. He'd also called Florrie so she could sit with her best friend until the ambulance arrived. He'd further stuck his neck out and offered a statement to the police as to the identity of the driver who had shot out in front of her so recklessly. It had been non-other than Jasmine's father-in-law, Gary Forster, who had fled the scene and denied it was him until paint samples taken from the bump in the side of his car proved to be a perfect match for Maggie's little vehicle. The statement had caused Ando a huge amount of grief, with him being hounded by the Forsters for "wrecking" their lives.

'Aye, it hasn't been bad so far.' He nodded. 'You keeping okay, Maggie? You're looking well after... well... I mean since, you know.' He shuffled awkwardly from foot to foot.

'I'm doing fine, thanks, and so is the baby.' She beamed at him, patting her bump.

'That's grand news.' The warmth of his smile suggested he was genuinely pleased to hear it. His gaze fell to Jasmine. 'Now then, Jazz,' he said in a familiar Yorkshire greeting. 'You're looking fit there.'

'Now then, Ando. Thanks.' She gave him a small smile, her uncertain expression betraying she was anticipating his next question; the one he now asked on a weekly basis.

'Don't suppose you fancy letting me walk you home tonight? I can grab us a packet of pork scratchings to share on the way back, maybe stop off at my place, finish off the last of my home-brew. Admitted it's a bit rank, like, but it hits the spot if you can stomach the taste. I've called it Gut Rot, you know, like this is called Micklewick Mischief.' He flashed her a leary grin, waving his bottle of beer at her.

Stella fought to contain the bubble of laughter that was rising inside her. She pressed her lips together, resisting any eye contact with her friends.

'Thanks for the offer, Ando, but I'm afraid it's a no again,' Jasmine said kindly. 'Like I've said before, I haven't got time for a fella in my life, and I'll have to get home to the kids.'

'Aye, well, fair do. You know where I am if you change your mind. Have a good night, lasses.' With that, he turned and sauntered off back to the bar, pulling on his bottle of beer.

'Aww, bless. You've got to hand it to him, he's a trier,' said Lark in her familiar gentle tone.

'You're not kidding,' Jasmine said wearily.

'And how could you reject the offer of pork scratchings, Jazz?' said Stella, amusement dancing in her eyes.

'Or his home-brew, what was it? Ah, yes, Gut Rot. Yum,' said Florrie.

'Yep, who said romance is dead?' Stella added dryly.

'Well, at least he wasn't plastered this week, which is a consolation, I suppose,' said Maggie.

'That may be so, but why me? Why do I have to attract blokes like that?' Jasmine shook her head in disbelief. 'I don't want to be unkind, and I know Ando means well in a... whatever it is kind of way, but seriously, pork scratchings and "Gut Rot"? Who'd be tempted by that? Not that I'm looking for a fella at all, but why don't I get the ones who want to sweep me off my feet with flowers and boxes of chocolates and meals in fancy restaurants?' Jasmine looked around at them. Though her tone was light-hearted and she was smiling, there was a sadness in her eyes.

'Jazz, the honest truth is, you wouldn't want a bloke that fits that bill,' Stella said.

'I'm with Stells on that one, I'm afraid, Jazz.' Lark nodded in agreement.

Jasmine's expression was thoughtful for a moment, before a grin crept over her face. 'True,' she said with a chuckle. 'I hate that kind of mush, and as for fancy restaurants, they're so not me.'

'Especially not with those stinky plimsolls, Jazz.' Maggie chuckled into her lemonade.

Jasmine scrunched up her face. 'Hmm. I reckon you're not wrong.'

'Maybe you should stick 'em under Ando's nose; that'd send him running for the hills.' Maggie chortled.

'Good point.' Still smiling, Stella's gaze drifted across to the door, her eyes alighting on the tall, handsome stranger who'd just walked in. Her heart leapt and her mouth fell open. *Oh my days! Mr Hot!*

SIX

'You okay, Stells?' asked Florrie, her forehead creasing.

Stella swallowed and took a steadying breath, her pulse surging around her body. *Pull yourself together, woman! What the heck's got into you?* 'Hmm, er, yeah. I'm fine.' She smiled brightly at her friend. 'Just wondering when our fish and chips are coming.'

'Aye, they've been a while.' Jasmine twisted round, a slow grin spreading across her face. 'Fish and chips, eh?' She turned back. 'I reckon our Stells' ovaries have just exploded – *again* – lasses. Take a gander at the hot looking bloke who's just wandered in.'

'Which hot looking bloke?' Maggie peered over to the object of their interest, Florrie and Lark following her gaze. 'Ahh, I *see*,' she said, giving Stella a knowing smile.

'And just how many times can ovaries explode exactly?' asked Florrie.

'Numerous times if our Stells is anything to go by; hers are always going bang. Whenever she claps eyes on a fella that takes her interest, that's it. Boom!' Jasmine grinned, turning to take another look. 'Mind, I can see why; he's right up her street, tall, dark and delicious. That's the criteria, isn't it, Stells?'

Stella rolled her eyes, shaking her head good-naturedly.

'Ah, and he's got a gorgeous Labrador with him,' said Lark, peering around Florrie. 'If he's a dog-lover he must be nice.'

'See, he's already got Lark's seal of approval, Stells.' Maggie gave her an exaggerated wink.

'I reckon we need another bottle of wine.' Stella reached for the empty bottle in the ice-bucket and got to her feet. 'Won't be a moment.' She flashed them a smile before striding in the direction of the bar in her usual self-assured manner, aware of her friends watching her closely.

Standing beside Mr Hot, the fresh scent of his cologne wafted under her nose. It was clean and mossy, setting Stella's senses on high alert. It didn't take long before he turned to face her, their eyes meeting, sending a pulse of attraction through her. His mouth turned up in a smile that made her heart rate take off at an alarming speed.

'Hello there.'

'Hi.' She returned his smile, taking in the blue of his eyes, how they crinkled at the corners, the dark stubble of his strong jaw. He stood a good few inches above her, making him at least six-foot-three, and his shoulders, which looked decidedly good in his blue shirt, seemed even broader close up. He really was just how Jasmine had described, tall, dark and delicious.

'Seems we're destined to meet.' He gave a barely discernible hitch of his eyebrow, still holding her gaze. The Labrador looked up at her, its tail swishing back and forth.

'You would think so, wouldn't you?' Aware of her heart beating rapidly, Stella drew in a slow, deep breath. She was attracted to him and was in no doubt he was attracted to her; she'd been in this situation many times before, but this felt different. She needed to get a grip on the unfamiliar emotions currently hurling themselves around inside her. 'Are you new to town or just here for the day?'

'I'm new; just moved in this morning. Thought I'd leave the unpacking, head out and get a feel for the place.' She noted his North Yorkshire accent had a polished edge to it.

'Hmm. Good plan. And do you like what you've seen so far?' She wound a tendril of hair around her finger and tilted her head coquettishly.

His eyes fell to her full lips. 'Mmm. Very much so,' he said, his voice taking on a husky tone. A frisson of attraction danced in the air between them. The Labrador sat down, he clearly thought they'd be there some time.

'Who's next, please?' Mandy, the Jolly's landlady called, her cockney accent standing out amongst the local voices. 'Who's next in the queue?' she asked again. But her words had fallen unheard by Stella and Mr Hot, each apparently as reluctant as the other to break eye contact.

Stella was utterly lost in the moment.

'Oy, laddo, do you want to order a bloomin' drink or what?' The rough tones of Lobster Harry, who was standing behind Mr Hot, jarred them back to the present. 'Some of us are gagging here, while you're too busy making eyes at her ladyship.'

Stella snapped her gaze away from Mr Hot, shifting them to the fisherman, whose familiar mariner's hat she'd spotted earlier, hanging from the nipple of the reclaimed figurehead at the other end of the bar. The thought that he must be sweltering in the navy-blue gansey he always wore crossed her mind. 'Sorry, Harry, you're welcome to go before me if you're desperate.'

'Aye, too right I'm bloomin' desperate, 'specially with this red-hot weather we're having.'

'You might want to take that sweater off then, Harry, mate,' said Ando Taylor, looking down at his short, stocky friend. 'That'd cool you down a bit.'

'Don't be so daft, lad. I never take me gansey off! Our lass'd have me guts for garters. How else d'you think they'd be able to identify me if I had an accident somewhere out of town? Thought you knew this pattern's only worn by fishermen from Micklewick Bay! Soft lad!' Lobster Harry shot him a look of outrage.

'But you're hardly going to get swept out to sea in here, are you?' said Ando, wearing a confused expression. 'And I thought you said you'd never been out of Micklewick Bay other than in your boat.'

Lobster Harry gave him an unimpressed look. 'That's beside the point. Anyroad, out me way, I've got a pint glass here, needs topping-up with some of that Micklewick Mischief; right good stuff it is.'

Stella and Mr Hot stood back, sharing an amused smile as Harry pushed his way to the front of the queue.

'I'm Alex, by the way, Alex Bainbridge, and this young rascal is Fred,' Mr Hot said when things had quietened down.

'Hi, Alex, hi, Fred.' Stella bent to ruffle the Labrador's soft ears. 'You're cute, aren't you?'

'I assume you're addressing Fred and not me?' Alex said teasingly when she stood upright.

'You assumed right.' She couldn't help but laugh. 'And I'm Stella.' She held out her hand. 'Stella Hutton.'

'Good to meet you, Stella Hutton.' He took her hand, his touch sending a bolt of electricity shooting up her arm.

Wow! What was that? Her eyes flickered and she looked at him, wondering if he'd felt it too. Had his smile faltered momentarily, or was it just her imagination? she wondered, as colour rose in her cheeks.

'Good to meet you too,' she said when she'd gathered herself together. 'So which part of town have you move—'

'Sorry I'm late, Al,' said an out-of-breath female voice beside them, cutting Stella off.

'Oh!' She was startled to see a young woman with a dark ponytail and a pretty heart-shaped face link her arm through Alex's. She was gazing up at him, smiling broadly, affection in her eyes. Fred's tail-wagging went into overdrive. She was clearly a regular fixture in "Al's" life. Stella felt her anger spike. How could Mr Hot think it was acceptable to flirt so blatantly with her when he had a girlfriend? It was a perfect example of why she was right to keep men at arm's length. If there was one thing Stella really didn't like, it was cheating rats.

She was pulled out of the moment by Immy, one of the Jolly's servers, who leant into her, giving her arm a quick squeeze. 'Just so you know, flower, your fish and chips are waiting.' Her cheeks were flushed from dashing in and out of the kitchen.

'Oh, righto, Immy, thanks.'

'No probs.' Immy flashed a grin before hurrying off.

Stella glanced up at Alex, pushing her mouth into a smile. 'Right, well, it was nice to meet you but I'd best get back to my friends,' she said coolly. Giving him no time to reply, she turned on her heel and headed back to the table where she spotted her friends regarding her with interest.

'How did it go?' asked Florrie, her eyes wide.

'Who's that woman who just came in?' asked Maggie.

'More importantly, where's the wine?' Jasmine pulled a "seriously?" face.

'Oh, blast!' Stella bumped the heel of her hand against her forehead. 'I forgot it. Sorry, lasses.'

'No worries, we can ask Immy to fetch one when she brings the gravy and mushy peas.' Lark smiled at her. 'She'll be happy to do that.'

'Aye, good thinking.' Lark's suggestion seemed to appease Jasmine.

'So, in answer to your questions,' Stella placed her napkin on her lap, 'all was going swimmingly, and we were having a good old flirt, until...' She left a loaded pause, picking up her knife and fork.

'Until what?' asked Florrie.

'Until his girlfriend arrived.' Stella glanced around the table. 'Oh, and his gorgeous Labrador's called Fred, by the way,' she said matter-of-factly, hoping her friends didn't detect the disappointment that was, for some strange reason, clawing at her insides. It was annoyingly distracting.

'You're kidding?' Jasmine said, her face falling. 'He's seriously got a girlfriend? I mean, we all saw the way he was looking at you, didn't we, lasses?'

'Yeah, he looked like he was really into you, Stells.' Lark gave her a sympathetic look while the others responded with a series of nods and words of agreement.

Stella was relieved to hear it wasn't just her who'd got the body language so spectacularly wrong.

'Looks like you had a lucky escape there, flower. Thank goodness you found out before things went any further.' Florrie gave her a small smile.

'I wouldn't care but I can usually sniff out a cheating rat a mile off. My radar must be off-kilter with all this heat.' Stella gave a hollow laugh before tucking into her fish and chips, doing all she could to push Alex Bainbridge out of her mind. But it was proving difficult. His behaviour had got her stirred up. Stella already had issues with commitment thanks to her father walking out before she was born. As a teenager it had played on her mind relentlessly, his actions piercing her heart, though she'd never admit to it. He couldn't have expressed his lack of interest in her any more explicitly if he'd tried. The result of which had been that Stella had built a wall around her heart, it growing more impenetrable with every passing year. This, combined with her mother's attitude to relationships, meant Stella had never let a man get within reach of her heart.

One man had got closer than most, but as soon as she had felt the first stirrings of something that went beyond friendship or lust, Stella had backed off, warning sirens sounding loudly in her head. There was no way she was going to make the same mistake her mum had, and expose herself to hurt and heartache. Ben, a fellow barrister, had been devastated, telling her he'd fallen in love with her, but his words had only strengthened her resolve and she'd exercised greater caution since.

'Right then,' said Lark, pulling Stella back to the present, 'I think we're just about caught up with all our news except for our Maggie here. How's things going with the very fabulous Micklewick Bear Company?'

'I still feel like I'm dreaming actually.' A wide smile lit up Maggie's face. 'As you know, the logo for Campion's has been finalised as have the designs for their signature teddy bear. I'm also just about caught up with my orders thanks to Jean's help; she's amazing I don't know what I'd do without her.'

Maggie created handmade bears out of reclaimed luxury wool and had recently been approached by Campion's of York – a once luxury store that was undergoing a renaissance under its new mystery owner. Their flagship store was now based in the quaint market town of Middleton-le-Moors, and Maggie had been approached by their head buyer with a proposal to make a range of signature teddy bears as well as designing a new company logo. She'd been initially torn about whether she could accept such an offer with a baby on the way, but a well-loved local lady by the name of Jean Davenport had stepped in with an offer of help. Long-since retired, Jean had been a close friend of old Mr and Mrs Harte of The Happy Hartes Bookshop and, as a consequence, had become a good friend of Florrie's, helping out at the bookshop's readings and book club. It turned out she was also a proficient seamstress and now worked for Maggie on a part-time basis.

'Wow! Sounds like things are really taking shape for you, Mags.' Stella smiled at her, pleased to see her friend seemed to have put her accident behind her.

'And Jean's loving working with you,' said Florrie. 'She called in this morning, full of chatter about it.'

Maggie smiled. 'That's so good to hear.'

* * *

The evening passed in a bubble of banter and laughter as it always did with Stella and her exuberant group of friends of a Friday evening. Alex Bainbridge had only sneaked into her mind a couple of times but she'd refused to dwell on what might have been. She'd been relieved to see him leave the pub with his girlfriend a good hour earlier, allowing her to relax.

Before they knew it, Mandy was ringing the old ship's bell that hung above the bar, calling for last orders.

'Blimey, is that the time already,' Lark said, draining her glass.

'Time seems to run away with itself when we get together,' said Jasmine.

Their drinks finished, Maggie fished into her bag for the Land Rover keys. 'Right, lasses, who wants to try out Bear's new Landie and have a lift home?'

All but Lark, who lived no more than two strides away in Seashell Cottage along Smugglers Row, and Stella, who said she wanted to clear her head, accepted the offer.

'Much as I'd love to have a whizz around in it, I'll decline for now, thanks, Mags,' Stella said. She regularly walked home alone, the streets of Micklewick Bay being safe to do so.

Standing outside the Jolly, darkness had descended and a

clear sky splashed out above, the pub lights stretched out, illuminating the garden area. The gentle hush of the tide inching towards the sea wall was punctuated by the cries of a solitary seagull.

Lark pulled Stella into a hug, setting her bangles jingling as they slid down her arms. 'Good luck for Sunday, Stells. I'm sure it'll go well, Rhys must be nice if your mum likes him.'

'I reckon Lark's right,' said Maggie, the others all agreeing.

'Thanks, you lot.' Stella was grateful for their support. She'd texted her friends earlier in the week and shared the news about her mum's invitation to meet the new man in her life. They'd all replied with a slew of positive texts and calls, no one being judgemental or issuing warnings. Their responses had gone some to easing the doubts that had lurked in her mind.

'Let us know how you get on,' said Florrie, resting her hand on Stella's arm. 'And you're always welcome to pop and see me if you feel you need to chat.'

'Thanks, Florrie, that's kind.' Stella smiled down at her.

'Sure you don't want a lift?' Maggie asked. 'It's gone a bit nippy.'

'Positive, thanks, Mags, I've got my cardigan.'

Stella watched as the Land Rover's lights disappeared around the corner on its way to Skitey Bank, the low rumble of its engine growing distant. Drawing in a deep breath, she made her way towards the bottom prom, the cool air creeping in from the sea slipped over her skin, triggering an eruption of goosebumps and making her shiver.

She'd just shrugged her cardigan on when she heard a voice behind her.

'Don't shposhe I can tempt you to a glash of Gut Rot, can I, Shtella?'

Stella's heart sank. Sharing a ropy glass of Gut Rot with a stewed Ando Taylor wasn't quite how she'd hoped to end her

Friday night, especially when she'd anticipated getting to know a certain tall and handsome stranger a little better.

'Not tonight, thanks, Ando.' She hooked her cross-body bag over her shoulder. 'Night then,' she said, striding off before he had a chance to engage her in any further conversation.

SEVEN

Stella pushed her earbuds into her ears as the main door of her apartment building clicked shut behind her. Dressed in her running gear, with her hair tied back in a high ponytail, she jogged across the road. With a quick check of the time on her activity tracker, she began her run. She relished this time of morning, before the town properly came to life and started to buzz with activity. From up here on the top prom, she could see that the beach was practically deserted but for the odd dog walker and the die-hard pod of surfers bobbing about on the waves. A haze hovered over the horizon, while a pale-blue sky stretched out above, the sun shimmering on the sea; the promise of another gloriously sunny day ahead. But for now, the air held on to the crispness of dawn, making it the perfect temperature for an early morning run. It was something Stella did every Saturday and Sunday morning without fail, provided the weather wasn't prohibitively inclement. On such days she put her treadmill to good use. She could forget about work and fill her lungs with fresh sea air. For all she would be pushing her body to the limits, it was a time when her mind was calm. It was how she switched off best.

She pounded the pavement, her long legs making short work of it, soon passing the impressive feat of Victorian engineering that was the cliff lift – or funicular, to give it its proper title; a complex structure involving pulleys and water-filled weights. In no time, she reached the one-hundred and ninety-nine steps that led to the bottom prom. She tripped effortlessly down each one, music from her earbuds thrumming in her ears. Reaching the bottom, she crossed the wide path and hurried down the handful of steps where she made her way nimbly over the broad bank of pebbles, seaweed-infused air filling her lungs. In the distance, Thorncliffe loomed over the bay exuding its familiar air of brooding power. With her feet sinking into the soft sand, making progress slow, Stella followed her usual route, heading towards the retreating sea where the sand, dotted with wormcasts, was still damp, making it a firmer base on which to run.

With a broad arc of golden beach stretching out in front of her, Stella upped her pace, running parallel to the tide, arms pumping like pistons, breathing hard through her mouth. Soon, beads of perspiration peppered her brow and she felt a trickle of sweat make its way between her shoulder blades and travel down her back. A sense of euphoria pervaded her body as she ran through the burn, pushing herself ever harder, faster. Stella was in her element. She liked nothing better than to challenge herself whether it be in the courtroom or here on the beach. Running like this, driving herself on, her lungs and muscles burning until endorphins surged through her, gave her a huge buzz.

As she ran, Alex Bainbridge crept into her mind, the memory of his blue-eyes twinkling at her, causing her wayward heart to give an unexpected – and unwelcome – lilt. What had he been playing at? she wondered. From the first, albeit brief, moment their eyes had met the previous day, he'd sent out the kind of signals that said he was available, that he liked what he saw, that he was interested. They were the sort that tested the water, wanting to know if his interest was reciprocated. Stella had had enough experience of men to understand the rules of this dance and in her book, they definitely weren't the kind of signals a man who was in a relationship should be giving out. Her blood began to boil at the thought. *The arrogance of the man!* And what a foolish risk he'd taken, flirting so openly with her when he was expecting his girlfriend to arrive at any minute. Stella scrunched up her eyes and gave a shake of her head. 'Loser!' She spat the word out in an angry gasp. And, no doubt, in typical fashion, though she'd been the innocent party, she would have been the one to look bad, not him. Unjust as it was, that's how it often went in such situations. She felt anger churn in her stomach. She'd had a lucky escape there. And one thing was for certain, if she had the misfortune to bump into Alex Bainbridge again she'd be sure to give him a very wide berth. Not for the first time, her brush with him had only served to confirm her decision not to get emotionally attached to a man.

Steaming on, she glanced at her activity tracker, a sense of achievement rushing through her as she realised she'd reached the long, angular limbs of the pier in her quickest time so far. Her anger with Alex Bainbridge had clearly spurred her on. *At least he's been good for something!* That thought raised a smile from her.

She pushed on, seagulls wheeling and screeching overhead, the sound of a dog barking in the distance. She wiped her brow with the back of her hand, puffing out her cheeks as she drove herself faster, harder. *Come on, Stella, you can do this!*

In the next moment she spotted a gangly black Labrador lolloping towards her, ears flapping, tongue lolling. Stella's eyes went to the figure running behind it, her heart sinking as she gave an inward groan. *Ughh! No! Please tell me it isn't him.* The Labrador leapt up at her, pressing sandy paws all over her running gear, amber eyes shining happily, and bringing her to a halt. 'Hello, Fred,' she said, through gasps, ruffling his ears, unable to resist his friendly greeting.

'Fred! Sit!' Alex Bainbridge finally reached them. He was panting heavily and sweat from his forehead had turned his dark hair wavy. Though she did all she could not to stare, Stella couldn't help but notice his impressive biceps and strong, muscular legs. Why did he have to be so attractive? Somewhat annoyingly, she found herself thinking it a shame he was taken.

'I'm really sorry. Has he made a mess of your running gear?' Alex asked, his breathing coming in short bursts, concern creasing his brow.

'No, it's just sand, it'll brush off.' Her tone was cool, her chest heaving as she caught her breath.

'Ah, good.' He rested his hands on his hips, a half-smile on his lips. His eyes searched her face, clearly sensing something was wrong.

Fred looked up, glancing between them, his tail still wagging hard, oblivious to the air of awkwardness between his dad and his new friend.

'Right, I need to get off.' Stella tightened her ponytail before bending to give Fred a pat. 'Bye, Fred, nice to see you.'

'Oh, okay.' Alex looked at her nonplussed, the usual sparkle in his eyes dimming as his smile faltered.

'Bye,' Stella said curtly, before setting off at a trot, quickly upping her speed, eager to get out of earshot in case he had anything further to say. The urge to turn round was agonising but she was determined not to give him the satisfaction. She wasn't playing his games anymore.

Before long, she was back at her apartment building, her heart thudding, Alex Bainbridge still occupying way too much of her mind. *Why have you let the loser get under your skin?* She slipped her trainers off at the main door, banging the sand off them before she went inside; there was no way she was going to leave a trail behind her and risk the wrath of Andrea who cleaned the communal area. That done, she ran up the stairs, a feeling of happiness enveloping her as she stepped inside her apartment. She'd have a quick shower, do a spot of shopping and then head over to the village of Danskelfe on the moors where she was booked in for a hot-stones massage and a facial at her new favourite beauticians. After the week she'd had, she couldn't wait.

* * *

With the top down on her sporty Mercedes, Stella headed towards the moors, the wind rushing over her skin and ruffling her hair. It was an area she'd visited many times since childhood, enjoying trips out with her mum or her friends and their families. Today, the heather was out in all its glory, covering the moors in a dense blanket and filling the air with the sweet scent of honey. As she negotiated the twisting, narrow roads, Stella delighted in the stunning scenery, the broad dales peppered with farmsteads, the little chocolate-box-pretty villages. Lytell Stangdale was a favourite, with its quaint thatched cottages, their gardens brimming with blowsy summer flowers. Sheep roamed freely around the moors and its villages, and she found herself having to slow down on several occasions while a ewe and its lambs made their way idly across the road. Game birds were another thing she was sure to keep an eye out for, pheasants in particular had a happy knack of scuttling out in front of you, as if out of nowhere.

Soon, Stella found herself at the beautician's, stretched out on the beauty bed, a towel over her, inhaling the soothing scent of aromatherapy oil while tranquil music murmured softly in the background. She'd had her facial, which had been wonderful, the luxurious products had smelt sublime. Now Rachel was running hot stones over Stella's back, the penetrating warmth soothing her muscles. It was bliss, and just what she needed after her nightmare of a week.

Though her mind had wandered, she'd made a concerted effort to keep thoughts of Alex Bainbridge at bay, as well as her mum's new boyfriend. Instead she'd focused on her new apartment, picturing the amazing view of the cliffs and sea.

The soothing rhythm of the massage had worked wonders at clearing her head. Before she knew what was happening, Stella was aware of Rachel speaking softly. She blinked slowly. Had she drifted off?

'All, done, Stella, I'll leave you to get dressed. Don't feel you have to rush, just when you're ready.'

'Thanks, Rachel, that was wonderful.' Stella inhaled slowly, she felt so chilled she could quite happily stay there all day.

EIGHT

The metal gate gave a reluctant groan as Stella pushed it open, the soothing scent of lavender swirling in the air as the skirt of her dress brushed against the plants that lined the path to number five Magnolia Gardens; her mum's Victorian terraced house on the other side of town.

A wood pigeon cooed from a nearby rowan tree, joining the muted rumble of a lawnmower further down the road. Uncertainty bloomed in Stella's chest as she clicked the gate shut, wondering how the afternoon would pan out. She'd tried to imagine her mum in the company of a man since she'd first learnt of her relationship with Rhys Baker, wondering how she'd behave. It had proved a difficult image to conjure. Thus far, Stella had only ever seen her mother in the company of men whom she'd believed to be no more than friends. She'd never been introduced to the few who'd taken her mum out to dinner; they'd never lasted more than five minutes anyway, but now she was beginning to wonder if she'd been given a true picture. After all, thirty-three years was a long time not to have had a romantic relationship. But then again, Stella had countered, she couldn't imagine herself being tied down to someone for even a fraction of that time! She and her mum were cut from the same cloth, she'd told herself, so maybe it wasn't so unbelievable. One thing she did know for sure was, as much as she was keen to get to know the man who'd so suddenly become a feature in her mum's life, she hoped she'd like him, for her mum's sake more than anything else. Stella would struggle to hide her feelings if she didn't.

She was halfway down the path, when the door was flung open, and her mother appeared, her cheeks flushed. 'Stella!' Alice's shoulder-length, highlighted blonde hair had been fluffed out and she was smiling broadly. Only her blue eyes betrayed the fact that she was feeling anxious. It was an expression Stella had rarely seen from her usually self-assured mother. And if the pretty dress that flattered her trim figure and her carefully applied make-up was anything to go by, Stella could see that her mum had made an extra effort today.

'Hi, Mum.' Smiling, she stooped to kiss Alice's cheek, inhaling an unfamiliar perfume. 'Ooh, you smell nice, and you look very pretty; I'm loving that dress.'

'Thank you, lovey.' Alice's hand went to the floaty fabric of her sundress, smoothing it down. 'I spotted it in a shop window when I was in York last week; thought I'd treat myself, got some new sandals too. The perfume's a present from Rhys.' Stella noted the tiny quaver in her mum's voice and how her gaze flickered momentarily away.

'Ah, must be serious if he's buying you perfume,' Stella said, teasing gently.

'Oh, I don't know about that, it was just a gift.' Brushing away the comment, Alice gave her daughter's arm a squeeze, the colour in her cheeks deepening. 'Thank you for coming, we're just in the garden. Rhys thought with it being such a lovely day, we could have a barbecue; better than sweltering away indoors over a roast dinner.'

'Mmm. Couldn't agree more.' Stella pushed her sunglasses

up onto her head and followed her mum down the neat, high-ceilinged hall, the delicious aroma of a barbecue floating down to greet them.

'Can I give you these, Mum?' She fished the bottle of white wine, encased in a padded cooler, and box of chocolates from the leather tote bag she'd had slung over her shoulder. 'The wine should still be chilled but I'm not so sure about the chocolates. I reckon they've probably melted in this heat. Sorry.' She pulled an apologetic face as she handed them over.

'Ooh, thank you, lovey, I'm sure they'll be fine, but you really needn't have bothered.' An air of distraction hung around Alice, a nervous smile hovering over her mouth as she set the gifts down on the table. 'Rhys is outside, come on, let me introduce you to him.' She paused, fixing Stella with a pointed look. 'And please give him a chance, no courtroom cross-examinations, okay?' she said reprovingly, her voice low. 'He's nice. I like him and I don't want you to scare him off.'

Stella raised her palms. 'As if I would. I'll be sweetness itself.' She grinned, resisting the urge to say that if he genuinely liked her, he should be able to withstand a little close questioning. Though Stella had already made a mental note to keep the tone of her enquiries gentle, there was no way she wasn't going to take the opportunity to do a little fishing, due diligence and all that. It was her mum's heart they were dealing with here, and Stella needed to be sure it wasn't going to get broken, needed to satisfy herself that Rhys's intentions were nothing less than honourable and that he was worthy of her lovely mum.

'Hmm.' Alice regarded her, a hint of doubt in her eyes. 'Just make sure you are.'

After Alice had first announced the news of her fledgeling relationship with Rhys, Stella had embarked on a round of subtle questioning in which her mum had revealed that, not only was Rhys eight years her senior, but he was also a widower with two grown-up children – a daughter and a son – and a doting grandfather to two little girls. He was comfortably off – 'So he's not after my money, before you head off down that route,' Alice had said, giving her daughter a knowing look – and ran his own business as a financial advisor – that part had set alarm bells ringing, though Stella had done all she could to hide the fact from her mother – and had moved to the area six months earlier. The details had been basic, barely fleshed out at all, but, most importantly, this Rhys Baker appeared to be making her mum happy, so Stella hadn't pushed any further.

But today, seeing her mum like this, she found herself hoping he wasn't going to let her down.

Stepping out into the sun-filled garden, Stella took in the thoughtfully set table with its striped, waxed tablecloth and matching linen napkins, a jug of colourful flowers from the garden placed in the centre. Her eyes went to a tall man, with swept back salt-and-pepper hair who was tending the barbecue. His attire was smart but casual, the quality of their cut lending him a well-groomed air.

Shielding her eyes with her hand, Alice said, 'Rhys, I'd like to introduce my daughter, Stella.' She followed up with a smile, her body language revealing how nervous she felt. She and Stella negotiated the sandstone steps down to the garden, classical music murmuring softly from the speakers on the window ledge.

'Hello there, Stella, it's delightful to finally meet you.' Rhys set down the tongs he was holding and headed over to her, his hand outstretched, his fresh, citrussy cologne wafting under her nostrils. His warm smile set wrinkles fanning out at the corners of a pair of kind, brown eyes. 'Your mother has told me so much about you.'

'Hello, Rhys.' Stella resisted the urge to say she wished she could say the same about him, her mum having furnished her with only the scantest of details, and that was only because Stella had pushed, albeit gently. 'It's lovely to meet you too. I hope my mum hasn't told you anything scary.' Returning his smile, she took his hand, noting the strong, but not overpowering, grip and spotting the expensive watch at his wrist.

'On the contrary, I've heard nothing but good things. Your mother's very proud of you.' His smile deepened.

'Phew! That's a relief,' Stella said jokingly. She stole a quick glance across at her mum, noting the smile she was sharing with Rhys. It triggered a squeeze of affection in Stella's heart.

'Thought it best to save stories of your teenage years until you know each other a little better,' Alice said with a chuckle.

Stella pulled a face of mock horror. 'Quite right too. I can't deny, I had my moments. Don't think Rhys is quite ready to hear them yet.' Her mum didn't know the half of it, sneaking out of her bedroom window at night and meeting up with boyfriends. As for university, Stella would be the first to admit she'd been pretty wild. But, despite this party-loving side to her, she'd always managed to buckle down and take her studies seriously.

'Don't worry, I think I'm pretty unshockable after what my two put me through.' Rhys gave an affectionate shake of his head. 'I can laugh about it now, though at the time, I have to admit, it was pretty challenging.'

'S'good to know I'm not alone,' Stella said with a smile.

'And, rebellious streaks aside, have you had a good day so far? Your mum tells me you go for a run on the beach every Saturday and Sunday morning. I have to say I'm full of admiration for you. I stick to the solid pavements of the top prom; so much easier, and which probably explains why our paths have never crossed.'

'Oh, I think I'm just a glutton for punishment.' She laughed. 'And nothing beats running by the sea, the breeze coming off it is so refreshing on days like these, not so much in the winter though, it can be pretty bracing then.'

'I can believe that,' he said, giving a hearty laugh.

Standing beside her, Alice's relief was palpable. 'Can I get you a drink, lovey?' Her voice was light as she smiled happily at her daughter. 'Glass of wine okay?'

'Mmm. That'd be good, thanks, Mum. Just a small one.'

'And I'd better take a look at the barbecue; we don't want anything burnt to a frazzle,' said Rhys, his tone easy. Stella marvelled at how effortlessly he appeared to have slotted into the dynamic, his presence seeming in no way awkward or uncomfortable. It made her think he must have been to the house several times before.

'Right, I'll leave you two to get to know one another a little better while I go and grab you that glass of wine and check on the quiche.' Alice shot a brief-but-pointed look in Stella's direction that said, 'Behave yourself!'

Stella watched as Alice hurried off in the direction of the kitchen. She moved closer to the barbecue where Rhys was turning golden pieces of chicken breast sprinkled with herbs. Helping herself to half a cherry tomato from the salad as she passed the table, and reminding herself to heed her mother's warning, she said, 'I gather from Mum you moved to Micklewick Bay only recently.' She gave him a friendly smile.

Rhys nodded, lifting his gaze to hers, smoke rising in a cloud around him. 'That's right, well, it's getting on for six months ago now.'

Stella nodded. 'And what was it that tempted you here? Do you have connections to the town, and do you plan on staying?' *Softly, softly, Stella.* If her mum heard her, she'd be sure to pin her with another of her warning looks.

Rhys smiled. 'No, I don't have any connections to the town, didn't know anyone before I moved here. My reason was, well, I expect your mother will have told you that I lost my wife a year ago.' His smile faltered and sadness briefly clouded his eyes.

Stella winced inwardly as a shard of guilt shot through her, making her instantly regret putting him on the spot. 'Yes, she mentioned it.' She pressed her lips together in a sympathetic smile. Though her mum had shared the fact that Rhys's wife had passed away, she hadn't gone into any detail, but if he had grown-up children, they must have been married for a while, providing she was the mother of his children, of course. 'I was sorry to hear of your loss, it can't have been easy for you, especially if you'd been together a long time.'

'Thank you, that's very kind. We'd been together for thirty-five years, married for thirty-two of them.' He drew in a deep breath. 'In truth, it was a blessing when it happened. Theresa had been ill for such a long time.' He paused, turning the chicken once more. His smile reappeared a moment later. 'Anyway, it was the catalyst that brought me here. I felt I needed a complete change, needed to move on, and a friend recommended I check out Micklewick Bay. He and his family had spent a week in a holiday cottage here and waxed lyrical about it. So, on my next free day, I jumped in my car and ventured over here. I found myself quite taken with the feel of the town; and who wouldn't love that beach and those cliffs? Anyway, as luck would have it, I spotted a house for sale that looked like it had quite a bit of potential, so I wangled a viewing that day.'

'You were clearly keen.'

'I was.' Rhys nodded. 'As soon as I got over the doorstep, I knew it was exactly what I needed. And, even better, it was empty and chain-free which meant the sale proceeded swiftly. It's a bit of a project, for want of a better word, and requires some renovating here and there, but I enjoy turning my hand to that kind of thing. Has a good-sized garden too, perfect for growing vegetables and for my grandchildren to enjoy a run around.' He gave a shrug and smiled across at her. 'So, there you have it, the reason I found myself here in Micklewick Bay.'

'Sounds like a good one to me.' Stella was just about to ask whereabouts in town he lived when Alice's voice made them both turn.

'Here we are. Sorry I took so long.' She was walking down the steps, a glass of wine in one hand, a quiche in the other. Judging by the expression on her face, Stella guessed her mum was inexorably relieved to see her daughter and Rhys appeared to be getting along.

* * *

The afternoon passed quickly in the suntrap of a garden, birds twittering in the hedges, the industrious hum of bumble bees in the borders. Conversation flowed easily, punctuated with a generous sprinkling of laughter. Stella couldn't deny the chemistry that danced between her mum and Rhys, and she found herself rather liking him with his affable manner and open expression. He'd spoken warmly of his children and grandchildren, and she'd surprised herself by thinking how lucky they were to have him. He was attentive without being overbearing and she felt confident there was no ulterior motive or shady side to him. Thanks to her profession, she'd encountered a whole variety of personalities in the witness box, from serial charmers to dangerous manipulators, and everything in-between, and had developed a sense of those who were genuine and those who most definitely were not. She felt able to rest easy that her mum had, at last, allowed herself to enjoy a romantic relationship – though Stella still made a conscious decision to monitor things, just in case...

With the sun beating down, and despite being careful not to partake in too much wine, Stella found herself feeling just a little too comfortable stretched out in her generously padded chair. It would have been oh-so easy to spend the rest of the afternoon here, chatting away to her mum and Rhys but, as with every Sunday, she had prep to do for her case the following day. She was about to announce it was time she headed back to her apartment when Rhys cleared his throat. 'Um, I have something to ask you, Stella, if that's okay?' He looked directly at her from the sofa opposite where he was sitting beside her mum, his arm thrown casually around her shoulder. For the first time during the afternoon, Stella detected an air of uncertainty about him.

'You do?' She looked from Rhys to her mother, whom she noted also looked a little uncomfortable, fidgeting away and fiddling with the stem of her wine glass. Stella couldn't begin to imagine where this was heading.

'Yes, you see, the thing is, I'd rather like to take your mum on holiday. Um... I have a villa in Tuscany and I've asked if she'd like to spend a couple of weeks there with me, but I... er, we wanted to check you'd be okay with that before we booked our flights.'

Stella took a moment to assimilate his words. Her mother was going on holiday with a man? *Wow!* She swallowed, her gaze flicking to her mum who was looking back, concern in her eyes. *Get a grip, Stella. Why wouldn't she go on holiday with Rhys?* She fixed a wide smile on her face and said, 'Of course I'm okay with it. Why wouldn't I be? And it's not as if you need my permission to go on holiday, Mum, you know that.'

'I know I don't, lovey, but with me only ever going away with friends before, I just thought it would be nice to run it by you first.' She smiled uncertainly. 'Well, it was Rhys's idea I do that, actually.'

Where had her confident, self-assured mum gone? she wondered. This new-found romance appeared to have put her out of her comfort zone, and she was clearly finding it awkward to discuss it with her daughter.

'Honestly, Mum, you don't have to run anything by me. I'm not a little girl. I just want you to be happy. And I'm so chuffed for you, it's time you lived a little and enjoyed yourself. A holiday in Tuscany will do you the world of good.' Stella spoke with more conviction than she felt and hoped her mum hadn't picked up on it. More than anything she wanted her mother to be happy – which she very clearly was from what she'd seen that afternoon – she couldn't help but think that a new relationship was all very well, but spending two weeks with someone you barely know, and in a different country too, was a big step. At least, it was to Stella's mind. A couple of years ago, Ferdy had invited her to spend a week with him at his villa in Nice, but she'd turned him down flat. The prospect of being cooped-up with a man twenty-four hours a day was more than she could bear. She'd always thought her mother had felt the same way. Not that Stella was going to bring that up right now; there was no way she was going to throw cold water over her mum's new-found happiness. *And besides, it's none of your business anyway.*

Alice's shoulders dropped as she visibly relaxed, a smile spreading across her face. 'Thank you, sweetheart, I'm so relieved you feel that way. I have to say, I've found myself very much looking forward to it.'

Stella looked on as her mum cast her eyes up at Rhys, happiness radiating from her. He smiled back, giving her shoulder a reassuring squeeze.

'I'll get our flights booked tomorrow, darling, see if there are any still available for a week on Saturday.

A week on Saturday? His attentiveness to her mum warmed Stella's heart. After all her years of being unattached it was good to see her looking so undeniably happy. Who'd have thought it could happen after all these years?

NINE

Leaving the large Victorian houses and the quieter, more genteel part of town behind, Stella sound found herself weaving her way through the small, characterful terraces that fanned out from the centre like satellite shoots. Reaching the street that offered the quickest route home, she decided to take a detour, opting instead to go the long way round. She needed to clear her head and feel more awake before she could even think about tackling any prep on her brief.

Soon, she found herself on the top prom where the temperature was a few degrees cooler. A light breeze blew in from the sea, brushing refreshingly over her skin. It was a welcome relief after the intense heat of her mum's garden.

Though she'd enjoyed the afternoon, and finally getting to meet Rhys Baker, Stella still felt the need to assimilate her thoughts on her mother's relationship with him. Today, she'd learnt that they'd been "friends" for around five months – apparently hitting it off when Rhys had called in at Spick 'n' Sparkle's small premises on Endeavour Road with a view to enlisting the company's cleaning services as well as having his laundry done. According to Rhys it had taken him three of those months to get Alice to agree to go out on a proper date with him and move their relationship up to the next level – something Stella hadn't wanted to think too much about. And though she'd never profess to being an expert on relationships, she couldn't help but think that things seemed to be moving pretty quickly – was it wrong of her to think *too* quickly? Or was this nothing more than her lawyer's brain stepping in and over-analysing the situation? It wouldn't be the first occasion if it was.

As she walked on, her thoughts swimming around her mind, the screeching of seagulls barely registered in her ears, nor the caterwauling busker who'd attracted a small, amused audience at the top of the one-hundred and ninety-nine steps.

Stella was jolted out of her musings when her gaze unexpectedly landed on a familiar tall, broad-shouldered figure ambling in her direction. Alex Bainbridge! Her heart leapt in the way it usually did when she set eyes on him and she cursed its inappropriate timing. He had a jaunty looking Fred on the end of a lead, and was walking alongside the young woman who'd arrived at the Jolly on Friday night. From her quick appraisal, Stella noted the woman was chatting away animatedly as Alex gazed down at her with what looked unmistakably like affection. *Rat!* At that moment, the pair laughed heartily at something the woman had said. Alex gave her a nudge with his shoulder. She reciprocated with a playful whack on his arm which set him laughing even louder. Out of nowhere, a pang of jealousy squeezed in Stella's chest, making her face burn, more with annoyance at herself for letting her feelings get carried away in such a ridiculous manner, than with him. Her nostrils flared and her breathing intensified. *Gah! He really is a player!*

It wasn't her style to avoid a situation; she preferred to tackle things head on, but right now there was no way she wanted to come face to face with either of them. She wasn't in the right frame of mind to deal with his self-assured manner, never mind have him introduce her to his girlfriend. Before either of them had a chance to spot her, Stella quickly slipped across the road and into the shade of the tall, Victorian houses, striding briskly in the direction of her apartment building, apparently unnoticed by Alex Bainbridge and his girlfriend.

Back home, her anger abated, Stella flung open the doors to the balcony, admitting the sea breeze before heading to the kitchen and her coffee machine. She'd have a quick kick of caffeine before getting stuck into her work. She not only had her brief to prepare for the following day, but also several forms relating to other cases to complete. She'd be working well into the evening which was why she'd gone easy on the wine at her mum's. If only she didn't have so much other stuff buzzing round her head.

As she sipped her coffee, gazing out to sea, comfy in her seat on the balcony, Stella's thoughts drifted back to Alex Bainbridge. Much as she'd decided unequivocally he was a rat, she couldn't help but feel a pang of regret that things hadn't panned out the way she'd hoped. Even she couldn't deny the sparks that had danced between them, nor the way he'd made her heart race so wildly. Maybe it was a good thing that he had a girlfriend, that whatever had been stirring between the two of them hadn't gone any further. She was only just getting her head around her mum having a boyfriend; she wasn't sure it was the right time to try and work out why Alex Bainbridge had triggered such a dramatic response in her, and in a way she'd never experienced before.

Her gaze fell onto a couple walking along, arm-in-arm, the man dropping a kiss to the top of the girl's head. Stella drew in a sigh, trying to imagine if she'd ever change her attitude to relationships as her mum appeared to have done. Tried to picture herself walking along with someone, looking as loved-up as the couple down on the prom clearly were. 'Ain't happening!' she said aloud and with great conviction. Stella would be the first to admit she didn't have a romantic bone in her body, she couldn't bear all that mushy hearts and flowers stuff. Her job was her first priority; she was too busy to factor having a man in her life on a permanent or serious basis. If they weren't reasons enough, there was the fact that she liked her home neat and tidy; under no circumstances would she be able to tolerate smelly socks lying around the place, or underpants that haven't quite made it to the laundry basket, strewn over the floor as Maggie so often complained about Bear, albeit affectionately. 'No thank you!' Stella shuddered at the thought, it was single all the way for her.

Her mind wandered its way back to the afternoon at her mum's house. From the various conversations they'd had, it was evident Rhys would be staying the night at Magnolia Gardens, and Stella surmised it wouldn't be the first time. This was new territory for her to navigate with her mum, and she couldn't deny it did feel a little strange, not that she wanted to think too much about it. On the other hand, it had been good to see her mum looking so happy. It was just that it had come so out-of-the-blue after she'd stressed to her for as far back as Stella could remember that there was no way she'd ever let a man into her life again after what Stella's father had done. And, much as she'd liked Rhys, the niggle that he might just be a bit too good to be true was starting to creep in.

TEN

Half an hour later, Stella found herself still rooted to her seat on the balcony when her eyes were drawn to the familiar relaxed amble of Alex Bainbridge, with Fred trotting along on the end of his lead. This time, there was no sign of the pretty young woman who'd been making Alex laugh so heartily earlier. Frustratingly, Stella's pulse surged, unleashing a flurry of butterflies in her stomach. *Dratted man!* How could he have this effect on her from this distance? It was ridiculous and totally unwarranted. There was something clearly amiss with her emotions right now. She must have had too much sun that afternoon.

With her traitorous heart leaping about in her chest, Stella watched as Fred brought them to a halt, sniffing around the legs of a wooden bench that faced out to sea. Just then Alex's gaze wandered in the direction of her apartment building, his eyes travelling upwards. Giving a sharp intake of breath, she leant back into the shade, her heart pounding for a different reason this time. The last thing she wanted was for him to think she was staring at him or spying on him. That would only serve to inflate his already enormous ego!

He glanced away, apparently ignorant of her presence and

she seized the opportunity to slink inside, telling herself it was time she made a start on her work.

'Lucky escape,' she said, puffing out her cheeks. As she headed towards the kitchen to rinse her mug her mobile phone pinged from where she'd left it on the worktop. Scooping it up she saw it was Florrie asking how everything went with her mum. Stella was just about to fire off a quick reply when something stopped her. Before she knew it she found herself selecting the call icon; it would be good to talk to Florrie, she was often the calm voice of reason – as Lark could be too, but she liked everyone, saw the good in everything. As lovely as this trait was, it didn't always help in situations like these.

The five friends acknowledged that she and Lark were the most different personality-wise, Lark's gentle, laid-back nature the polar opposite to Stella's drive and assertive manner. Maggie and Jasmine both shared a wicked sense of humour but could get quite hot-heated at times – Jasmine particularly so – whereas Florrie fell somewhere in between. She had the knack for putting things very clearly into perspective, which was something Stella felt in need of right now.

Florrie picked up on the first ring. 'Hi, Stells,' she said cheerily, the sound of a lawnmower rumbling away in the background.

'Hi, Florrie, are you okay to talk for a few minutes?'

'Course, Ed's just mowing our postage stamp of a lawn, and I was about to sit down with a cup of tea and a book.'

'Sounds like you've got the work distribution spot-on there,' Stella said with a laugh. 'Sure I'm not intruding on your reading time?'

'I so have.' Florrie giggled. 'And no, you're certainly not intruding, I'm keen to know how it went at your mum's.'

Stella made her way over to the lounge area and flumped down onto the sofa. 'It went well. Rhys Baker seems very nice, and mum looked happy. It's just...' She paused, drawing in a deep breath.

'It felt a bit weird.' Florrie finished her sentence for her.

'It did, and you know what I'm like, my mind starts going off down all sorts of avenues, wondering if he's a genuinely decent bloke or if he's a charmer who's trying to inveigle his way into her life so he can fleece her of all her money before doing a disappearing act. And I'm sure, as much as I did my best to hide it for my mum's benefit, they'll both have detected a hint of my mistrust; I'd just hate for her to end up hurt.'

'Listen, Stells, I really don't think you should beat yourself up about this. You're only thinking what everyone else would in your position, and I totally get why you're feeling the way you are. I mean, it's just been the two of you your whole life and your mum has always said a romantic relationship wasn't for her; you're bound to feel a little wary. And it's not as if you know this Rhys; he's just arrived in the area and into your mum's life. If I was ever in your shoes and one of my parents started a relationship with someone new, I'd be exactly the same, worse probably. Knowing your mum as I do, I'm sure she'll understand. She's a reasonable person; she'll know you've got her best interests at heart.'

Florrie's words had an instant soothing effect, helping to assuage Stella's guilt. 'I suppose you're right. Mind, her saying a romantic relationship wasn't for her is clearly a thing of the past after what I witnessed today. You should've seen the way they were looking at each other, all puppy-dog eyes. And she seemed so different around him, so much more carefree and light-hearted. It felt good to see her that way actually.' A smile spread over her face at the thought.

'Aww. That's so nice to hear,' Florrie said, gulping down a mouthful of tea. 'You never know, maybe it's just taken until now for the right man to come along for your mum. And don't forget, she's no fool, she's not some giddy young girl who's desperate to fall in love for the sake of it. She'll have given it a great deal of thought before she dipped her toe into the relationship pool. Like you, she's a pretty good judge of character and I honestly can't see her letting herself get sucked in by some unscrupulous bloke.'

Florrie had summed up Alice so well. Stella hadn't considered either of those points. 'I hope you're right.'

'I'm sure that's how it is.' Florrie paused, Stella could almost hear the cogs of her friend's mind working down the phone line. 'And am I right in thinking you might be a bit worried about how the dynamics between you and your mum will be affected if Rhys does become a permanent fixture in her life? That he'll have a hand in her decision-making? It's only natural, by the way, flower, I'm not criticising.'

Florrie had hit the nail right on the head. 'I know you're not. And, yeah, I suppose I am a bit bothered about it, especially if they end up moving in together.' Her heart jumped as another thought segued into her mind. 'Or if they end up getting married.' She pulled a concerned face at that.

'I think you're getting a bit ahead of yourself there. Your mum's a level-headed woman. Look at it from this perspective, it'd be like you meeting a fella, falling in love and suddenly announcing you're getting hitched – which we all know is something that's never going to happen!' Florrie gave a hearty chuckle. 'Can you honestly see your mum doing that?'

Florrie's analogy seemed to have the annoying effect of conjuring Alex Bainbridge into Stella's mind. Scowling, she shoved the unwelcome image firmly out of her thoughts and said, 'When you put it like that, no, I definitely can't. And you're right, Mum is level-headed and a good judge of character. Which reminds me, from what I picked up today, it would seem I'm not the only one who's got concerns.'

'Oh?'

'Hmm. I get the impression there's a more than a whiff of disapproval coming from his daughter's camp.'

'What makes you think that?'

'It was more that I gained a sense of something.' Stella gnawed on her bottom lip.

Nothing had been overtly said, but the loaded looks that had been exchanged between her mum and Rhys whenever Suzie's name had cropped up had been hard to ignore. Thinking about it now, it rankled that someone out there should be viewing her lovely, kind-hearted mum in a disapproving way. She wondered if she'd been introduced to Rhys's children yet; something told her she hadn't and she made a mental note to put this Suzie straight if things progressed between their parents. There was no way Stella would tolerate anyone being unkind to her mum; any negativity needed nipping in the bud and sharpish. She'd rather got the impression that this Suzie had been more than a little indulged if the warmth in her father's voice whenever he mentioned her was anything to go by, as well as the number of times he'd brought her up. 'Suzie thinks this, Suzie wants that, Suzie's getting the other. Suzie, Suzie, Suzie.' Granted, the expression Rhys had worn when he spoke of his son Josh had been warm, but it hadn't matched the one he wore when speaking of Suzie; that had definitely been cranked-up a notch or two. The term "daddy's little princess" sprang to mind, quickly followed by what felt annoyingly like a stab of jealousy. Ignoring it, Stella told herself that it was just down to feeling irritated; she had no time for women like that.

'Sounds like this Suzie's feeling pretty much the same as you, just she's been a little more vocal about her concerns,' Florrie said, when Stella had finished.

'I suppose so, but I was friendly and polite to Rhys. Plus, I haven't given my mum a hard time about him.'

'Yes, but if you think about it, Stells, their situation is a little different. I mean, your mum isn't *replacing* anyone – for want of a better word. I should imagine it can't be easy for Suzie and her brother to think about someone potentially...' Florrie paused, as if considering a suitably sensitive way to express herself. 'I don't mean filling their mum's shoes, but maybe filling a gap in the family dynamic as well as in her father's heart. It might feel all a little bit too soon after losing their mum.'

Sympathy flooded Stella's chest. She hadn't thought of it like that. 'Oh blimey, that's a really good point. A year's not a long time at all, though I should imagine it's felt a whole lot longer for Suzie and Josh.'

'Yeah, poor things, must be hard.'

'It must. I'll be sure to keep that in mind.' Stella couldn't even begin to imagine what they were going through. The prospect of being without her mum didn't bear thinking about. In fact, now she thought about it, growing up with her mum as her only relative, Stella had got to the age of thirty-three without experiencing the loss of anyone close, not even her grandparents, having never met them. She didn't even know if they were still alive. A shiver ran up her spine, sending a rash of goosebumps pinging up over her skin. *Time to move the conversation along.* Stella didn't want to consider a time when her mum wouldn't be around anymore. It had been her biggest fear growing up; if anything happened to her mum, she'd be on her own. It was a scary prospect for a young child.

'You okay?' Florrie's voice drew her back to the present.

'I'm fine, there's just a lot to think about, but most of all, I wish I knew what had changed Mum's outlook on relationships. Her going all lovey-dovey with Rhys is the polar opposite of what she's espoused about getting involved in a relationship for as far back as I can remember. I'm just not used to seeing her like this.'

'I totally get that, and I can't argue, it is quite hard to imagine but people change. Maybe she's never felt this way about anyone before. Maybe it was an instant, intense attraction. You know, like a love at first sight scenario? We know it happens, Mags and Bear are a perfect example.'

Love at first sight? That her mum could have been struck by such a concept was something else that hadn't crossed Stella's mind.

'True, they are.' Even a cynic like Stella couldn't deny that it had been the case in that relationship. Infuriatingly, an image of Alex Bainbridge sprang from nowhere and into her mind yet again, those deep-blue eyes twinkling at her, making her heart flutter and her face grow warm. *What the heck is he doing here?* Huffing noisily, she forced his image out of her thoughts. 'Clear off!' she muttered angrily.

'Oh... um...I didn't mean to upset you by saying that, Stells,' Florrie said, sounding concerned.

'Oh, no, flower, I didn't mean you! I was talking to myself. I'm just annoyed at the suspicion that keeps creeping into my mind, I wish it would stop.' She shook her head, rolling her eyes at herself. 'It'll be because of my job, I've developed a habit of assuming the worst of people, or treating them warily until I get to know them.'

'I'm not surprised, it's cos you actually do see the worst that people can do. I'd be the same.'

Glad to have smoothed that over, Stella sat up straight, swinging her legs round and placing her feet back onto the floor. 'Anyway, that's enough of me wittering on, are you and Ed still on for the auction night at The Cellar on Wednesday?' Time to move on to a more positive topic, she didn't want to put the dampeners on Florrie's peaceful afternoon.

'Ooh, too right we are. How about you?'

'Can't wait, should be a laugh.'

Bill and Pim, the proprietors of The Cellar, were hosting a charity auction for a local family whose daughter was suffering from a rare illness and they were doing all they could to raise enough funds to send her to the States where she could receive some pioneering treatment that was only available there. Stella made a mental note to pick up a voucher for a meal for two at Oscar's, the town's local bistro, as her way of donating an item to be auctioned.

'It should, Bill and Pim always put on a good do. I think Jazz has managed to get a babysitter so we should all be there.'

'Fab!'

The friends ended the conversation and Stella glanced across at her desk, her heart sinking as she was reminded of the Dixon family and her dodgy opponent, Vaughan Elliott. Monday morning couldn't look less appealing if it tried. As a rule, Stella usually tackled her work with vigour and laser-like concentration, but after the week she'd had, it was beginning to feel as if her enthusiasm was slowly draining away. And, much as she was loath to admit it, the look in Gavin Dixon's eyes as he'd glared at her from the public gallery, and the subsequent words he'd hurled at her as she'd left the court for the robing room, had been bothering her, slowly creeping under her skin and triggering a little voice of anxiety clamouring for her attention. It wasn't like her to be affected like this at all; she had a reputation for having an impenetrable shell, letting nothing get to her, moving on without a second thought. When her work was finished for the day, she very neatly packed it away in a mental box and forgot about it until the following morning. But there was something sinister about the Dixon family and if rumours were to be believed, their unscrupulous ways had stooped to worrying depths, with talk of them being involved in a particularly notorious gang from out of the area.

'*Ughh!*' Stella flopped back into the sofa. 'As if I need anything else to think about!' She found herself beginning to regret not taking a holiday this summer. Instead, she'd got stuck into a run of back-to-back heavy trials which, as a rule, she'd thrive on, the pressure giving her a buzz. But now the thought of a break from the intensity felt suddenly rather appealing.

She'd turned down the offer of a week at a villa in Sorrento with some of her single female friends at the bar, which was something a handful of them did each year, letting their hair down, savouring an escape from the stresses that came with their line of work. Having plunged a huge chunk of her savings into the purchase of her new apartment, Stella felt she couldn't justify blowing money on an expensive holiday in the sun – the villas the group chose were always exclusive and cost a fortune, the argument being that they'd worked for it so they deserved a little bit of luxury. She told herself it would probably be wise to forgo a summer break for this year, especially since she still needed some extra furniture for her new apartment, it being considerably bigger than her old one.

'Right,' she said out loud, pushing herself up from the sofa, 'time to stop dwelling on things. You need to get cracking. The sooner it's done, the sooner you can treat yourself to a soak in the bath with those amazing bath salts.' At her trip to the beautician's yesterday, she'd bought a jar of bath salts that promised to "set you adrift on a cloud of blissful relaxation". Stella hoped they wouldn't disappoint.

ELEVEN

Monday morning in court hadn't turned out to be quite as Stella had expected. Four of the jurors in the Dixon trial had phoned in sick, which had immediately alerted her suspicions, especially since there'd been no talk of stomach bugs or viruses doing the rounds. Judge Hoskinson, who was infamously grouchy at the best of times, appeared most displeased by this turn of events; he'd been keen to crack on with proceedings, get the Dixon trial finished and make a start on the next one in his list.

If pushed, a trial could run with a quorum of ten of the twelve members that made up a jury, but eight was unthinkable. It didn't help His Honour's ill humour when it was revealed that there were no courts available to accommodate the swearing-in of a completely new jury, allowing the trial to start afresh. Judge Hoskinson was left with no option but to discharge the remaining jurors and adjourn the trial to a date in the future, grumbling about the "abhorrent" waste of public money as he stormed off the bench.

Stella had felt torn. Part of her was keen to see the back of the case, albeit temporarily, but another part was relieved she didn't have to spend the day dealing with Vaughan Elliott and the dreaded Dixon clan.

Gavin Dixon had given a victorious cheer when Judge Hoskinson had announced his decision, earning him a withering look from His Honour, but Gavin Dixon had been undeterred and left the public gallery punching the air, flaunting his lack of respect for the judicial system.

Stella's suspicions were confirmed once she returned to the robing room where gossip was rife that Gavin Dixon and his family had spent the weekend nobbling members of the jury involved in the case, threatening them with unspeakable things if they dared to find his son guilty.

'Thought as much, there's no other explanation for it,' Stella said, sliding her wig off and dropping it onto the table. 'That whole family needs locking up and the key throwing away; they're a menace to society.' She'd need to draw her suspicions to the attention of the CPS and the police officers involved in the case – whom she knew to be gutted that the trial couldn't go ahead today, particularly DC Stephens.

'I'd be very careful what you say about my client and his family, if I were you, Hutton.' Vaughan Elliott entered the room with a supercilious swagger, instantly setting Stella's hackles up.

'Oh come off it, Elliott! We all know it's true, and so do you for that matter. That family is notorious and have no respect for the law or the people whose lives they ruin.' She shot him a look of utter disdain.

But Vaughan Elliott was undeterred. 'Have you ever considered that they could merely be the victims of malicious gossip?' He unfastened his bands and proceeded to disrobe, arrogance oozing from every pore. He had a reputation for bandying about baseless, controversial remarks, seeming to thrive on the reaction they generated.

Stella snorted in disbelief. '*Victims? Malicious gossip?* Are you serious?'

'Of course he's not, he's just talking a load of rubbish!' Ferdy said, his face growing red with anger. He threw down his pen. 'And he shouldn't be hob-knobbing with them either, it's unethical and he knows it.' It was no secret at the bar that Elliott was a regular visitor to his clients' homes, including that of the Dixon family. There were even rumours that he sneaked items into prison on their behalf. It didn't seem to bother him that he floated perilously close to being disbarred.

'I don't know what you're talking about, but what I do know is that now the trial's gone off I'm free for the rest of the day and intend to enjoy a delicious lunch at the Wig and Pen. Anyone care to join me?' He turned to Stella. 'Oh, and I'm afraid that doesn't include you, Hutton. You seem to have made a bit of an enemy of my client's father and it wouldn't be good to be seen socialising with you. I'd think very carefully about getting on the wrong side of someone like Gavin Dixon, you know.'

'And what exactly are you trying to tell me?' Stella pinned Elliott with her infamous death stare.

'Did I hear right?' asked Tim Bentley-Harris – or BH as he was known to his fellow members of the bar on the North Eastern circuit. He was a formidable silk from chambers in Leeds. He was wearing a grave expression. 'You're spouting-off some highly inappropriate claims there, Elliott, one of which, quite frankly, sounds like a threat. Talk like that just isn't on between members of the bar. I strongly suggest you desist or I'm afraid you'll find yourself being hauled in front of the Bar Council.'

Elliott, who'd now joined them at the table, leant back in his seat, his top lip curled in a lopsided snigger. 'We're not in the playground now, you know, BH; we don't go telling tales to the teacher. And besides, no one's foolish enough to report me.'

'Oh, is that right?' BH glared at him, hostility emanating from him.

'Don't worry, BH, he's not worth rising to,' Stella said, anger thrumming through her. Elliott had a reputation for taking pleasure in winding up other members of the bar, and he was doing a good job of it right now. He didn't appear to mind that it had resulted in him being universally disliked. On the contrary, he appeared to get a kick out of it.

'There's no need to get your pretty little knickers in a knot, Hutton. I was merely making an observation, that's all.'

Stella clenched her fists. *Arghh! Irritating man!* Fighting to keep a lid on her anger, which was now at boiling point, took every ounce of her courtroom skills. Her jaw tightened. There was no way she was going to be goaded into losing her temper which was exactly what Elliott was aiming for, she knew. Instead, she shook her head in distaste, rolling her eyes as she headed to her locker. Retrieving her red bag she set it down on the table, her breathing heavy as she stuffed her robes inside. Though she was aware of Ferdy's eyes on her from his usual seat opposite, she didn't look up; she needed to save every ounce of her strength to keep her anger reined in.

'You might want to reconsider how you converse with women, Elliott.' Speaking calmly but firmly, Stella turned her gaze from her brief bag and pinned the defence barrister with a steely glare.

'And you might want to reconsider your stuck-up attitude, Hutton.' Elliott glowered at her. 'No one likes a pinch-faced shrew.'

Ferdy pushed himself up, his eyes narrowed. 'Now just hang on a minute, you low—'

'Ferdy!' Stella cut him off. 'He's not worth it.' She pulled herself up to her full height, pushed her shoulders back and adopted her familiar confident stance. 'He's still bitter that I turned him down. Several times, actually.' She arched a challenging eyebrow at Elliott. 'He even resorted to pinning me into a corner at the court Christmas party last year, trying to force me into letting him "show me a good time in the bogs".' She used finger quotes around his words. A murmur of disapproval ran around the robing room.

'How very unappealing,' said Fay Norton.

Stella watched, a sense of satisfaction slowly replacing her anger as Elliott's smile faltered. He licked his lips nervously. 'I was only having a laugh.'

The robing room fell silent, the other members of the bar looking on with interest as events unfurled.

'Oh really? It didn't feel like you were joking at the time, and I certainly didn't find it funny. Quite the opposite in fact. As I recall, you were pretty persistent, and wouldn't listen when I told you, quite *forcefully*, and repeatedly, that I wasn't interested.' Stella sensed she'd hit a nerve and it sent a feeling of victory surging through her. It was time he was called out for his inappropriate and unwelcome behaviour.

He pushed himself up, his chair scraping noisily across the wooden floor. 'You're a hard-faced cow, Hutton, I've no idea what you're talking about.' All trace of his arrogant expression of earlier had vanished as he stole an uneasy glance around the robing room.

'Oh, I think you do. It wasn't the first time you'd made a pest of yourself with me either, and I know for a fact I'm not alone, you've got quite the reputation.'

'Rubbish!' He glared at her, his eyes full of fury, a nerve twitching at his temple. 'From what I remember, it was you who came onto me. Desperate for it, you were. Offering yourself up on a plate like you do with every man who crosses your path.' He puffed himself up, seemingly pleased that he'd opted to give this tactic a try. 'And I'll bet I'm not the only bloke who thinks that.' He cast his gaze around the men in the robing room as if looking for support, his face falling when none was forthcoming.

Ferdy shook his head in disgust.

Stella gave a shallow laugh of disbelief. 'Why would anyone

in their right mind be attracted to someone as unscrupulous as you with your dubious morals?'

'That,' said Fay Norton, 'is a very pertinent question.'

'Certainly not me,' said Alice Wiggins, a barrister with a broad Leeds accent who'd swept into the robing room and caught the tail-end of the altercation. 'Nor any other woman in my acquaintance, they all run in the opposite direction when they hear you're around.' She slid her laptop onto the table beside Stella and shot him a distasteful look. 'When are you going to stop making a nuisance of yourself, Elliott? You might want to consider behaving yourself before someone takes you to task about it.'

'My thoughts exactly,' said Stella.

Elliott glowered at Stella. 'I don't know what your problem is, Hutton, but you've always had some kind of vendetta against me, always had a high opinion of yourself,' he spat the words out. 'You'll be sorry you ever started this.' With that, he grabbed his cabin case and stormed out, slamming the door behind him.

'Wow,' said BH. 'His sort really shouldn't be at the bar.'

'I very much doubt he will be for much longer,' said Fay Norton. 'And well done for tearing a strip off him on behalf of the sisterhood, Stella.'

'Bravo, Hutton, our fearless, kickass lass!' said Ferdy in his cut-glass accent.

'Yes, Hutton, that was something to see. Remind me never to get on the wrong side of you,' said Peter Theobald, a highly respected King's Counsel who'd walked in halfway through the exchange. 'Having said that, he's had that coming to him for a long time.'

'He has. It's about time somebody put him in his place,' said Alice Wiggins. 'He's starting to act like he's untouchable; above the law.'

'Yes, well done, Hutton.' BH gave her a smile. 'No man should make a woman feel uncomfortable like that.'

'Ughh.' Stella's shoulders sagged with relief. She pulled out a chair and sat down, rubbing her temples where she could feel a headache beginning to brew. 'I'm just glad the trial's gone off and I don't have to deal with him any more today.' She knew her colleagues were right, and much as she was glad to have got the better of him, his warnings about his client's family had sent a ripple of unease running through her. Had it really been such a good idea to spar with him? she wondered.

* * *

Stella headed to chambers once she'd gathered her stuff together in the robing room, including her brief bag since she was in court in Newcastle the following week and didn't want to have to detour to York to collect them. After the nightmare of the Dixon trial and her unpleasant interaction with Vaughan Elliott, she'd made up her mind that she was going to take the rest of the week off.

After updating Allegra her clerk on the situation with the Dixon case and Allegra had passed on a handful of messages, Stella said, 'Since I've had to return the trial I had for this week thanks to the Dixon trial running over, I'd like my diary kept clear for the rest of the week, so please don't accept any further instructions in my name. I'm going to take the opportunity to unpack the rest of the boxes at my new place.'

'Are you sure?' Allegra looked surprised. 'I was just about to say the CPS have been on, asking if you'd take a section eighteen trial for them. Counsel for the prosecution has to go to the Court of Appeal tomorrow, so he's had to return it.'

Normally Stella would snap Allegra's hand off but nothing could tempt her today. 'No,' she said resolutely. 'Somebody else in chambers will have to do it.'

'Are you coming down with something, Miss Hutton,' asked

Jacob, looking as if he'd heard wrong. He was one of the junior clerks who'd been listening from his desk.

Stella laughed. 'Don't think so. But I have had an overkill of Vaughan Elliott and the Dixon family.'

'*Ughh!* That explains everything.' He rolled his eyes.

'Actually, things got quite heated in the robing room,' she said. 'I'm expecting repercussions as far as Elliott's concerned – nothing I can't deal with,' she added, seeing their concerned expressions. 'Right, who fancies a cuppa before I head off?' Stella asked, eager to move on from the unsavoury topic of Vaughan Elliott. She was met with a resounding chorus of yeses.

Before long, Stella was driving back to Micklewick Bay, the top down on her car, savouring the refreshing breeze that was doing a good job of clearing her head. It had been an intense day and she was looking forward to having a break from it. The driven and determined Stella Hutton was taking a back seat and her counterpart, the more relaxed version, was taking her place. Stella couldn't remember the last time that had happened, if at all.

TWELVE

Stella was strolling down the aisles of the supermarket in Micklewick Bay, having decided to stop off before she went home. She had plans to have lunch, launch into some unpacking, then treat herself to a walk along the beach – the thought of breathing in the salty air and having a paddle in the sea was growing more tempting by the minute. Her fridge needed stocking-up on ready meals – Stella would be the first to admit her culinary skills were basic at best, and consisted of salads or microwave meals. She also wanted to get a few ideas for what pre-prepared nibbles to lay on for her housewarming party on Saturday night. And, as the wine aisles came into view, she decided she might as well scoop up a few bottles in readiness for it too.

Leaving her trolley at the end of the aisle, which was blocked by a couple bickering about which wine would go best with fish and couple of women who appeared to be putting the world to rights, Stella made for the white wine section and lifted four bottles of Pinot Grigio from the shelf. Setting them down in her trolley, she headed back for a couple of bottles of Cabernet Sauvignon. That done, she selected some beers. As she was making her way back to her trolley she looked up to find none other than Alex Bainbridge wearing an amused smile. *Unbelievable!* Micklewick Bay may be a small town, but Stella didn't think it warranted bumping into him as frequently as this! Was he following her?

'Hello there,' he said in his deep, rich voice that, annoyingly, sent a tingle running right through her.

She stopped in her tracks, taking in his black slogan T-shirt and khaki combat-style shorts. 'Oh!' Her heart responded as if it had been jump-started, her pulse taking off at a gallop. And there was that feeling speaking to him seemed to trigger, mixing up her insides. *Get a grip of yourself, woman!* Reminding herself he was a shameless flirt despite having a girlfriend, she took a calming breath and pulled her mouth into a tight smile. 'Hello.'

'Doing a spot of shopping, I see.'

'Yes, anyone would think we were in a supermarket,' she quipped. Despite her cool tone, she couldn't help but think he really did have the most gorgeous eyes, a mesmerising ocean-blue flecked with gold. The sort she could very easily lose herself in, given half the chance.

'Hmm.' He nodded, his grin growing wider, his eyes dancing.

The feeling that he was laughing at her, or that there was some joke she wasn't a party to started to creep over her. 'Right, well, if you'll excuse me, I need to get on,' she said, bristling.

'Yes, of course, but before you go, can I just check that you meant to put all of that in my trolley?' He nodded towards the bottles of beer she'd just set down, his smile twitching.

Stella's brow creased with a frown. *What's he talking about? And why does he have to be so out of the way attractive when I'm trying to play it cool with him?*

'I mean,' he gave a shrug, 'I'm very happy to pay for it, but I thought I'd–'

'What d'you mean? I'm not expecting you to pay for

anything.' She looked down at what she'd assumed was her trolley to find it contained not only the wine and beer she'd selected but also a variety of other items she certainly hadn't placed in there. 'Oh. Oops!' She pushed her lips together as her frown deepened. She glanced around for her trolley to see it had been pushed out of the way and was now next to an elaborate display of chocolate biscuits. 'Sorry about that.'

He followed her gaze. 'No worries, it's easily done.'

'So it would seem.' She hitched her black designer bag up on her shoulder and bit down on a smile, refusing to soften towards him despite what her insides were telling her, not to mention her thudding heart.

'So, is this a shopping dash in your lunch break?' he asked.

'Not quite, I just managed to finish early for the day.' Stella cut a striking figure in a fitted, crisp white collarless shirt and smartly tailored trousers which, thanks to the addition of her high heels, made her legs appear to go on forever.

'In that case, I hope you're going to do something more exciting with the rest of it than have a whizz around a supermarket.'

Was he hitting on her again? she wondered, her hackles rising. 'Yes, I most certainly am. And now, if you'll excuse me, I really must get on,' she said curtly.

His smile fell as she went to reclaim her trolley.

'Stella, can you just give me a moment, please?'

She turned to him, meeting his eyes, noting the frown that now furrowed his brow. 'Why? I can't imagine we have anything left to say.' *He's a tryer, I'll give him that.*

'Oh, wow! Blunt! I kind of get the feeling I've done something to annoy or upset you – which, if I have, has been completely unintentional.' He raked his fingers through his hair. 'I mean you were friendly one minute and in the next you were giving me the cold shoulder. Forgive me if I got the wrong end of the stick, but I kind of thought we had a connection.' He pushed his mouth into an uncertain smile.

Though the appealing look in his eyes tugged at her insides, she was determined not to fall for it. 'I'm not in the habit of flirting with, never mind dating, men who are in a relationship,' she said sharply.

'Sorry, you've lost me.' He rubbed his fingers across his brow.

'You have a girlfriend, or have you conveniently forgotten about her – again?'

He looked utterly confused. 'What girlfriend? I don't have a girlfriend to forget about. I've been single for the last six months.'

It wasn't the response Stella had been expecting. As she marshalled his words, she searched his face for any telltale signs that would reveal he wasn't telling the truth, her senses screaming at her that he was being honest. If she was wide of the mark, then he was a convincing liar. The thought that Rhys could be fooling her mum in such a way flashed through her mind. Blinking, and telling herself that her eyes hadn't deceived her – she had seen him with another woman – she said, 'What about the girl you met at the Jolly last Friday. You know, very attractive, dark ponytail, petite? The one you were apparently overjoyed to see.' She hitched a questioning eyebrow at him. 'Surely she can't have slipped your mind.'

A smile slowly spread across his face. 'Ah, that one.'

'Yes, that one.' Why was he smiling like that?

'Zara.'

'I've no idea what she's called, you didn't introduce us – not that I'd expected you to under the circumstances, that would've been way too weird.'

She watched in confusion as Alex threw his head back and laughed heartily.

'I'm not sure why you find that so funny.'

'That explains it,' he spluttered.

'Explains what?' Stella narrowed her eyes at him. She was beginning to feel really rattled now.

'Zara's not my girlfriend.'

'Oh really?'

'Really.'

'What is she then? You looked pretty close to me.'

'That's probably because she's my sister; my twin sister. She was coming to see my new place but was late – as Zara always is.' He rolled his eyes affectionately. 'So I'd arranged to meet her at the Jolly. She'd only just landed when you and I were talking at the bar.'

'Oh. So... so, does that mean you're single?' A feeling of relief washed over her mingling with a generous dash of embarrassment. It was quickly followed up by an unexpected surge of happiness.

'Yup, well and truly. Well, unless you count Fred, we come as a package, I'm afraid.'

'Sounds like a nice package.' Stella smiled at him, her heart dancing, he had a way about him that she found herself drawn to; a mix of his easy manner, his friendliness, not to mention his sense of humour. That, along with the fact there was no edge, or arrogance to him – unlike most of the men she encountered in the robing room – all added up to make him undeniably appealing.

'Why thank you, you're not the first woman to have complimented me on it.' He gave a mischievous grin.

'I didn't mean *that*!' She giggled. Though she had to admit, she wouldn't mind getting a bit of first-hand experience of it. He did, after all, look mighty fine, even more so with this new information he'd just shared.

They stood smiling at one another for several moments, emotions swarming around Stella's insides. Alex was the first to break the silence. 'So,' he said, 'if you're free this afternoon, don't suppose you fancy grabbing a coffee somewhere, do you? Or a bite of lunch, even? I quite like the idea of playing hooky for a few hours.'

Her mind went to the boxes back at her apartment, waiting to be unpacked. She figured they could wait a little longer. Smiling, she said, 'I'd really like that.'

'Great.' He beamed at her. 'Don't suppose you can recommend anywhere? With me being new around here, I'm still finding my feet as far as eateries are concerned.'

'How about the Jolly? They do a great Lite-Bite menu that runs from lunchtime right through to about five p.m. I was planning on heading down to the beach this afternoon anyway.'

'Sounds good. Shall I meet you down there, say, one o'clock?'

'Perfect.'

'Great.'

They struggled to break eye contact, both grinning inanely until an impatient voice broke into their moment. 'S'cuse me, you're stopping anyone getting to them chocolate biscuits.'

'Oops, sorry.' Alex flashed an apologetic smile as he stood back, Stella doing the same. 'See you at one then. Oh, and do you mind if I bring Fred?'

'I'd be disappointed if you didn't,' Stella replied.

'You mean there's two of you?' asked the woman reaching for the chocolate biscuits. Before Alex could answer, she turned to Stella and said, 'By, aren't you a lucky lass?' She gave her a saucy wink before ambling off, leaving Stella and Alex dissolved in a fit of the giggles.

THIRTEEN

Stepping inside The Jolly Sailors, Stella pushed her sunglasses up onto her head, the cooler temperature of the pub a welcome relief after the intense heat of the sun. She'd swapped her court suit for a pair of olive-green cigarette trousers and a loose-fitting cotton top. Her hair had been released from its neat French pleat and was left to hang in relaxed glossy waves over her shoulders. Never one to get overexcited for a date – if, indeed, that's what this was – she'd found herself feeling a little fluttery as she was getting ready to meet Alex, and unusually indecisive about what to wear. Should she opt for her new chambray dress with the shoestring straps, or her knee-skimming playsuit? Or would that send out the wrong message? she'd wondered, before giving herself a talking to and telling herself to get a grip. '*It's just a casual bite to eat with someone you've just met, it's hardly the date of the century!* She'd chosen to ignore the excitement that had been fizzing away in her stomach.

Unsurprisingly for a glorious summer's day in the middle of the school holidays, the bar was heaving. Jaunty music Stella recognised as that of one of the local folk bands who played there of a Friday evening was filtering through the speakers, adding to the upbeat, happy vibe. She glanced around the room, spotting Alex at a table by an open window. Seeing her he raised his hand in a wave, his smile sending a pulse of attraction shooting through her. She headed over, her stomach doing its now-familiar somersaults whenever Alex was in close proximity. It really was a novel feeling to her. As soon as she arrived at the table he got to his feet and greeted her with a kiss on the cheek, his hand resting on her forearm. Butterflies took off in her stomach adding to the chaos there, and her knees felt in danger of buckling at any minute. He smelt delicious, all soapy-fresh-from-the-shower with a dash of crisp cologne. The brush of his stubble against her skin and the touch of his hand combined to send her hormones into overdrive. *Oh my days! What's happening to me?* She was reluctant to focus too much on what made her body react in this out of character way when she was around him – other than his obvious good looks – but there was no denying the chemistry that danced between them.

Fred jumped up, wagging his tail, nudging at her leg. She bent to stroke him, momentarily glad of the distraction, allowing her to regroup and rein in her wayward senses. This was *intense*.

'Hi,' Alex said, his smile warm and relaxed, his eyes locking onto hers. 'What can I get you to drink?' He'd changed into a striped linen shirt – a pair of sunglasses peering from the pocket – and navy chino shorts, and was sporting a pair of canvas shoes. He looked impossibly handsome.

'It's okay, I can get my own, thanks. I just came over to see if I could get one for you.' She glanced at the table to see he had a bottle of beer. Her heart thudding hard beneath her top, she did all she could to appear nonchalant and cool.

'I'm fine, and I've set up a tab at the bar, so please allow me.'

'Oh, okay, in that case, I think I'll have a glass of Pinot Grigio, thanks.'

'Coming up, I'll grab us a couple of menus while I'm at it.'

'Sounds good.' Smiling, she turned her attention to Fred, hoping her galloping heart would calm itself down. 'Hi there, Fred, how are you doing?' She ruffled his ears and he pushed his head into her lap as she made herself comfortable in the chair opposite Alex's. She hoped she wasn't going to feel like this all the way through their meal. She was in danger of not being able to concentrate on the conversation.

Moments later, Alex returned. 'I hope Fred's been behaving himself. He's just over a year old and can get a little overenthusiastic sometimes; thinks everyone's his best buddy.'

'Ah, he's adorable, and he's been as good as gold, haven't you, lad?' Stella smoothed Fred's head, two amber eyes blinking up at her happily.

'That's what I like to hear. Anyway, Cheers,' Alex said, raising his bottle.

'Yeah, cheers to Monday afternoons spent in the Jolly rather than at work.' Smiling, she clinked her glass against his bottle before taking a sip.

'So, what does work involve for you then? What would you usually be doing right now?' Alex asked as he indicated for Fred to tuck in closer to the table and sit down. The Labrador obeyed instantly.

Stella swallowed her mouthful of wine. 'I'd be in the Crown Court over at York.'

'Oh, right. Okay.' His eyebrows shot up. 'In what capacity, if you don't mind me asking?'

'I'm a barrister, not a defendant,' she said, laughing as she realised he was mulling over the possibility of her being on the wrong side of the law. 'And I only take prosecution briefs; I'm not keen on defending.'

'Ah, so I'm guessing you work for the CPS?'

'Nope.' She shook her head. 'I'm at the independent bar; I'm self-employed, but the CPS do employ their own court advocates.'

'Oh, right, I see.' He sat back as if appraising her. 'And I can imagine you're absolutely terrifying for anyone in the witness box. I've only known you five minutes and I'm already scared of you.' He grinned, his eyes crinkling appealing at the corners.

'What? You're scared of me? No way! I'm a pussycat, honest.' She laughed. In truth, it wasn't the first time she'd been told this.

'Yeah, a pussycat with extremely sharp claws and teeth if you cross her.' Alex laughed too, taking a glug of his beer.

'Look, before we go any further, I just want to clear something up.'

'Okay.' He leant forward, resting his arms on the table. 'Fire away.'

'I suspect I know the reason you've already formed the opinion that I'm scary, but I have strict rules about who I date, or even flirt with. I won't go near anyone who has a girlfriend or is married, which is why I backed off from you so quickly when I thought your sister was your girlfriend. I – albeit wrongly – assumed you were flirting despite being in a relationship, so my respect for you plummeted. And I'm guessing my frosty reaction is probably why you think I'm fierce, which I know I am, but only when necessary.' She grinned.

'Good to know, and I hope I'll never put you in a position so you'll find it necessary to be fierce around me.' He grinned back. 'But that aside, you do have a general air of kick-ass about you. I sensed it the moment I first set eyes on you. I liked it.' His eyes twinkled at her.

'That so?' A smile tugged at the corners of her mouth. She liked nothing better than a bit of no-strings flirtation.

'Mm-hm.' He took another swig of his beer, his expression turning serious. 'And for the record, I share your values. I steer well clear of anyone who's in a relationship; they're strictly off-limits as far as I'm concerned. And I'd certainly never cheat on a partner. I value honesty and fidelity. In fact, my last relationship ended because my ex cheated on me.' An expression of regret flittered over his face.

'I'm sorry to hear that,' said Stella, feeling a squeeze of sympathy in her chest.

'Don't be.' He gave a shrug. 'But it did reinforce that I'd never want to be responsible for causing that kind of hurt. It was poor Zara who had the unenviable job of telling me.'

Stella winced at that. 'That can't have been easy, though I do think honesty is the best policy.' Her mind swept back to a time she'd found herself in a similar situation. She'd arrived back at her student house to find one of her housemates in a compromising position on the sofa with the boyfriend of another of her housemates. Lola and Bruno had been more concerned about being found out than how their actions might hurt Tori, which had enraged Stella. She'd demanded that they come clean and tell Tori, warning that if they didn't then she would. They both knew Stella didn't make hollow threats. Much as she'd hated the prospect of the pain it would inflict on Tori, Stella had refused to be a party to any deception. The ensuing atmosphere had been horrendous but Stella hadn't regretted her decision; if she'd been in Tori's position she would have wanted to know, no matter how painful the truth.

'Anyway, I think that's enough doom and gloom from me.' Alex's wide smile reappeared. 'How come you're not in court this afternoon.'

'Ah, well...' Stella gave him a brief rundown of what had happened in the Dixon case, being careful not to mention the threats or the menacing looks she'd been given by Gavin Dixon.

'I thought that sort of thing was just reserved for gritty television dramas.'

'Sadly not, though jury nobbling's not that common.' She leant forward, placed her elbow on the table and rested her head in her hand. 'Anyway, how do you earn your bread and butter?'

'I'm an architect; I'm self-employed, like you.'

'A creative,' Stella said, impressed. 'So would I know any of the buildings you've designed?'

'Actually, I did the—'

At that moment, Immy appeared at their table, order book in hand. 'Just to let you know a table's come free outside if you're interested. I've slapped a reserved sign on it for you. It's the one in the far corner on the right with a sun umbrella.' She smiled between them. 'While you're making up your mind, how about I take your order?'

* * *

'That was delicious.' Alex set his knife and fork down on his plate and leant back in his seat, patting his stomach. He'd had fresh crab salad with a side of the Jolly's legendary triple-fried chips. 'It was like a work of art on a plate, it was almost a shame to eat it, but I couldn't resist.' He glanced across at Stella and chuckled.

Stella dabbed her mouth with her napkin. 'Mmm. I have to say, the scallops were sublime.' She'd opted for a light meal, the heat of the day taking the edge off her usually hearty appetite. It hadn't stopped her from stealing a couple of Alex's salty chips though. Much to her delight she'd found they were perfectly crisp on the outside and as light and fluffy as a cloud on the inside, just the way she liked them.

'Don't suppose I could tempt you to a pudding?' he asked.

'Ooph! No thanks, I'm stuffed right now.' She laughed. 'Might be a different story in half an hour, mind.'

'Coffee then? Or tea?'

Stella shook her head. 'No thanks; too warm. And I'm awash with sparkling water.' Stella had only had the one glass of wine, with a view to working later. She was keen to keep her wits sharp.

'Okay, how about a stroll along the beach? You mentioned earlier that's what you had planned for this afternoon. How d'you feel about a couple of well-behaved companions joining you?' He glanced down at Fred, who was looking up at him adoringly, his tail swishing over the floor. 'Hmm. Having said that, I'm not so sure I can guarantee this one will be well-behaved. He tends to lose all sense as soon as he gets near the sea.'

'Funny, he said the self-same thing about you when you were getting the drinks,' she said with a giggle.

They settled the bill with a brief argument over who was paying – Stella reluctantly backed down and let Alex pay.

'I'll get this one and you can get the next,' he said.

'Ah, that's confidence for you. You think there's going to be a next time?' She gave an amused grin, her gaze locking on his. Much to her surprise, she found herself secretly thrilled that he was thinking along those lines.

They made their way down to the beach, negotiating the bank of pebbles before heading to the shoreline. Alex had thought it best to keep Fred on lead until they got closer to the sea and the Labrador trotted along, his ears pricked as he watched the seabirds bobbing about on the waves.

'Did you grow up in Micklewick Bay?' Alex asked, looking around him appreciatively, the background sound of the waves rushing up to them.

'I did; spent hours down here as a kid.' The gentle breeze lifted Stella's hair and she drew in a fresh lungful of the salty air.

'I love the sea, always wanted to live beside it, which is why I jumped at the chance when I got it.'

'Yeah, I can't imagine living anywhere else.' Her hand brushed against his, sending a jolt of electricity through her. Their eyes met and she knew he'd felt it too.

'So do you have lots of family here? I'm guessing you're

about fifth generation, or something like that. Unlike my family, who are scattered all over the place.' He turned to her, smiling.

'Not at all. My mum moved here when I was a very small baby. We've got no relatives here, it's always been just the two of us.' Rhys's face filled her mind but she pushed it away. Now wasn't the right time to think about her mum's relationship with him.

'What? No siblings?'

Stella shook her head. 'Nope. No father, no grandparents. Just my mother and me.'

'Oh, okay.' A frown flittered across Alex's brow as they paused to let a handful of children race down to the sea, squealing as the chilly water lapped over their skin. 'I can't imagine not having Zara around, though I suppose that could be a twin thing.'

'I don't feel deprived, if that's what you're thinking.' Her pride suddenly kicked in. 'My mother is an amazing woman, she was both mum and dad to me when I was growing up – my father did a runner when she told him she was pregnant and she didn't let that faze her. We didn't need anyone else. She's been a wonderful role model, built her business up from nothing and now it's a huge success with multiple employees. She instilled her work ethic into me, encouraged me to strive to be the best I can be.' Though she meant every word, she hoped she didn't sound like she was ranting or preaching.

Alex paused, as if absorbing her words. 'She truly sounds like an amazing woman. I'm not surprised you're so proud of her.'

'I am,' she said, her tone softening.

'And you've never met your father?' He turned his head to her. 'Tell me to mind my own business, if you like.'

'It's okay, and no, I've never met him.' Stella wasn't keen to share that she didn't even know his name. Her mum had always appeared a little shifty whenever Stella brought the subject of her father up, so Stella hadn't pushed it, fearing it could cause a huge argument, the sort from which there'd be no going back. She couldn't do that to her mum, and she didn't want to be responsible for creating a rift between them. Her mum had a determined stubborn streak, and Stella had learnt when to back down. 'My mum's always been enough, plus, I've had the same tight-knit group of friends since primary school; they're like family.'

'I take it that's the group you were with on Friday night?'

'That's them. Maggie's the newest recruit. Florrie met her at university but she slotted in like she's always been there. She lives at Clifftop Cottage on Thorncliffe.' Stella turned to Alex, smiling. She brushed her hair out of her eyes, 'So, tell me about your family.'

'Well, you've – albeit briefly – met Zara. We're thirty-four and I'm the oldest by ten minutes. We're very close and have always looked out for one another. She's a research doctor and is based in London. We've got a younger brother called Leo, he's thirty-two and is currently working in IT in Germany; he was always the wild one, always up to mischief when he was younger. Our parents now live in Cumbria and our grandparents live in a village called Skeltwick on the edge of the moors. And we've got aunts and uncles and cousins all over the place; Scotland, Australia, Canada, Cornwall.'

'Wow! I see what you mean about being spread far and wide.' Stella secretly thought it must have been overwhelming if they'd all ever lived closer together in this country. She would have found it stifling.

Arriving at the pier, Alex stopped, his gaze travelling to the ice-cream shack on the bottom prom where a small queue was snaking its way over the path. 'Don't suppose I can tempt you to one now?' He nodded towards it, grinning.

Stella didn't need to think twice. 'Mmm. You certainly could.'

Ten minutes later, ice creams in hand, they walked along, Stella filling Alex in on the history of Micklewick Bay, how Old Micklewick was steeped in stories of smuggling, the most infamous smuggler being Jacob Crayke whose decommissioned pistol hung in a glass display cabinet in the Jolly. He'd been arrested and tried in York, then hanged for his many crimes against the tax man. She went on to tell him of the local gentleman, Benjamin Fitzgilbert, who'd led a double life as a member of the local landed gentry and a prolific smuggler. 'Rumour has it there's a tunnel that runs from beneath the Jolly right up to what was once his rather fancy home.'

'Wow! It's fascinating stuff. I'm surprised there's not a little museum about it,' said Alex, fighting a losing battle with his ice cream that was now running down his hand thanks to the heat of the sun.

Laughing, Stella popped the remains of her cone into her mouth and reached into her handbag, pulling out a hand wipe. 'There you go,' she said, chuckling.

'Thanks,' he said, taking it gladly.

They walked on, chatting away. 'Right, this is me,' said Stella, stopping at the foot of a flight of steps that curled their way up to the top prom.

'It's me too.' Alex smiled at her, beads of sweat on his brow. 'Do you have far to go after this?'

Stella shook her head. 'I'm just along at Fitzgilbert's Landing.'

Alex froze, his expression one of utter disbelief.

'What's the matter?' she asked, concern firing inside her.

'I live at Fitzgilbert's Landing. I'm the architect who worked on its conversion.' His voice was loaded with surprise.

'What?' Stella looked at him, his words sinking in. 'You mean to say we live in the same apartment building?'

'Seems we do.' He gave an amused laugh.

'Which floor is your apartment on?' she asked.

'The second, on the left-hand side. Why, where's yours?'

'The second, on the right-hand side.'

'In that case, it looks like we're neighbours.' A smile broke out on his face.

'It seems we are.' Though Stella fixed a convincing smile to her face, she wasn't one hundred per cent sure she was keen on that idea, for a whole variety of reasons.

'At least I know where to call if ever I need to borrow a cup of sugar,' he said.

'Yeah,' she replied, uncertainty filling her chest. Having Alex live so close had the potential for a whole load of awkwardness, especially when their dalliance ended; which it invariably would.

* * *

Reaching their floor at Fitzgilbert's Landing, Alex turned to face Stella. 'Here we are.'

'Here we are indeed.'

'Well, good luck with the unpacking, I dare say you're way ahead of me. It's chaos in there.' He pulled a face, jabbing towards his door with his thumb.

'I'm sure it's not that bad.' She forced a smile, telling herself to just focus on the here and now and not let their close living arrangements spoil their time together. They were both adults, and besides, she was still friends with most of her exes, even worked alongside some of them. Ferdy was a prime example. *Just enjoy your time with him.*

'Oh, trust me, it is.'

He leant in and placed a kiss against her cheek, sending her emotions into a frenzy and her doubts scattering. *Calm your jets, woman!* This was all so very confusing.

'Thanks for a lovely afternoon, I've really enjoyed myself. Any time you fancy some company on a walk, just holler. Fred and I are happy to oblige, we don't know too many folk around here yet.'

'Thanks,' she said, still recovering from his kiss, and half-expecting her knees to buckle at any moment. 'Bye for now.' She gave a small wave, turning to face her door. 'Actually,' acting on impulse, she turned back, 'there's a fundraising event on at The Cellar on Wednesday night. I've got a ticket going begging, you're very welcome to join me and the gang, if you like?' A colleague from chambers had asked Stella to get a ticket on her behalf but had discovered she was needed in the Court of Appeal in London that day and doubted very much she'd be able to get across to Micklewick Bay in time. Hence Stella being in possession of a very convenient spare ticket.

Alex's face lit up with a smile. 'Sounds fun, I'd love to, thanks.'

'Great!' Stella gave him the time and filled him in on what to expect. 'Oh, and it's likely to be packed so it might be best if you leave Fred at home.'

'Fair enough. And I'm happy to walk down with you, if you like? Not pushing, or anything.' He splayed his hands. 'I'll understand if you'd rather head out on your own.'

'Not at all, I'd like that.' She returned his smile. 'See you later.'

FOURTEEN

Inside her apartment, Stella leant against the door, waiting for her stampeding heart to slow down, wondering how a man could affect her in such a way. She closed her eyes and inhaled slowly in an attempt to steady her breathing. She was used to being in control of her emotions, used to being cool, calm and collected, but this? This was something completely new, and she wasn't sure she liked it.

And now she'd discovered Alex Bainbridge didn't just live in the same apartment building as her, but on the same floor and directly opposite? Lark would say it was the universe talking to her. Despite her misgivings, that thought made Stella laugh. She pressed her hand to her chest, there was definitely something talking to her, Stella very much doubted it was the universe; her rampaging hormones more like. She'd be sure not to let them get out of hand; she needed to stay focused on her career and not get distracted.

She headed to the kitchen and poured a long, cool glass of water. Had she really just invited Alex to join her and her friends at The Cellar? What had she been thinking? His presence would result in a load of ribbing from them, particularly

Jasmine and Maggie. She could only imagine what they'd say. She took a sip of water, consoling herself with the knowledge that they at least didn't know what effect he was having on her insides, how her emotions were thrown into turmoil whenever he was near. Only she knew that. As far as her pals were concerned, Alex was just another man she was attracted to, and if they dated, their liaison would have the same finite lifespan of all the others that littered her dating history. She only hoped the sparks she felt flying between them weren't visible to anyone else.

'Right,' she said out loud, setting the glass down on the granite worktop. 'Time to tackle these boxes.'

* * *

Stella had made great in-roads with her unpacking by the time the intercom buzzer sounded. Slotting the last of the books into the bookcase, she headed over to it, surprised to see her mum's image on the screen. Though she'd sent a text earlier, saying how she'd taken the week off, Stella hadn't expected a visit from her mother quite so soon. But then again, Stella had a sneaking suspicion she knew the reason behind it.

'Hi, Mum,' she said, smiling as she opened the door. She noted the pretty tea dress her mum was wearing, and how she was still radiating the same happy glow that had been evident the day before.

'Hello, lovey.' Alice beamed up at her daughter, offering her cheek for Stella to kiss.

'This is a treat. Can I get you a cup of coffee? I was just about to have one. We can drink it sitting out on the balcony, if you like?' As soon as the words were out, Stella wished she could take them back. What if Alex was out on his balcony? Wouldn't that be a bit embarrassing or awkward? Telling herself it didn't matter if he was, she headed towards the kitchen.

'Mmm. A coffee would be great, thanks.' Alice set her handbag down on the table and glanced around her. 'I love the atmosphere of this place. You were so right to snap it up when you did, it's a sound investment.' Her eyes landed on the stack of empty boxes alongside reams of bubble wrap and paper. 'Mind, I don't think Andrea would be too chuffed at having all her handiwork undone.' She laughed jokingly.

Stella followed her gaze and smiled. 'Don't worry, it looks worse than it is. That can all go to the recycling centre in one fell swoop. And, actually, there wasn't much for Andrea to do this morning with me having just moved in a week ago.' She set about frothing a jug of milk.

Her mum nodded. 'Andrea said to tell you she's done some of your washing while she was here, by the way; just some undies. Said she thought it was such a lovely day, she might as well make a start on it and get it hung out in the garden.'

'In the garden?' Stella frowned, popping a coffee capsule into the machine and selecting the lungo button; she quite fancied a large cup of coffee.

Raising her voice to be heard above the noise of the coffee machine, Alice said, 'Yes, she mentioned that since there was no washing line, she grabbed a spare clothes airer from her van and hung the washing on that. Said the garden's a right little suntrap and it'd be dry in no time.'

'Oh, right, okay.' Stella had always had her washing and ironing taken care of through Spick 'n' Sparkle. As a rule, it was taken away in one of the company's laundry bags by Andrea on a Monday, and returned freshly laundered and pressed the next. She really didn't mind that Andrea had made a start on it here at the apartment. Stella always felt guilty that she paid her mum reduced rates for the cleaning and laundry services anyway, but she wasn't sure how she felt about having her expensive silk underwear hung outside. Wouldn't the sun bleach it? She hoped not, some of it cost a small fortune.

Anyway, that was something to think about for later; she'd go and retrieve it after her mum had gone. Next Monday, she'd leave a tactfully worded note to Andrea saying that she'd prefer it if they could just revert back to their usual arrangement as far as her laundry was concerned. 'There you go, Mum.' She handed her a cup of coffee.

'Thanks, lovey.'

They'd just got themselves settled outside when her mum said, 'Rhys thinks you're wonderful by the way. Says you're a chip off the old block.' Smiling, she looked over at Stella, her eyes shining happily.

Stella smiled back, her heart squeezing for her mum. 'Lots of people say that, don't they? And I'm always proud to hear it.'

'Thanks, lovey, that's kind.' Alice took a sip of her coffee, her expression thoughtful. She took a few moments before she spoke again. 'So, what did you think of Rhys? Did you like him?' She turned to face Stella, meeting her eyes.

'I did actually, he came across as a decent bloke and from what I could gather, he seemed genuine.'

'Oh, he's most definitely a decent bloke and completely genuine,' Alice added quickly. 'You know I'm not the sort to get taken in by anyone's flannel. You and I are the same in that regard. And you know better than anyone how wary I've been of having a relationship. There's no way I'd consider getting involved with anyone I didn't think was one hundred per cent genuine and had high moral standards. No way at all.'

'I totally get that, Mum.' From her mother's almost defensive tone, Stella felt the need to take things gently.

'I've honestly given it a lot of thought, which is why I waited as long as I did before I introduced you to him. I wanted to be certain, didn't want to rush things.'

'I know you'll have thought long and hard about it, Mum, and it really is great to see you looking so happy.' She reached over and took her mum's hand, giving it a squeeze.

'And you're really okay with me going on holiday with him?'

'Of course I am! And anyway, it's not up to me.' Stella couldn't help but laugh at that. 'I'm sure you'll have a fabulous time. Tuscany's a wonderful place. It'll do you good.'

Visibly relaxing, Alice breathed a sigh of relief and said, 'Thank you. I'm really quite excited about it. Rhys has booked the flights.'

They sat in contemplative silence for a moment, the only sound the cries of the gulls overhead and the rumble of the traffic below. Stella's mind drifted to the conversation she'd had with Alex about family, in particular her father. She stole a look at her mum, watching as she sipped her coffee, a contented expression on her face. Maybe now would be a good time to ask a couple of the questions she'd been mulling around in her head for some time. Her curiosity had gained momentum ever since her mum had mentioned Rhys, her father occupying an increasing amount of her thoughts.

Conscious of not wanting her mum to feel she was being interrogated about her ex, Stella opted for a more subtle approach, hoping she'd be able to glean the odd scrap of information about him. With that in mind, she asked, 'What was it that made you come to Micklewick Bay all those years ago? I mean, why pick here out of everywhere else you could've chosen? Did you know someone who lived here at the time? Do we have some kind of connection to the town?' Though Stella kept her tone casual, she observed her mum closely.

'Well...' Alice took a slow sip of coffee, the pause instantly alerting Stella's suspicions. 'It's such a long time ago, I can't really remember to be honest. And no, I didn't know anyone from the town at the time.' She gave a shrug, suddenly avoiding eye contact with her daughter. 'I've always liked the seaside, so maybe that was it.' Her body language had switched from being open and happy, to closed and defensive. A familiar pose Stella had seen many times before, particularly when she'd been asking about her father.

'Oh, right. You chose well then.'

'Hmm.' Her mum's lips were pinched, her fingers clutching tightly onto her coffee cup.

Though Stella felt a prickle of guilt for making her mum uncomfortable, something made her determined to plough on. 'And what about your parents – my grandparents – are you never tempted to get in touch with them?'

'No,' Alice said firmly. 'Definitely not. They made it very clear that they wanted nothing more to do with me so there'd be no point. They were very stubborn people, they'd never back down from a decision they'd made.'

Sounds familiar.

'I get that.' Stella nodded, she could understand her mum's point of view. She couldn't even begin to imagine how much it must have hurt, or how scared it had made her mum feel when they'd reacted how they had. It would have taken some pretty cold-hearted person to turn their back on their eighteen-year-old daughter who'd just given birth, the father having walked out. Though she could never imagine being in that position with her mum, she had to concede, she could see why she was reluctant to resume contact with them. 'But what about my father?' *Tread carefully!* 'Whenever I ask about him, you clam up. Have you mentioned anything about him to Rhys?' Stella could have kicked herself at jumping in, but she'd been unable to stop herself.

A cloud fell over Alice's face, her mouth setting in a hard line. 'No, I haven't told Rhys anything about him. Why would I need to? There's nothing to tell, as I've told you many times,' she said, a hint of irritation in her voice. 'I really don't know why you're asking these questions all of a sudden. It's not as if he's going to make any difference to my relationship with Rhys.'

Her mum may have turned prickly, but Stella was undeterred. Didn't she have a right to know who her father was? And surely, wouldn't Rhys at least wonder where Stella's father fitted into the picture? Their relationship may have been brief, but it had produced a child. 'Surely you can tell me his name? Tell me what he looked like,' Stella said imploringly. 'Do I look like him? Is he where I get my height from?'

'Please, Stella!' Alice shook her head and rolled her eyes, refusing to be pushed on the matter. She gave her daughter an imploring look.

Stella's hand flew to her mouth as an abhorrent thought came to her, bile burning in her stomach. 'Oh my God, Mum, you weren't a victim of–'

'Oh, for goodness' sake! Don't be ridiculous! Trust you and your lawyer's brain to go down that route! Of course I wasn't,' she said impatiently. 'I was in a relationship, albeit for a short time, and your father is just someone I'd rather forget. That's all. As soon as he found out I was pregnant he wanted nothing more to do with me. I'll never forgive the fool for not hanging around so he could get the chance to get to know, or play a part in the life of the most wonderful little girl and the wonderful young woman you've become. He's not worth you wasting another second of your thoughts on him, Stella!' Her bottom lip wobbled and she swallowed down a sob. 'I understand that you want to know who your father is, but you've got to trust me on this, lovey, it's best left alone.'

Stella's heart twisted. She rushed over, squatting down beside her mum's chair, taking her hand in hers. Surely there must be something more to the story to generate a reaction like this? 'Oh, Mum, I'm so sorry, please don't cry. I didn't mean to upset you. I was just having a conversation with someone about families earlier and it piqued my curiosity again, that's all.'

'It's okay, flower. It's me who should be sorry, I overreacted. It's just, whenever I think of what he's missed out on because of his selfishness, it makes me so angry.' She patted Stella's hand, tears clouding her eyes. 'I'd hate for you to track him down and for him to reject you all over again. That would be too cruel and you're worth so much more than his pathetic, arrogant rejection. And I'd hate for his puffed-up ego to get some kind of kick out of you going to the trouble to find him.' She sniffed, swiping her tears away.

Talk of her father certainly roused some strong feelings in her mum. 'But surely that's something for me to decide,' Stella said gently. 'I'm a grown woman, not a little girl. I'm tough and I'm rational, and you know I'm not one for being emotional. I won't care if he doesn't want to know me, and I'd quite happily tell him that.'

'Yes, my love, but I'll care. Very much. And I'll want to throttle the living daylights out of the silly old fool.'

'That, I don't doubt.' They looked at one another and laughed. 'And the first thing I'd want to do would be to tear a strip off him for leaving you the way he did. You were so young. There's no way he'd get away with that lightly.'

'Like I said before, my love, he's not worth wasting your energy on.'

That's a classic cop-out response, Mother!

'Right then,' Alice said, clapping her hand on her thigh, apparently drawing the conversation to a close. 'I really need to be going. I'm interviewing a new candidate to add to the Spick 'n' Sparkle team in half an hour. She comes very highly recommended, so I'd best get to the office. Don't want to create a bad impression.' She pushed herself up, her body language back to being assertive and confident.

'Oh, right.' This was the closest Stella had ever got to her mum opening up about her father, and now, it would seem, the chance was trickling away.

'Okay, one last attempt. Are you sure you won't give me his name?' She looked at her mother, imploringly. 'Please, Mum. It would mean such a lot to me; give me some sort of closure, if you like.'

Alice threw her head back, exasperated. She huffed out an impatient breath. 'Stella, we've been through this a hundred times. I don't even know where he is or what he's doing now, so how the heck would you manage to track him down?'

Had she conveniently forgotten about the small matter of the internet? Stella wondered.

'And I'm absolutely positive no good would ever come of you knowing him. He's a selfish, self-centred man. If he wasn't, he'd have come looking for you years ago,' she said bitterly. 'I was well aware of his many failings when I was young and seemingly in love with him, I just chose not to see it – bigger fool me. So I'm afraid it's a firm and final no, and I'm not prepared to discuss the matter further.' She set her coffee cup down on the kitchen worktop and headed for the door, scooping up her bag en route. Reaching the door, she turned back. 'Oh, and I'll see you on Wednesday evening at The Cellar. Rhys and I have tickets for the auction. He bought them a while ago, thought it sounded fun,' she said, though there was no trace of humour in her voice. The door closed behind her with a firm click.

Her mother's revelation stopped Stella's thoughts in their tracks, her mind processing what she'd just heard. *Wow!* She was going to The Cellar with Rhys? She really must be serious about him if they were going public.

Stella sucked in a deep breath. It had been quite a day, from events at court, to her sparring session with Vaughan Elliott in the robing room, to the lovely time she'd had with Alex – it had been more than lovely, actually – not that she was keen to dwell on that. And now this. 'Talk about extremes,' she said aloud.

Feeling suddenly restless, her mind full of such an odd mix of thoughts she was unable to settle on a single one to even make an attempt at processing it, she started to gather the cardboard boxes and packaging together. She'd take them to the recycling centre on the outskirts of town, get the place looking tidy.

As she worked, her mind kept running over the conversation she'd had with her mum. Much as she felt bad to have annoyed her so much by pushing, the lack of knowledge about her father was becoming increasingly frustrating. What reasons, beyond the ones she always gave whenever Stella confronted her about them, could her mum have for not wanting her to track him down? Couldn't she see how unreasonable she was being? Surely he couldn't be a serial killer or something equally unsavoury? And what was responsible for her mum's hesitation before giving her reason for moving to Micklewick Bay?

Whatever it was, Stella made the decision she was going to do all she could to find out.

FIFTEEN

Back from the recycling centre, Stella locked her car away in the garage and headed to the garden at the rear of the building to gather up the washing Andrea had hung out. Her heart sank at the sight that greeted her. '*Ughh!* You've got to be kidding me!' Instead of it being discreetly positioned and tucked away at the side near the hedge – as she'd hoped – the clothes airer had been positioned slap-bang in the middle of the garden, for all the world to see what Stella wore beneath her sober court suits. If that wasn't bad enough, a large herring gull was perched on top of the frame.

On seeing Stella, the bird gave a shriek of consternation, before extending its huge wings and taking flight.

Hurrying over, and desperately hoping she wasn't going to have to contend with any unpalatable seagull deposits, Stella threw the items of washing into the laundry bag she'd had the foresight to bring with her. It briefly crossed her mind that there were far fewer pieces of her underwear than she'd expected as she hooked the clothes airer over her arm. She'd have to make sure she got the message across to Andrea that she'd prefer her washing to be dealt with at the Spick 'n' Sparkle premises. She treated herself to expensive silk underwear as a contrast to the austere clothes she wore for work and knowing what she had on beneath such a stern exterior made her feel good, but it didn't mean she wanted to share her secret with her neighbours.

By the time she sat at her desk, armed with another cup of coffee, Stella's thoughts had found their way back to the conversation she'd had with her mum. Before she knew it, she was typing the name "Alice Hutton" into the Google search bar. Of course, she'd made half-hearted attempts at trying to track down her father many times before now, but there was something about her mother's reluctance to share even a scrap of information about him that seemed to be driving her on more than ever before. And despite what her mother had said about Rhys not being interested in who he was, Stella wasn't so sure. She'd bowed down to her mum's wishes for too long. This time, she was determined to make some headway into finding the man who caused her mother so much distress every time Stella brought him up. And, she figured, a good a place to start as any would be by delving into her mother's past. Surely there'd be the odd photo of her time at university online, even if it had been brief. And if there was one of her mum, there was a good chance it might even feature a certain man too.

Stella's heart started pounding with anticipation as she scrolled down the results of her search.

* * *

Feeling more than a little despondent, with her searches not throwing up anything of any use at all – there'd only been an undated, grainy old photograph of a large group of who she assumed were students, a handful of names beneath, one of which was "Alice Hutton", but it was difficult to make out which one, if any, was her mum – she was ready to call it a day, when a knock at her apartment door startled her. She glanced at her watch, surprised at the time looking back at her and how the light had faded. She'd been so consumed by trying to find even the tiniest nugget of information about her mother – and potentially her father – she hadn't done a stroke of work on any of her briefs. She quickly shut her laptop and headed to the door.

Peering through the spyhole, her heart leapt as she saw Alex standing on the other side.

She opened the door. 'Hi.' She smiled at him.

'Hi,' he said back, looking impossible handsome. 'Okay, so I'm going to start off by saying please feel free to say no, I'll totally understand, but I wondered if you fancied joining Fred and I for a glass of crisp white wine on my balcony? It's such a beautiful evening, and the sunset's brewing up to be a stunner.' The heart-melting smile he gave meant he could have offered her a glass of ditch water while taking in the view of the sewage-treatment works over at Lingthorpe, and she'd have found it impossible to refuse.

'Fred drinks crisp white wine?' A playful smile danced over her mouth.

'I'll have you know, Fred has a very discerning palate. That rotting seagull carcass on the beach that he was showing so much interest in earlier today was totally out of character. I promise.'

'I sensed that about him.' Stella couldn't help but giggle at that.

'So what do you say? Tempted to join us?'

Those eyes! That smile! Oh my days! Could he get any hotter? 'Sounds great. Give me two ticks to change out of this lot.' She indicated to the grey cashmere loungewear she'd thrown on when she'd returned from the recycling centre. In truth, she'd be glad of a moment to calm herself down, get her surging pulse rate in check.

'You look perfectly fine to me. No need to change on our account. Being comfy is good, especially on your days off.'

'In that case, I'll grab my keys.' She'd just have to keep her burgeoning emotions under control as best she could, especially when Alex always seemed so laid-back and impossibly chilled. In fact, though she didn't know much about him, she couldn't imagine anything ruffling him.

In Alex's apartment, and after fussing Fred, who greeted her warmly and with much tail wagging, Stella said, 'So I'm guessing this is pretty much a mirror-image of my apartment?' She glanced around an identical layout to her home, imagining the bedroom/bathroom distribution to be the same. They'd even opted for a similar colour-palette – something that was offered as part of the sale – and the décor was minimal just like hers. He had the balcony doors flung open onto the very same view she enjoyed every day. And he'd been right, from the colours gathering together in the sky, the sunset had every promise of being stunning. She was glad he'd called, she'd been so engrossed in her searches, she'd have missed it.

'It is, yeah.'

Her eyes went to a vintage architects' drafting table and an array of pens and pencils beside it. The tools of his trade. 'Oh, and I should have said this before, but you've done a brilliant job of redesigning the place. I could never have imagined how such a shabby, run-down building could end up looking like this. What's so appealing about it is how you've managed to keep the character of the place and yet bring it up-to-date at the same time. I should think that was quite a challenging prospect.' She smiled, her voice filled with awe. 'It's fantastic. I'm told it's the most desirable property in town, and it's easy to see why. It's greatly improved the kerb appeal of the area.'

'Thank you. Your approval means a lot.'

She turned towards him, her plait snaking over her shoulder. 'It does?'

'Yes.' He nodded, their eyes locking.

Stella's already lively pulse suddenly started stampeding through her body, as her libido surged. The urge to lean in and kiss him hard was becoming increasingly hard to resist. She felt inordinately pleased she'd decided to put her doubts about him living so close to one side; deciding to let their liaison simply run its course.

'Right,' he said, breaking the spell with an unexpected snap. 'I do recall I lured you over here with the promise of a glass of crisp white wine.'

'Indeed you did.' Stella couldn't decide what she felt most, relief or disappointment. Relief at not lunging at him, or disappointment that he hadn't seized the initiative and taken her in his arms and kissed her passionately. Either way, she was glad of having a moment to recover. She glanced down at Fred who was looking up at her, a curious expression on his face. Something told her he knew exactly what was going on in her mind. She raised a finger to her lips and said, 'Shh. Our secret. Okay, Fred?' She winked at him, hearing movement behind her.

'Here you go. One glass of Pinot Grigio, chilled to perfection.' She turned to see Alex, a glass covered in beads of condensation in his hand.

'Mmm. Looks perfect.' She took it, clinking it against his. 'Cheers.' Her gaze swept over his face, hoping to see a trace of the expression he was wearing just moments ago, but there wasn't so much as a hint.

'Cheers to new neighbours,' he said, hitching his eyebrows and smiling.

'Cheers to new neighbours,' she said, her smile matching his.

They sat a while, chatting away and sipping wine as the gentle glow of the sun morphed into the most glorious sunset. It was as if the sky was on fire such was the intensity of colours splashed across it, from blazing orange to rich purple, and numerous shades in between. The wispy, candyfloss clouds had been swirled with colour that reached down and poured its molten ink over the gentle undulations of the sea, the sun slowly sliding towards the horizon.

Stella couldn't remember seeing a sunset like it. 'Oh, wow! That's stunning.' She breathed out, the glow reflecting in her face as she took in the full display, a sense of calm washing over her. 'I'm so glad you knocked on my door when you did or I'd have missed this.' The light breeze ruffled the fine tendrils of hair around her face.

'I'm glad I did too.' His eyes found hers and he leant towards her, his expression changing.

Instinctively, she moved closer to him, her heart hammering in the familiar way it did when Alex was in close proximity. He reached out his hand, cupping her face, his skin warm against hers.

SIXTEEN

With her breathing shallow and her libido raging, their faces were mere centimetres apart when a deep, booming bark sliced through their moment.

Startled, Stella sat back, pressing her hand to her chest.

They both glanced across to see Fred looking at them. He was wagging his tail and looking inordinately pleased with himself. He barked again, his tail wagging even harder and thudding against the table.

'Jeez, Fred, you scared the life out of me!' Stella said.

'Fred! You little horror. Always have to be the centre of attention, don't you?' Alex gave the Labrador a stern look. Undeterred, Fred barked once more. 'I think that's quite sufficient, don't you, young man? Unless you fancy a bit of time-out in your bed?'

At the tone in Alex's voice, Fred's ears flattened. He blinked, and looked away, aware his participation hadn't been well received.

Much as she was disappointed their moment had been ruined, Stella couldn't help but laugh at the Labrador's expressive face. Though it didn't stop her from wondering how it would feel to have Alex's lips pressed against hers, and if she'd get another chance to find out that night.

Just then, his mobile phone started ringing from the living room, sending her hopes of any further kisses scattering.

Alex clapped his hand to his forehead, rolling his eyes in disbelief. 'You've gotta be kidding me!'

'I think that's probably my cue to leave.' Stella gave a regretful smile. She drained her glass and went to push herself up.

'There's really no need, you're more than welcome to stay for another glass, if you'd like, that is.' Alex looked at her hopefully.

She was about to ask if he was going to answer his phone when the ringing stopped. Checking her watch, she considered his suggestion – it wasn't that late – when he said, 'In case you're wondering, I don't intend to return that call this evening and I'm going to turn my phone off. I should imagine it will have just been work-related; it's surprising how many clients struggle with the concept of me having a life outside of being an architect, or that I might actually choose to take some time off, and expect me to be at their beck and call twenty-four seven.'

'I can empathise; sounds like the bar, and chambers to a lesser degree.'

'The not-so-great side of being self-employed,' he said ruefully.

'Have you considered getting a separate phone for work?'

'I have, but it might be a good idea to move on from simply *thinking* about it and actually *doing* something about it. Anyway, back to the matter in hand, what do you think? Can I tempt you?'

Oh, you have no idea! 'Hmm. Yes, why not?' Stella's wayward musings made her cheeks burn with unfulfilled desire.

'Great!' Alex grinned. He was clearly oblivious to the wicked thoughts running through her mind.

Back in their comfy chairs on the balcony, dusk had sneaked in further. The vintage streetlamps had flickered on, illuminating the road along the top prom. Lights from the pier stretched out into the sea and in the distance the odd light from ships punctuated the increasing darkness. A little cluster of lights nestled below Thorncliffe indicated the location of Old Micklewick, while the first stars started twinkling in the sky. It made for an achingly cosy sight.

Stella and Alex settled effortlessly back into their chat, their near-kiss almost forgotten – though not by Stella. It was still very firmly at the forefront of her mind and she couldn't stop wondering if they'd get back to it. Fred was curled up contentedly at their feet. Alex was interested to learn more about her; what her hobbies had been when she was younger, what had made her want to become a barrister? Had she been a swot at school, he'd asked jokingly? That question had made her laugh. 'I suppose some of my classmates would have considered me a swot, yeah, but it wasn't as if I spent every night poring over my schoolbooks. Sure, I was keen to do well, and my mum certainly encouraged that, but I liked to enjoy myself too, and I was sporty as well as academic. I was fortunate enough to have a brain that seemed to retain relevant information, which made life easier for me and meant I could be a part of the sports clubs the school offered. I've always enjoyed being outdoors and I loved being part of a team.'

He nodded. 'Which teams were you a part of?'

'Hockey, athletics – running was a passion – and netball.' A smile spread over her face as she recalled days spent on the school sports field, winning medals and trophies for her achievements. She'd always loved the buzz of competition.

'I'm guessing you were tall in your teens, so you'll have been a much-in-demand player on the netball team!' He grinned at her.

'Yep, by the time I was twelve years old, I was already five-feet-eight and easily head and shoulders taller than all my friends, especially my pal Florrie who has the bookshop. She's always been a little scrap whereas I was so long and lanky; I felt like a giraffe!' she said with a giggle. 'But you're right, it came in very handy playing netball, basketball too.'

Stella had also been a keen swimmer – something she still enjoyed regularly today – passing all the levels in her swimming lessons, joining the local swimming club. 'When I was old enough I enrolled for life guard training and, when I'd qualified, I managed to get myself a weekend job as a life guard down on the beach; I did more hours in the summer. I loved it, despite the sea being absolutely freezing cold!'

'Sounds like you've always been driven, if you could fit that lot in as well as studying hard,' Alex had said.

Stella nodded. 'My mum was my role model. I'd seen what she'd achieved by sheer determination and hard work and I wanted to be the same. I think if you get yourself in that mind-set, you're halfway there.'

Alex nodded, absorbing her words. 'And what does your mum do?'

When Stella had explained about her mum's cleaning company, it clicked that she had the contract for cleaning the communal areas of the apartment, having seen one of her vans parked around the corner.

'Ah, this may sound like I'm telling tales out of school, but I think it was the lady who was cleaning the communal area who left the door open to the back entrance here.'

'The door was left open?' Stella asked, surprised.

'Yes, earlier today. I only know because Fred had managed to sneak out of my apartment door before I'd got his lead on and shot off downstairs.' Fred's ears twitched at mention of his name, his eyes opening briefly. 'He's never one to miss an opportunity for mischief, spotted the door was open and made a break for it in the garden. It was another of the residents here who pointed me in the little monster's direction.'

Stella realised it could have been when Andrea had hung out her washing. Leaving the communal back door open was another reason for her not to have her laundry done there. The fact that visitors had to be "buzzed-in" would no doubt be something the residents of Fitzgilbert's Landing found reassuring, not that there was much in the way of crime in Micklewick Bay, but all the same... Plus, she didn't want such oversights to have a negative impact on her mum's business, especially with it being so easy for people to voice their complaints and niggles on the many rating sites the internet had to offer.

'Thanks for the tip-off. I'll bring it to my mum's attention tomorrow; she won't want it to happen again. Anyway, I've told you loads about me, what about you? What made you want to become an architect?'

'Ah, well...' Alex went on to explain how he'd wanted to be an architect as far back as he could remember. 'I was always drawing buildings, creating elaborate affairs out of my toy building bricks and when I realised you could actually make a living out of designing buildings, then that was it. I never wavered, never wanted to be anything else. Helped that I loved maths.' He pulled an apologetic face.

'Ooh, me too. I love the patterns.' Her smile morphed into a frown. 'Hmm. I've just realised how geeky we sound. I mean, seriously? Who talks about loving maths over a glass of wine?' They both chuckled at that. 'Moving quickly on, what about hobbies? I assume you're not too consumed with your work to allow yourself some time for those,' Stella asked, fiddling with the star-shaped diamond stud in her ear. The earrings were a twenty-first birthday present from her mum and Stella always wore them.

Alex told her how he liked nothing better than a run for a spot of head-clearing, especially if it was along the beach. He reminded her that they'd bumped into one another when they were both doing just that.

'I remember,' she said, smiling. How could she forget? He'd looked so delicious even with sweat pouring down his face.

He'd gone on to say how he used to enjoy climbing until a shoulder injury had meant he'd had to avoid the sport for a while, and he was beginning to resurrect his love of surfing. 'My skills are a little rusty, but it hasn't damped my enthusiasm. Yet.' He grinned at her.

The sound of voices and laughter drifted up from the beach where a small campfire had been lit. It was soon joined by the thud-thud of dance music, and the smell of woodsmoke wafting in the air. Stella and Alex looked on at the shadowy silhouettes eking every last bit out of the day. She smiled, recalling the days when she and her friends had enjoyed such summer evenings.

'So,' Alex said, sitting back in his seat and swirling the remains of wine around his glass, 'it would seem we have quite a bit in common. We're both driven professionally, we're both guilty of being secretly – or maybe not so secretly – geeky, and we like to switch off by being physically active.'

'I think that's a fair assessment.' Stella pulled her eyes away from the beach, doing all she could to keep her mind off heading down a route of just how she'd like to get physically active with Alex. Her gaze rested on his arm, the muscle rippling beneath the sleeve of his T-shirt making her heart ping. She gave an inward sigh of longing.

'And what about relationships? Ever had your heart broken?'

She shook her head, holding his gaze. 'Never been in love, never had a long-term relationship, and never had my heart broken. Which is just the way I like it.' She figured she might as well be honest, she wasn't ashamed of feeling this way.

'Wow!' His eyebrows shot up. 'You've never had a long-term relationship?'

'Nope.' She gave an amused smile. 'I've never wanted to get involved with anyone.' *Until now*, said a little voice at the back of her mind. *You'd very much like to get involved with delicious Alex Bainbridge, wouldn't you?* 'How about you?'

'Well, I've had two long-term relationships. The first one was in my early twenties; lasted a year-and-a-half, I hadn't been long out of university when it started and just sort of fizzled out. Ended amicably, which was good, so no hearts broken there. Erin and I are still in touch from time-to-time actually. She's married now to a great guy called Jacques, has a couple of kids; they live in France.' He sucked in a slow breath. 'And as you already know, I've not long since broken up with someone. Cerys...' He drew in another deep breath, making Stella wonder if he was still hurting from the break-up. 'We'd been together for just over four years and had been going through a bit of a rough patch for a good few months. If I'm honest, it had never been the easiest of relationships, but, against my better judgement, I kept telling myself everything would work itself out. We'd been on the point of breaking up when we agreed to give the relationship another go with the proviso that if at any point either of us felt it wasn't working, then we'd call it a day.' He gazed out to sea, his expression inscrutable in the soft glow cast by the discreet uplighters either side of the balcony doors. 'A week later, Zara spotted her getting up-close and personal with another bloke. And despite Cerys saying it meant nothing, that she still wanted to give us another go, there was no way I could ever trust her again. So, that was the end of it.'

'I'm sorry to hear that.' Stella didn't know what else to say.

'Don't be. It was the right thing to do, just a bit of a shock at the time. We should've just broken up when we first talked about it, instead of dragging things out. Cerys cheating was proof of that. And I wouldn't say my heart was broken as a result, more a little bit bruised.' He turned, flashing his familiar smile. 'Anyway, that's been quite an information-packed few hours. I think I've learnt more about you tonight than I did about my ex in a whole year!'

'Yep, can't argue, it's been a bit of an info-splurge.' Stella laughed too. 'Apologies if you feel I've overshared.'

'On the contrary, I've enjoyed talking to you, finding out about you. You're a fascinating woman, Stella Hutton. And you know what?'

'What?' she asked. He looked impossibly handsome, dark-stubble peppering his strong jaw.

'I'd pretty much decided that, the first moment I saw you walking towards me in the street last Friday, with that confident, kick-ass spring in your step.'

'You did?' Her heart looped-the-loop as happiness flooded her chest.

'I did. Couldn't take my eyes off you, and not just because you're incredibly attractive, by the way. It was like "boom", who *is* this woman? You were giving off this aura of...' He glanced around him, as if looking for the word. 'Oh, I don't even know how to describe it, but I felt drawn to you, compelled to get to know you. I've never felt that way before.' He turned to her. 'Imagine how pleased I was when we kept bumping into one another. I was even undeterred when you'd gone frosty on me. Just made you all the more intriguing.' A smile spread across his face, lighting up his bright-blue eyes. 'And you've got to admit, fate must be playing a part here, putting us in the same apartment building, on the same floor.'

Stella could barely believe what she'd just heard. She swallowed. 'What you've described is something similar to what I felt when I first saw you.'

'You felt the same?' His smile grew wider.

She nodded. 'Mm-hm. I was instantly attracted to you, but on a much deeper level than I've ever experienced.' She felt suddenly vulnerable at revealing this part of herself. She'd never done anything like it before, never felt anything like this before.

She hesitated, considering whether to go on. *Don't forget, Alex has just bared his soul to you.* 'I... um... Oh!' Before she knew it, Alex was standing before her, offering his hand. Looking up at him, she took it, letting him pull her to her feet.

'Stella,' he said, his voice husky as he cupped her face in his hands, stars twinkling in the inky-blue sky above.

'Alex,' she said in a whisper. In the next moment, his mouth was on hers, all hot and sensual. She closed her eyes as a groan escaped her lips, a bolt of electricity shooting through to her core with such an intensity it took her breath away. She pushed her fingers into his hair, their kiss deepening, growing more urgent by the minute as he pulled her closer to him. Fireworks started going off down at the beach, but they were no match for the ones currently exploding in her heart.

SEVENTEEN

Stella lay in her king-size bed, the thoughts that had been crashing around her mind for the last hour had been making sleep frustratingly elusive. At almost one a.m. a balmy warmth lingered in the air. She'd cracked open the balcony door a little, in the hope of tempting in even the smallest breath of the tiny breeze that whispered in from the sea. From what she could hear, the party on the beach was winding down, the music having long-since been silenced, the voices thinned out.

She peeled off her short, silk nightdress and switched her pillow for the one on the opposite side of the bed, savouring the crisp coolness of the twelve-hundred count Egyptian cotton. She puffed out a sigh. Stella would never have guessed her day would end the way it had. It was hard to believe that her morning in court and the following confrontation with Vaughan Elliott had been part of the same day that had finished off with Alex. She closed her eyes, savouring the feeling of his kisses all over again. Wow! She'd never experienced anything like them. Never felt her body react with such an intensity, every inch of her had tingled. No one had made her feel like that before. But then again, no one had ever made her heart lift in the way it did by simply looking at him, and that was before his lips had ever touched hers. It unnerved her slightly, but not for long. She found herself craving the feeling all over again.

Was this what her mum had meant when she'd said Rhys had made her feel different? she wondered. Because, if Stella was being truthful with herself, even though she'd only just met him, something about Alex Bainbridge felt very different indeed. It was as if they were meant to meet. It was as if she wasn't meant to fall for a man until their paths had crossed. Was he the reason she'd never had a long-term relationship? Had fate been waiting for the right moment to throw them together?

'*Ughh!*' Stella punched her pillow and turned over roughly. 'You're beginning to sound like Lark!' All the same, Alex had said something pretty similar, she reasoned with herself. And he didn't strike her as someone who would believe in airy-fairy stuff like that. Not that she was saying Lark was "airy-fairy", but... Well, maybe she was... A little bit... Not that Lark would mind one jot. She was happy being that way. But these feelings for Alex Bainbridge had to be explained somehow. They couldn't just "happen"! She had to be experiencing them for a reason.

How about love at first sight? said a tentative little voice.

'Go away! Stella pulled the duvet over her head. She wondered if she'd wake up in the morning and discover it had all been a bizarre dream. After all, she didn't believe in love, never mind at first sight! What utter rubbish!

She closed her eyes, her mind leading the way to Alex and his rather fine kisses.

* * *

Adding one more thing to her to-do list, Stella scooped up her coffee cup and headed out to the balcony. She was fresh from the shower, dressed in a light, silk dressing gown, her hair wrapped in a towel as she gazed out towards the sea. Cradling her cup in her hands, she stole a sideways glance in the direction of Alex's balcony to see that, though his door was open, there was no sign of him. She felt a pang of disappointment, but it was soon nudged out of the way by the memory of how his kisses had made her feel the previous night. As usual, her heart flipped the way it did whenever she thought of him, though she did her best to ignore it. It didn't stop her from hoping it wouldn't be long before they got a chance to pick up where they'd left off.

At not quite seven thirty, an early-morning haze still hung over the horizon as the sun gained strength before burning its way through – if the forecasters were to be believed, it was going to be another hot day with temperatures soaring to record-breaking levels; the warmth already circulating certainly hinted at it. Despite the early hour, there were already people on the beach, including the usual keen surfers, and a clutch of ladies who went sea swimming several times a week. Though she was a keen swimmer, taking an early-morning dip had never appealed to Stella. The North Sea was bitingly cold even during a heatwave – as her paddle previously had reminded her. These days, with her lifeguarding well behind her, she much preferred a pool, particularly if it was under a Mediterranean sun. Her mum, also a keen swimmer, had mentioned she'd been invited to join a sea swimming group – The Goosebump Gals, she'd said they'd called themselves, the mere name made Stella shiver. As she sipped her coffee, she wondered if her mum was amongst the gaggle of ladies on the beach. She certainly seemed keen to try new things recently. Relationships, foreign holidays without her group of friends. Sea swimming. Whatever next? Stella wondered.

* * *

With an hour-and-a-half's form-filling under her belt – an increasing bugbear of the bar owing to how much it ate into brief prep time – Stella headed out of her apartment building, the heat hitting her like a brick wall. 'Phewph!' She slid her sunglasses on, glad that she'd opted for a cool, knee-length linen dress, the aquamarine shade complementing her colouring.

Arriving in the town centre, she felt just about ready to melt and was glad of the air-conditioning when she reached Oscar's Bistro. She grabbed a refreshing drink while she waited for the preparation of a gift voucher; her contribution to the auction at The Cellar. The place was busy with customers enjoying the bistro's hearty breakfasts, an easy-listening playlist murmuring away in the background.

As Lark's shop was just around the corner, Stella decided she'd head there next. 'Thanks, Theo,' she said, downing the last of her drink, the ice cubes rattling, before heading out of the door.

The window display of Lark's Vintage Bazaar was as deliciously quirky as Stella expected it to be. There were a couple of mannequins dressed in an array of bohemian summer clothing, set to a backdrop of a tropical-looking beach, and decorated with an eclectic range of props, including several colourful faux parrots. You couldn't help but smile; it had Lark's handiwork written all over it.

Pushing the door open, Stella was met with the sound of magical chimes and a powerful waft of essential oils. Her eyes were treated to a host of clothing displays in bright, jewel colours. Lark had always been artistic, and here, in her domain, it showed.

'Stells, flower! It's fab to see you.' Stella turned to see Lark heading towards her, a wide smile on her face. She was achingly pretty. Her small, heart-shaped face made her look a good decade younger than her thirty-three years. Her long, blonde hair hung in loose waves, but for the fine plaits that were threaded through it. She was wearing a loose-fitting pair of cotton dungarees in shades of mermaid-green and had a pair of silk jewelled slippers on her feet. Her armful of bracelets jangled as she pulled Stella into a hug.

'Hiya, Lark. I'm afraid I might be a bit sweaty, it's absolutely scorching out there.'

'Hey, no worries, flower.' She stood back, her hands resting on Stella's shoulders. 'Hmm. *Interesting.*' She gave a mysterious smile.

Stella knew instantly what Lark was referring to. *You don't hang around, do you?* 'What's interesting?' she asked, knowing full-well what it was.

Lark's smile deepened, lighting up her pale-green eyes. 'I've never seen your aura like this before, young lady. It's positively radiant. And as for that sparkle in your eyes, I think we both know what I'm referring to.'

There was no point denying it. 'Okay, I've been rumbled.' Stella laughed, holding her hands up in defeat. 'It's Alex.'

'Alex? The one who was with his girlfriend?'

Stella nodded. 'The very one, only the girl we saw him with wasn't his girlfriend, she's his twin sister.'

'Ah, I thought you couldn't be right about him being a rat.' She reached for Stella's hand and led her towards the room behind the counter. 'Come on, let me make us a drink and you can tell me all about it.'

'Hmm. Okay, but just water for me, thanks.' Lark favoured herbal teas which Stella thought tasted like the juice from a compost heap.

'Come on then, missus, fire away.' Lark grinned at her from her squishy seat.

Once Stella had arranged the many vibrantly coloured cushions on her chair, she said, 'Well, after last Friday at the Jolly...'

'Wow!' Lark said, her eyes wide when Stella had finished

telling her. 'You actually live in the same building, on the same floor?'

'I know, you couldn't make it up, could you?'

'You do realise this is fate, don't you, Stells? I mean, I know you don't believe in things like that; a load of "old rot" is how I seem to recall you've described it on several occasions.'

'Was I really that harsh?' Stella asked with a giggle.

'You were.'

'Sorry.' Stella pulled an apologetic face.

'No worries. Anyway, surely you have to believe there's something in it after all that? There's really no disputing it. The planets have finally aligned for you – and for your mum by the sound of things – which is just amazing.' Lark's face was wreathed in smiles.

'I suppose it is pretty compelling.'

'It's wonderful, Stells! I always had a sense you'd fall in love and have a happy-ever-after.' She clapped her hands together excitedly.

'Now let's not get carried away, Lark. I've only known him five minutes.' Stella shook her head, amused.

'Ah, but what a five minutes they've been! You've never felt this way before; you've always mocked love and romance, but now look at you, you're positively glowing with it.'

Stella couldn't help but smile as her heart swelled with happiness. She knew there'd be no point trying to fool Lark with all her extra-sense malarkey, but it was time to move the conversation in a different direction; she was still struggling to get her head around her feelings for Alex. 'Anyway, my reason for popping in, other than to say hello, is to ask if you've still got that black and white print of Thorncliffe?' She asked, when Lark had eventually stopped enthusing about her Alex news.

'Ah, sorry, Stells. If you mean the vintage photo, I'm afraid it's gone. Old photos are always very popular when they come in,' she said regretfully.

'Drat. I wish I'd snapped it up when I first spotted it. If I hadn't been so distracted, I would've done.' Stella had been heading down Station Square, waiting for the car in front to slip into a parking space, when she'd glanced across at Lark's window display, and the photograph instantly caught her eye, the dark tones emphasising the cliff's power, white, foaming waves crashing at its base, a sky full of brooding clouds above, the odd shaft of sunshine reaching down. She thought it would look perfect in her apartment, hanging above the fire and had meant to text Lark, asking her to put it to one side for her. Unfortunately, she'd been bombarded with work-related phone calls and emails when she'd returned home and it had slipped her mind.

'If any more come in, I'll check with you before putting it out in the shop.'

'Thanks, Lark.'

'Actually, with all the excitement about you and Alex, I've only just realised you're here and not at work.' She giggled. 'How come? I thought you were in the middle of that dreadful trial with that dreadful man opposite that dreadful barrister.'

'That's a lot of "dreadfuls" coming from you, Lark, flower.' Stella chuckled. As a rule, you never heard Lark say anything negative about anyone. 'To cut a long story short, the trial had to be adjourned so I decided to take the rest of the week off. Thought I could do a bit of catch-up with all the forms we get, and also tackle the rest of the boxes in readiness for you all coming round on Saturday.'

'Fab, and how's it going?'

'Not as well as I'd hoped, I should probably be heading off. I still need to drop my auction contribution off with Bill and Pim.'

* * *

'Hey, Stella, it's good to see you.' Pim beamed at her, his blue eyes crinkling warmly as she made her way over to the bar of The Cellar. Tall, broad-shouldered and blond, he fitted the Dutch stereotype perfectly. He and his husband Bill had opened the microbrewery with attached bar just a few years ago and it had instantly become a roaring success, with its taste-bud-tempting beers and "contemporary-saloon" décor. The lite-bites they'd added recently had added to its popularity.

'So, what can I do for you?' he asked in his lilting Netherlands accent, ceasing his polishing of the beer pumps.

'Hi, Pim. I've just come to drop this off for tomorrow night's auction.' She handed him the envelope containing the voucher. 'Should cover a three-course meal for two with a bottle of wine.'

'Thanks, that's really generous of you.'

'Hey, it's for a good cause.'

'Hi, Stella.' Bill slipped behind the bar, his neatly trimmed beard and close-cropped hair standing in contrast to Pim's clean-shaven appearance and casually floppy, jaw-length bob. 'Looking forward to tomorrow night?'

'Very much so. I've just dropped off my contribution, apologies if it's a bit late.'

'The timing's perfect. Pim and I are going to go through all the gifts and promises later this afternoon. Oh, and did he tell you we've reserved your usual table?'

'Not yet, I haven't had a chance.' Pim rolled his eyes good-naturedly. 'By the way, Stella, we've reserved your usual table,' he said with a chuckle, making Bill return his eye roll.

'Why, thank you, Pim.' She giggled.

Pim resumed his polishing. He had his shirtsleeves rolled up revealing a smattering of tattoos. One in particular caught her eye, triggering the faint flutter of a memory.

'Pim, I don't mean to be nosy, but can I ask, does that tattoo have a meaning?'

'What? This?' he asked pointing to what appeared to be a shield of some sort, a set of initials above.

She nodded. 'Yeah.'

'It's my family crest, and these are my initials,' he said, pointing to them. 'My full name's Pim Johan de Groote.'

'Oh, right,' she said, suddenly distracted.

'Wanna know something funny?'

'Okay.' She pushed her mouth into a smile, putting her thoughts to one side.

'The name de Groote actually means the tall one or the big one.' He grinned broadly, revealing even, white teeth.

'Well, it definitely suits you, Pim.' She laughed, thinking he must be at least six-feet-four and positively towered over his husband who was lucky if he scraped five-feet-seven.

'Doesn't it just?' Bill chuckled. 'In fact, you're tall, you could be a de Groote too, Stella. I, however, certainly couldn't.'

'Ah, but you're perfect the way you are,' said Pim, flashing him a cheesy smile, earning him a quick backhander from Bill.

* * *

All the way back home, Stella hadn't been able to stop thinking about where she'd seen the family crest that also adorned Pim's arm, but no matter how hard she racked her brains, nothing would come to her. It was frustrating; she usually prided herself on being able to remember such things.

Inside the entrance area of her apartment building, she collected the post from her pigeonhole and headed upstairs, her heart lifting as she wondered if she'd bump into Alex.

She was to be disappointed, the only sound was the lift rising to the floor above, making her wonder if any more of the apartments had been occupied and as to the identity of the lucky person who'd managed to snap-up the one occupying the top floor.

Inside her apartment, she slipped the post onto the kitchen worktop and headed over to the balcony windows, throwing them open. She took a moment to savour the view and, naturally, take a peek over at Alex's balcony which was empty, the doors now closed.

The thought that she needed to get in touch with her mum about organising a last-minute clean of her apartment on Friday in lieu of the get together popped into her mind. She flopped down onto one of the balcony chairs and fired off a quick text, ignoring the barrage of work-related messages that had been arriving steadily all morning. While she was texting her mum, she also mentioned that the back door to the building had been left open and that it had very probably been Andrea.

A matter of seconds after the text had sent, a reply landed.

> Hi Stella, thanks for letting me know. Got you booked in for a clean on Friday morning. I'm out with Rhys & have had notification of a delivery. Needs signing for and I wondered if you'd be able to pop to my house & be there for me? Should be arriving between 1-3pm today. Thanks so much xxx

Stella checked the time on her phone. At twelve thirty, it didn't give her long, she'd have to drive there, she didn't want to risk it arriving at the earlier end of the estimate. She fired off a quick reply, confirming she'd be happy to, then grabbed her keys and dashed out of her apartment, a sudden thought swirling around her mind.

EIGHTEEN

Number five Magnolia Gardens was cloaked in silence, the metronomic ticking of the grandfather clock in the hallway the only sound. With her heart thudding hard in her chest, Stella quickly stole upstairs, heading across the landing to her mum's bedroom. She hesitated a moment, her hand on the Bakelite handle of the door, guilt squeezing in her stomach. Should she be doing this? *No, of course you shouldn't! Your mum would have a fit if she knew!* But something stronger urged her forward.

She pressed down on the handle and stepped into the room. It had been years since she'd ventured in here she realised as she cast a cursory glance around the bedroom. It had recently been redecorated with a fashionable colour-scheme and bold, statement wallpaper. Her eyes went to her mum's jewellery box – the one she'd once told Stella had been a gift from someone special but had refused to elaborate on when her daughter had pushed her – relieved to see it was still in its usual place on the dressing table. It was flanked by a photograph of Stella on her graduation day and another in her wig and gown to commemorate the day she was called to the bar. Stella felt a tug in her heart, her guilt increasing at what she was about to do.

Stealing across the room, Stella gently lifted the lid of the jewellery box. With her pulse thrumming in her ears, she took a quick photo with her phone as a reminder of how everything was set out. She knew her mum would be able to spot if anything was even slightly out of place. As she gingerly lifted out the top layer, her eyes alighted on the very thing she'd been looking for. Anxiety swirled in her stomach as she carefully picked up the delicate silver locket. She swallowed the lump of nerves that had taken up residence in her throat. *Do you really want to do this?* She took a fortifying breath and before she could think any further, pressed the release catch.

Her brow furrowed when nothing happened. She tried once more, but the catch remained reluctant to give. It was hardly surprising, she supposed. It probably hadn't been looked at for years. After a couple more tries, the two halves finally popped apart just as there was a loud hammering on the door.

'Arghh!' She gasped, panic lurching through her, the necklace slipping out of her fingers.

Pressing her hand to her chest, she turned quickly, knocking over the photograph of her graduation day. 'Oh no!' She glanced at it quickly before rushing downstairs and flinging the door open to see the delivery man and a large parcel on the doorstep.

With the parcel signed for and safely deposited in the kitchen, Stella hurried back upstairs. She went to pick the locket up from the floor but was horrified to discover she couldn't find it. 'No! Don't do this to me!' She carefully lifted out the dressing table stool and felt around the carpet, but it revealed nothing.

Pushing her hands into her hair, with panic prickling over her, she swept her gaze over the cream flooring, but nothing leapt out at her. 'How could this be happening?' Her mother was going to be furious, and Stella couldn't blame her; she'd been snooping and she had no right.

Her stomach was churning violently when something caught the corner of her eye. She glanced down to see the necklace had somehow become snagged on her dress and was hanging there. A tidal wave of relief washed over her. 'Oh, thank goodness!'

With trembling hands, she unhooked it, relieved to see no damage had been done. Taking a deep breath, she gazed down at the images looking back at her from the locket. Her heart leapt when she spotted the initials *JPdeG* above a family crest. It was an almost identical image of the one on Pim's arm, only here the "J" and the "P" had switched places. 'What could this mean?' Stella said, her voice a whisper.

In the other side of the locket was the photograph of a striking young man with blond hair. He looked uncannily familiar, but she couldn't think where from.

Stella's mind was in turmoil as it dawned on her that she'd discovered something significant and she was convinced it had something to do with her father. She set the locket down on the dressing table before taking photographs of each image using her phone. Being careful to return everything to its original position, she closed the jewellery box.

She lifted the photograph she'd knocked over in her haste and went to set it back down when she noticed the back had come loose a little. She couldn't explain what it was that drove her to do what she did next, other than she felt an overriding compulsion. She slid off the back of the frame and set it to one side, before removing the piece of card that was holding the photo in place. It revealed what appeared to be a carefully folded letter. Stella removed the note and set the frame down, instinctively knowing she'd happened upon something of great significance.

With her heart racing she opened the letter out, her eyes running over the words.

The colour drained from her face. 'Oh my God!' She clapped her hand over her mouth as a mix of emotions bombarded her body. She could scarcely believe what she was reading.

NINETEEN

Stella quickly put the photo frame back together, all fingers and thumbs – minus the letter; she was going to hang on to that for now – then stood it back in its position on the dressing table. That done, she hurried out of her mum's bedroom, barely registering the masculine dressing gown hanging next to her mother's on the back of the door.

As she drove away, the guilt of snooping around her mother's bedroom was at loggerheads with the fact that her mum had been keeping secrets from her. 'How could she?' Stella cried, hitting the steering wheel as tears scorched their way down her cheeks. It took a lot to make Stella cry. In fact, she couldn't remember the last time she'd shed a tear, but now the urge to release the rising tide of hurt and deceit was too overwhelming, too great to hold back and she gave in to great wracking sobs.

It didn't take long for anger to become the dominant emotion, pushing its way through hurt, confusion and innumerable others that were swirling around inside her. What right had her mum to keep this from her for so long? And as for the link to Pim, well, she didn't even know where to start thinking about that. What she'd found had only added to the list of questions Stella had about her father. But how the heck was she going to broach this with her mother? She was going to have to confront her at some point. She couldn't leave something as significant as this unspoken, couldn't leave it to burn away in her gut as her anger intensified.

Stella snatched the tears away from her eyes. She couldn't go back to her apartment right now, she didn't want to risk Alex seeing her like this. And besides, her head was too full of what she'd just learnt to simply switch off and hold any kind of normal conversation with him. She wouldn't want him to think she'd gone off him again.

Heading out of town, Stella drove until she arrived at the long road that led to the moors, continuing along until she came to a suitable place to park her car, too consumed by stress to notice the stunning scenery that usually captivated her. She indicated right and slowed down.

The car that had been behind her for much of her journey – tailgating her at times – swerved around her and shot off, the driver revving the engine aggressively. If she didn't know better, she'd have thought whoever it was had been following her. She watched as it reached the crest of the hill, almost taking off it was travelling so fast.

Pulling up, sending a handful of the free-roaming sheep scattering, Stella stilled the engine and sat back in her seat. She took a moment, gazing out at the miles upon miles of undulating moorland, her mind going to the letter and what she'd found at her mother's.

She pulled out her phone and enlarged the photos she'd taken of the locket, confirming to herself that the initials were almost identical to those of Pim's tattoo. She scrutinized the photo of the young man, noting the laughter in his eyes, the unsettlingly familiar expression. Where, exactly had she'd last seen that face. Realisation slowly dawned and she pulled down the visor, taking a moment before she looked in the mirror. She gasped, pressing her hand to her mouth. There, gazing back at her were those self-same eyes, the resemblance so strong, it was uncanny.

When she was finally able to pull her gaze away from the photo, Stella set her phone down and turned to the letter she'd tucked into her handbag. The words on the page leaving her in no doubt she'd finally discovered the identity of her father. Johan de Groote. The only problem was, how could she track him down and get in contact with him, if that's what she decided to do? And what the heck was she going to say to her mum?

TWENTY

As she drove home, Stella arrived at the uncomfortable conclusion that she was going to have to be honest with her mother. There was no other way she could tackle the conversation or tell her she'd discovered the identity of her father. And it was a conversation she was keen to have sooner rather than later. There was something else niggling her too, and it was her mum telling her she'd had no reason to settle in Micklewick Bay other than she thought it looked pretty. If that was the case, how had Pim found his way there? It was too much of a coincidence that he'd just turned up by chance. And what was the connection between them, other than the obvious initials? They had to be related, of that she was certain. Stella had a lot of questions and she was determined her mum wasn't going to wriggle out of answering them this time.

Parking up in her garage, she checked her reflection in the mirror on the back of the visor. She wanted to make sure all traces of her tears had gone. The pale blue eyes looking back at her triggering a reminder of the young man in the photo. Satisfied she'd removed all tearstains, she climbed out of her car and made a dash for the front entrance of her apartment block.

Much as she'd love nothing more than to see Alex, she felt now still wasn't the right time, so she hurried up the stairs and rushed to unlock her door, glad to be in the quiet sanctuary of her home.

Massaging her temples, she headed over to the balcony doors and threw them open, though she had no intention of sitting out there right now, the refreshing, salty air that flooded in was more than welcome. She'd make a coffee first, then start her internet trawl; work would have to wait.

Now she had a name, she felt buoyed by optimism that she'd have some success in the search for her father. That thought made her heart jump.

As she was waiting for her cup to fill, the aroma of coffee beans swirling around her nose, her eyes landed on the clutch of letters she'd collected from her pigeonhole earlier that day. She scooped them up and quickly checked through them. There were a couple of circulars – they went straight into the recycling bin – a magazine from one of her favourite clothing companies and a letter in handwriting she didn't recognise.

She ripped the envelope open and unfolded the single piece of paper it contained. Her stomach clenching as the words, written in large, uppercase letters leapt out at her.

I KNOW WHERE YOU LIVE

She stared at the paper, her chest heaving, her breathing short. Her mind raced through a mental list of who would send her such a thing. Gavin Dixon and Vaughan Elliott jumped out as the most likely candidates. Dixon would be trying to scare her off pursuing the case against his son, the threat – it couldn't be construed as anything other – to push her into advising the CPS to drop it. Vaughan Elliott would no doubt be smarting about their spat yesterday morning. But would he really stoop to doing something like this? she wondered. Actually, yes, she thought, he would, or at least get someone to deliver the note on his behalf. His reputation for being unscrupulous had mushroomed over the last year.

The next thing to cross her mind was how whoever it was knew where she lived? She hadn't lived there long. She must have been followed. That thought sent a prickle of anxiety running up her spine. If Vaughan Elliott was responsible, then he was risking being disbarred, not that she could see that bothering him much. He was so slippery, he'd have convinced himself that he'd get away with it; blame someone else. If it was Gavin Dixon, he risked a prison sentence. He probably hadn't even thought that far ahead, and had just assumed she'd bow down to his threats, just as his daughter-in-law and certain members of the jury in his son's trial had no doubt done.

She snatched up the envelope again, checking the postmark to see there wasn't even a stamp. 'How did—' Anxiety squeezed in her chest. Of course, the back entrance door! Whoever it was must have sneaked in when it was left open, found the pigeonhole with her name on and posted the note. A rash of goosebumps broke out over her skin. 'Flipping Andrea!' The fact that someone who bore her ill will had been in her apartment building didn't sit easily with her.

Her mind went to the car that had been driving so closely behind her earlier that day. Could the two be linked? she wondered, her concerns building. She really hoped not; she had enough to deal with without having to worry about someone who had an axe to grind. She'd have to call chambers, bring them up-to-speed with the threats Gavin Dixon had made to her before the trial was adjourned. She'd also have to contact the CPS as well as the police officer in the case. And now she'd become potentially personally involved like this, she'd have to step away from the Dixon case; someone else would have to take over the brief. One thing she knew for certain, she wouldn't be sorry to see the back of that family.

She released a juddery sigh, the thought crossing her mind that she'd need to find out who to contact to access the CCTV to the premises. All entranceways to the property were covered by cameras which offered her a grain of reassurance that whoever had sneaked in would be captured on film.

But for now, she just needed a minute to regroup and let her heart rate settle.

She grabbed her coffee and eased herself onto the sofa, feeling utterly bombarded, wondering what else could possibly happen that day?

TWENTY-ONE

With her clerk and the officer in the Dixon case contacted, Stella sat down at her desk and lifted the lid of her laptop. She was going to put all thoughts of the Dixon family out of her mind for now, she needed to clear her head to focus on other matters. Her stomach churned as she typed in the name she'd seen mentioned in the letter she'd taken from the back of her graduation photograph. She hesitated a moment, her hand hovering over the return key. Before she could change her mind, she tapped on it quickly, her eyes widening at the number of results it churned up.

After quickly scanning through the list, she was disappointed to find that, at first glance, none leapt out at her as she'd hoped they would. Her heart sank; this could take some time.

There were several men with the name Johan de Groote, most of them based in The Netherlands, though none seemed to fit the age group she was searching for, and none of them resembled any of the grainy images in the photographs she'd seen. But though her father was proving a difficult man to track down, Stella wasn't going to give up. She'd toyed with the idea of asking Pim about his father, wondering if he could be somehow related to hers, with Micklewick Bay apparently being a common factor between them, whatever that could be. But she decided against that; she'd rather keep what she'd learnt to herself for the moment. As for what she was going to say to her mother, she couldn't even begin to think about that right now. All Stella knew was that she wasn't looking forward to seeing her at The Cellar tomorrow night, she wasn't sure she'd be able to hide her feelings. She'd just have to remind herself that tomorrow night wasn't about her and her mum, and it wasn't about the mysterious, elusive Johan de Groote. It was about a family trying to raise funds to send their daughter to the States for some pioneering, life-saving treatment. That put things well and truly into perspective for Stella. She'd be sure to keep it in her mind for tomorrow night.

Confronting her mum was inevitable, but it had to be when there was just the two of them and definitely not when Rhys was around. It would probably be best done at Magnolia Gardens where Alice wouldn't feel so wrong-footed or ambushed as she might if Stella invited her here to her apartment to discuss it. It went without saying that she'd have to be very careful how she approached it, that it would be best when the shock didn't feel so raw with her, when the heat of her anger didn't burn so intensely. The last thing she wanted was to risk having a huge argument with her mum, it was bad enough she'd have to come clean about her snooping – though that would be a weight off her chest. One thing was for certain, however Stella tackled it, it wasn't going to be received well. Not after all these years of keeping it a secret.

Stella had had enough and decided she needed a break from trawling the internet and wasting hours looking for something she wasn't going to find. She told herself she'd be better off channelling her energy into her work, provided she could concentrate on it. So, she made a fresh coffee and pushed the, albeit scant, information about her father into a file and into the top drawer of her desk.

Almost two hours later, Stella was surprised to find she'd made decent inroads into a manslaughter brief she'd been sent by Newcastle CPS. In the midst of her work, she'd had a text from her mother, thanking her for signing for the delivery, but Stella hadn't had the stomach to reply. She'd have to soon, before her mum started wondering what was wrong. The last thing Stella needed was her mum coming round; the risk of her recent findings rushing out in an angry torrent was too high right now.

With a headache brewing at her temples, Stella flipped down the lid of her laptop and headed to the balcony where she took a much-needed lungful of fresh air.

'Hi,' said a familiar voice, sending a ripple of excitement through her and chasing her tension away.

She turned to see Alex leaning on his balcony railings, a warm smile on his face, his gorgeous eyes squinting in the bright sunshine. Fred, who was sitting beside him, started wagging his tail as soon as he saw her. 'Hi.' She couldn't help but return Alex's smile.

'Had a good day?' he asked. Stella noted he had his phone in his hand; she thought she'd heard the sound of someone talking a few minutes ago.

'Mixed.' She demonstrated, tipping her hand from side to side. 'How about you?'

'Not bad.' He nodded. 'I've been dealing with a particularly challenging client, but I think I've finally come up with something he's happy with.'

'That must feel good.'

'Yeah, it does. He had to accept some things are just impossible and would never get past the planners.'

'Well, I'm glad for your sake he did.'

'Yeah, me too. Wasn't easy, I'm sure he's given me some grey hairs,' he said, laughing. 'Anyway, you saved me from having to knock on your door. I don't suppose I could tempt you to join me at Oscar's Bistro? I've just been onto them, managed to get an early table. Thought, as you're not in court, you might be up for it.' His tone was hopeful.

Stella took a moment before she answered. Did she really fancy going out after the day she'd had? Actually, yes, she did. She fancied it very much. 'I'd love that, thanks.'

'Great!' He beamed at her. 'The booking's for six o'clock. Is that doable for you?'

She glanced at her watch, it was already five thirty. 'Yep, I'll go and get changed. Give me twenty minutes and I'll be ready.'

'Cool, I'll give you a knock then.'

Stella shot back into her apartment, scooped her hair up on top of her head and ran into the shower. That done, she hurriedly wrapped a towel around her, quickly brushed her teeth and washed her face before applying a flick of mascara and eyeliner, finishing with a dusting of highlighter. After a spritz of perfume, she slipped on another of her linen dresses and was good to go. Just as she'd pushed her feet into her sandals, there was a knock at the door.

'Hi,' she said, opening it and greeting Alex with a smile.

'Wow!' He ran his gaze over her. 'You look amazing.'

'Thank you.' Her heart lifted. 'You don't scrub up too badly yourself.' She smiled up at him.

Stella loved the ambience of Oscar's, it had a laid-back, easy air, the excellent food belying its casual atmosphere. They followed the manager who led them to a cosy table for two in the corner, the sound of their feet tapping over the wooden floor. Already, the bistro was heaving, lively chatter mingling with the playlist of traditional French music. The mouth-watering aroma of seafood filled the air. Stella felt the stress that had gripped her body for the afternoon slide away. Sitting them down, the manager handed them each one of the large menus. 'Nikki will be with you shortly. Hope you have a lovely evening with us.' He smiled warmly.

Moments later, a fresh-faced young girl appeared before them. She was dressed in black trousers and a fitted white shirt, and had a basket of bread in her hand. 'Hi there, I'm Nikki and I'm your waitress for the evening. I wondered if I could get you any drinks while you peruse the menu?' She flashed them a cheery smile as she set the bread down.

'How about we go for a bottle of Pinot Grigio?' Alex asked, peering over his menu at Stella.

'Sounds good to me.' She nodded.

'Great. A bottle of the Italian Pinot Grigio, please, Nikki.' He smiled up at her.

'Coming right up.' She beamed between the two of them. 'And can I get you a carafe of water for the table?'

'That would be nice, thanks,' said Stella.

With Nikki heading over to the bar, Alex asked, 'So, I don't suppose you fancy elaborating on the sort of day you've had? You described it as "mixed" when I asked you earlier.' He helped himself to a chunk of bread and started spreading butter over it.

Stella sat back in her seat and puffed out her cheeks, wondering how she should answer that.

Before she had a chance, Alex glanced across at her, concern furrowing his brow. 'That sigh doesn't bode well. I hope you're not finding my company boring already.' He grinned at her, making her heart flutter.

'Not at all, I'm really glad to be here.' She smiled back. 'It's been quite a day actually. Not at all what I expected.'

'In a good way or a bad way?' He sat back, giving her his full attention.

'Definitely a bit of both.'

'Care to share any of it? I'm a good listener, I'd like to be able to help if I can.'

Before she could answer, Nikki returned with their bottle of wine in a metal cooler. Stella and Alex looked on as she poured them each a glass once Alex had tasted it and declared it delicious.

'I'll be right back with your water. I can take your order then, if you're ready,' said Nikki.

True to her word, she returned, nodding her approval as both Stella and Alex ordered the hot smoked salmon salad starter. 'Ooh, that's my favourite. The hot smoked salmon is to die for.'

For her main course, Stella opted for Oscar's legendary fish pie with sea herbs and a side of samphire and seared vegetables, while Alex plumped for a steak with chunky chips and salad.

Stella's stomach growled loudly, reminding her she'd had no lunch that day. She helped herself to a chunk of bread, telling herself it was best not to drink on an empty stomach.

With Nikki out of earshot, Alex asked, 'Have you had a chance to think if you'd like to talk about your day? Maybe start with the good stuff?'

Stella chewed thoughtfully on her mouthful, wondering which part she could ideally describe as good. 'Well...' she said, swallowing, 'cutting a long and very messy story short, today I discovered who my father is; his name at least.'

Alex was about to take a sip of wine but paused, setting the glass down on the table instead. He didn't attempt to hide his shock. 'Wow! That's major news. Are you happy about it?' The look in his eyes, revealed he'd sensed her uncertainty.

'Confused might be a better word, I think.'

'Right,' he said slowly.

She looked at him, holding his gaze. Did she really want to tell him she'd been snooping around her mum's house? She didn't want him to think badly of her, but it was going to be difficult to tell him the full story without sharing that piece of information. After a brief wrestle with her thoughts, she decided a slightly edited version would suffice. 'I'd rather not say how I found out, but I discovered his name is Johan de Groote.' It felt rather strange saying his name out loud. 'Anyway, it would appear he has a link to Micklewick Bay, and maybe even...' She paused a moment.

'Maybe even?'

She heaved a sigh and lowered her voice. 'Maybe even to Pim, who's joint-owner of The Cellar, but I'd be really grateful if you could please keep this to yourself; I haven't mentioned anything to Pim yet. I'm sure it'll come as much of a shock to him as it has to me.'

'Course, my lips are sealed.' Alex nodded, his expression calm as he absorbed her news. 'And you've really never had a clue about a connection before now?'

'No.' She shook her head. 'Not one. Had no reason to.'

'So what kick-started it, if you don't mind me asking?'

Stella found she didn't mind him asking at all. In fact, it felt good to share it with him. She already knew from their chat yesterday he was easy to talk to, a good listener; didn't judge. Something in her gut told her she could trust him. She went on to explain how she'd noticed Pim's tattoo when she'd called round earlier that day, and how it had triggered a distant memory. She kept out the part where she'd gone snooping and taken the letter from her mum's, and instead merely said that it was Pim mentioning the name Johan de Groote which had led to her putting two-and-two together, and finally realising who her father was.

'It's certainly quite a way to find out,' Alex said, taking a sip of his wine.

Stella gave a wry laugh. 'Tell me about it. The name's never cropped up before, and it was the first time I'd spotted Pim's tattoo.' She paused. 'The only problem is, my mum doesn't know I've discovered this yet, so I'd appreciate you keeping this to yourself too.' She didn't want to say how she was concerned it was going to cause a huge rift between them and how that thought absolutely terrified her. Part of her also felt bad about sharing this with someone she'd known for barely five minutes before speaking to her mum about it. It set her wondering if her mother had told her the truth when she'd denied telling Rhys anything about Stella's father. He's bound to have asked about him.

'Don't worry, your secret's safe with me.' Alex gave her a sympathetic smile and reached across the table, taking her hand, weaving his fingers through hers. 'This can't have been easy for you. I'd have understood if you hadn't wanted to come out tonight, you must be feeling a bit punch-drunk with it all. Though I have to admit, I'm impressed at how calm you seem, as if you're taking it in your stride. You're a strong woman, Stella.'

She smiled and gave a small laugh, enjoying the feeling of her hand in his. 'Thanks, though I'm just managing it as I do my work-related issues. I've learnt to pack challenging situations up and put them away until I need to tackle them. My brain seems to do it without me having to think about it. Helps keep the unpalatable stuff out of my mind. The last thing I want is the grim details of the cases I deal with bothering me in my down time. Sounds heartless, but it keeps stress at bay.' It was also helping to keep her from dwelling on the letter she'd received today, that and telling herself it was just an idle threat, designed purely to intimidate.

'I totally understand; no one could criticise you for that. In fact, I'm sure most people would envy that skill.'

'Maybe. Some people think it makes me look cold and hard.'

'I wouldn't worry what other people think.'

'I tend not to,' she said with a laugh. 'The exception being my mum and my close circle of friends.' Stella was surprised to find that she'd added Alex to that select group.

Just then, Nikki arrived with their starters. And, just as she'd described, they looked mouth-watering, beautifully garnished with an array of sea herbs and edible flowers. The chef here was clearly creative.

'Mmm. Looks fantastic!' Alex said enthusiastically.

'It so does,' agreed Stella, her mouth watering in anticipation.

'Enjoy, guys!' Nikki said, walking away, her ponytail swishing from side to side.

'Anyway, I think I've hogged enough of the conversation,' said Stella, dropping her napkin onto her lap and picking up her starter knife and fork. 'Tell me about what other wonderful places you've worked on. I mean, you must have a pretty impressive portfolio if you were given the brief for the warehouse. I've heard the guy who originally bought it is a real stickler for detail and design.' She pushed her mouth into a smile and pushed thoughts of her mother – and her new-found father – out of her mind.

'You're bang on the money, there. He is a real stickler, but has great vision too. He really cares about getting things right, using sustainable materials and keeping as much of the original features in buildings as possible. I'm working on a few other projects for him, not that I'm at liberty to say.'

'Ooh, sounds intriguing. And I don't suppose you're allowed to say who he is either, are you? I gather he likes to foster an air of mystery around himself.'

Alex chuckled. 'I'm not so sure that's the reason. And I couldn't tell you if I wanted to. I don't know his name, I just deal with his next-in-command.'

'And is that okay? I mean, don't things get a bit lost in the process if you're having to use a go-between?'

'On the contrary, it's very straightforward. I've got to know what he likes, and what he doesn't like. We've never had any problems in that regard. And from what I can gather, he's very well-respected by his staff; treats them well apparently.'

'That's good to hear.'

The evening passed pleasantly, the bistro was buzzing with the staff busy tending their tables. Stella found herself relaxing despite the background hum of stress she hadn't quite managed to squeeze into the "box" as effectively as she usually did, but then again, the issues she'd been tackling today had been mostly of a personal nature, their impact potentially huge. As ever, Alex was easy company, making her laugh at his self-deprecating jokes and tales of Fred's mischievous ways. She'd never encountered a man like him, the boundaries she usually had up, keeping romance at bay, could very easily tumble away. She found herself wanting to get close to him, imagining how it would feel to melt into his arms. It was most un-Stella-like and right now, she didn't want to fight it. Instead, she wanted to embrace it, give herself up to these new, unfamiliar feelings, yet something still held her back. And she knew exactly what it was: her mum's warnings, not to let a man into her heart were never far away, particularly when there was someone new on the scene. Stella reached for her wine glass and took a sip, peering over at Alex as she did so.

Before she knew it, they were ordering dessert. Stella had opted for ice cream while Alex hadn't been able to resist the rice pudding with rhubarb puree and ginger shortbread crumb.

'Oh, this is sublime, you've got to try some,' he said, offering her a spoonful.

He was right, the intense creaminess of the vanilla-infused rice pudding was cut through by the sharp tang of the rhubarb, the ginger crumb offering the perfect texture and kick of heat to finish. 'Mmm.' She closed her eyes and savoured the mouthful. 'Heaven.'

'I chose best,' he said, grinning at her. The flickering light from the candle in the old wine bottle on the table cast a warm glow over his face. He seemed oblivious to how attractive he was, and the appreciative looks that were regularly directed his way.

'You definitely did.' She couldn't help but grin back, her eyes falling to his mouth that looked irresistibly kissable.

They were sipping coffee when the bill arrived on a small white plate, Nikki setting it down on the table between them. Before Alex had a chance to think, Stella quickly reached for it. 'This is on me.'

When he went to complain, she said, 'That was the deal; you picked up the bill for our meal at the Jolly, so I said I'd get the next one, which is this. No arguments.'

'But I invited you out.'

'I don't care, doesn't mean to say I can't pay. You can get the next one.' She flashed him a cheeky smile, making him laugh.

'It's a deal.'

Outside on the street, Alex slipped his arm over Stella's shoulders as they made their way to the top prom, having decided to head home the scenic way. Hearing footsteps bearing down on them, her heart suddenly upped its pace and she turned anxiously to see a tall youth wearing a black sweatshirt, the hood pulled up, obscuring his face. She gripped tightly onto Alex, inadvertently alerting him to her concern.

The youth loped by them, Stella breathing a sigh of relief.

'You okay?' Alex asked, concern drawing his brows together.

She nodded, feeling silly for overreacting. 'Yeah, just thought we'd better get out of the way of such a determined walk. Sounded like he was going to trample us.' She laughed hoping to make light of it, but she could see from his expression he wasn't buying it.

At eight thirty, the top prom was still teeming with people, the air balmy. A lone seagull was perched on the railings, letting vent to its feelings with a screeching cry. A moment later, it had taken flight before swooping on an unsuspecting man who was sitting on a bench looking out to sea while he tucked into a portion of fish and chips. The man sat in disbelief for several moments, looking at his empty lap where his fish and chips had been only seconds before, all those around him, including Stella and Alex, hooting with laughter.

The excitement over, the couple strode along hand-in-hand, Alex regaling her with tales of his surfing disasters. 'I was seriously, *seriously* bad for ages. I got pretty close to giving up until one day it just seemed to click. I love it now, though I don't get as much time to put my surfboard to use as I'd like.'

'You should make time, if you enjoy it,' she said.

'True.' He smiled down at her, before pressing a kiss to the side of her head and pulling her close to him.

This feels good.

Soon, they were back at their apartment building, loitering on the landing between their doors.

'Can I tempt you in for a drink?' Alex asked.

Much as the offer was tempting, Stella found herself saying, 'Not tonight, thanks, Alex. It's been a really lovely evening but I'm suddenly feeling shattered. Think I'll get an early night.'

He nodded. 'I totally understand. I dare say today will have been emotionally exhausting for you.' He reached out and squeezed her shoulders. 'Can I ask though, is everything okay? It's just you seemed a bit edgy when we were walking back, checking over your shoulder all the time. There's nothing worrying you, is there?'

'Oh, no. Not at all. I wasn't aware I was doing that.' She hadn't realised she'd been so obvious. 'Sorry to have worried you.'

'No need to apologise.' His face broke out into a smile. 'But if you feel you need a finely tuned killing-machine to protect you, Fred's your man. Don't be fooled by his happy-go-lucky exterior, I can assure you it belies the highly trained protector beneath. He's not known as "The Assassin" for nothing.'

Stella fell into a fit of the giggles as she conjured up an image of Fred in his role as protector. 'I'll be sure to keep that in mind.'

'You do that.' Alex's expression turned serious. 'You know where I am if you need to talk, or if there's anything causing you concern. You've got my mobile number, you can call me any time, day or night.' He stepped closer, closing the gap between them and took her face in his hands.

'Thanks, Alex.' She gazed up into those deep-blue eyes, wondering if she'd been right to turn down his offer of a drink. In the next moment his lips were on hers, sending a whoosh of emotions shooting right through her. Butterflies swooped and dived inside her and her knees buckled. The intensity of his kiss literally took her breath away. By the time they pulled apart she half-expected to find herself in a molten puddle on the floor. *Wow!* This was a whole new experience for her.

'Thanks for an awesome evening. I'll see you tomorrow.' He gave a lopsided smile as he headed for his door.

'See you tomorrow,' she said, though her heart was screaming for him to come back, that she'd changed her mind and wanted to join him for that drink, and so much more.

It was unlike Stella not to give in to her urges, to resist the prospect of falling into bed with Alex – her usual mantra that "it's only sex" not seeming to fit her feelings for him. What she had with him – though she wasn't fooling herself, this was early days – felt so very different to her previous encounters, which were no more than dalliances. She shared something with Alex she'd never shared with anyone before; they had a *connection*. She'd already accepted that her feelings went way deeper than simply fancying him – which she did, like crazy. If she'd gone to bed with him tonight, which she was sure was where they were destined to end up, it would have felt no different to her usual dates, the ones where she'd had no emotional attachment. And she badly wanted it to be different with Alex, wanted to treat what was blossoming between them with care; nurture it. Though it scared her if she thought too much about it, she sensed Alex was going to be someone special in her life, if she'd let him. And that was the crucial thing, *if* she'd let him.

* * *

Stella woke with a start, sitting bolt upright, her heart hurling itself against her chest. She glanced around to see her bedroom was in darkness thanks to the thick curtains at her window. She lay still for a few moments, listening, but all she could hear was the sound of her pulse thudding in her ears. Reaching for her alarm clock on the bedside table she saw it was one fifty a.m. What could have woken her at this hour?

Easing the sheet back, she climbed out of bed and tiptoed across the floor in her silk nightdress, her steps muffled by the thick carpet. Opening the bedroom door a crack, she paused, listening hard, her breathing sounding noisy in the silence.

Hearing nothing untoward, she slipped through the door and into the hallway, inching towards the living area. A loud thud out on the balcony made her start and set her already racing heart galloping frantically.

Reasoning with herself that she lived two-storeys up and no one would be able to access her apartment from outside, she tiptoed over to the balcony window, peering through a gap in the curtains. It was impossible to see anything so, feeling bold, she flicked the switch for the outside lights and opened the curtains a little wider.

Relief washed over her as her eyes alighted on one of the outdoor seats that had blown over. 'Oh, thank goodness,' she said, pressing her hand to her chest. She'd deal with it in the morning. On the other side of the road, a car flicked its lights on and slowly drove away. It sent a shiver running through her. If she wasn't mistaken, under the glow of the vintage streetlight, it looked like the same kind of vehicle that had been tailing her when she'd driven out to the moors. 'It's just your imagination playing up,' she told herself before turning out the light and heading back to her bedroom, doing all she could to convince herself she was right.

TWENTY-TWO

Wednesday dawned with rain beating against the windows, the blue skies of the last week replaced with sullen grey clouds. Stella peered through the glass of the balcony door. The sea was dark and brooding, waves hurling themselves at the shore culminating in a mass of spray and foam. It was the perfect sort of day to stay indoors and attend to her paperwork. She also intended to delve a little further into tracing her father. The internet was bound to churn up something about him if she looked hard enough.

Her mind went to her mum and the realisation that she'd be seeing her tonight at the auction at The Cellar. Pim too. She closed her eyes, marshalling her thoughts. It was going to be difficult to resist the temptation to say something to either of them. She'd gone from her family consisting of no more than her and her mum, to suddenly knowing the name of her father and potentially being related to Pim. That took some sinking in.

She was distracted by her mobile phone ringing and snatched it up from the kitchen worktop. 'Hi, Allegra.'

'Hello, Miss Hutton, I just wanted to let you know the CPS have been on and booked you as junior in a murder brief. It's the case that's been making the headlines here recently, the one with the man who'd been on the run. The silk for the prosecution is Aiken Ferdinand. Thought you'd like to know.'

A thrill ran through her. It was always a boost to be briefed in such a high-profile case. 'Thanks, Allegra, I appreciate that. Do you know when I should be getting the brief?'

'I'm afraid I'm not sure of that yet, but rest assured, I'll let you know as soon as I do,' said Allegra. 'And, just to keep you up-to-speed with your situation, I've been informed the police have asked for the CCTV footage of your apartment and they've been questioning Gavin Dixon. He of course denies all knowledge, but he would say that. Interestingly, he was arrested for assault yesterday and has been in police custody ever since, so if it was him who sent the note, then you can breathe a sigh of relief. He's locked up and won't be making any trouble for anyone for the foreseeable future.'

Stella's heart sank at hearing this. Much as she was glad that Dixon had been locked up, if he'd been in custody for the last couple of days, then it begged the question, who had been tailgating her and who had been parked across the road from her apartment in the early hours of this morning? The more she'd thought about that, the more she'd come to the conclusion she was the reason they'd been there. Had Dixon got one of his heavies to bother her?

Not wanting to throw cold water over her clerk's news, she said, 'Thanks, Allegra, that's good to know.'

Deciding to put the Dixon family out of her mind, Stella grabbed the list she'd made and left the apartment. She was going to head to the supermarket with the intention of gathering up some more essentials for her apartment-warming party on Saturday. She also wanted to place an order at the local deli for a selection of their locally renowned dips, cooked meats and artisanal breads.

* * *

Arriving back at Fitzgilbert's Landing, glad that it had stopped raining so hard, Stella spotted a young woman in a green raincoat. She had deep copper hair that was tied back in a high ponytail, and was looking flustered as she struggled with an armful of boxes, attempting to press the buttons of the lift.

'Here, let me give you a hand.' Stella rushed forward and pressed the "up" button, noting several more boxes stacked on the floor beside the young woman.

'Oh thank you. I'm struggling to see anything from behind these.' She gave a good-humoured laugh, her smile friendly, her face pink with exertion and speckled with raindrops.

'Tell you what, I'm guessing these other boxes are yours, so why don't I grab them and travel in the lift with you? Save you having to come back for them.'

'Are you sure it's not too much bother?' The young woman asked, her eyes going to the bulging tote bag filled with shopping hanging from Stella's shoulder.

'Honestly, I'm happy to help.' She smiled at the young woman before squatting down and gathering up the boxes.

Moments later, the lift pinged open.

'After you,' said Stella.

'Thank you so much.' The young woman looked inexorably relieved at Stella's help. 'I've lost count of how many times I've been up and down in this lift today.' She chuckled.

'I feel your pain. I was in your very shoes last week.' Stella smiled. 'What floor number is it?' she asked when they'd both stepped inside.

'Three, please. I know I should probably have taken the stairs, but I'm sure I would've fallen flat on my face and sent these boxes scattering everywhere.'

'Which is never good.' Stella laughed. 'And the reason the lift's definitely the most sensible option when you're lugging a load of boxes around. I'm Stella, by the way. I live on the second floor.'

'Oh, right. Pleased to meet you, Stella. I'm Brooke.'

'Pleased to meet you, Brooke.' Stella wondered if Brooke was moving in on her own but didn't like to ask for fear of sounding nosy.

Stopping at floor three, the lift doors slid open. Brooke stepped out onto the landing, the boxes tumbling from her arms. 'Arghh! No! I could feel that happening but couldn't stop it in time.'

'Are you okay?' Stella peered over her armful of boxes. 'I hope there's nothing breakable in there.'

'I dare say I'll find out soon enough.' Brooke pulled a regretful face. She hurried over to her apartment, unlocked the door then made her way back to Stella who was gathering the scattered boxes together. 'Thanks for your help, I really appreciate it.'

'No worries. I'm happy to help.' With the boxes scooped back up, Stella followed her neighbour into a mirror-image of the layout of her own apartment, which was directly below. The only apparent difference was the décor which was slightly more feminine with hints of dusky pink off-set with sage green. There were boxes piled-up everywhere. Where would you like these?' she asked.

'Oh, just pop them over next to the others, thanks,' said Brooke, who was making her way to the kitchen. 'Most of my stuff might still be stashed away in boxes but I made sure to unpack the most important items first.' She grinned waving a kettle at Stella. 'Can I make you a cup of tea by way of saying thank you for helping me?'

'I didn't do much, just carried a few things.' Stella chuckled. 'And are you sure you've got time?' She glanced around at the chaos. She'd be itching to get things tidied away if her apartment looked like this. She'd kept her boxes piled neatly against one wall as she'd worked through unpacking them, and all were clearly labelled so she knew exactly what they contained and where the contents needed to go. She couldn't see any such labels on Brooke's boxes.

'It's the least I can do.' Brooke said over her shoulder as she filled the kettle. 'I'd be making one anyway, I'm gasping.'

'In that case, I'd love one, thanks.'

As they sat and drank tea and tucked into a packet of chocolate-dipped oat biscuits Brooke had also kept handy, Stella learnt that her neighbour – who looked to be in her late twenties – had moved to Micklewick Bay from York. She'd bought the apartment with her fiancé, Marcus, who was currently away on a business trip in Frankfurt, sourcing goods for their online luxury homeware store, and wouldn't be back until Saturday morning.

Stella warmed to Brooke instantly. She was chatty and friendly and had already shown a glimpse of a wicked sense of humour which Stella found appealing.

'Don't worry, as soon as Marcus gets here, he'll have everywhere ship-shape. He's as tidy as I'm messy,' Brooke said with a giggle. 'He actually loves cleaning, can you imagine that? And I'm happy to leave him to it.' She grinned.

'Don't blame you,' said Stella. 'Actually, I'm having a bit of a housewarming get-together on Saturday night, just a few friends, but you're both welcome to join us if you'd like. My apartment's directly below you, so I'm easy to find.'

'Sounds great! I'd love to. Thanks.' Brooke beamed, her dark-green eyes shining. 'Will any of the other residents be there?'

Stella nodded. 'Alex from the apartment opposite me will be there, but other than you and him, I haven't met anyone else here yet. I've heard the lift go a couple of times though.'

'I suppose it's to be expected, us all moving in at staggered times; we'll all have different completion days.'

'True.' Stella got to her feet. 'Right, well I'd best be off. I've got a mountain of work that I was hoping to be much further through than I am by now. Good to meet you, Brooke. See you Saturday.'

'See you Saturday, and thanks again for the help.'

At six thirty on the dot, Stella heard a knock at her apartment door. Her heart leapt at the prospect of seeing Alex again. She opened it, her stomach looping-the-loop as she saw him standing before her looking achingly handsome in a teal-coloured shirt and jeans. He really was easy on the eye, stubble grazing his chin affording him a rugged air.

'Hi,' she said, not bothering to rein in the huge smile that was tugging at her mouth. His appearance had chased away the anxiety that had been building at the prospect of seeing her mum after what she'd learnt. And then there was Pim. Stella couldn't even begin to work out where he fitted into it all. But now, with Alex on her doorstep, a lightness washed over her.

'Hi,' he said, leaning forward and pressing a lingering kiss to her lips, her hormones launching into a happy dance. 'Ready to head to The Cellar?' he asked once he'd reluctantly, pulled away.

'Mm-hm.' She nodded, feeling slightly dazed from the touch of his mouth on hers. She could have quite happily dragged him into her apartment and led him straight to the bedroom – despite her resolution to take things slowly. That was a much more appealing prospect than facing her mum.

'I'm pleased to say it's stopped raining for now, so I suggest we make a dash for it, much as I could stand here kissing you for way longer.' He pressed his forehead against hers before giving her a last passion-filled kiss, leaving her feeling more light-headed than ever.

Out on the street, having gathered her wayward emotions together, Stella was relieved to find that Alex was right about the rain. The wind, however, was still hurling itself around, making the sea look decidedly choppy. It was such a difference to the warm and balmy days they'd been enjoying. Stella fastened her coat, glad that she'd had the foresight to tie her hair back into a low ponytail to keep it from ending up in a tangled mess.

Alex took her hand and they hurried along, taking the shortcut through the narrow streets to Endeavour Road where The Cellar was located rather than savouring the walk along the top prom, buffeted by the wind as they went. They spotted a woman battling against the elements with a large golf umbrella on the opposite side of the road. In the next moment a powerful gust blew the thing inside out and the woman let out a shriek. Stella stole a sideways look at Alex, and from the amused look in his eye she guessed he was struggling to keep his laughter in just as she was.

Stella let out a sigh of relief when they arrived at The Cellar, it was good to get out of the wind. Alex held the door open, the hostelry's familiar playlist of rock/folk fusion spilling out onto the pavement. Though they were early the place was already buzzing with eager customers. 'There's Florrie and Ed.' Stella waved over to where they were sitting in a large semi-circular booth. Florrie's eyes lit up as she spotted her friend. She nudged Ed and the couple waved back, smiling broadly.

Alex ordered their drinks from a cheerful-looking young server with a neatly clipped beard. He was sporting The Cellar's uniform of fitted waistcoat over a crisp white shirt, black skinny jeans and a long apron bearing the bar's logo, tied at the waist.

Stella's gaze stole to Pim who was pulling a pint from the gleaming Micklewick Mischief beer pump. He was chatting away in his usual friendly manner. She wondered what he would think of the prospect of them being related. She looked more intently, trying to see any trace of family resemblance other than blond hair, blue eyes and, of course, the height. She noted his long, straight nose, just like hers – which she didn't get from her mum; hers was turned up at the tip. As if sensing her watching him, he turned and nodded, his smile widening. Stella started, feeling her cheeks flush, embarrassed at being caught staring. Recovering quickly, she nodded and returned his smile.

'Right, here you go, one Pinot Grigio.' Alex handed her the glass while he reached for his pint of The Cellar's famous Micklewick Magic beer.

Arriving at their booth, Stella smiled and said, 'Hi, folks, can I introduce my neighbour, Alex Bainbridge.' She turned to Alex. 'This is Florrie and Ed, they have The Happy Hartes Bookshop in the square.'

'Ah, yes, the shop with the amazing window displays.' Alex nodded.

'Hi, Alex, good to meet you.' Florrie gave him a friendly smile. 'And it's Ed who's responsible for the window displays. I just look on in awe.' She laughed.

'Hi, Alex,' said Ed, smiling. 'It's great that you could join us. And it's good to hear you like the window displays, they're fun to do.'

'Ed's an artist,' said Stella, sliding along the leather seat beside Florrie, Alex following her.

Alex nodded. 'Ah, that explains why the displays are so awesome.'

They'd just got settled when they were joined by Maggie and her husband Bear.

'Ey up, folks,' Bear beamed at them. He was built like a brick proverbial, with an unruly head of hair and thick, bushy beard. He was often described as looking like a Viking though his muscular stature belied his gentle nature.

'By 'eck it's bloomin' nippy out there. I don't know what's

happened to the sun, but it can get its backside back in that sky.' Maggie giggled, unbuttoning her coat and revealing her growing baby bump.

'Mags, Bear, this is Alex,' said Stella. 'He's my neighbour.'

Smiling, Bear held out his hand. 'Hi, Al–'

'Flippin' 'eck, don't tell me I'm not the last one to arrive.' Jasmine's voice sliced through the introductions. 'I don't think I've ever turned up anywhere before Lark.' She giggled. 'Ooh, hello.' Her eyes widened when she spotted Alex. She clearly recognised him from Stella's brief encounter with him at the Jolly. She turned to her friend, giving a quick waggle of her eyebrows.

'Jazz, this is Alex.' Stella gave her a warning look. 'Alex, this is my friend, Jasmine.'

'Hi, Jasmine, it's good to meet you.' Alex gave an amused smile. He was clearly picking up on the two friends' non-verbals.

'It's fab to meet you too. Hope you're prepared for a night with us lot. It's not for the faint-hearted.' She grinned at him as she unfastened her coat. 'Especially when we start grilling you.'

'Oh, right.' Alex shot Stella a vaguely concerned look.

'Take no notice, we're a very tame bunch,' said Maggie.

'Don't say I didn't warn you,' said Stella.

'Yeah, I'm just joshing.' Jasmine slid onto the bench beside Maggie. 'Shuffle up, missus.'

Lark and her friend Nate arrived five minutes later, quickly followed by Jean Davenport and her son, local author and poet Jack Playforth.

Before they knew it, the bar was heaving, the music battling with the hum of chatter. As she was chatting to her friends, Stella noticed her mum and Rhys squeezing their way in the direction of the bar. Her mum looked over and waved, Rhys following suit. Stella mustered up her best smile, waving back as her stomach started rolling. She looked on as her mother spoke to Pim who was taking their order, checking to see if there was anything in her facial expression that revealed she knew his identity, but it was too difficult to tell from where she was sitting. Stella could count on one hand the times her mum had mentioned she'd been to The Cellar so doubted she'd know Pim and Bill particularly well.

She watched as they made their way over to the table where Florrie's parents were sitting with Jasmine's, the friends falling effortlessly into conversation. From the greeting, it struck Stella that the two other couples were familiar with Rhys, they'd clearly met him before. The thought that her mum was pretty good at keeping secrets crept into her mind, triggering a squeeze of annoyance in her stomach. *Stay calm, Stella. Tonight's not the night for getting angry with your mum.* Inhaling a deep breath, she fixed a smile to her face and turned back to her friends, launching into telling them about how she'd met another one of the residents at Fitzgilbert's Landing.

'Right, ladies and gentlemen, can I have your attention, please.'

Everyone turned to see Bill standing in front of the bar, microphone in hand, looking as neatly groomed as ever. 'As you're all aware, the reason we're here tonight is to help raise funds so Chris and Hannah Readman can send their little girl Fleur for some pioneering, life-changing treatment over in the States. We've got some amazing lots – thank you to all who've donated so generously – so please, dig deep. And, without further ado, let's get started.'

A rousing cheer and round of applause followed, punctuated by the odd "whoop".

They were halfway through the auction, with bidding heating up on the latest lot before taking a break when the door opened, setting the bell above jangling. 'I'll give twenty pounds more,' said a voice with a melodic accent. Stella's head shot round to see a tall, broad-shouldered man with floppy blond hair amble across the room. He wore an air of confidence and a self-assured smile. Her brows drew together as something made her instinctively turn to her mum.

She watched as her mother's expression morphed from happiness to utter horror. Alice clasped her hand to her mouth, shaking her head in disbelief. Moments later, she muttered something to Rhys, grabbed her coat and bag, and fled the bar, her face ashen. Rhys, looking bewildered, followed close behind as Florrie and Jasmine's parents watched, wearing expressions of confusion.

'What the heck was all that about?' asked Florrie, who'd witnessed it too. 'Do you think your mum's okay? Sorry, daft question, she's clearly not, but do you have any idea why she looked so upset?'

Stella couldn't answer, her brain struggling to compute what Florrie was saying to her. She glanced back at the tall, blond man who appeared oblivious to the reaction his arrival had generated in her mother. He reached the bar and struck up a conversation with Pim whose usually friendly expression had been replaced by an uncharacteristically stern look.

'Everything okay, Stella?' she heard Alex say, the same question repeated by Florrie.

'I just need to... Sorry, can I just squeeze out?' Stella asked, her heart thumping as her friends looked on. She was too preoccupied by what she'd just witnessed to formulate a coherent reply right now.

She weaved her way around the tables on autopilot, nausea churning in her stomach. Finally, Stella found herself standing by the tall stranger. She glanced at Pim, the serious look in his eyes suddenly fading as realisation dawned.

'Oh, shit!' he said, pushing his fingers into his thick, blond hair. 'I don't know how I didn't realise...'

'Didn't realise what?' asked the stranger, turning to follow Pim's gaze.

'Stella... Oh, jeez... Seeing you like this, side-by-side, it's so obvious.' Pim swallowed hard. 'Stella, this is Johan de Groote. Johan, this is Stella, Stella Hutton.'

The stranger's smile faltered, his eyes roving her face. 'Did you say Hutton?'

'Yes, my mother's Alice Hutton. I believe you knew her once,' she said, a challenging glint in her eyes.

TWENTY-THREE

'Alice Hutton? Hmm. Yes, I believe I did,' Johan de Groote said.

He spoke far more calmly than Stella was expecting. She noted his lilting Dutch accent was stronger than Pim's. As for the lazy smile he was wearing, she found it infuriating. That, combined with the way he was resting so casually against the bar, lent him an arrogant air.

'So, tell me, how is dear Alice these days?'

Dear Alice? He's got a nerve! Stella felt her blood beginning to bubble as her anger levels inched up. 'My mother's doing very well, actually. In fact, you've just missed her.' She pinned him with her hardest stare. The pale-blue eyes looking back at her were unwavering, but she held firm.

He gave a small laugh. 'Yes, I'd heard she was doing very well for herself. As, from what I can gather, are you, Stella.'

That threw her momentarily off balance. She wasn't expecting him to know anything about her. Blinking quickly, she regrouped. 'And how would you know that?'

'Well,' he said slowly, an amused expression creeping over his face, 'it's surprising what you can find out on the internet.'

Stella couldn't argue with that, her profile was on the chambers website for all to see. She clenched her jaw, myriad emotions bombarding her body. She was fighting hard against the urge to scream at him, tell him to quit with his annoying, smarmy attitude! Did he think by being "amusing" it was going to make her like him? And what the heck did her mother ever see in him? He was *awful*! Surely she must have got it wrong; he couldn't be who she thought he was. She couldn't imagine her mum giving the time of day to a man like this, so full of his own importance, so infuriatingly arrogant.

Pushing her shoulders back, she said, 'So, you're the man who was dating my mother when she was at university?'

'Yes,' he nodded slowly, 'we dated in our first year at university.' There was that annoying smile again.

'And you're the man who turned your back on her when she told you she was pregnant, am I right?'

His eyes flickered away and he pushed his lips together, taking a moment to formulate his reply. Stella was pleased to see she'd dented his confident air, albeit slightly. 'Hmm. That's not *quite* how I remember it, but yes, we split up, if that's what you mean; hadn't been together long, it wasn't anything serious.' He gave a casual shrug.

'Is that right?' She glared at him, keeping her voice low, reminding herself of the reason they were at The Cellar. *Tonight's about the Readman family.*

Pim, who'd been observing events unfold, concern hovering in his eyes, leant across the bar and said, 'Would you like to come through to the back? Might be better to talk there?'

'Good idea,' said Stella, just as Florrie appeared by her side, squeezing her arm.

'Stells, are you okay?' she asked, her petite face full of concern. 'Alex was wanting to come over to see that you were all right, but I put him off; I wasn't sure if you'd want that.'

Stella sucked in a deep breath and shook her head. 'Thanks, Florrie. I'll explain everything when I'm finished. I'm just going through to the back for a few minutes. Tell everyone not to worry.' She mustered up a small smile.

'Okay, but you know where we are if you need us.'

Pim led them to a small room just off the kitchen. 'I'll just be in the bar if you need me.' He gave a tight smile before heading through the door.

Stella turned to the tall man standing before her. It was easy to see their shared resemblance in this brighter light, and that his slightly unkempt blond hair was streaked with white. 'So, getting back to what we were talking about in the bar, are you telling me you don't think your girlfriend at the time telling you she's pregnant with your baby is *serious*?' Her chest was heaving, her breathing short.

He splayed his palms. 'Hey, now let's not get things blown out of proportion here, and please don't twist my words.'

Stella gave a scornful laugh. 'Tell me how it was then, because that's how it sounded to me.'

She folded her arms defensively in front of her. 'This isn't at all how I expected meeting my father for the first time would be.' In truth, it was about as far removed as it was possible to be. Ever since she was a small girl, she'd dreamt about this day, imagining him greeting her with open arms, scooping her up, telling her he loved her and had missed her and had been so desperate for the day he could actually meet her. That dream had changed as she'd grown older, grown more cynical, but even so, she hadn't ever imagined she'd feel such hostility towards the man whose genes she shared.

'I'm sorry if I disappoint you, Stella,' he said, sounding anything but.

'You're sorry you *disappoint* me? What an utterly futile comment.' A look of disgust distorted her features. 'It's not about you disappointing me, it's what you did to my mum! Walking away like that, leaving her on her own to fend for herself. What kind of man does that?' *And you walked away from me.*

'You're describing a very black and white situation, but, as with so many things, it wasn't quite as straightforward as that.'

'Oh, and how was it then? Come on! Now's your chance! You've had thirty-three, almost thirty-four years to think of an answer. Go for it!'

'I'm not sure now is the right time to explain. Emotions appear to be running high.' He looked away, rubbing his hand over the back of his neck.

Is he for real? 'Something tells me there would never be a right time for you to face-up to your actions.'

'What you don't realise is that I'm dealing with a lot of difficult stuff right now. My health isn't great and I haven't got anywhere to—'

'Is everything okay with you guys?' Pim's voice made them both turn.

Stella shook her head, pinching the bridge of her nose between her forefinger and her thumb. 'I'm really not sure how to answer that, Pim. This whole situation seems surreal.'

'I thought I should let you know the auction's about to resume.' He looked between them, giving a concerned smile.

'Thank you, son.' Johan's words stopped Stella's train of thoughts.

Son? Of course, why hadn't she realised? *That would mean Pim wasn't only related to her, he was her...? Oh, jeez, this is too much to get my head around right now.* 'Thanks, Pim. We're done here for now.' With that, she turned and headed back to the bar, her mind reeling, her chest squeezing. She didn't know how she was going to explain any of this to her friends, never mind Alex. As for her mother... Her stomach clenched at that thought. What on earth was she going to say to her mum?

TWENTY-FOUR

Stella arrived back at the table, a sea of worried faces looking at her. She squeezed back in to where she'd been sitting earlier, reaching for her glass of wine and taking a glug.

'Is everything okay, Stella?' Alex asked, his eyes soft with concern.

'I'm not sure,' she said, releasing a long breath.

'What's happened, flower,' asked Maggie.

'If it's that arty-farty-looking bloke that's upset you I'll go and kick his backside,' said Jasmine, her green eyes flashing and her cheeks flushing as they did when something had angered her. 'He certainly seemed to put the wind up your mum.'

'I got a very strange vibe from him, Stells, and from the brief glimpse I got of his aura, it left me feeling a bit concerned.'

That Lark rarely ever said anything negative about anyone meant her comment struck a chord with Stella.

'Is everything all right?' her friend asked softly.

'I think so, and you're not the only one who got a strange vibe from him. I'd appreciate it if you'd keep this to yourselves for now,' she said lowering her voice, 'but that "arty-farty-looking bloke" – I can't believe I'm about to say this – turns out he's actually my father.' She figured there was no point hiding it from her friends.

An almost deafening silence followed, her friends looking back at her, unmistakable shock on their faces. Jasmine's mouth was hanging open while Florrie had clamped her hand over hers. Alex wrapped his arm around her, pulling her close and rubbing her arm. She leant into him, his strong reassurance soothing.

Lark was the first to speak. 'Do you think his appearance is linked to your mum rushing out the way she did?'

She nodded. 'I think it has everything to do with why she rushed out.'

'Oh, Stells.' Florrie reached for her hand, squeezing it tightly. 'It must be a huge shock for you, him turning up out of the blue like this.'

'You could say.' Stella glanced around at them all, feeling numb. 'It's going to take some sinking in.' She held back from mentioning Pim, unsure if he wanted to broadcast the news just yet, if at all.

Jean Davenport, sitting opposite, said, 'I'm sure it'll all come right, lovey. Look how everything turned out for Jack and me.' She smiled kindly.

Jack, who was sitting beside his mother, nodded. 'Aye, I have to agree,' he said in his gravelly North Yorkshire accent. 'It was a heck of a shock for me to find my birth mother and hear her story after all these years, but look at us now.' He put his arm around Jean and hugged her, indisputable affection in both their eyes. 'Neither of us could be happier with how things turned out.'

Jack Davenport had only learnt he was adopted after his adoptive parents had died. What he'd found out had led him to Micklewick Bay where, quite by chance, he discovered the identity of his birth mother. As an unmarried young woman, Jean had found herself pregnant at a time when it was viewed with much disapproval, not least by her parents. With her boyfriend, who was the father of her unborn child, running off with her so-called best friend, Jean had found herself with no alternative but to give up her baby. It was something she'd done secretly, and with the help of Ed's grandparents. It had given her great comfort to know her little boy had gone to a couple who would love him as their own. And she'd always hoped, one day, he'd come looking for her.

'But you had your reasons to give up your baby, Jean. My so-called father turned his back on me and my mum, not caring what happened to us, you made sure Jack went to a family who would love him.'

'I can understand why you feel that way right now. You've had a shock, but things will settle down,' Jean said kindly.

'I wonder why he's turned up now, after all these years?' Jasmine voiced exactly what had started running through Stella's mind.

'He mentioned something about his health not being great, and that he was dealing with a lot of stuff.' Stella nibbled on the corner of her mouth.

'And you think that might be why he's landed here in Micklewick Bay?' asked Maggie.

'I don't know.' Stella's heart sank at the thought. After being so desperate to find him, she suddenly found herself wishing he wasn't here.

'Just be careful, flower,' Lark said. The unfamiliar warning note in her words sending anxiety shooting up Stella's spine.

'Don't worry, I will.' She gave Lark a shaky smile.

'And don't forget, we're here for you whenever you need us,' said Florrie, the others agreeing wholeheartedly.

* * *

'Are you sure you're okay?' Alex asked when they arrived outside her apartment door.

Stella mustered up a smile and nodded. 'Yeah, I just need to process it all.'

'Well, you know where I am if you need to talk.' He rested his hands on her shoulders. 'I can't imagine what you're going through right now, but please feel free to call, text or knock on my door any time, I really won't mind.'

'Thanks.' She looked up into his eyes, the kindness she saw there making her throat tighten.

He wrapped his arms around her, holding her tight and she let herself melt into his embrace, blinking back the tears that threatened. She rested her head on his shoulder, breathing in his comforting scent, savouring the feeling of reassurance that suddenly overwhelmed her. No man had triggered such a feeling in her. Uncharacteristically, she found herself glad of it.

With her emotions under control, she lifted her head, gently – and reluctantly – releasing herself from his embrace. 'Thanks for being so understanding.'

'Hey, it's nothing.' He smiled before pressing his lips to hers and kissing her softly. 'Try to get a good night's sleep if you can – easier said than done, I'm sure, but everything will look better in the morning. And if you fancy joining me for breakfast, just holler.'

'Thanks.'

Inside her apartment, Stella threw her keys into the bowl on the console table by the door, then scrunched up her eyes and scrubbed her face with her hands. 'What a mess!' Tonight hadn't turned out to be anything like she'd expected. She'd thought the evening would be spent with her being on the receiving end of a slew of loaded looks and teasing from her friends on account of her taking Alex along. Part of her had been dreading that, but it would have been far more preferable than what had actually happened.

She padded to her bathroom and turned on the taps of her large free-standing bath, adding a generous dash of soothing bubble bath. She felt the urge to soak away the negative emotions that currently gripped her body.

With her hair piled on top of her head, Stella stepped into the scented bubbles, sliding down into the soothing warmth and closing her eyes. She needed to work out what she was going to say to her mother but at this very moment, she just wanted to let the warmth envelop her and relax her mind. She very rarely acted in haste, and this situation was no exception. She needed to think it through from every angle, consider the best way to break it to her mum that she knew the identity of her father, and when to do it. She hadn't decided what to do about the letter, but with Johan de Groote turning up, it had somehow lost its urgency.

Wrapped in a snuggly dressing gown and armed with a mug of hot chocolate, Stella grabbed her phone from the kitchen worktop and made herself comfortable on the sofa. Though it was just gone eleven o'clock, she felt compelled to call her mother. In fact, she'd half-expected to receive a call from her mum, explaining her hasty exit, but there'd been nothing. There had, however, been a slew of messages from her friends, offering words of support and telling her not to worry. Reading them had made her smile, they really were the best bunch. Selecting her mum's mobile number Stella pressed the call icon, wondering what Rhys knew of the situation. After all, rushing off the way she had was going to take some explaining. When the call went straight to voicemail, Stella called her mum's land-line, disappointed to find the answerphone kicked in straight away. Her mother, who rarely went to bed before midnight, clearly didn't want to talk to anyone tonight.

Heaving a sigh, Stella threw her phone down on the sofa and flicked the television on. She'd watch something mindless while she drank her hot chocolate; anything to take her mind off the thoughts that were crowding her mind.

TWENTY-FIVE

A feeling of dread filled Stella's chest the moment she opened her eyes. She'd barely slept a wink the previous night, her mind buzzing with the events of the evening. It felt like she'd only been asleep for a couple of hours and now her mobile phone was trilling away on her bedside table. She reached for it, surprised to see The Cellar's number on the screen.

'Hello,' she said, her voice groggy with slumber.

'Hi, Stella, it's Pim. Sorry, is this a bad time?'

'No, not at all, it's fine. I didn't sleep too well last night, that's all.' She pushed herself up onto her elbows. The reason for his call could only be one thing: Johan de Groote. Her stomach clenched at the thought.

'Listen, I just wanted to say I'm so sorry about... Well, how everything went last night. It must've been a massive shock for you. I just wanted to make sure you're okay.'

Her heart squeezed for him. If he really was who she thought he was, it can't have been easy for him either. 'You have nothing to be sorry about, Pim, but it's kind of you to be concerned. I'm fine, but how are you in all of this?'

She heard him sigh down the phone line. 'Well, a funny

kind of mix of confused, angry – at Johan, not you – and even a bit glad about certain things. But, hey, I'm okay.'

'Well, it's good to know you're all right,' she said kindly.

'Thank you. So, the reason I'm calling is, I wondered if you'd like to pop in here sometime this morning. I mean, there's so much needs to be talked about between all of us. I've asked Johan to be here, and I wondered if your mum would like to join us too?'

Stella sat up straight, pushing her hair off her face with her free hand, her mind racing. 'Oh, right. Wow. Well, yeah, you're right, it probably would be good for all of us to talk. Though I'm not sure about my mum. She left the auction in a bit of a hurry last night.'

'Yeah, I noticed that. Must've been a huge shock for her too. Is she okay?'

A flutter of nerves made themselves known in her chest. 'I'm not sure. I tried to ring last night, but couldn't get hold of her. I'll try again just as soon as we've finished this call. What time were you thinking of for us to head round?'

'Is ten o'clock okay?'

Stella glanced at her alarm clock to see it was eight fifty-five. 'Yeah, that should be fine.'

'Great! See you then.'

With the call ended, Stella flopped back onto her pillows. She needed a moment to think how best to broach the subject with her mum. Would she have gone into work this morning? she wondered. She could hardly see her mother letting anything affect her business, but these were extenuating circumstances, and Stella had a feeling they would make her mum want to hide away; pretend last night hadn't happened. Rhys was her next thought, wondering what he'd made of it all.

Scooping up her phone, Stella called her mother's mobile, relieved when her mum picked up.

'Stella, hello. Sorry but I'm just about to rush out, so I don't have long to chat.'

It was exactly the response Stella had expected. 'Morning, Mum.' She sucked in a deep breath. 'Um... I saw you leave the auction in a hurry last night and wanted to check you were okay. I rang a couple of times last night, but both your phones went to voicemail.'

A long pause followed. Stella could almost hear the cogs of her mum's mind whirring down the phone line. 'Mum, are you still there? Can you hear me?'

'Oh, yes, yes. I can hear you, lovey, I'm just rushing, that's all.' She paused again. 'I, er... I suddenly came over feeling unwell last night and had to leave quickly. Very embarrassing.' Alice gave a nervous laugh. 'I think it was some dodgy prawns I'd eaten earlier in the day.'

Stella closed her eyes and shook her head. It was time to bite the bullet. 'Are you sure it wasn't because of that man who walked in, Mum?'

An awkward silence stretched out.

'Mum?'

'What man? I didn't see anyone walk in, I was too preoccupied with the most horrendous stomach ache to notice anyone else.'

'Mum, please, it's time to be honest.' Her mother certainly wasn't making this easy. 'It was seeing Johan de Groote that upset you, wasn't it?' she said softly.

She heard her mother gasp. 'You know his name?' Alice's voice came out in a whisper, tugging at Stella's heartstrings.

'Yes, Mum. I know his name.' She took a fortifying breath. 'And I know who he is; I know he's my father.'

'Oh, right. I see.' Her mother's breathing sounded heavy down the phone line. 'Just give me a second, I need to sit down.'

'Of course. Are you okay?'

'Yes, I'm fine. Just shocked, that's all.' Stella thought she sounded as though she'd had the stuffing knocked out of her.

'That's understandable after all this time. Is it the first you've seen of him since...?'

'Mm-hm, yes. I recognised him straight away, he has a certain way of carrying himself.'

Doesn't he just? 'I'd noticed.'

'Did you speak to him?' her mum asked.

'Briefly. He wasn't at all what I expected. Well, apart from I'd always thought he was a tosser for walking out on you, and the impression he created last night did nothing to change my mind on that score.'

That raised a laugh from Alice. 'And, in light of what you've just said, I'm guessing it wasn't you who tracked him down, and you weren't the reason he turned up last night.'

'No, not at all!' Stella hadn't thought that was how it might have looked to her mum. 'I was a shocked as you when I realised who he was. If I'd had anything to do with it, I'd have spoken to you first before inviting him to turn up, and I certainly wouldn't choose anywhere as public as an event at The Cellar. I'd like to think you know that, Mum,' she added softly, the locket and the letter fleeting across her mind, a squeeze of guilt in her chest.

'Of course I do, sweetheart. Sorry, I'm still making sense of it all.'

'I get that. Anyway, Pim's been on the phone this morning – he's actually connected to all of this – and he wondered if we wanted to meet in the back room at The Cellar so we could all chat. Johan de Groote will be there.' She couldn't bring herself to refer to him as her father. 'Pim suggested ten o'clock.' She couldn't decide whether she thought it would be a good idea for her mother to join them or not. The last thing she wanted was for the feelings that would inevitably be dredged up to cause any new heartache, especially when her mum seemed so happy with Rhys. But then again, she might appreciate the chance to give Johan de Groote a piece of her mind. If there was one thing Stella knew about her mum, it was that she liked to get things off her chest. Have her say and move on. Just like Stella herself.

'Pim's involved?' Alice sounded shocked.

'It's a long story, I'll explain all at The Cellar, if you can make it, that is.' Her mum evidently hadn't put the Dutch connection together, but then again, Stella wasn't sure if her mother would know where Pim was from if she hadn't frequented The Cellar that much.

'I'm really sorry, lovey, I can't, I've got an important appointment at that time and it's too late to change it; it would be rude if I did.'

'That's a shame. I thought you'd be glad of the chance to get closure after all these years.'

Alice gave a scornful laugh. 'Closure? That man isn't worth me wasting another second of my time on. I shut him out of my thoughts years ago; it's only you who keeps reminding me about him with your incessant questions.'

Stella winced at the bitterness in her mum's voice.

'Mum, I—'

'Trust me, Stella, I've had all the closure I need with that man. If you want to form some kind of father-daughter relationship with him then that's up to you. But I warn you, don't believe the promises he'll no doubt make you; he'll let you down. Of that I'm certain.'

'I understand that. I'm not fooling myself about him.' It was true, especially after what she'd seen of him.

'Well, just in case, I'll be here for you when he does.' Alice huffed out a sigh. 'Right, sorry, sweetheart, but I'd really better be going. Let me know how you get on, won't you?'

'Yes, of course.' Stella didn't know whether to feel annoyed by their exchange or sad for her mum. Johan de Groote had clearly unsettled her.

TWENTY-SIX

Apprehension was building in Stella's chest as she turned onto Endeavour Road, her heart pumping hard. The grey sky overhead was doing a good job of reflecting her mood.

As soon as she arrived on the doorstep of The Cellar, Pim rushed to open the door for her.

'Morning, Stella,' he said, his face a picture of concern. 'Are you okay?'

'Hi, Pim.' She smiled up at him. 'Yes, I'm fine, thanks. How about you?'

'Yeah, I'm okay.'

Inside, she glanced around to see the bar was empty but for Bill polishing the beer pumps in readiness for the lunchtime opening. She wondered if Johan de Groote was already there or if he'd keep them waiting. Part of her wouldn't be surprised if he didn't turn up at all, something about him told her he wouldn't be too eager to be confronted by his past.

'Hi, Stella.' Bill looked up and gave her a sympathetic smile.

'Hi, Bill. I'm really sorry to disturb your morning.'

'Hey, no need to apologise. I just hope it all goes well for you.' He lay the polishing cloth on the bar. 'Can I get you a coffee?'

'Mm. That would be good, thanks.' Though she'd made a coffee at her apartment, she'd been too preoccupied to drink it. As for breakfast, she hadn't been able to face anything; her stomach had been in knots.

'No problem. I'll bring it through to the back for you.' Bill's smile widened. 'Flat white? Cappuccino? Macchiato?'

'Flat white would be perfect, thanks.' She returned his smile.

'Johan's already here,' Pim said, turning and making his way across the bar to the back room.

'Oh, right.' Stella followed, their shoes tapping over the wooden floor.

A tidal wave of anxiety flooded her body at the mention of his name. She braced herself as she stepped into the room. The feelings he triggered were worse than any she'd experienced facing even the most high-profile of her cases with the fiercest of opponents.

Johan was standing looking out of the window, his tall, broad-shouldered stature filling the frame. He turned when they walked in, a mug of coffee in his hand. 'Good morning, Stella,' he said softly, his eyes the same striking light blue as Pim's – and her own.

'Good morning,' she said coolly, her jaw tightening.

'Shall we sit down?' Pim gestured to the wooden table set with four matching chairs. It didn't escape Stella's notice how nervous he looked.

'Sounds like a good idea.' Johan gave a condescending smile which sent a spike of irritation through her.

'Here's your flat white, Stella.' Bill arrived in the room, handing her a rustic mug, the aroma of freshly ground coffee filling the air. 'I'll leave you to it,' he said, giving her shoulder a reassuring squeeze.

'Thanks, Bill,' she said, throwing him an appreciative smile.

'So, who'd like to start?' Johan asked as he looked between Pim and Stella, what appeared to be a mocking smile on his face.

Ughh! He clearly felt he was in charge of proceedings, which instantly made her bristle. Doing all she could to suppress the negative emotions stampeding around her body, Stella said, 'If it's okay with Pim, I think it should be you.'

Pim nodded. 'I agree.'

'I'd like to know everything, right back to when you were at university with my mother – who you may be relieved to know, won't be joining us here today.' Stella's assertive gaze didn't waver.

'Okay. Everything, eh? Very well.' Johan drew in a slow breath. 'So, as you know, I met your mother at university. We fell head-over-heels in love and the relationship moved super-fast. Before I knew what was happening, Alice was telling me she was pregnant.' His expression turned to one of disbelief. 'It was a huge, *huge* shock for both of us. We were so young; *too* young. I was honest with her right from the start, told her I wasn't ready to be a father, but she was a headstrong young woman; wouldn't listen to reason – she never did, always had to do things her way. Despite my opinion, she insisted she wanted to keep the baby. I felt I had no choice in the matter, felt I was being forced into fatherhood.'

Forced into fatherhood? Despicable man! Stella shook her head, his cold, detached words felt like a knife to her heart.

'I think you need to be very careful how you deal with this, Johan. After all, the baby Alice was pregnant with is right here with us.' Pim sent him a warning look.

Johan looked startled at being pulled up in such a way. 'Oh, yes, of course. I apologise, I was simply explaining how I felt at the time; it wasn't personal.' His eyes flicked quickly at Stella.

Wow! What a piece of work! Stella struggled to believe it

could be anything other than personal. 'So we've established you didn't want to be a father, which is why, I assume, you took off,' she said calmly. 'Where did you go?' She'd already decided the best way to deal with this man was to take a detached standpoint, treat the situation as though it was one of her cases. His cold-hearted comment had proved her right.

Johan went on to explain in a waffling, round-about way how he'd headed back to his home town of Harderwijk in Holland where he found work as an odd-job man. Stella and Pim listened, exchanging knowing looks from time-to-time. Finally, Johan arrived at the point where he met Pim's mother, Anouk, with whom he'd had a brief relationship. 'Pim is the product of the few short months Anouk and I were together. She wanted a child, I didn't.' He gave another of his lazy shrugs. 'She got her child, the relationship broke down soon after.'

'"*Her child*",' Pim said, shaking his head.

Pushing down her feelings of repulsion, Stella said, 'So, it would seem history repeated itself. Your girlfriend tells you she's pregnant with your baby, and you do a runner; the "child" in the case you've just mentioned being Pim.' Stella held him in a stony gaze. 'Even you must be able to see there's a pattern forming.'

Johan laughed, scratching his head. 'Well, I wouldn't describe it quite like that. It was different with Anouk. I stayed with her for a couple of weeks after the child, er, Pim was born, before I left.'

'That's big of you. Still sounds like you did a runner to me. And I'm interested to know how you would actually describe it,' she said, his patronising tone grating on her like nails down a blackboard.

'Yeah, I'd be keen to hear that too,' said Pim, sitting back in his chair and folding his arms across his broad chest.

A thought suddenly struck Stella, and before Johan could

answer, she jumped in, 'Can I just ask, can we expect any more Johan de Groote offspring to make an appearance?'

'Oh... I... um, a former girlfriend of mine has a set of twins in Roussillon in France.' He was suddenly reluctant to make eye contact. 'I ... er... I believe I'm their father.'

'Unbelievable!' Pim pushed his hands into his hair.

'Wow!' Stella couldn't hide her incredulity. 'You *believe* you're their father?'

He nodded sheepishly. 'According to Sylvie, their mother, I *am* their father.'

Stella shook her head. 'And how old are these twins?'

'I think they'll be about eight or nine; something like that.'

'"Something like that"?' Stella shot him a look of utter disdain.

'Yes, I'm not sure exactly.'

'And are they girls or boys?'

'A girl and a boy.'

'And is that it? That's all of us?' asked Pim, his tone stern.

'I have another daughter back in the Netherlands; Katrijn – her mother and I grew close when I was doing some odd jobs on her house – but that's it. That's all of you.'

'That's all of us.' Pim repeated his words, his face a picture of disbelief.

Johan's words tumbled around Stella's mind. She'd gone from being an only child, to suddenly having four half-siblings in an unbelievably short space of time. Something told her there was a chance there could be more, judging by the way she and Pim had had to drag this information out of him. She took a sip of her coffee, peering over her mug, working out how best to move forward with this situation.

Johan shuffled in his seat, looking decidedly shifty.

Was there anything about him that she'd inherited other than her physical appearance? she wondered. She sincerely hoped he hadn't passed on his appalling lack of conscience and deep-rooted selfish streak. He hadn't once said he was sorry for walking away from his children, for turning his back on his responsibility, for not caring what had happened to them. A thought hit her out of the blue. Had her reluctance to get involved in relationships passed to her from his genes? Her face paled at that, before sense kicked in, reminding her it was her mother's advice that was responsible for her keeping relationships at arm's length, and the reason was sitting right here in front of her; her father was the one with commitment issues, not her mum. Relief washed over her and she took another sip of coffee.

Setting the mug down, she turned to Pim who she noted was looking drawn, with no trace of his familiar ready smile. 'Are you okay, Pim?'

He looked over at her and gave a weak smile. 'Yeah, just a bit shocked, that's all. How about you?'

Despite the information Johan had, reluctantly, delivered, Stella found she felt decidedly robust, her lawyer's persona had served her well, providing her with some necessary bolstering. 'I'm fine.' She smiled back at him.

'You're a tough cookie, but I suppose I didn't expect anything less.' Johan gave a hollow laugh. 'And I suppose no one is going to ask me how I'm feeling in all of this? After all, I'm the one who's sitting here, being interrogated by two people, being ganged up on. I've just taken it on the chin.'

Stella and Pim exchanged looks of disbelief. The memory that her mum had described her father as a selfish man who didn't care about anyone else's feelings, crept into her mind. 'And how exactly *are* you feeling, Johan? Please do enlighten us, we're dying to know,' Stella said calmly, not bothering to hide the note of sarcasm in her voice.

Johan hung his head. 'Well,' he gave a self-pitying sigh, 'I'm not doing too good actually. About a month ago, I was diagnosed with a heart condition and prescribed medication. Just days after that, I learnt I was going to lose my home in Leiden. My landlord told me he was wanting to sell the apartment I was living in, so he served me my notice.' He pushed his floppy blond hair back with his hand. 'To make matters worse, my health has meant I've been struggling to work which means I've been finding it virtually impossible to raise the funds for the deposit on a new flat. I haven't been able to keep up payments on my medical insurance so I'm also struggling to afford my medication, which I desperately need.' He looked forlornly from Stella to Pim. 'I don't know what to do, things are feeling pretty hopeless for me. I've been crashing on friends' sofas; it's why I've ended up here in Micklewick Bay.'

If anyone else had imparted such news, her heart would have gone out to them and she'd have offered to help, but there was something about this man sitting before her that didn't evoke a single feeling of sympathy or affection. Her years of experience at the bar told her when things didn't add up, and something in her gut told her to be wary. Instead, he just looked pathetic and inordinately sorry for himself. Did that make her cold or hard? Stella caught Pim's eye, trying to read his expression, wondering if Johan's speech had evoked the same feelings in him as they had in her. Before she could give it any further thought, Pim spoke.

'So how have you ended up in such a mess? Didn't you have any savings to help tide you over?'

'Good point. I dare say you won't have been helping support the children you have dotted around all over the place, so your money won't have been going on that.' Stella reached for her mug again, sipping her coffee slowly, observing Johan's reaction over the rim.

He flinched at her words. 'I don't know how it's happened, it just has. It doesn't help that rent is expensive in The Netherlands. And despite what you suggest, the women who have had my children refused to accept any money from me; they wanted to be independent, didn't want me to stick around. It was almost as if I'd served my purpose like some kind of champion stud.'

Stella and Pim shared a look of utter mortification.

What the...? This man had a seriously inflated opinion of himself. If his comment hadn't been so repellent, it would be hilarious!

'Oh, don't worry, I understand how it happened; a tall, strong, good-looking guy is very appealing to some women, especially when their biological clock is ticking. Tick, tock, tick, tock. They see my genes as desirable. I fall for it every time. They use me for what they want, then when I've served my purpose, out I go. Bye, bye, Johan, we don't need you anymore.'

Is he for real? His arrogance knew no bounds. 'Anyone would think you'd have learnt your lesson from the amount of times it's happened.' Stella wasn't giving him an inch.

'Ah, but I hate to disappoint the women in my life. And like I said, I fall for it every time.'

Johan pushed up the sleeve of his grey and white striped linen shirt, revealing the same tattoo Pim had imprinted on his wrist. Johan caught Stella eyeing it with interest. 'It's my initials and my family crest.'

Before she could reply, his mobile phone, which was face down on the table beside him, pinged. He picked it up and read the message quickly. 'Okay, I have to go now.' He pushed himself up and turned to Stella. 'It's been good to talk to you. Perhaps I could visit you at your apartment; I've heard it's very smart, I'd quite like to see it.'

Though his request surprised her, her expression remained impassive. 'If we do meet again, I'd prefer to do it elsewhere,' she said matter-of-factly. The last thing she wanted was to have this man set foot in her apartment. He may be her biological father, but emotionally, he was nothing more than a stranger with an inflated opinion of himself, and one who most certainly wasn't going to slither his way into her home. It was transparently obvious that his reason for visiting was to serve his own needs, and nothing to do with the fact that he wanted to get to know her.

He pushed his hands into the pockets of his crumpled cotton trousers. 'Okay.' He held her gaze, as if pushing her to change her mind, but she stood firm. 'Right, well, I'll say goodbye for now. I hope to see you again soon.' He pulled a creased beige jacket from the back of his chair and pushed his arms into it, hovering a moment again as if waiting for her to change her mind. When she didn't he loped off, Pim following behind.

As soon as Johan had left the room, Stella breathed out a sigh of relief. She felt drained. Meeting her father should have been a monumental moment in her life. Instead it had felt surreal, the overriding emotions being those of disappointment and annoyance.

When Pim returned from seeing Johan out, he sat back down at the table and put his head in his hands. 'That was exhausting.'

Stella's heart went out to him. 'She reached across and touched his arm. 'It was, but at least we've spoken to him now.'

'For what good it did. I'm not so sure I feel any better for hearing all he had to say.'

Stella couldn't argue with that. 'Amongst all of his bluster, there's one thing that I'm very glad to have found out, and it's that I have an awesome half-brother living in the same town as me.' A smile pushed its way over her face.

Pim looked up. 'You really think that?'

'Yeah, I really do.' Her smile grew wider. 'Please tell me you feel as happy having a half-sister living here.' She laughed.

He smiled as he absorbed her words. 'Yeah, I think it's actually pretty cool.' He paused a moment before saying, 'Big sis.'

'Little brother,' Stella quipped back, making them both chuckle. At six-feet-five, Pim was anything but little.

'You guys okay?' Bill peered around the doorway. He looked relieved to hear them laughing.

'We're fine, my love.' Pim beamed at his husband. 'We were just saying how cool it is to have a sibling living close by.'

'And a brother-in-law,' Stella added, smiling over at Bill and pushing aside the turmoil Johan had created, her heart feeling suddenly so much happier.

'Oh, yes, of course,' he said, his face lighting up. 'I hadn't thought about that. I have a brand-new sister-in-law. That *is* very cool.' He strode over to her and enveloped her in a warm hug.

Sitting in Johan's vacated seat, Bill said with a chuckle, 'I know it's a little early, but you two look as though you could do with a stiff drink.'

'It was pretty intense.' Pim nodded in agreement. 'Though I think another caffeine hit will have to suffice rather than any of the hard stuff.'

'Ooh, I totally agree,' Stella said with a laugh. 'If I had a drink this early I'd be in danger of sliding off my chair and ending up in a heap on the floor, snoring loudly. It so wouldn't be a good look!'

'You paint a wonderful picture, Stella.' Bill laughed as he pushed himself up from the table. 'Coffee it is then. Another flat white?' He gave Stella an enquiring look.

'Great, thanks, Bill.'

Moments later, he brought three steaming mugs of coffee through on a tray, setting them out on the table with a plate of cookies. Between them, Pim and Stella shared what had been said, Bill listening with interest, his eyes growing wide at times. It was agreed that the two half-siblings had much to catch up on, which both were keen to do. With that in mind, Pim and Stella arranged to meet up on Sunday morning – a quiet time for The Cellar – and maybe go for a walk if the weather was kind. 'You guys need time to talk, just the two of you,' Bill said.

As Stella drained her mug, thoughts of her mum began filtering into her mind. She needed to speak to her as a priority. She may have declined the invitation to meet with Johan, but Stella knew she'd be anxious to hear what had been discussed. Stella was also worried that Johan might seek her out and fill her in on what had been said; she wanted to be the first to share it with her mum, not some man whom she had a sneaking suspicion would give some one-sided version of the conversation.

Stella couldn't deny, she was still smarting that she'd been left in the dark about her father for so many years, but she had to concede, her mother had been right about him. The impression he'd created was that he was a selfish, self-absorbed and conceited man who too easily absolved himself of anything he considered unpalatable. That he had several children scattered far and wide with whom he had no contact was evidence of that, as was the fact that not once during their conversation had he asked anything about Pim or her. He was clearly only interested in one person, and that was himself.

While the three were chatting away, an urgent rapping at the door caught their attention.

'Who the heck could that be?' asked Bill, checking his watch before pushing his chair back.

'I sincerely hope it's not Johan coming back to deliver more of his crap,' said Pim. 'I've had about as much of that as I can take for one day.'

'Same here,' said Stella, just as her mobile started ringing from her bag. She rummaged for it as Bill went to see who was knocking at the door. 'Oh!' She was surprised to see the call was from her mum. She went to press the answer icon, frowning as she became aware of a familiar voice in conversation with Bill in the bar. It couldn't be, could it?

TWENTY-SEVEN

The voices drew closer and moments later, Alice appeared in the doorway, looking flustered and short of breath.

Stella's mouth fell open. 'Mum! I thought you couldn't make it?'

'Sorry, lovey, I didn't think I was going to be able to.' Alice glanced around the room, wringing her hands together. 'But it looks like I'm too late anyway. Or didn't he turn up?'

'If you mean Johan, oh, he turned up all right.' Pim rolled his eyes. 'Left in a bit of a hurry not five-minutes ago.'

Alice's face fell. 'Oh, I'm so sorry, Stella, sweetheart. I got here as quickly as I could.'

'It's okay, Mum.' Stella didn't like seeing her usually confident mother looking so harassed. Johan de Groote most certainly wasn't worth that.

'Can I get you a coffee, Alice?' Bill asked, resting his hand on her arm.

Stella spoke before her mum could reply. 'Actually, Bill, you've been so kind, but I think I've taken up enough of your time; you'll need to open the bar soon. I think I should head back to my apartment, get my head around all we've heard this morning. I can update my mum there. If you've got time, that is, Mum? There's quite a lot to tell.'

'I've got time, sweetheart. My car's parked just outside, I'll drive us there.'

Stella smiled at her mum, feeling a rush of love for her. It meant more than she could express that she'd turned up, even though she'd missed Johan. And a part of Stella was actually glad she had. Something told her he'd do all he could to get under her mum's skin. Stella would have hated that, especially now Rhys was in the picture; she didn't want Johan to cause problems there. She found herself thinking he wasn't a patch on Rhys.

* * *

Stella and her mum were heading up the steps to her apartment when they encountered Alex making his way down with a jaunty-looking Fred on the end of a lead. They paused on the half-landing, the Labrador wagging his tail happily, evidently pleased to see Stella.

'Hi there, Fred.' She bent, giving him a sound pat. She noted Alex was looking achingly handsome in a V-neck sweater, the white of a T-shirt peering in the gap, and a pair of well-fitting jeans. His familiar aroma sent her senses dancing.

'Stella, how are you doing?' he said, resting his hand on her arm, concerned eyes searching her face.

'I'm fine, thanks.' She smiled up at him. 'Are you and Fred off out for a walk?' Her heart flipped as their eyes met. It was quickly followed by a warning note that threaded its way through her thoughts. Since meeting her father her doubts about relationships had begun to gain strength.

'We are. I've just got back from seeing a client, thought I'd whisk this lad out before I head out on my next appointment.'

His gaze switched to Alice. 'Hello there.' He smiled, giving her a polite nod.

'Hello,' said Alice.

'Oh, how rude of me. I'm so sorry. Been a bit of a morning.' Stella rolled her eyes at her lack of manners. 'Mum, this is my neighbour, Alex. Alex, this is my mum, Alice.'

'Good to meet you, Alice.' Alex held out his hand.

Alice took it. 'Hello, there Alex, it's good to meet you too.' She gave her daughter an enquiring smile. Stella quickly averted her gaze.

'Right well, much as I'd love to catch up with you,' he said, looking meaningfully at Stella, 'I'm afraid I'm going to have to dash or I won't make my appointment.'

'Oh, yes, of course.'

'Catch up later?' he asked.

'Yeah, that would be good.' Stella was conscious of her mum observing the interaction.

'Great. I'll give you a knock when I'm back.'

'He seems nice,' Alice said, once they were in Stella's apartment, the door safely closed behind them. 'Didn't I see him sitting with you at The Cellar last night?'

'Yes, he is nice, and yes you did.' Stella busied herself filling the coffee machine with fresh water, doing her best to ignore the knowing glint in her mother's eyes. She didn't want to offer any further explanation right now, there was enough for them to discuss without her mum quizzing her about Alex and her feelings for him.

With the coffee made, mother and daughter made their way over to the sofa. Alice, who'd been stunned when Stella had told her how she'd discovered Pim was her half-brother, listened intently as her daughter recounted the conversation she and Pim had had with Johan de Groote, her eyes growing wide at his arrogant comments. There was a lighter moment when Stella had mentioned how he'd compared himself to a champion stud.

Alice had almost choked on her mouthful of coffee, the two of them falling about laughing once she'd recovered. 'Oh my days! I can just see him saying that too.' Tears of mirth had fallen down Alice's cheeks. 'Champion stud indeed. That man always did have an inflated ego.'

It had been a different matter when Stella had touched on the fact he couldn't remember the age of his twins.

'Shameful! Sounds like he doesn't get any better,' Alice said, not hiding the bitterness in her voice.

'What did you see in him, Mum? If he was always like that, I'm amazed you gave him the time of day. He's so not you. I can't picture you together at all.' She stopped short of saying how he was nothing like Rhys.

'Ah, but he knew how to turn on the charm – still does if his string of prodigy scattered around Europe is anything to go by,' Alice said with a shake of her head.

'Hmm. Good point. Having said that, I didn't see any evidence of his charm today. He was pretty heavy-handed with the self-pity though. *So* unappealing.'

They sat thoughtful for a moment, sipping their coffee. Alice eventually broke the silence.

'I don't regret the time I had with him, you know.' She looked directly at her daughter.

'You don't?' Stella wore an expression of disbelief. How on this earth could her lovely mum not regret wasting time on such a man?

'How could I when he gave me the best thing that's ever happened to me? If I hadn't had my time with him, I wouldn't have you, lovey. And that's something I wouldn't change for the world.' She reached for Stella's hand, wrapping her fingers around it and squeezing it gently. 'From the very first moment I set eyes on you, oh my days, I couldn't believe the overwhelming feeling of love that just washed over me with an almighty whoosh!' She chuckled. 'Honestly, it knocked me for six. And if anyone had told me the love I felt then could grow stronger, I wouldn't have believed it was possible. But that's exactly what it's done. The love I have for you, my darling... well, I can't even begin to put it into words.'

Stella felt her throat tighten. 'Oh, Mum.' Tears started burning at the back of her eyes.

'I mean it, lovey. I often find myself thinking about it. And I know I don't say it as often as I should, but I'm so very proud of you, sweetheart. I'm proud of what you've achieved with your sheer hard work and determination, and proud of the wonderful, kind-hearted and thoroughly decent young woman you've become.'

Stella had been battling to compose herself but her mum's words caught her off guard, tipping her tears over the edge. She put her head in her hands and sobbed.

'Oh, lovey, I didn't mean to make you cry,' Alice said softly. She inched closer to her daughter, rubbing soothing swirls over her back as Stella's tears flowed.

Finally composing herself, Stella swiped her tears away with her fingers and sniffed. '*Ughh!* I'm not sure where that came from.' Her voice was still thick with emotion. 'But thank you, Mum, your words mean a lot. I feel the same about you. You've been an amazing role model for me – mind, you do set the bar pretty, flippin' high.' They both chuckled at that. 'And when I look at what you've achieved on your own, without any help from anyone, I'm in complete awe.'

'You were my motivation,' her mum said. 'I just wanted to give you the best of everything without having to rely on anyone else.'

'And, after meeting my father, I can understand why you didn't want him in our lives.'

Alice stroked her hand over her daughter's hair. 'I was just terrified he would hurt you, but looking at it now, I can see my protective instinct went into overdrive, mushroomed out of proportion. I was worried he'd work his infamous charm on you, suck you in, and then do one of his vanishing acts. As a child, that would have been absolutely devastating for you. I never wanted you to have to experience that.' Alice sighed. 'But I can understand by not telling you about him, it must have been incredibly frustrating for you. All I can say in my defence was that it came from a place of love.'

'I can see that now, and it doesn't matter anymore. I've met him. I'm not sure how long he'll stay in Micklewick Bay for. I'll probably meet him again, but I can't see my feelings changing towards him, if I'm honest,' she said matter-of-factly, her eyes still puffy with tears. 'I can't speak for Pim, of course; I don't know what their relationship is like or how long they've actually been in contact for. I kind of get a feeling it's not been long.'

'Well, from what I've seen of Pim, he's a nice lad,' Alice said. 'I think you'll like having him in your life.'

Stella's mind ran over her mum's words. She was right, Pim was a nice lad, with his easy-going nature, ready smile and kind heart. And though the thought of having someone else she was related to living close by felt a little odd, there was also something so very appealing about it. 'Yes, I think I will.'

They looked at one another and smiled.

'I'm just glad you're okay, lovey.' Alice pulled her daughter into a hug, pressing a kiss to her cheek.

'It's going to take more than Johan de Groote to bring me down, Mum,' Stella said jokingly. She felt a sudden pang of guilt rush over her as she recalled how she'd been snooping in her mother's bedroom. *Snooping!* The word didn't sit well with her at all. She'd have to confess her misdemeanour to her mum at some point; she needed to get it off her chest, but now didn't feel like the right time. But should she mention the letter she'd found? She wasn't so sure about that either. It was probably best left for now, especially as it no longer served a purpose; Stella was in full possession of her father's name and his whereabouts!

She didn't even want to think how she was going to get it back to where she'd found it. She only hoped her mother wouldn't go looking for it before then.

'That's good to hear.' Alice sat back and drew in a shaky breath, glancing at Stella.

'You okay, Mum?'

'Well, as we're having a day of getting everything out in the open, I have something to tell you.' Alice swallowed nervously, her fingers knotting in her lap.

Stella's heart started pounding.

TWENTY-EIGHT

'Is everything okay, Mum?' She couldn't begin to imagine what her mother was about to tell her.

Alice nodded. 'It is now.'

'It is now?' What did that mean? Stella's stomach started churning. 'Is it Rhys?'

'No, no, it's nothing to do with Rhys, everything's fine with him. It's...' Alice heaved another sigh. 'I wasn't actually going to say anything; especially with everything you've had on your plate, what with moving house, your workload and now *that man* turning up out of the blue, but Rhys thought I should be open and honest about it, said you'd want to know. So...'

Stella grabbed her mum's hand, nausea swirling in her stomach. 'Mum, you're scaring me, please tell me what it is. I want to help. You're not ill, are you?'

'I'm fine, but the reason I couldn't come to the meeting this morning was because I had an appointment at Middleton-le-Moors Hospital.'

Stella's heart stilled, her hand flying to her mouth. 'Hospital? Oh my God, Mum! Why did you have an appointment there?' Tears misted her eyes once more.

Alice patted her daughter's hand. 'This is exactly why I didn't want to say anything, lovey. I didn't want to worry you unnecessarily.'

Stella latched onto the word "unnecessarily", a tiny glimmer of relief sneaking in.

'I'm absolutely fine. I just went to get the results of a recent biopsy.'

A recent biopsy? Fear surged through Stella, snuffing out the small glimmer of relief. She blinked, listening as her mum went on.

'I found a lump in my breast about a month ago. I wasn't going to do anything about it. It was really quite small; didn't think it was worth troubling the doctor about it. Anyway, I mentioned it to Rhys who told me I should get it checked out, just to be on the safe side, and to put his mind at rest if nothing else, especially after what he'd been through with Theresa. After a week's-worth of nagging from him, I made an appointment with our GP who then referred me to the hospital. It all seemed to happen very quickly from there. As I said, I got my results this morning, and I'm thrilled to say they're clear, it's just a cyst.' She smiled broadly at her daughter, relief evident in her eyes.

'Oh, Mum! You should've told me!'

'What? And worry you unnecessarily? I really couldn't see the point in that.'

'But what if it had been...' Stella couldn't bring herself to say the word. 'What if the results hadn't come back clear? Would you have told me then?'

Her mum looked at her sheepishly. 'Probably not. I'd have waited to see what the prognosis was. Having said that, I had a strong feeling it was going to be okay.'

'That's beside the point, Mum. I'd want to know,' Stella said softly. 'You've got to promise you'll tell me if you're ever in that situation again. You'd say the same if I was in your position.'

'True.' Alice nodded. 'I'm sorry I kept it from you, I promise I'll share things like this with you in the future.'

'Good.' If it hadn't been for Rhys, Stella dreaded to think how long her mum would have ignored the lump before doing anything about it. 'Thank goodness for Rhys nagging you. It might not have been okay, and that doesn't bear thinking about.'

'Oh, he certainly nagged me all right.' Alice said with a chuckle.

'Yes, well, it can't have been very nice for him, after what he went through with his wife.' The thought of her mum going to hospital alone, potentially to receive some devastating news crossed Stella's mind, sending a shiver up her spine.

Her mum's smile fell. 'No, it wasn't. Poor man was walking around looking so worried. Which is why I made the appointment. Rhys insisted on coming with me.'

'Good. That was kind of him.' Once again, she found herself glad that her mum had Rhys to support her.

'He's a very kind man, very thoughtful.' Alice's expression softened as she spoke of him. 'And I'm so glad he's in my life, lovey, it's taken me quite by surprise.'

Stella turned to her mum, scrutinising her face. She noted how her eyes were shining and the glow that emanated from her when Stella had joined them for the barbecue had returned. 'I'm really happy for you, Mum. I've never seen you like this before, but being in a relationship with Rhys certainly seems to suit you. You're positively sparkling!'

Alice's cheeks flushed pink. She clapped her hands on her knees and said, 'Well, I don't know about that, but anyway, I'm ravenous. How about we rustle up some sandwiches and a bit of salad for lunch? You can tell me all about your charming young man while we're eating.'

Crafty, Mum, turn the attention back on me! The mention of food cut through Stella's thoughts; a timely reminder that she'd only had a couple of biscuits all day. Her stomach rumbled perfectly on cue. 'I like the sound of the sandwiches, but I think I should clarify before you get carried away, Alex is not my "young man".'

'Are you sure about that, sweetheart? I'm not the only one who's sparkling, you know.'

It was Stella's turn to blush.

* * *

Over a meal of chicken pesto sandwiches in crusty granary bread accompanied by a crisp salad – all ingredients courtesy of the local deli – mother and daughter chatted away, perched opposite one another on bar stools at the island. Stella's mood had softened towards her mum since the day of the auction, and she happily told her about Alex and Fred, her face animated, her insides dancing as she spoke.

Alice dabbed her mouth with her napkin. 'The thing is, lovey, listening to you talk, seeing how happy you are, is exactly how Rhys makes me feel. And I know it's early days for you but I—'

'Mum, I've barely known Alex any time at all. How can I know for sure? I've never felt like this before, but what if I've got it all wrong?' The warnings had begun to creep in again, Johan de Groote and the obvious impact he'd had on her life, hovering at the corners of her mind.

'I don't think it matters how long you've known him, especially if being around him is triggering those kind of feelings. I knew there was something different about Rhys from the first moment we spoke to one another. No one has ever made me feel that way, not even Johan de Groote, with all his smarmy charisma and "champion stud" genes.' She chuckled, pressing her hand to her mouth. 'Sorry, I shouldn't speak to you like that about your father.'

'No need to apologise at all on that score.' Stella set her

knife and fork down on her plate. She was interested to hear her mum's take on her feelings for Alex.

Alice looked thoughtful for a moment. 'I know I've drilled it into you not to depend on a man, that you should avoid getting bogged down in a relationship, and how you'll only risk being disappointed or hurt. But I realise now how wrong that was of me. I let my experience with Johan cloud my judgement and influence you.'

'It's understandable after what happened, but it's a shame you've been on your own for such a long time.'

Alice nodded. 'I can understand why you think that, but in truth, I'd never met anyone I wanted to build a relationship with.' She raised her eyes to meet Stella's. 'Until I met, Rhys, that is.' Her face flushed again. 'I always say everything happens for a reason. Seems I had to wait for Rhys to come along for me to find love, so it's the perfect time for me. I suppose it meant I could focus on you and setting up the business without the distraction of a relationship.'

'Well, I'm happy for you, Mum.' Smiling, Stella reached across the countertop for her mother's hand.

'Thank you, that means a lot, sweetheart.' Alice's face was wreathed in smiles. 'Which is why I want to tell you that if Alex makes you feel the way Rhys makes me feel, then don't let what I've told you in the past get in your way. Let love into your heart. You'll know if it's right, and if it is, just go for it! You deserve to be loved, my darling, and from the way Alex was looking at you, I think he could be "the one".' She put finger quotes around the words.

Butterflies fluttered in Stella's stomach. 'I do really like him, Mum. No one has ever made me feel the way he does. I honestly never expected this.' Her heart started dancing, Alex's handsome face appearing in her mind. 'I never thought I'd fall in love.' *Oh my days!* Had she really just said that out loud? Had she fallen in love with Alex? A surge of emotions flooded her chest as she realised, yes, she'd fallen head-over-heels in love with Alex Bainbridge, just like Maggie had done with Bear all those years ago, and just how Stella, the "lovephobic" as her friends had regularly described her, had found difficult to comprehend.

'Well, grab it with both hands and let yourself be happy.' Alice beamed at her daughter. 'Tell you what, why don't you and Alex come over to Magnolia Gardens, join Rhys and me for a meal? Did I tell you Rhys is an *amazing* cook? His chicken curry is to die for.' Watching her mum speak so animatedly warmed Stella's heart.

'Much as I think that sounds great, Mum, I think it's a bit early days for dinner with a parent and her partner. I mean, I don't want to scare Alex off before we've even got properly started. You'll be rushing us down the aisle at this rate; that'd be guaranteed to have him running for the hills.'

Both women looked at one another and burst out laughing.

'Sorry, lovey. Looks like I've got a lot to learn with this rules-of-dating malarkey,' Alice said through her giggles. 'Tell you what, you shout up and let me know when you're ready to come round and I'll book Rhys for cooking duties. How does that sound?'

'Much better.' Mother and daughter exchanged happy smiles.

TWENTY-NINE

Rain had been lashing against the windows for the last couple of hours, the overcast sky had meant Stella had needed to use her desk lamp. It lent a cosy air to her apartment. She'd added to the ambience when it had turned a little chilly, flicking the switch on the uncannily realistic electric fire set in the wall; it even emulated the sound of crackling wood which she loved.

Once her mum had left, Stella had spent the afternoon at her desk, catching up with her work as much as her concentration would allow. She wasn't one to be distracted easily, but with the events that had unfurled over the last few days, she'd found her mind wandering. Would she hear from Johan de Groote again? she wondered. They hadn't exchanged contact details, though with Pim being in touch with him, Johan would be able to get a message through him. She still struggled to refer to him as her father, still didn't think he deserved the title.

She'd spent several hours researching the law on a particularly complicated aspect of a murder brief she been instructed in as junior counsel. The silk she was working with on the case had asked her to look into it, content in the knowledge she'd be thorough. She was pulled away from her online lawbook by a knock at her door, making her jump, her thoughts immediately springing to Alex.

Stealing a quick glance in the mirror in the hallway, Stella smoothed down her hair and checked her eyes for smudges of mascara – she hadn't replaced her make-up after she'd been crying earlier and didn't want to open the door to him looking like she was an extra in a Halloween movie.

'Hi.' Alex was leaning against the doorframe, his deep voice sending a fizz of excitement through her. He really was easy on the eye.

'Hi, come in.' She beamed a smile at him. Her conversation with her mum had gone some way to easing Stella's concerns about the strength of her feelings for him, allowing herself to enjoy them instead.

'Thanks. I can't stop long, I've got a few work-related phone calls to make, but I just wanted to check in with you first, see if you fancied joining me for a bite of supper?' He followed Stella into the lounge.

She stopped and turned to him, unable to keep the smile from her face. 'I'd love to, thanks.' He always smelt so *good*.

'That's great.' Alex closed the gap between them. He brushed her hair off her face and looked deep into her eyes. 'You okay?'

'I'm fine.'

He quickly scrutinised her face. 'You sure?'

'Positive. I'll bring you up-to-speed with everything later.'

'Okay.' He nodded, smiling. Moments later, he lowered his mouth to hers, kissing her deeply, the fizz of excitement now a blaze of fireworks inside her.

'Wow!' she said dizzily, when they finally pulled apart.

'Does six thirty suit you?' he asked, his eyes dark with lust.

'Perfect.' *Now would be good actually!*

'Good.' He smiled. 'I'll see you then.' He went to walk away, but turned back, evidently having second thoughts. 'I just need another one of these...' With that, he cupped her face in his hands and kissed her tenderly. 'Mmm. That's better,' he said before flashing her a smile and heading out of the door.

Stella stood rooted to the spot, her lips burning, as she tried to bring her swirling emotions under control, something she was finding almost impossible to do.

* * *

The time for her to head over to Alex's apartment had finally arrived, much to Stella's relief. Despite everything that had been going on, it was his delicious kisses that had dominated her thoughts that afternoon, the warmth of his lips, the graze of his stubble. It was intoxicating. Taking the time to prepare herself, she'd showered and washed her hair, which she'd styled in loose waves before carefully reapplying her "no-make-up" make-up. That done, she'd put on a dusky pink wrap dress that seductively accentuated her curves.

Adding a spritz of perfume and a final slick of lip gloss, she grabbed a bottle of Pinot Grigio from the fridge and left her apartment, a thrill dancing around inside her.

'Mmm. You smell so good.' Alex didn't waste a moment, kicking his apartment door shut and pulling Stella close to him. His muscular body pressed against her combined with the hot kisses he was delivering sent her pulse sky-rocketing.

The feeling of Fred nudging at her legs pulled Stella out of the moment. She glanced down to see two eager eyes looking up at her. 'Hello, young man, are you feeling left out?' she said with a giggle.

Fred wagged his tail excitedly and gave a happy whimper.

'Ah, good old Fred, always likes to be in the thick of it, don't you, fella?' Alex released Stella from his arms so she could ruffle the Labrador's ears.

She was grateful for the opportunity to bring her raging

hormones under control. If Alex kissed her once more like that, he was in serious danger of being dragged off to the bedroom, but it would be a shame if it meant the food he'd been preparing would be burnt while she had her wicked way with him, she reasoned. 'There are some delicious smells coming from the kitchen.' She stood up straight, ignoring the urges of her hormones that were causing such mayhem in her body, focusing instead on the mouth-watering aroma of food that was dancing around her nose and setting her taste buds tingling.

Apparently oblivious to the wayward thoughts his kisses had aroused in her, Alex said, 'So to start, we have baked camembert, garnished with caramelised onion chutney and a sprig of rosemary, accompanied by flatbreads. That's followed by pan-roasted hake, new potatoes and salad for main.'

Stella groaned with delight. 'Wow! Sounds heavenly.'

'There's crème brûlée for afterwards, if you can manage it. Though I can't take credit for that, I picked it up from the deli earlier.'

'I've always got room for pudding, and anything from the deli is amazing.' Stella smiled, her lust shrinking to a background simmer.

Alex took her hand and led her through to the living area, gentle music tinkling away in the background. Her eyes landed on the table set for dinner where a candle flickered invitingly in a mini lantern, casting its glow over the rustic crockery and linen napkins. That Alex had gone to such effort was touching.

'Glass of wine?' he asked.

'Love one. Oh, and can I give you this?' She handed him the bottle she'd brought.

'Thanks, but you needn't have. Just you would've been enough.' The look he shot her made her tingle from her head all the way to her toes.

'Sweet talker,' she said with a smile, struggling to quash her desire that was on the rise again.

'It's true.'

Stella followed him to the kitchen where he poured her a glass of wine. She watched as he smothered a bowl of potatoes in butter, threw a sprinkling of freshly chopped herbs over them and popped them in the oven. 'They shouldn't take long,' he said.

Perched on the bar stools at the island, Alex asked, 'So, how are things with you? I have to say, you look much brighter than you did when I saw you on the stairs with your mum.'

'Things are good, thanks.' She took a sip of her wine, thinking how right it felt to be here with him. 'My mum and I had a real heart-to-heart, cleared the air about a lot of things – namely the enigmatic Johan de Groote.'

'Yeah, I can imagine he provided quite a bit of fodder for discussion.'

Stella snorted. 'Just a bit!'

She went on to share an edited version of the conversation she'd had with her mum, Alex listening intently.

'That's a pretty intense twenty-four hours you've had there, Stella,' he said, when she'd finished. 'A lesser person would've crumbled having all that piled on top of them, me included.'

'I'm not so sure you would. It's amazing what you cope with when you're faced with it, without the luxury of having time to think about it. It's sometimes better that way.' She twirled her wine around as Alex slipped off his stool and popped the camembert into the oven. 'What's most important out of everything that's been going on is my mum. I'm just so relieved she's okay.'

'Yeah, I can imagine. And Rhys sounds like a really decent bloke.' Alex glanced over his shoulder as he closed the oven door.

'I think he is; he's certainly making my mum happy.'

'I sense there's a "but" coming.' Alex slid back onto his bar stool and scooped up his glass of wine.

'Oh, it's not about Rhys; the more I know about him, the more I really like him.' Stella exhaled noisily. 'It's my father. Johan de Groote. I know my mum had given me plenty of warnings, yet I can't help but be disappointed by my first impression of him.' She glanced up at Alex. 'Does that make me sound hard and unkind?' She'd given much thought to what Johan had said about not being in good health and being unable to afford his medication. Her gut had told her not to take what he said at face value, that things were not quite as they seemed, but it still managed to tug at her conscience.

'Not at all,' he said firmly. 'It makes you sound honest. It's good that you're not trying to fool yourself, convince yourself otherwise. Though, for your own peace of mind, it might be a good idea if you met with him again, see what he has to say for himself. That way you might get a better idea of what he's really like.'

Stella nodded. 'Yeah, I'd thought that too.' She flashed him a smile. 'Anyway, that's way too much about me, how has your day been? What exciting designs have your clients asked you to come up with?'

'Before I get onto that, I'll just add that as far as your father's concerned, trust what your gut's telling you. The times I've ignored mine I've always ended up regretting it.' He swapped his serious expression for a smile. 'And as for it being way too much about you, I beg to differ. I like hearing about you, helps me get to know *you* better.'

'You sure it's not scaring you off?' she asked, giggling into her glass.

'It'd take a lot to do that,' he said, holding her gaze.

* * *

The meal passed with the couple chatting and laughing. Stella had been fascinated as Alex described some of the designs he'd been commissioned to work on, from creating luxury homes out of old water towers, to converting an ungainly row of storage units into a bold, contemporary house. When they'd finally finished their meal, with Stella devouring her crème brûlée and declaring it to be delicious, they moved to the large L-shaped sofa in the lounge. Alex flicked the table lamp on in the corner, it cast a cosy glow around the room.

Stella leant back, savouring the subdued lighting and the easy atmosphere, a cup of decaffeinated coffee in her hand – she thought it would be wise to avoid caffeine this evening in the hope of getting a good night's sleep – watching as Alex changed the playlist for something more soothing.

Fred was stretched out on the large rug in front of the fire, identical to the one in Stella's apartment. The Labrador was snoring contentedly, his paws twitching every now and then, making Stella smile. She'd never considered getting a dog before, the hours she worked making it unfeasible, but Fred, with his upbeat, affectionate personality, had really grown on her.

Alex reached for the remote control for the fire and selected the option to have the flames glowing for aesthetic effect, adding to the cosy atmosphere.

'I'm just going to pop to the bathroom,' Stella said, setting her cup down next to the books on architecture that were laid out on the coffee table. 'Don't worry, I can find my way.' She grinned.

The bathroom, filled with the clean, fresh aroma of Alex, was almost identical to Stella's but for the masculine products dotted about. She took a moment, breathing in his scent. Glancing around, her eyes were drawn to a laundry basket with what appeared to be a pair of silk knickers peeking out of the top. Another pair were on the floor beside it. They looked disconcertingly familiar. Unease prickled its way up her spine as she walked over to them. Lifting the lid of the laundry basket, her eyes grew wide. There, looking back at her, was her missing underwear. She bent to take a closer look. 'What the heck are these doing here?'

Without waiting a moment, Stella snatched up her knickers and stormed back into the living room, anger propelling her forward.

Alex turned, his face falling as he took in her expression. 'Stella, what's happened?'

'What's happened?' she said, her chest heaving, eyes blazing. Fred leapt up, alerted by her angry tone, glancing between Stella and Alex. 'I'll tell you what's wrong, finding my knickers in your bathroom when *I* haven't left them there!' She threw the handful of silk at him, a tiny G-string landing on his head, part of it covering his right eye. If she wasn't so consumed by rage it would have made her giggle. 'What is *wrong* with you? I didn't have you down as some sort of knicker-stealing pervert but it seems I should have!'

'What?' Alex scraped her knickers from his head and threw them to the left of him where this time, they landed on Fred's head. The Labrador sat statue-still for several seconds, eyes wide, blinking at the arguing couple. 'You think I...? No! Stella, please, you've got to believe me, it's not like that!' Alex cried, frustrated.

'How else is it, then?'

'If you could just calm down a minute, I'll tell you.' Alex got to his feet, raising his hands in a placatory gesture. 'I honestly didn't know they were yours.'

Stella gave a scornful laugh. 'Oh, so that makes it all right then.'

'No, no. What I mean is, I didn't know *whose* they were.'

'It's not sounding any better.' She jabbed her hands onto her hips.

Alex pushed his hands into his hair and let out a loud groan. 'Stella, please, you've got to listen to me, got to let me explain!'

'You're not doing a very good job of it so far.'

'I found them, I've no idea how they got into my apartment, and no idea where they came from.' He started to make his way around the sofa towards her.

She stepped back. 'You really are pathetic! I can't believe I ever let myself get sucked in by a knicker-nicking weirdo like you.' She went to walk away but stopped. 'And you can keep my underwear, I don't want any of it back. I don't even want to think about what you've been doing with it.' She caught sight of Fred with her knickers perched on his head, a comical expression on his face, and felt a laugh bubbling up inside her.

'*What? Oh come on*!' Alex looked appalled when he realised what she was insinuating, his words quashing her giggle before it had the chance to leave her mouth.

She shot him a look of pure disgust, turned on her heel and stomped out of his apartment, closing the door firmly behind her, her chest heaving with rage.

On the stairs, Brooke from the flat above stopped in her tracks. Judging from her soaked appearance, the rain evidently hadn't let up.

'Oh hi, Brooke.' Stella rustled up a smile, doing all she could to affect an air of calm.

'Hi, Stella.' Brooke gave an apprehensive smile. 'Everything okay?'

'Everything's just fine and dandy, thanks.' Stella forced a smile. Much as she'd rather disappear into her apartment, she was reluctant to come across as rude. Instead, she asked, 'Are you getting settled into your new home?'

'Pretty much. Just a few boxes left to unpack.'

'Cool. And are you still okay for Saturday night?'

'Definitely.' Brooke beamed. 'It'll be good to get to know a few more Micklewick Bay locals.'

You'll be getting to know one less person at my party after what I've learnt tonight!

'Great.' Stella forced another smile. 'Right, well, if I don't see you before, I'll see you then.'

'Yeah, see you then.' Brooke gave her a quizzical look as she continued up the stairs.

In her apartment, Stella threw herself on the sofa. '*Ughh!* Why did he have to turn out to be a creep?' she said, angry that she hadn't picked up on it. He'd seemed so open and likeable and funny and gorgeous and... perfect. And he'd completely fooled her. She threw her head back and let out a groan. Was she losing her touch? Had her intuition become dulled? Or had he been so successful in worming his way into her affections that she'd been blinkered to the signs? Frustration gripped her and she scrubbed her face with her hands. '*Arghh!*'

But it wasn't just anger and frustration that was boiling inside her. A deep ache had taken hold in the pit of her stomach, the pain radiating outwards and encompassing her whole body. She'd let herself fall in love with him, shared her deepest thoughts with him, and now her heart felt like it was breaking, the pain becoming unbearable. *What a fool I've been*, she thought sadly, as tears misted her eyes.

She vowed, there and then, never to let it happen again.

THIRTY

Stella had headed into town before Andrea had arrived to give her apartment a quick once-over. Armed with a list of things she needed to pick up for her small get together the following evening, and relieved that the sun had decided to make a reappearance, she made her way to the little gift shop that stocked an array of her favourite scented candles. With those taken care of, the next stop was the florist's to pick up her weekly order of a pre-arranged bouquet. Treating herself to a bunch of flowers was something she'd been doing for a few years now, usually collecting the floral arrangement on a Saturday morning, but she'd given the florist, Maisie, the heads-up that she'd need it a day early this week.

After calling in at the deli, where she selected a range of dips, cheeses and continental meats, Stella headed to the supermarket to stock up on more drinks – top of the list there were a couple of bottles of traditional lemonade which was something Maggie had developed an insatiable craving for during her pregnancy.

Stella was pushing her trolley towards the tills when she spotted Alex wandering along with a half-filled basket in his hand. Her stomach leapt. He was wearing a troubled expression and there was no trace of his usual confident demeanour. Annoyance prickled through her, tempered by a tinge of regret.

Since yesterday evening, she'd found herself wondering if she'd maybe overreacted to finding her underwear in his bathroom. She'd been quick to jump to the worst of conclusions, hadn't been prepared to listen to his explanation. It made her embarrassed at her behaviour. She'd even wondered if her extreme reaction was linked to her reluctance to be in a relationship. She was used to being in control and had struggled to get used to the fact that her emotions had taken the lead – or at least tried their hardest to. It had ruffled her usually cool, level-headed disposition. Maybe she'd subconsciously thought that a way of regaining control was to get rid of the cause. It was easier to walk away than get involved and risk getting hurt. Even she had to admit, this line of thinking had all the hallmarks of an exercise in self-sabotage. But then again, she had found her missing underwear in his bathroom and he hadn't even tried to tidy it away! The reminder justified her actions to herself.

As she went to turn in the opposite direction, he looked her way, their eyes locking. He froze on the spot, his troubled look exchanged for one of sadness. Stella felt a tug in her heart, the urge to go over to him gaining pace, until a little voice reminded her she'd found a stash of her knickers in his bathroom. *Don't be fooled, he's a pervy knicker-nicker!* In the next moment, she swung her trolley round and strode to the till furthest away.

Boy, did she have a lot to tell the lasses at their Jolly session tonight!

By the time Stella landed back at her apartment, Andrea had gone, leaving the citrussy smell of cleaning products in her wake, the place neat and tidy, just the way Stella liked it.

After putting her shopping away and placing the bouquet in a vase, being careful not to disturb the arrangement, she settled down to a couple of hours' work at her desk. Rather annoyingly, Alex made regular appearances in her thoughts, the hurt look in his eyes triggering a pang of guilt. It frustrated her no end; *she* shouldn't be the one feeling guilty, *he* was the one with her missing underwear in his bathroom. She really needed to forget about him. That was going to be easier said than done with him living in the apartment opposite, but she was determined to do just that, telling herself the passage of time would make the situation easier. *You're a strong woman, you can do it!*

* * *

Stella always looked forward to her Friday nights at the Jolly, but tonight she found herself even more so.

With the weather being a little cooler, she'd opted for a jumpsuit in a bold floral print, teamed with her favourite designer ankle boots and a black cotton utility jacket. She'd fixed her hair in a messy "up-do", leaving soft tendrils framing her face.

A chilly breeze was blowing in off the sea, a hint of mizzle in the air, as she strode briskly across the old cobbles, passing the ramshackle stack of lobster pots that lined the path to the Jolly. A couple of seagulls wheeled overhead, their screeching cries carried along the beach. She welcomed the blast of warmth that hit her when she opened the heavy oak door of the pub, her eyes going to the fire that was dancing in the grate of the old inglenook.

Spotting Florrie and Lark at their usual table, Stella headed over to them. 'Hiya, lasses, how're you diddlin'?' She beamed a smile, glad to see them.

'Hiya, Stells,' Florrie and Lark chorused back, both wearing happy Friday night smiles.

'Tell you what, it's a bit nippy out there now.' Stella was aware that both her friends were regarding her closely which didn't surprise her after everything that had been happening, and they didn't even know the half of it yet.

'You're not wrong there. I had to fish out my thicker jacket,' said Lark.

'Yeah, me too,' said Florrie. 'Jazz is on her way, says she's adding the finishing touches to a cake for a fiftieth wedding anniversary. We're expecting her to arrive covered from head to toe in golden glitter.' That made them chuckle; Jasmine regularly sported some sparkly evidence of her cake-decorating.

'Poor old Jazz, she works her socks off.' Stella slipped in beside Lark on the settle, laying her jacket beside her.

'She does,' said Lark, inching up for her. 'Which reminds me, as it's her birthday coming up soon, I was going to suggest we book her in for a pamper session at that place you go to over in Danskelfe, Stells. You're always raving about it. What do you reckon?'

'Ooh, fab idea, she could do with a treat like that,' said Florrie, reaching for the bottle of white wine in the ice bucket and pouring a glass for Stella.

'Thanks, Florrie.' Stella picked up the glass and took a sip, the crisp flavours dancing on her tongue. 'I agree, it is a fab idea. Rachel is *amazing*. Her hot stones massage is so *dreamy*, I defy anyone not to feel relaxed after one. It'd do Jazz the world of good, providing she can sit still for long enough, that is. We could take her for a meal at The Sunne Inne in Lytell Stangdale after. I've had a Sunday dinner there and it's absolutely amazing, and Mags is still raving about the meal she and Bear had there.'

'Aww, that would be a fab way to finish her day off, she so deserves some "me time".' Lark pressed her hands to her heart. 'I suggest we tell her it's all been paid for in advance and that it's our treat; you know what she's like about not letting folk pay for things for her. We don't want to make her feel like we think of her as a "charity case" as she calls it.'

'Heck, no, we don't want that,' said Florrie.

'How about we don't let on any of the details at all?' said Stella. 'We could just tell her we're taking her out on a surprise trip for the day, that way she won't have the chance to dissuade us or try to get us to cancel it.'

'Good plan.' Florrie nodded and Lark agreed.

'Now then, lasses.' Just then, Maggie appeared at the table, oozing radiance, her baby bump standing proud in her brightly coloured jersey tunic dress. 'I just caught the tail-end of that, but I'm guessing you're plotting our Jazz's birthday.' She inched her way in beside Florrie.

'We are.' Stella nodded as they filled Maggie in on their idea.

'We'll need to make sure her parents are free to look after the kids that day. I can run it by them when we settle on a date,' said Florrie.

'Ey up, the woman in question has just walked in,' said Maggie. 'Time to change the subject.'

'Flippin' 'eck it's good to see you lot.' Jasmine puffed out a sigh as she flopped onto the chair at the end of the table, her brow glistening with perspiration. Her hair was shimmering with gold sparkles, the soft lighting of the bar picking out a dusting of gold edible glitter on the end of her nose. Despite her smiles she looked exhausted. 'So what have I missed? Owt or nowt?'

'Nothing really,' said Stella, 'we haven't been here long ourselves; you've made good time.'

'I'm not surprised! I belted down Skitey Bank as fast as my little legs could carry me. I'm jiggered now,' she said with a chuckle. 'Anyroad, how's things with you, Stells? Have they settled down after Wednesday night's drama at The Cellar?'

'Yes, that can't have been an easy night for you. Have you seen any more of your father?' asked Lark.

'And how's your neighbour Mr Dishy?' Jasmine waggled her eyebrows mischievously at that, raising a smile from Stella.

'Hmm. There's so much to tell, I'm not sure where to start,' Stella said, before pointing her finger between her nose and Jasmine in an attempt to alert her friend to the smudge of gold glitter adorning her nose.

Jasmine's brows knitted together before she clicked what Stella was doing. 'Ahh, the bloomin' stuff gets everywhere. I dare say I'll find it in my knickers when I take them off.'

'Please tell us you're not going to do that now, Jazz.' Maggie feigned a worried expression just as Ando Taylor's shrieking laugh rang around the bar. The friends glanced over at him and burst out laughing. 'Ando clearly agrees.'

'Trust me, my belly-whackers will be staying firmly in place on my bum. No one in their right mind wants to see those things.'

'Phew!' Stella mimed wiping sweat from her brow. Jasmine responded by poking her tongue out at her friend.

'Anyroad, getting back to you, Stella, we're all dying to know how things went with your father after his dramatic appearance on Wednesday night. Have you seen or heard from him since,' asked Florrie.

'I met him at The Cellar yesterday morning, Pim was there too.' Stella went on to share what followed.

'Wow!' said Jasmine. 'That's some heavy stuff.'

'Tell me about it,' said Stella. She was still trying to get her head around it and reliving it had got her feeling a little churned up again.

'So you've gone from having no siblings to a whole load of them,' said Lark.

'Pretty much sums it up.' Stella nodded. 'Though, in all of this mess, learning that Pim's my half-brother has been kind of nice.'

'Yeah, Pim's a really decent bloke,' said Jasmine.

'He is, he's got a good heart; you can see it in his face, and his aura,' said Lark.

'And now I think about it, you really do look alike, and I don't just mean that you're both so tall; facially you're very similar, especially around the eyes,' said Florrie. The others scrutinised Stella's face, making sounds of their agreement.

'How come we didn't notice this before?' said Jasmine.

'Probably because we weren't looking for it,' said Florrie.

'And how's your mum in all this, Stells?' asked Maggie.

'She's taken it surprisingly well actually. Though she'd shared the details of their conversation concerning Johan de Groote and Pim, Stella hadn't mentioned her mum's visit to the hospital, knowing she'd want to keep it private. 'Anyway, I'm sick of talking about myself and I'm sure you're getting fed-up of hearing about me, so what have the rest of you been up to?' Stella glanced around the table; she'd save telling her friends about Alex and her knickers after they'd had had a chance to speak. 'Mags, I take it you haven't been troubled any further by that dreadful cousin of yours?'

Maggie's face dropped at the reminder. 'Thankfully, all's quiet on that score, and I really can't see me hearing any more from her. Touch wood.' She tapped her fingers against the table.

'Good,' Florrie said firmly.

Earlier in the summer, Maggie's estranged cousin, Robyn, had arrived on their doorstep armed with an elaborate story of how her marriage had broken down and she'd been left homeless and penniless. The two cousins shared a troubled history and despite Maggie's misgivings, Maggie and Bear had found themselves inviting her to stay for a couple of days. It had soon become clear that she had no intention of leaving and, worse, had designs on Bear. Her passive-aggressive behaviour and endless lies had taken a worryingly short space of time to cause a rift between the usually contented couple. Things came to an unpleasant end when Robyn's lies were exposed and she was asked to leave, which she did, but not before she'd caused a final flourish of trouble. The whole drama had coincided with Maggie being desperate to share the news of her much-longed-for pregnancy with Bear, after the couple had suffered a heart-breaking series of miscarriages. The stress had been enormous and she'd worried it would affect her unborn baby. It was fair to say, the couple were still reeling a little from it.

'If she shows her face around here again, she'll find herself getting chased out of town before she can cause any more trouble,' said Jasmine, her pixie face flushing with anger.

'Too right,' said Stella, the friends murmuring their agreement.

'Thanks, lasses. I'm hoping it won't come to that.' Maggie gave an appreciative smile.

After Florrie had updated them on the preparations for romance author, Thea Carlton's, reading, Lark had shared how she and Nate had booked a trip to France to trawl the markets there in search of items for her shop and more pieces for his upcycling business – Lark's revelation had resulted in an exchange of knowing looks.

'We're *just friends*!' she said, laughing.

'Oh, aye. And I'm a multimillionaire,' Jasmine said dryly before turning to Stella. 'On the subject of *lurve*, how's things going with you and Mr Hot?'

Stella snorted. 'They're not and never will be. We're over before we got properly started, and I won't be troubling the idea of a relationship again, that's for sure.' Though she was putting on a brave front, it did nothing to stop the ache in her heart.

'No!' said Florrie, her smile falling. 'What happened?'

'I think I need my lugs cleaning out,' said Jasmine, waggling her finger in her ear. 'I could've sworn you just used the "relationship" word. Thought you didn't go in for them.'

'What happened, Stells?' asked Lark, her face wreathed in concern.

'Well, we seemed to be getting on fine; I'll even admit to quite liking him.' She caught Lark's eye and quickly looked away. She didn't want to run the risk of her friend reaching in and reading her thoughts in that other-worldly way of hers.

'So what went wrong?' asked Maggie. 'I thought he seemed really nice, and from the way he was looking at you the other night, I got the impression he was very keen on you.'

Stella gave a scornful laugh. 'In love with my knickers, more like.'

Jasmine spluttered, almost choking on her glass of wine, while Lark's eyebrows shot up to her hairline. 'What d'you mean, in love with your knickers?' asked Florrie.

'I don't think I'd mentioned that some of my underwear had gone missing; there's been so many other things going on. Anyway, Andrea, the woman who cleans my apartment, popped some washing in for me, and had apparently hung a load of my knickers and a couple of bras out in the garden on a clothes airer.' Stella rolled her eyes at the memory.

'There wouldn't have been much fabric in your drawers, so I doubt they'd have taken long to dry,' Jasmine said with a snigger, earning herself a look of mock disapproval from Stella.

'And are you saying someone nicked it?' Maggie asked in disbelief.

Stella nodded. 'Yep, that's exactly what I'm saying.'

'But I don't get what this has got to do with Alex, and why you don't want anything to do with him anymore,' said Florrie.

'The thing is, I found them.' Stella glanced around at their faces, using a lengthy pause for dramatic effect; a much-used courtroom tactic of hers. 'In Alex's bathroom.' She sat back, awaiting their reaction.

'No!' Florrie's eyes were wide with disbelief.

'Are you sure they were yours?' asked Lark. 'I mean, hadn't his sister been staying with him? Don't you think there's a chance they might belong to her?'

Stella shook her head assertively. 'Nope, they were definitely mine.'

'Flippin' 'eck, I'd never have had him down as a perv,' said Maggie, shocked.

'So what did you do with them? Did you take them back? I dare say they'll have cost a fortune; you wouldn't want to just leave them there,' said Jasmine.

'Did I heck take them back! I chucked them at him after I'd told him what I thought. I don't care how much they cost, there's no way I'd want to wear them again.'

Her friends looked at one another before dissolving into a fit of giggles. Despite her indignation, Stella found herself laughing along with them. 'I told him he was a "knicker-nicker",' she said when she was finally able to speak. His horrified expression bloomed in her mind, momentarily distracting her. 'And what's worse, when I'd thrown them at him, a pair landed on his head.' Her words came out in a splutter of laugher. 'And he whipped them off, throwing them inadvertently at Fred. Poor lad just sat there with them on his head, an ear sticking out of a leg-hole. Honestly, I had all on to keep a straight face.'

The friends collapsed into another round of raucous laughter, attracting bemused attention for nearby customers.

Once their giggles had subsided, Florrie wiped tears of merriment from beneath her glasses and said, 'Well, I'm really sorry to hear that, Stells. Seems he fooled us all good and proper.'

'Didn't he just,' said Stella. 'Anyroad, that really is enough about me tonight; I don't want to think any more about Johan de Groote or Alex Bainbridge.' She turned her attention to Maggie. 'So, Mags, how's things going with you and Baby Marsay, not to mention your bear-making company?'

'Well,' Maggie was busy fishing the slice of lemon out of her drink. She popped it into her mouth, pulling a face as she sucked the flavour out of it, then plopped it back into her drink. 'Not bad, thanks.' She flashed a smile at her friend.

'I see the lemon craving's still in full swing.' Stella couldn't help but chuckle.

'I think it's actually getting worse.' Maggie grinned.

THIRTY-ONE

Stella was standing at the bar, waiting to order another bottle of wine, tapping her foot to the music provided by the lively folk band in the corner, when the pub door opened. Her stomach leapt as Johan de Groote walked in. He was in conversation with a man of a similar age, with thinning sandy hair. From the way they were talking, it was clear they knew one another well. She watched with interest as Johan pulled back, letting the sandy haired man join the queue at the bar, Johan scanning the packed room as if looking for a table. He appeared to be dodging paying for the first round of drinks – why didn't that surprise her? His gaze landed on her and he looked startled for a few moments. Regrouping himself, he simply nodded and turned away, continuing his sweep of the room as if she was no more than a casual acquaintance. Stella watched as his eyes alighted on a table for four where a couple of attractive young women, who looked to be in their mid-to-late twenties, were sitting. He leant into his friend, saying something in his ear, before swaggering over to the young women. He'd evidently said something appealing as, in no time, the women were smiling up at him, laughing heartily at whatever he was saying. In the next moment, he gestured to the two empty seats. The two women responded with enthusiastic nods, and he wasted no time pulling out one of the chairs and sitting down, continuing his charm offensive.

Unable to watch any more, Stella turned away and waited to place her order. She didn't know how to feel about his reaction to seeing her, that he didn't even say hello. Maybe, after their last meeting, he was wary of any further confrontation. He wasn't the only one; it was the last thing she wanted, especially here in the Jolly.

As she made her way back to her friends, Stella toyed with the idea of going over to Johan, just to say hello, but thought better of it when she heard the flirtatious tone of the conversation he was having with the young woman sitting nearest him. *Ughh!* That he was laying it on so thick made her stomach curdle. It was taking some getting used to, him being her father.

Back at her table, Stella gave a quick update, her friends taking it in turns to surreptitiously take a look as her father held court, the two young women hanging on his every word. She guessed he was using a well-worn style of patter that had proved to be successful in the past, including with her mother.

Over the next hour, Stella did all she could to get on with enjoying her evening, listening as Jasmine shared the details of the latest comedy celebration cake she'd been commissioned to make for a couple in their late sixties who lived near her parents. 'I mean, who even thinks about asking someone to make an anniversary cake like that?' I was mortified when Mrs Marsh showed me the photo she wanted me to replicate; didn't know where to look. And, judging by her husband's *appearance* – if you get my drift – it was clearly a *very* chilly day.' Her green eyes twinkled with mischief.

Mrs Marsh had told her how she and Mr Marsh were

seasoned naturists and were regulars at a private naturist caravan camp over on the opposite coast. It was where the photo she'd passed to Jasmine had been taken, and where the couple would be celebrating their anniversary.

'Honestly, I'll never be able to look at her and her husband again. I've known them all my life, always thought they were both very prim and proper. Pfftt! Totally fooled me there. And why she wants me to have them on a tandem beggars belief. Talk about having to deal with lots of fiddly bits and not knowing where to put them.' Jasmine shook her head, giggling at the face Florrie was pulling. 'And, let me tell you this, gravity has been no friend to either of them. In fact, I'd go so far as to say it's absolutely bloomin' ravaged them. Which begs the question, do I copy them exactly, or do I enhance things; be kind, if you like? Make things a little *perter*?' She sat back in her seat and looked at her friends. Only Jasmine could tell a story so dryly and have everyone hooting with laughter.

Movement from the direction of where her father was sitting caught the corner of Stella's eye. She turned to see him and his friend getting to their feet along with one of the young women. The young woman nearest Johan quickly finished her drink and stood up too, smiling as she said something to him, making him laugh. Johan placed his hand on the small of her back, glancing over at Stella before quickly turning away. She watched with interest as he and his friend headed towards the door, the two women following. *Talk about a fast worker.* Stella felt an unexpected twinge of hurt that he hadn't wanted to speak to her, quickly telling herself that it would've been awkward anyway. The hurt was suddenly tempered by a feeling of irritation.

'You okay, Stells?' Lark's gentle voice pulled her out of her musings.

'Hm? Oh, yeah, I'm fine thanks, flower.' Stella nodded.

She'd got the feeling he hadn't turned up in Micklewick Bay by chance; he had a reason for it, and she had her suspicions as to exactly what it could be.

* * *

Heading along the bottom prom, Stella fastened the buttons of her utility jacket and flicked the collar up, her mind teeming with thoughts of Johan de Groote. Mizzle was hanging in the air, swirling around in the muted glow of the vintage street-lamps. As she walked, she gradually became aware of footsteps behind her, the scrape of shoes on cobbles. Her heart jumped, triggering an unwelcome memory of the anonymous note that had been pushed into her pigeonhole. Stella felt herself regretting not accepting Maggie's offer of a lift home. A car was heading down the road, its headlights illuminating the footpath and she turned quickly, surprised to see no sign of anyone following her. She puffed out a sigh of relief. She may have taken self-defence classes and be a black belt in karate, but the thought that there was someone out there trying to intimidate her still didn't stop her from feeling uneasy.

Upping her pace, Stella made her way towards Skitey Bank, thankful it was well lit.

Reaching the top, she took long, purposeful strides towards the top prom, her mobile phone in her hand. She was about a third of the way along when she spotted a familiar dark car with tinted windows on the other side of the road. It had slowed to a crawl and appeared to be matching her pace. Anger rose inside her. No one had the right to make a woman feel intimidated. Her nostrils flaring, she marched towards the car, her body language exuding confidence and fearlessness. She was determined to find out who it was.

She'd almost reached the car when the driver revved the

engine before taking off with a noisy spin of its wheels, Stella looking after it, her hands on her hips. Whoever it was, they evidently wanted their identity to remain a secret. All the same, it was a reminder that she needed to get in touch with DC Stephens and see if they'd made any progress with the CCTV footage at Fitzgilbert's Landing.

THIRTY-TWO

Saturday morning arrived welcoming the return of summer. Stella threw open the balcony doors of her bedroom, sunshine and sounds of the seaside rushing in, including a vocal herring gull that was perched on the balcony above Alex's flat. She heard the rattle of a door handle over at his apartment and quickly ducked back inside. There was no way she wanted to come face to face with him for several reasons, one of which was that she didn't want him to see her in such a dishevelled state. Her hair had escaped its plait and she had the feeling her face bore the creases from her pillow. It was so not a good look.

It had taken her a while to fall asleep the previous evening, adrenalin pumping around her veins after her unpleasant experience on her way home. She made a mental note to contact DC Stephens; this attempted intimidation needed to stop, she had enough going on in her life right now.

As she set her coffee machine away, a ripple of excitement rushed through her; she was looking forward to having her friends round tonight, welcoming them into her new home. Much as she loved her apartment, it was a big space to fill. Stella had been taken off guard a couple of times when she'd detected an air of... not loneliness, but something hovering on the periphery of it. She wondered if her mum had ever felt that way at Magnolia Gardens after she'd left for university. That was a big house too, with generously proportioned rooms and high ceilings, the sound almost echoing around the place. The thought that it might have had something to do with why her mum had finally welcomed some romance – and Rhys – into her life crossed her mind. Her following thought was if she'd find herself in a similar position one day, but dismissed the notion before it had a chance to take root, moving swiftly on to Bill and Pim; she'd thought about inviting them this evening but Saturday night was always crazy busy at The Cellar and it was too short notice to get anyone to cover for them. Maybe they could get together over Sunday dinner at the Jolly some time? she mused.

Her father slipped into her mind, how he'd acted as if he didn't know her the previous evening. He could at least have said hello, rather than averting his gaze before either of them had a chance to speak. 'His loss!' she said resolutely, adding a dash of frothy milk to her cup of coffee. She'd got this far without his presence in her life and she'd continue without it just fine. She didn't need him; she'd satisfied her curiosity and that had been enough. What she'd witnessed hadn't made her want to get to know anything more about him. Perching on a bar stool, cradling her cup in her hands, she ignored the little pinch of hurt that had resurrected itself in her chest, turning her attention to her to-do list for that evening, she'd attend to its contents on her return from her Saturday morning run.

* * *

Stella's eyes swept the living room, taking in the kitchen area, pleased with what she saw; her apartment looked sleek and inviting. She'd selected an upbeat, poppy playlist at a volume that wouldn't hamper conversation. The scented candles had been lit for the last hour, their clean fragrance filling the air, the bouquet looked stunning on the sideboard, and the island was positively groaning with delicious looking nibbles from the deli. She'd flicked the fairy lights on in readiness for when the light had dimmed, adding to the ambience.

She'd already planned her outfit for the evening, selecting a grey silk slip dress with fine straps that crossed over at the back, and had swept her hair up into a chic chignon. On her feet were a pair of designer heels that fastened delicately around her ankles. She'd kept her make-up understated, adding a slick of deep pink lip gloss for impact.

She was taking a last check in the mirror when the buzzer of the intercom sounded, sending a frisson of excitement running through her. She strode over to it to see Florrie and Ed grinning back at her, with who she guessed were Florrie's parents standing in the background. 'Hiya, Stells,' they said in unison.

'Hiya, guys. Come on up.' Smiling, she pressed the entry button.

Moments later, she was greeting them cheerily at the door.

'By the way, flower, I thought I should mention there was a shifty-looking fella hanging around the door downstairs. Said he'd forgotten his key and asked if we could keep the door open for him, but we were having none of it, especially when we asked who he was and he was reluctant to give his name,' Paula, Florrie's mum, said once she'd released Stella from a warm hug.

'Aye, too right, we told him to sling his hook,' said Florrie's dad, Charlie.

'That's very good of you.' Stella smiled, hoping to conceal the alarm she felt; she was sure it must be the creepy man who'd been following her. But she wasn't going to let him spoil her evening with her friends. He'd proved he was cowardly by speeding off when she'd gone to confront him the previous evening. She didn't want to dwell on his motive for trying to gain entry into Fitzgilbert's Landing for a second time. He must be oblivious to the fact he'd be captured on CCTV again. She really must contact DC Stephens and get this sorted once and for all.

Not long after, Maggie and Bear arrived with Lark and Nate, as well as Jean Davenport and Jack Playforth. They'd scooped them up en route in their Land Rover. With Maggie being pregnant she was steering clear of alcohol so had volunteered to drive, allowing the others the option to enjoy a glass of wine.

'I think it's probably best if we wait for the others to arrive before we give you your pressies,' said Jasmine, who had a large cake carrier in her hands; she'd arrived with her parents just after Maggie and her carful.

'Who are we waiting for?' asked Maggie, looking around just as the buzzer went again.

'My mum and Rhys, and the couple from upstairs,' said Stella, handing Nate a bottle of beer before heading over to the intercom. She smiled to see her mum's face on the screen. 'Mum, you could just use your key, you know!' she said, chuckling.

'I know, lovey, but I don't like to be pushy and presumptuous.' Her mum's words sent a prickle of guilt rushing over Stella, reminding her of how only days ago she'd been creeping around her mum's bedroom and sifting through her jewellery box and pilfering a letter. Not her finest hour by any stretch of the imagination. *Best not dwell on that tonight!* She was saved from thinking any further of it by the arrival of Brooke and Marcus and the introductions that followed.

'Right then, Stells, now we're all here, I think it's time to hand over your apartment warming presents.' Jasmine beamed.

'You really didn't need to get me anything,' Stella said. 'I just thought it'd be fun to have a get-together now I've got unpacked, welcome you all to my new apartment.'

'Is Alex not coming?' Stella's mum asked, looking puzzled.

'No, he won't be here tonight, Mum,' Stella said firmly. 'I'll explain later.' She could feel her mum scrutinising her face but she didn't want to discuss Alex tonight, he was strictly off limits.

'Anyroad, here's my offering; it's chocolate cake, by the way.' Evidently picking up on the non-verbals flying between Stella and her mum, Jasmine jumped in, shooting Stella a knowing look.

'Thanks, Jazz, that's so kind.' Stella gave her a grateful smile as she lifted the lid off the cake carrier, a gasp escaping her lips as she looked down at the intricate creation. 'Oh, Jazz! It's stunning!' A series of wows ran around the room as everyone gazed in awe at Jasmine's handiwork. Before them was the Fitzgilbert's Landing building skilfully recreated in sugar paste and fondant icing, right down to the wrought-iron balconies and metal window frames. Standing beside the building was a sugar paste version of Stella in her barrister's wig and robes, a brief tied with pink ribbon tucked under her arm, vertiginous heels adorning her feet. Curling sugar paste waves trimmed the side of the cake, with biscuit crumb sand spread over the base. There was even a seagull on the roof. Though the mix of features could, on paper, be considered somewhat incongruous, in cake form, it worked brilliantly, with Jasmine's skill and personality shining through. 'Jazz, this is *amazing*! It must've taken you hours. Thank you so much.' Stella felt a rush of love for her friend, appreciating the busy – at times frantically so – life she had, yet she'd set time aside to make this for her. Stella swept her into a hug and squeezed her tight, Jasmine joking that she was getting dangerously short of breath.

'You really need to give up your other jobs and focus on this, Jazz. You're so talented,' said Florrie.

'Hear, hear,' said Maggie.

'That's what we keep telling her, isn't it, Steve?' Heather, Jasmine's mum, said, pride shining in her eyes.

'Aye, it is.' Her dad nodded, smiling fondly.

'It's just a bit of chocolate cake and fondant icing.' Blushing, Jasmine batted the compliment away as she always did. 'Mind, if I'd heard the story of your disappearing undies sooner, I might've been tempted to make one with a load of skimpy sugar paste knickers strewn all over it instead, but I'd already made a start on this so it was too late.' She gave a dirty giggle.

'Sounds like you had a lucky escape there, Stells.' Lark chuckled.

'What's this about your disappearing undies?' asked Brooke, her copper brows drawing together.

Stella quickly relayed the story of how her lingerie had gone missing but decided against mentioning Alex's involvement. Much as she was still furious with him – not to mention crushingly disappointed – she was reluctant to bad mouth him to their neighbours.

'I think I might know what's happened to it,' Brooke said, all eyes turning to her.

'You do?' Stella said.

Brooke nodded, her auburn ponytail swinging. 'I was out there this morning, just having a cup of coffee in the sun, when I spotted a black Labrador charging around; looked full of mischief. Anyway, next thing I know, it jumps up at the washing line in the garden next to mine, grabs a tea towel and starts running about with it in its mouth. It was having a whale of a time, tearing about.' She giggled, pressing her hand to her mouth. 'A couple of minutes later, I heard a man's voice shouting the name Fred or Ted – something like that. Fred or Ted dropped the towel and shot back inside and that was the last I saw of him. I reckon that's what probably happened to your silk undies.'

'You're kidding me?' Stella clamped her hand to her mouth. *No way!* She cringed inside, her stomach twisting in a tight knot as she realised how wrong she'd been. 'Fred's the knicker-nicker?'

'Ey up, what's this?' said Florrie's dad Charlie tuning in. Up to that point, he and his wife Paula had been deep in conversation with Stella's mum and Rhys.

'Did I hear right? There's a knicker-nicking Labrador about?' asked Paula.

Brooke laughed. 'Yep. I reckon Stella's relieved to know her undies haven't been pinched by some undesirable scrote with dubious intentions. It's just a mischievous black Lab.'

Stella swallowed, aware of the weight of everyone's gaze on her.

'Oops,' said Jasmine.

Oops indeed. Stella felt dreadful, the accusations she'd hurled at Alex replaying in her mind making her face burn with shame. She rubbed her brow with her fingertips. He'd tried to explain but she'd shot him down, refused to listen. From this vantage point she could see she'd switched into lawyer mode way too easily, and she wasn't proud of herself for it. She desperately needed to speak to him, but tonight wasn't the right time. She'd head over to his apartment first thing in the morning before she went for her run, apologise and hope he'd forgive her. But right now, she had an apartment full of guests and she needed to play hostess and put her horrendous mistake out of her mind until the morning. It was going to be easier said than done.

'Right, time for more pressies,' said Maggie. She'd clearly picked up on Stella's concerns and was keen to stop her friend from heading down that particular rabbit hole tonight. 'There you go, happy apartment warming from Bear and me.' She smiled kindly, handing over a gift bag.

'Thank you, guys.' Stella reached into the bag and carefully lifted out a wooden box bearing The Micklewick Bear Company logo, her spirits lifting instantly. She slid the lid off, revealing one of Maggie's exquisite keepsake cashmere bears. Her face lit up. 'Oh, Mags, you shouldn't have.' She knew just how much care and attention her friend gave to the construction of her bears, and looking at the detail in this one – whom Maggie had named Sibyl – Stella could see it was no exception, with its studious expression, complete with a pair of half-moon glasses perched on its nose. Smiling, Stella's eyes ran over the bear, taking in the detail of the courtroom attire which included a carefully constructed knitted replica of a barrister's wig. Maggie had even included a red brief bag. There was no doubting it would have taken days of Maggie's busy schedule to make it.

'Oh, Mags, she's gorgeous! Thank you so much, you too, Bear. I'll sit her on my desk so I can see her while I'm working.'

Maggie and Bear beamed back at her. 'Glad you like her, flower,' said Maggie.

Lark was next up, smiling broadly as she handed Stella a large, flat parcel. 'This is from Nate and me.'

Everyone looked on as Stella carefully removed the gift wrap to reveal the photo she'd been enquiring about at Lark's shop just days earlier. 'Lark! I thought this had been sold?'

'When I told you it had gone, it's because I'd tucked it away for you; I'd noticed how taken you were with it.' Lark smiled at her.

'I was! I love it! Thank you.'

With the picture propped against the wall, Florrie handed over the gift from her and Ed. It was an old book detailing the history of some of the oldest buildings in Micklewick Bay, including the warehouse that was now Stella's home, and the nearby terrace of houses. 'Wow! Thank you. This is going to look super cool on my coffee table.'

'Here you go, lass.' Jack Playforth handed her a gift bag. 'It's from my mother and me.'

'Goodness, I feel so spoilt.' Stella laughed, taking the bag.

'Thank you.' Inside was a large box of chocolates from The Chocolate Cherub Chocolate Shop over in Middleton-le-Moors. 'Ooh! These are my favourites! Thank you both so much.'

'Glad you like them, lovey,' said Jean Davenport, smiling. 'We didn't really know what to get you, but Maggie said these were your favourite chocolates so we thought we couldn't go far wrong with them.'

'And it's good to see you like these,' said Brooke, holding an elegantly wrapped box out to her. She and Marcus had brought a scented candle they sold on their website which was the very same brand as the ones Stella had bought earlier in the week and were currently perfuming the air of the apartment, while Florrie's parents had brought a pot plant for her balcony, as had Jasmine's parents.

'Our Florrie mentioned you were thinking about getting some plants for out there but weren't certain which ones would be hardy enough to withstand the sea air; these should be ideal,' Paula said.

'Thank you all, I really didn't expect any gifts but you've all been so thoughtful,' Stella said, touched by their kindness.

After a quick tour of her apartment, with everyone suitably impressed, it wasn't long before her new home was thrumming with chatter and laughter. Talk of the proposed new marina and the identity of the mystery man who'd renovated the warehouse and was apparently ruffling local disreputable businessman Dodgy Dick's feathers by snapping up property he'd shown an interest in were the most popular topics of discussion. Everyone seemed to be enjoying themselves as they tucked into the nibbles and sipped their drinks. But Stella found herself struggling to switch off completely, thanks to the little voice that kept telling her Alex should have been here. The thought that she'd hurt him, accused him, made her stomach clench.

She cast her gaze around at her guests, her eyes alighting on

Maggie and Bear. He had a protective arm around his wife's shoulders, absently bending to kiss her cheek as they chatted away. Maggie glanced up at him, indisputable love in their eyes. Stella felt a squeeze of something that felt uncomfortably like jealousy. It hit her like a bolt out of the blue, she wanted what they had. In the next second, her heart sank like a stone when she realised the only one she wanted that with was Alex.

But she very much doubted he'd want anything to do with her now.

THIRTY-THREE

The first thing that filled Stella's mind when she woke was Alex. Her chest tightened and she clamped her hand over her forehead as she recalled the previous night's conversation with Brooke. *What a hot-headed fool you've been, Hutton!* She reached for her alarm clock to see it was almost seven thirty; late for her. Throwing the duvet back, she leapt out of bed determined to get the day started; the sooner she got to speak to Alex the better. She'd spent hours lying awake last night, torturing herself, trying to think of what to say to him, how she could apologise and let him know she meant it, that she regretted what she'd said. Much as she hoped he'd accept her apology, part of her couldn't blame him if he didn't; she'd hurled a pretty unpleasant accusation at him. The memory made her wince.

What time would be deemed acceptable to knock on someone's door on a Sunday morning? she wondered, as she paced back and forth in her living room, nursing a mug of coffee. Was eight o'clock too early? Surely he'd be up with Fred. Or maybe she should go for a run and speak to him when she returned? She talked herself out of that option, not wanting to risk him heading out while she wasn't around to hear him leave. No, she'd forgo her Sunday morning run and wait until it got to nine then she'd head straight over to his apartment.

She glanced over at the clock, willing the hands to move faster.

Despite showering, washing her hair and changing into some cashmere loungewear, time appeared to be dragging its heels. And though she'd tried her best to summon her courtroom courage, nothing seemed to stop her heart from stampeding or the nerves jittering in her stomach. It mattered more than anything that Alex listened to her, that he'd give her the chance to apologise.

Johan de Groote had barely crossed her mind since the conversation with Brooke. *Pftt. That's no bad thing.* Her annoyance at his indifferent, arrogant attitude had increased, though she wasn't certain if it was being nudged on by her situation with Alex, making her channel her unsettled emotions in her errant father's direction.

The minute it got to nine a.m., Stella found herself standing in front of the door to Alex's apartment. She'd already knocked twice, getting no response. Impatience rippling through her, she listened carefully, hoping to hear to signs of activity. When she heard nothing, she knocked again. Still, the door remained unanswered.

Back in her living room Stella started pacing the floor once more, glancing down at her phone, toying with the idea of sending Alex a text, asking if they could talk. The thought that he might ignore her request prevented her from taking the plunge. She'd prefer to speak face to face anyway, that way she could be sure he fully understood just how sorry she was, that she wasn't using hollow words.

While she'd been waiting, a text had come through from Pim, asking if they could meet at ten thirty and maybe go for a walk. She'd replied, confirming she'd be at The Cellar for then. Much as she was desperate to speak to Alex, she very much wanted to talk to Pim too, and there was no way she'd countenance cancelling meeting up with him.

By the time it had got to ten o'clock, Stella had knocked at Alex's door a further two times, each time it had remained unanswered, silence lingering behind it. Gripped by frustration and anxiety in equal measure, she'd been unable to apply herself to anything and instead, had spent the time busying herself with small, undemanding tasks while listening out for any signs of movement on the landing, signalling Alex's return.

Giving one last knock as she headed out to meet Pim, Stella was to be disappointed yet again. He and Fred clearly weren't at home; surely the Labrador would have barked if they'd been in. She was just as well pleased since she'd have to rush off to meet Pim which wouldn't create the best impression of someone who was keen to apologise.

* * *

Dressed in a blue and white striped pullover, a pair of ankle-grazer jeans, and canvas trainers on her feet, Stella fell into step alongside Pim, listening as he started to tell her of his relationship with their father. It transpired that they hadn't been in contact for long at all, with Johan turning up at his mother's house in The Netherlands out of the blue one afternoon.

'You can imagine my surprise when I received a call from my mother saying he'd rocked up and was keen to meet me.'

'I can, but then again, he's got some brass neck,' Stella said, her words laced with disapproval.

'That's what Bill and I thought, but my mother seemed uncharacteristically eager for me to head over there and speak to him. She told me later she was keen for me to see what sort of man he was while I had the chance, said she didn't know how long before he'd disappear, that it might be my only chance to meet him.'

'He's certainly got quite the reputation.' Stella found the contrast between Pim's mother and her own interesting. Whereas his mum had been keen for him to meet Johan to prove how much of a disappointment he was; it was the complete opposite to her mother who wanted to shield her from him.

'You're so right. As you know, he left not long after I was born and as far as I was aware, he'd never returned.' They paused at the end of the road, waiting for a car to pass before they crossed to the other side. 'We'd never even spoken on the phone; he'd never kept in contact at all.'

Sounds familiar. 'So I assume you went over to Holland to meet him? How did that go?' She glanced up at him. The thought that he had a kind face crossed her mind.

'I talked it over with Bill and we both agreed that it would be good if I met him at my mother's house rather than have him coming here. So I booked a flight and headed over there. I was absolutely bricking it.' He laughed. 'The prospect of meeting a total stranger who was actually my father, the man whose DNA I share, felt too bizarre to comprehend. It really took some getting my head around.' He turned, looking down at her. 'But I don't have to tell you how that feels, do I, sis?' he said softly.

'No, you don't.' She smiled; that he'd called her sis warmed her heart.

In what felt like a matter of moments, they were walking along the beach, seagulls wheeling overhead, the rush of the waves in the background. A brisk, salt-laden breeze was blowing in off the sea, making Stella glad she'd worn a jumper. A stray lock of hair had escaped her plait and she tucked it behind her ear, watching as a couple of wetsuit clad surfers ran in front of them, surfboards tucked under their arms, their feet slapping over the wet sand. Despite the cooler temperature, the beach was already beginning to fill with families and walkers.

'So how did it go, meeting Johan de Groote for the first time?' she asked.

'Well,' Pim stuffed his hands into the pockets of his jeans and gave a wry laugh, 'put it this way, it didn't take long before he came crashing down from the pedestal I'd sat him on ever since I was a small boy.'

'I'm sorry to hear that, Pim.' Stella glanced up at him, giving a sympathetic smile.

'Oh, don't be. It's not as if I'm a child – I'd have been devastated if it had happened then. Though I didn't think so when I was growing up, it was a good thing he'd stayed away; forgot he had a son. That way he didn't have the chance to cause unhappiness and disruption to mine and my mother's lives.'

'I can understand that, it's the reason my mum didn't want me to have anything to do with him.'

'Your mum is very wise.' Pim nodded. 'I'd tried on numerous occasions to find him when I got older, but with no luck; it was as if he'd just vanished into thin air, didn't want to be found.'

'I got that impression too, in my brief searches for him.'

'When I met him at my mother's house, I found myself actually feeling more shocked by his self-absorbed attitude than hurt by his lack of interest in me. All he talked about for the three hours of his visit was himself. He wasn't interested in how my mum had been or what I'd been doing with my life, though his ears pricked up when he heard I owned a bar here.'

Stella shook her head sadly.

'Would you believe he even asked my mum if he could stay with her for a while until he got himself "sorted out"? Had the nerve to ask for money too.'

'You're kidding me? And the last time your mum had seen him was not long after you were born?' Their so-called father certainly wasn't looking any better in her eyes.

'That's right. She hadn't seen or heard anything for almost

thirty years.' He paused, gazing out to sea, pushing his thick, blond hair off his face. 'It didn't take me long to reach the conclusion that he was the most selfish person I'd ever met. And I know it might sound harsh, but I didn't care if I never saw him again. He didn't fill my heart with love the way I thought he would. There was no rush of the father/son bond that I'd expected to feel. Just a great big disappointment instead.' He turned to face Stella. 'Does that make me sound bad? Unkind? Make me sound like him?' he asked softly, his face wreathed in concern.

'It doesn't make you sound bad or unkind at all.' Stella rested her hand on the top of his arm, the sadness in his eyes triggering a rush of pity. 'And it most definitely doesn't make you sound like him.'

'Thank you.' His expression brightened. 'That's what Bill says, but I wondered if he was just being nice.'

'He wasn't just being nice, Pim, you're a genuinely good guy, everyone says so.' She smiled up at his gentle face. 'And what you just told me is exactly how I feel about Johan de Groote, there's no getting away from the fact that he's an inherently self-absorbed man with a shocking lack of conscience. In fact, I saw him in the Jolly on Friday night.'

'You did? Did he join you and the other girls? Please tell me he wasn't holding court and spoiling your evening, boasting about himself.'

Stella gave a scornful laugh. 'Quite the opposite; he'd have got short shrift from the lasses if he tried, especially Jasmine.'

Pim chuckled. 'Ah, yes, that I can believe.' He caught her eye, a mischievous smile lighting up his face. 'Would've been fun to see. For one so small, she's pretty fierce.' They both laughed at that.

'And loyal,' Stella added. 'They all are, we all look out for each other.'

'I know, Bill and I think that's so cool.'

They resumed walking in the direction of the pier as Stella recounted what had happened on Friday evening, Pim shaking his head in disbelief.

'I expect he'll be looking for somewhere else to stay once his pal Guy gets sick of him. I should imagine he was hoping to charm one of the young women he was talking to at the Jolly,' he said.

'Oh, from what I saw, he was definitely pulling out all the stops to get them wrapped around his little finger, seemed to be working too.'

They watched as two dogs of indeterminate breed raced by them, chasing a ball their owner had thrown, kicking up lumps of sand in their wake, before plunging into the sea after it.

'I guess he's had years of practise to hone his charm,' said Pim.

'Hmm. If that's what you can call it. I rather think it's more like manipulation.'

As they made their way along the beach, Pim told her how on his return from Holland, Johan had been in touch, asking if he could stay with him and Bill for a while, telling him it would give them a chance to get to know one another, to build a bond. In the next breath, he'd asked if Pim could transfer him some money.

Stella's face was burning with anger. The man really had no shame or self-respect. 'I know it's none of my business, but please tell me you told him what he could do with his request.'

Pim chuckled. 'Tempted as I was to put it in blunt terms, I simply said I didn't think it was a good idea. It didn't go down well but, hey,' he shrugged, 'I don't owe him anything.'

'You certainly don't! The man's no more than a stranger.'

'The next thing I know, he rocks up in the bar telling me he's staying at his friend's place for a few days, orders a load of beers and doesn't put his hand in his pocket once, not that I would've asked him to, but the fact that he just presumed they'd be on the house and doesn't offer a word of thanks, well...'

'Why doesn't that surprise me? I'm getting the impression he's a seasoned freeloader.' Stella shook her head. 'And this mate he's referring to is Guy, right?'

'Yep, apparently they know each other from way back – he did say how, but he told me in such a vague, convoluted way I couldn't make sense of it. Top and bottom of it is that Guy's family used to live here in Micklewick Bay years ago and Johan used to visit them. This Guy has recently bought a holiday cottage over in Old Micklewick and is here for a couple of weeks, so Johan is staying with him.'

Stella absorbed this new information. So that was why her mother had headed to Micklewick Bay just after Stella was born. She must have still held a torch for Johan de Groote, must have hoped there'd be a chance she'd bump into him when he visited Guy. Stella couldn't help but think things wouldn't have turned out quite so well for her mother if she had. Keeping this thought to herself, she turned to look up at Pim. 'I wouldn't be surprised if he hopes Guy will let him stay on for a bit longer after he's gone.'

Pim nodded. 'That thought had crossed my mind too, but then I wondered if Guy was wise to him; they've known each other for a long time.'

'I dare say we'll find out soon enough.' A feeling of doom sat heavy in the pit of Stella's stomach. For all he seemed keen to create the impression he was laid-back and happy-go-lucky, something told her Johan de Groote's visit was going to cause ructions.

THIRTY-FOUR

By the time Stella was making her way along the top prom the temperature had dropped, the wind had picked up and lumpen grey clouds had crept over the sky, smothering any last traces of sunshine. Now, large, chilly drops of rain were splashing down. A rash of goosebumps erupted over her skin, urging her to push forward, her long legs making short work of it.

Though her conversation with Pim was running through her mind, thoughts of Alex had started to nudge their way in the closer Stella got to home. She wasn't used to her personal life occupying so much headspace, her cases were usually responsible for that, leaving her emotions unscathed. But now...

Ughh! She sucked in a lungful of fresh salty air as she contemplated this new set of circumstances. Now it felt as if her emotions had been set adrift on a choppy sea and given a thorough tossing about.

Arriving back at Fitzgilbert's Landing, she ran up the stairs and headed straight for Alex's apartment, knocking urgently on the door, her chest heaving as she tried to catch her breath. Her face speckled with rain, she didn't care that she'd look windswept and bedraggled. What was more important was that she spoke to him, cleared the air between them and apologised. If he'd let her, that is.

When there was no answer, she knocked again, disappointment squeezing tightly when she realised he still wasn't home. Pulling her phone from the back pocket of her jeans, she searched for his number and pressed the call icon, listening for sounds of a phone ringing behind his door. But all she heard was a frustrating silence, the call eventually going to voicemail.

* * *

Having changed back into her loungewear, Stella had been at her desk, working for the last hour and a half when her phone pinged with a text. She snatched it up, hoping to see Alex's name, but her eyes landed on Florrie's instead. Much as she loved her friend, she couldn't help but be disappointed. She opened the text, her eyes widening as she read it.

> Hi Stells, just a quick message to say I hope your talk with Pim went well. Also wanted to mention that Ed and I saw Alex looking in the estate agent's window when we were at the bookshop earlier. Might be nothing, but thought you'd like to know. Fxx

With her heart thudding Stella reread the message, her mind running over the implications. He might have just been looking in the window out of general interest –or nosiness – she was no stranger to that herself. Or – the least palatable option – he might have been looking for property to move to. She couldn't deny the allegations she'd hurled at him that fateful night had been pretty unpleasant, and it didn't take a genius to see why he'd want to move house with his accuser living a matter of feet away.

She scrunched her eyes tight shut. *Why did I have to wade in like that, adopting full-on barrister mode, accusing him and pointing the finger? I didn't even give him a chance to speak, didn't stop to listen.* She huffed out a frustrated sigh. 'Stella Hutton, you've been a complete and utter fool! You've let your fear of commitment take over and now you've blown it with the only man you've ever cared about!'

The need to speak to Alex had suddenly taken on a new urgency. She *had* to get hold of him. *Had* to make him understand how utterly sorry she was.

With her fingers flying over the screen of her phone and her heart pounding hard against her ribcage she found Alex's number, her hand shaking as she pressed the call icon. Unsurprisingly, it rang out before going to voicemail so she sucked in a deep breath and left a message, asking him to get in touch with a view to them meeting up, explaining how she wanted to apologise. Ending the call, and feeling she'd been uncharacteristically gabbly, she hoped she wouldn't have long to wait before he returned her call. If, indeed, he would.

Taking a break from her work, Stella stood at her balcony window, mug of coffee in her hand, watching as the rain lashed against it, running in rivulets down the glass. The sea had turned a dark shade of pewter, trimmed with frothy white breakers. The beach was now empty of people but for the odd foolhardy dog walker. In the distance, a small fishing boat chugged its way back inland, a swirl of seagulls following in its wake.

She'd managed to get more prep done than she'd expected, especially with her mind being all over the place, but she was still glad of the extra day off work thanks to it being the August Bank Holiday weekend; she'd be working through that.

The sound of her mobile pinging to life pulled Stella away from her thoughts, sending her pulse racing. *Please let it be*

Alex. She hurried over to her desk, quickly setting her mug down and scooping up her phone. Her heart dropped to her cashmere socks when she saw that the message was from her clerk Allegra. Stella's brow crumpled. Allegra may be uber efficient, but she wasn't one for texting on a Sunday unless something of great urgency had cropped up.

Curious, Stella opened the text.

Hi Miss Hutton, I can't begin to imagine what's given you the impression that I've been stealing your underwear, but I can assure you I'm definitely no "knicker-nicker"! Hope you find the real culprit! Allegra

Stella pressed her hand to her mouth, her face burning. 'Oh no!' In her haste to speak to Alex she must have tapped on the wrong name. She could see how it had been done with Allegra being the one directly below Alex in her list of contacts. She cast her mind back to the voicemail message, recalling it had been generic, giving no clue as to the identity of the person she was calling. Little did she know it was her clerk's number. *What is wrong with you, woman? You're going to pieces!* She consoled herself with the fact that it could have been so much worse. *Imagine if it had been someone like her stuffy head of chambers. She doubted very much he'd have been impressed.*

At least Allegra had taken it in good spirits, especially if all the jokey emojis were anything to go by. Allegra may be supremely efficient and professional, but Stella was glad of their friendly working relationship, with a generous dash of good-natured banter. That was something at least.

Stella sent a quick reply, her blushes fading.

Oops! Sorry about that, Allegra! Wrong number! I'll explain later. Enjoy the rest of the long weekend. I promise to leave you in peace! Stella

She added a couple of emojis and pressed send, smiling to herself; that was going to be an interesting conversation in chambers next week.

Despite her smiles, Stella took it as a stark warning to herself. She needed to clear her head, regain her focus and stop allowing herself to be so distracted by the non-work-related things going on around her.

But she'd be the first to admit it wasn't quite as straightforward as that. It hadn't been easy to accept just how deeply her feelings for Alex had run, how he'd broken through the many, hitherto invincible, barricades to finally reach her heart. Hadn't been easy to admit to herself that she'd fallen for him, and fallen hard. And then, after all that, accepting the idea that maybe they could develop a relationship, she had to go and hurl some fairly unpleasant accusations at him. Her stomach twisted at the memory and she put her head in her hands.

As if that wasn't enough, her father turning up the way he had, then finding out Pim was her half-brother, had all taken turns in chipping away at her famously rock-solid exterior in a way she hadn't expected or experienced before. Not to mention the fact she was being followed by some creep. Unlike the tough, unpalatable subjects she was used to tackling, it wasn't so easy to place these matters into an imaginary box and file them away for dealing with another day. They were too personal, and they were stacking up. She needed to face them, needed to get them out of her head.

Which was exactly what she was determined to do. And she was going to start by leaving a calm and composed message on *Alex's* phone, with no mention of her knickers whatsoever. She inhaled a calming breath and called his number.

THIRTY-FIVE

Stella woke early, an agonising ache gnawing in her heart. Alex hadn't returned her call and there'd been no sign of him back at his apartment. She'd blown it. Blown her chance with the only man she'd ever had feelings for, the only man she'd ever had a connection with. What a fool she'd been. She pulled the duvet over her head and turned over. She wasn't ready to face the day, wasn't ready to face the loss of a potentially wonderful relationship.

Less than five minutes later, she threw the duvet back and pushed herself out of bed, a new-found resolve spurring her on. 'Stella Hutton, you do not do sentimental feelings and you most certainly do not do relationships,' she said resolutely. 'It's time to forget about Alex Bainbridge. You've tried to apologise and he clearly hasn't accepted your apology. He's ignoring you and there's nothing else you can do. It's time to move on, you don't need him in your life. You don't need any man in your life, you've managed perfectly well without one; they only bring trouble.' Adding as an afterthought, 'And that includes Johan de flaming Groote!' With that, she strode into the kitchen and set about making herself a large mug of coffee, ignoring the pesky ache in her heart that clearly hadn't taken heed of her words.

Sipping her coffee, she headed over to her speakers, sat her phone in the dock and selected a playlist of happy songs and turned up the volume. That done, she padded over to the balcony door, peering out at the damp, grey day that held Micklewick Bay in its grip. Much as she hated to admit it, it appeared to reflect her mood, not that she was going to dwell on it. She half expected to see the dark car with blacked-out windows parked in its now familiar spot across the road. She was relieved when it wasn't. Its absence strengthened her resolution to head out for a run, despite the inclement weather, telling herself it would help exorcise the final vestiges of her feelings for Alex.

Stella returned from her run, out of breath and red faced. She was also soaked to the skin thanks to the permeating mizzle that had hung in the air, clinging to all it touched. But there was no doubting she felt better for it thanks to the endorphins currently pumping around her body. Pushing herself on had cleared her head as well as her lungs, and now she felt ready to tackle her prep for court tomorrow.

Peeling her wet running gear off, she stepped into a zinging hot shower, the jets of water pummelling her skin, the crisp scent of her shower gel filling the air. That done, she pulled on a pair of dusky pink yoga pants, teamed them with a matching slouchy sweatshirt, slipped her feet into a pair of fluffy socks and headed to her desk.

She was engrossed in her case, making notes, when the buzzer to her apartment sounded, making her start.

Peering at the intercom screen, her heart sank when she saw Johan de Groote looking back at her.

Myriad thoughts began darting around her mind. She

hadn't expected to see him again and the last thing she wanted was to invite him up to her apartment, especially after what Pim had told her about him asking to stay with him and Bill. She most certainly didn't want to give him ideas about getting his feet under the table here. Should she answer? Or should she pretend she wasn't in? Reminding herself that he would more than likely have seen the light from her desk lamp, she thought it was probably best to reply. Plus, she'd never been one to shy away from anything and she wasn't about to start now, errant father or no errant father.

She buzzed him up, telling him which floor she was on, then quickly slid the papers relating to her brief into the drawer of her desk and flipped the lid on her laptop. The details of her case were of a sensitive and highly confidential nature and she couldn't afford to have anyone sniffing around them.

The knock on the door sent her pulse jumping. Opening it she was greeted by the man she still couldn't get used to thinking of as her father. Her eyes fell to the large holdall in his hand.

'Stella.' He gave a lazy smile and stepped inside, towering over her. Dumping his bag, he headed down the hallway towards the living room in a self-assured manner. Irked, Stella closed the door and followed up behind.

She noted his blond hair was damp with beads of mizzle, as was his raincoat which he took off and threw over the back of the sofa, sending another dart of annoyance through her. She scooped it up and hung it on a peg in the hall.

Returning to the living room, she found him glancing around, his hands pushed into the pockets of his jeans, as if appraising the place. He wandered over to a carved dark stone bowl on the coffee table. Picking it up, he checked the stamp on the base, his eyebrows lifting. 'Expensive.'

'It was a gift.'

He nodded, pursing his lips together as he cast his eyes over the furnishings. 'Nice place you've got here. You're clearly doing very well for yourself.' He had a lazy, almost soporific air about him; so at odds with her motivated demeanour.

She folded her arms. 'I work hard. You reap what you sow. Someone once told me it's the same with kids.' She knew she shouldn't have said that, but she couldn't resist.

'Ouch,' he said, giving a sardonic laugh that didn't reach his eyes.

'To what do I owe this surprise visit?' she asked. 'I get the feeling this isn't just a social call.' She wondered how he'd managed to track her down; she hadn't told him her address and she couldn't imagine anyone she knew sharing it with him.

'How about we have a nice chat over a coffee from that fancy machine I can see over there?' He nodded in its direction. 'I can tell you then.' He gave her a smile that could only be described as smarmy.

'Okay.' Much as she would rather he hadn't turned up like this, a part of her couldn't help but be intrigued by what he had to say.

With the coffee made, she headed over to the sofa where Johan had made himself comfortable and had stretched out his long legs and rested his feet – which were encased in annoyingly muddy shoes – on the coffee table, scattering the books that were there, including the one from Florrie and Ed.

She set his mug down in front of him and took the seat furthest away but which afforded her a full view of his face. She was keen to read his expression, hoping to pick up on any telltale signs that would reveal what he was feeling and whether he was telling the truth. The fact that his pale blue eyes were so like Pim's – and her own – she found slightly disconcerting. The similarity was further emphasised by the thick, straight, blond eyebrows the three of them shared, though hers had been tamed by regular appointments at the beautician's.

'So,' she said, taking a sip of her coffee, watching him all the while, 'you were going to tell me why you're here.'

'You don't beat about the bush, do you?' He gave another of his small laughs. There was something about their tone that were beginning to grate on her. 'Straight in there, no niceties. Boom!' He jabbed his fingers as if to demonstrate. 'Just like your mother.'

Stella bristled. 'I'm proud to be like my mum, she's an amazing woman and someone I've looked up to all my life. She's the reason I'm "doing well" for myself.' She added emphasis to his words.

Johan nodded, the small smile hovering over his mouth venturing into the realms of a sneer. He reached for his coffee and slumped back into the sofa, one arm slung casually over the back, his body language in no way suggesting he was a stranger here. 'Nice coffee,' he said. 'Good and strong.'

'Glad you like it.' Stella couldn't recall the last time she'd seen anyone so arrogantly comfortable in their own skin. She tried to quell her rising irritation. 'You were about to tell me why you're here.' Her North Yorkshire accent stood in stark contrast to his lilting Dutch tones.

'Well,' he said, drawing out the word as his gaze slowly swept around the room once more, 'isn't a father allowed to pay his daughter a visit?'

Stella almost choked on her coffee. 'Excuse me?'

'My reason for coming here is that I think it would be a good idea if we got to know each other after all these years.' His eyes met hers; the look she saw in them could easily have been construed as challenging.

Was he kidding? She held his gaze, there was no way she was going to back down, give him the slightest impression he was in charge, had the upper hand. She knew his game; she'd seen way too many people like him in the witness box, expert manipulators. 'That's interesting, because that's the very last impression you gave on Friday night in The Jolly Sailors when you blanked me,' she said, her voice firm.

A shadow of discomfort flittered across his face, but Johan was undeterred. 'If I remember the situation correctly, it was you who ignored me. You turned away and headed back to your friends without even saying hello. But I'm prepared to be the bigger person, to let it go and move on for the sake of our relationship.' The calm tone he used and the way he'd raised his palms at her was seriously beginning to grate.

Stella set her jaw, shaking her head in disgust. It was a blatant lie. 'As far as I can see, we have no relationship; by staying away for thirty-three years, you've made sure of that. And please refrain from coming into my home and telling barefaced lies, accusing me of something I did not do.'

'I'm not lying.' He gave a shrug. 'I'm simply saying that's how it seemed to me.'

There was clearly no getting through to this man

'Whatever,' she said, batting his comment away. 'I'd like to know the *real* reason you're here. No more beating around the bush.'

He laughed again, shaking his head, tutting. 'Stella, Stella, Stella, you really need to soften up a bit. You're all hard edges, sharp corners, primed for battle. I haven't come here to fight with you, I've come to talk, get to know you, let you get to know me.'

'So you keep saying, but we don't seem to be getting anywhere.' She wished he'd hurry up and get to the real reason behind his visit. Pim's words started ringing in her ears, the request for a place to stay, asking for money. Surely he hadn't come here for that, had he? She'd only spoken to him once before; they were little more than strangers.

'That's because these things can't happen in a hurry, they take time.' He brushed his damp hair off his forehead and smiled.

In that moment, she knew exactly where the conversation was going.

Uh-oh! 'In that case, we'd better get started then.' She kept her tone cool.

He gave another dry laugh, making himself more comfortable on the sofa. The man was so laid-back he was almost horizontal.

'I don't suppose we could chat over a bite to eat? He flashed his languid smile at her. 'I'm feeling quite hungry.'

Not speaking, she got to her feet, marched over to the kitchen, returning moments later with a plate of biscuits, placing it on the table in front of him.

'Oh, okay,' he said with an unimpressed snort, reaching for one of the biscuits and examining it as if it were something inedible.

Stella looked on as he took a bite, before launching into giving her a potted history of his life.

As she listened, she found herself wondering yet again what her mother could possibly have seen in him. They were polar opposites; her mum was driven and hardworking, he gave the impression he was bone idle, a loafer who'd spent his life simply bumming around from place to place, sofa surfing, with no direction, no aspirations. To Stella, these were deeply unattractive traits.

'So,' he said, swallowing the last of the biscuits and wiping crumbs from his hands, 'I thought it would be good for both of us if I spent a bit of time here with you. That way we could start building a bond between us.' The way he spoke, she rather got the impression he was telling her that's what would happen, that there was no option for her to refuse. The disingenuous smile he gave confirmed her thoughts. 'If you could point me in the direction of a bedroom where I can put my bag. You can make a start on lunch while I take a shower; that plate of biscuits wasn't enough to fill a man.' His mocking laugh made Stella grit her teeth.

'There's no room for you here; that's not going to happen,' she said firmly. 'I use the spare room as a mini gym. I keep my treadmill and spinner bike there.' Yet again, he hadn't asked a single question about her. The only thing that appeared to interest him about her was the amount of money she must be earning to afford an expensive apartment and a fancy car.

'Oh, Stella, don't be like that. I'm here now, you've seen I've brought my bag with all my stuff, you might as well let me stay. What harm can it do? I've already told you I'm not a well man. I need somewhere warm and calm to stay where I can rebuild my strength.'

What harm can it do? She got the feeling if she let him stay even for one night, she'd struggle to get rid of him. Maggie's recent unwelcome houseguest sprang to mind. Maggie had thought she'd never leave. That most certainly wasn't going to happen here. And that was something else, she couldn't help but doubt what he'd told them about his illness, there was something in the way he couldn't make eye contact when he mentioned it. She'd noticed it when she'd first met him at The Cellar with Pim.

'You're not staying here and that's final.' She got to her feet. 'You'll have to stay with your friend, Guy, is it? If we're going to get to know one another, I'd prefer to do it slowly, rather than have you staying in my home.' She'd be interested to hear what had happened between them that meant Johan was suddenly looking for somewhere to stay.

Johan's gaze slid away from her as he mumbled something indiscernible. She'd clearly hit a nerve. 'Guy isn't being a great friend to me at the moment. He's heading back home, says I can't stay at the cottage any longer. He can be a very selfish man. He has two homes, I have none. It wouldn't hurt to let me stay, it's not as if he lets it out, it's only him that uses it.'

And there it was, the reason Johan de Groote had landed on her doorstep. He needed somewhere to stay. The man really was something else.

'If you're wanting to stay in Micklewick Bay there are plenty of bed and breakfast places. I know for a fact that there are several with vacancies.' Stella had been told this by her mum who'd heard it directly from some of the owners whose properties Spick 'n' Sparkle cleaned for. They'd expressed their disappointment at the lack of last minute bookings considering it was a Bank Holiday weekend, blaming the bad weather.

'Staying in a bed and breakfast is hardly the same as staying in a proper home.' Johan coughed, patting his chest. 'I'm not in the best of health, the doctors say I should really have someone to look after me, but instead I just plough on alone, never complaining.' He looked at her, the self-pity in his eyes making her stomach turn over.

From what she'd witnessed, Johan de Groote was more than capable of looking after himself. 'Most of the bed and breakfast places are nice and homely.'

He heaved a sigh, drumming his fingers impatiently on the back of the sofa. 'Well, this really isn't what I'd expected. I thought you'd welcome me into your life with open arms; your long-lost father shows up, the man you've been desperate to see all your life.' He shot her a disapproving look, his arrogant smile finally slipping away.

Stella could hardly believe what she was hearing, her anger was inching up to boiling point. Telling herself to stay calm, she gritted her teeth and said, 'I'm not sure how you ever arrived at such an assumption. But anyway, I think we've talked enough for one day.'

'That causes me a bit of a problem.' Rubbing his hand over the light stubble of his chin, Johan paused, as if running something over in his mind. 'If you're not going to let me stay here, I don't suppose you could help me out with some cash? Just a couple of thousand. Only, I haven't been able to afford my medication, and if I'm going to have to pay to stay somewhere else...' He gave in to an elaborate bout of coughing. 'My heart isn't strong. I don't know how much longer I've got...' He stole a look at her from beneath his fringe that was now flopping over his eyes.

This performance was something else. It begged the question, if he had such a bad heart, why had he just stuffed his face with a load of chocolate biscuits?

The ringing of her mobile spliced through Stella's thoughts. Johan ceased his coughing and sat upright. Stella got to her feet.

'You're going to answer it?' he asked in disbelief. 'But we're talking.'

'I'm going to see who it is.' She headed to her desk and picked up her phone, surprised to see her mum's name. She tapped her fingernail on the screen, answering it. 'Hi, Mum, you okay?' She was glad to have her attention diverted away from Johan for a moment.

Stella turned to look at him. 'Yes, he's here,' she said, her words eliciting a frown from him. She fell silent, her eyes never leaving him as she listened to what her mum had to say.

'What did your mother want? Was she talking about me?' he asked when the call had ended.

Stella didn't answer. Instead, she strode out into the hall, returning with his coat, holding it out to him. 'You can gather up your holdall as you leave.'

THIRTY-SIX

'What's going on? I demand to know what your mother has been saying about me.' Johan got to his feet and headed towards her, hands raised in question. 'She's trying to poison your thoughts about me which I suspect from my cold reception is what she's spent your whole life doing.'

He could demand all he jolly well liked, Stella wasn't going to tell him anything. 'Don't talk about my mum like that.' She pushed the coat at him. 'Please leave now.' Though she was shaking inside, she kept her voice calm, her gaze steady.

'What? No, I'm not going anywhere. When you've had a minute to calm down, we can talk. I'll give you my side of things.' The laugh he gave had a patronising tone that did him no favours with Stella. 'I know you don't really want me to leave, you're just acting in the heat of the moment. I'm your father.'

'I think you'll find I very much want you to leave.' She looked him directly in the eye. 'I know what you've done, I know the sort of person you are. I want you to go.' She refrained from telling him it was a shame he hadn't remembered he was her father when she'd been a little girl.

'I'm afraid it's not so easy for me to do that,' he said casually, apparently reluctant to make eye contact with her.

'Why not?'

'I have no money.' He shrugged, his eyes returning to hers. 'If you want me to go, you're going to have to give me some.'

Did this man have no shame? 'Wait there!' Seething, Stella headed to her bedroom, grabbing her purse from her handbag. 'There, that's all I have.' She held out a handful of notes. 'Now you can go.'

He snatched the money out of her hands, counting it quickly, shaking his head in disbelief. 'That is all? What am I supposed to do with this? There's not even enough for me to get a train to London.'

Was he for real? 'No one carries much cash around these days. I've given you all I have on me.'

'I noticed a bank on—'

'It's a Bank Holiday, it's closed.'

'There's an ATM.'

'I won't be making use of that,' she said, unyielding. 'Now you have to go.'

He leant towards her, the air around them filling with tension. 'You're no daughter of mine. You're not what I expected at all.' He spat the words out. 'I thought you'd at least show some compassion; I'm your father, I'm ill. But no, you're too wrapped up in your own life, your high-flying career. You're just like your mother, bitter and twisted.'

'I'd rather be like her than like you. Now just go.' The steel-strong look in her eyes told him she'd brook no further argument.

He snatched his coat out of her hands, his face distorted with spite. 'You're a foolish woman. No man will ever want you, you'll end up on your own, just like she has.'

That hit a nerve. She took a moment to reply, steadying herself. 'She's not on her own, she's found someone wonderful, someone who treats her well and makes her happy,' she said more calmly than she was feeling.

His words had landed like a knife to her heart, Alex looming in her mind. Battling the emotions that were swirling frantically inside her, Stella said calmly, 'I'd like to say you're not what I'd expected, but it turns out you are.' She pushed past him and headed down the hallway, holding the door open for him to leave. She closed it firmly when he'd gone, her chest heaving as she blew out a breath of relief.

Back in the living room, her heart still pounding, she made for her desk and picked up her phone. When she'd taken the call from her mum, she'd noticed a slew of missed text messages. She must have been so focused on her conversation with Johan de Groote she hadn't heard them arrive. Disappointment raced through her as it registered that none were from Alex. However, she noticed one was from Pim. She scanned it, her pulse thrumming in her ears. Just when she thought their father couldn't scrape any lower in her opinion. Swiping the message shut – she'd reply to Pim later – she called her mum, wondering if she'd heard the news.

THIRTY-SEVEN

Pulling up outside number five Magnolia Gardens, Stella stilled the engine of her car and sat for a moment, bracing herself for the unabridged version of the story her mum had quickly given her on the phone. She felt a pinch of sympathy for her mum; her day out with Rhys that she'd been so looking forward to had been scuppered. He'd surprised Alice with tickets to go around Danskelfe Castle and its grounds over on the moors, and had booked a table in the restaurant of the legendary Sunne Inne at nearby Lytell Stangdale. She'd been bubbling with excitement about it ever since.

'Oh, lovey, come in.' Alice gathered her daughter into a tight hug as soon as Stella stepped into the hallway.

'Hi, Mum, you okay?' A hug from her mother always felt good, whatever the circumstances.

'I'm fine, it's you I'm worried about.' Alice released her daughter from her embrace, her hands slipping to her shoulders while she scrutinised Stella's face.

'Oh don't worry about me, I'm fine,' Stella said, her light tone belying how she was really feeling; the cocktail of emotions still pulsing around her body had her senses on high alert.

Her mum's smile told her she wasn't convinced. 'Come on through, Rhys has just made a pot of tea.'

She followed her mum to the kitchen where Rhys was pouring tea into a mug. He looked up, his face breaking into a smile. 'Stella, my love, how are you?'

'I'm okay, thanks, Rhys.' She hooked her bag over the back of a chair at the table and sat down, her mother sitting opposite. 'I'm sorry your plans have been spoilt.' It dawned on her she rather liked being in his company.

'It's fine, we can do it another day.' He smiled again, an air of calm and kindness about him, so very different from the assured arrogance of Johan de Groote. 'There you go, get that down you.' He set a mug on the table in front of her, patting her shoulder. 'Things always look better after a cup of tea.'

Stella looked up at him and pressed her lips into a smile. 'Thanks, Rhys.'

'Right then,' said her mum, as Rhys took a seat beside her, 'tell us what happened.'

Alice and Rhys listened quietly as Stella shared the details of how she'd been blanked by her father at the Jolly, right up to him reluctantly leaving her apartment. Even to her ears, it sounded like something from a soap opera.

'The man's got no shame,' said Alice, her face flushing red with outrage. 'He clearly hasn't changed, I'm just really angry he had the audacity to turn up at your home and speak to you like that, especially after what had gone on here.'

'Don't worry about it, Mum, you'd warned me about him plenty, it wasn't as if I wasn't prepared. And at least he left.' Stella gave a reassuring smile. 'So how come he ended up here?'

Alice and Rhys exchanged loaded looks.

Her mum inhaled deeply before she spoke. 'I've no idea how he got my address, but you can imagine my surprise when I found him snooping around the back garden.'

'He was snooping around your garden?' Stella said in disbelief.

'Oh, yes, having a right good nosy, he was, had a great big holdall with him.' Alice gave an incredulous laugh. 'Mind, he didn't half get a shock when he spotted me watching him, laughed it off in that annoying way he has when I confronted him about it.'

'I was out at the time,' Rhys added.

'So what did he have to say for himself,' Stella asked.

'Well, after he'd made some weak excuse about having knocked at the door but couldn't get a reply so had headed round to the back – which was clearly a load of rubbish – he then launched into telling me how it had been a wonderful "surprise" to find I was living in Micklewick Bay; the place he just so happened to be visiting.' Her tone was laced with sarcasm.

Alice went on to explain how he'd managed to wangle his way into the kitchen where he'd wasted no time in utilising his well-worn smarmy techniques, telling her she was still beautiful, how a day hadn't passed when she hadn't been in his thoughts. 'Did he really think I was going to fall for that?' she said. He'd then launched into an over-sentimental speech, talking of their days together when they were "young and carefree and in love". 'He seemed to have conveniently forgotten that he'd walked out on me when I'd told him I was pregnant, leaving me penniless.'

Rhys placed his hand over hers, squeezing it gently, the gesture sending a wave of warmth through Stella.

Alice then described how his attention had quickly turned to her home, commenting on how much room she had, wondering as to the value of the property, saying how she'd made a success of her life. From what he'd been spouting about her financial situation, he'd clearly done his research on her cleaning company. 'Didn't take long for him to sneak in with the suggestion that he move in for a while, giving me the same spiel he gave you about his health diagnosis, how he couldn't afford his medication.'

'Wow,' Stella said, eyebrows raised, wondering at the nerve of the man.

'Told me it'd be just like old days, us living together. Like *that* was ever going to tempt me,' Alice said, rolling her eyes. 'And then, the next thing I knew he'd grabbed hold of me and was telling me he still loved me, even tried to kiss me, can you believe? "For old times' sake." Saying one kiss was all it would take to make me fall in love with him all over again. Cheek of the man! He's deluded!'

'He did what?' The colour drained from Stella's face. 'There's absolutely no excuse for that kind of behaviour.'

'Oh, don't worry, lovey, he got a stiff knee to the testicles for his trouble.' Alice said, reminding her daughter just what a tough cookie she really was. 'One kiss indeed.'

'And that's when I returned,' Rhys said.

'And thank goodness you did.' Alice looked at him, rubbing her hand over his arm.

It transpired that the couple had asked Johan to leave but he'd turned hostile, demanding money before he left. When they'd refused to give him anything, he'd threatened to sue Alice for denying him contact with his daughter, his argument being that she'd moved away, leaving no forwarding address and no way for him to contact her. 'Stood there, bold as brass, shouting the odds. Unbelievable,' Alice said. 'But Rhys was amazing.' She turned to him again, affection shining in her eyes. 'Told him he'd get nothing from us and frogmarched him out of the house.'

'Go, Rhys!' Stella said, her admiration for the man who'd captured her mother's heart growing by the minute.

'So,' Alice sat back in her seat, 'he'd already tried his luck here before he landed at your place. It was Rhys who said we should warn you, it hadn't even crossed my mind that he'd end up on your doorstep.'

'Yeah, thanks for that, Rhys. It definitely put the wind up him when my mum rang.'

'Happy to help,' he said. 'I'm just sorry things have turned out the way they have for you.'

'Don't be, it's no more than I expected.' And it was true.

'I don't know about you, but I reckon this calls for another cup of tea before you tell us what Pim had to say.' Alice pushed herself up and headed over to the kettle.

'Best make it extra strong, Mum.'

What Johan de Groote had done in his short time in Micklewick Bay was bad, but what Stella was about to share was a whole lot worse. His misdemeanours weren't going to improve his already tarnished reputation.

THIRTY-EIGHT

Armed with a fresh cup of tea, and with her mother and Rhys eager to hear what she had to say, Stella retrieved her phone from her bag and opened the text from Pim. She read the contents out loud.

> Hi Stella, don't let Johan in your apartment!!! Just heard from my mum & she says he's been stealing from people back in The Netherlands!! He's also lying about his illness! Sorry this is so short but it's very busy here. I'll give you more details later. Much love Pim x

'Goodness, that was punchy and to the point,' said Alice.

'It's good of Pim to warn you,' said Rhys, his expression grave.

'Seems Johan de Groote is leaving a trail of destruction in his wake.' Stella set her phone down on the table and looked between them. A thought suddenly struck her. 'He didn't take anything from here, did he, Mum?'

'I haven't noticed anything... actually, now you come to mention it...' Alice glanced over to the worktop by the door. 'I'd left my purse on—' She gasped, her hand flying to her mouth.

'It's not there.' She got to her feet and started looking around the kitchen, colour draining from her face. 'I could've sworn I'd left it there.'

Rhys joined the hunt around the room. 'I don't recall seeing it, Alice.'

'Maybe you put it back in your handbag, Mum.' Despite her suggestion, Stella had a bad feeling about this.

'I'll check, but I'm sure I didn't. I was putting some raffle tickets away and can just remember thinking I'd put it back in my...' She stopped her search and turned to face them. 'I put it down when I caught sight of Johan in the garden, didn't cross my mind that he'd end up in the house.'

'You think he's taken it?' asked Rhys, clearly shocked.

'After hearing what Pim said in his text, I'd say there was a pretty good chance he's lifted it, yes. He used to take money out of my purse when we were students.' Her voice tailed off.

'Was there much cash in it?' asked Stella, taking in her mum's wan expression.

'I think there was about fifty pounds, plus all my bank cards.'

Anger blazed inside Stella. How dare he come back and disrupt her mother's life again? To think, she'd been desperate to find him, desperate to know who he was. Now she wished she'd never set eyes on him. The only saving grace was that he wasn't here because she'd tracked him down and brought him to Micklewick Bay. That would have been too much to bear. The sooner he left town, the better. But first, her mum needed to get her purse back.

* * *

Stella drove into town, slowly scanning the streets for any sign of Johan de Groote, the windscreen wipers swishing back and forth as the rain teemed down. He'd be easy to spot; being so tall meant he stood out, as did his slightly bohemian style. It also helped that the inclement weather meant there weren't many people kicking about for him to melt into.

She'd left her mum's house determined to track her father down and get the missing purse back. She was going to give him a piece of her mind too. She'd take great pleasure in wiping that arrogant smile off his face. The man clearly had no conscience.

As her car nosed its way down Victoria Square, the rain thrumming ever harder against its roof, her heart jolted as her eyes landed on a familiar figure. Alex! Her pulse took off at a gallop. He appeared to be taking shelter in the station buildings along with a young woman she recognised as his twin sister Zara. There was a soggy-looking Fred sitting beside them, watching the world go by with interest.

Stella looked around frantically, searching for a parking space, the urge to speak to Alex setting nerves wriggling in her stomach. Spotting one, she quickly parked up and ran towards the station, head bowed against the driving rain that was slicing at her cheeks. Water splashed up from the puddles, soaking her plimsolls as she raced over the pavement.

'Alex!' she called as she drew closer, fearful he'd walk away. He turned, his smiles morphing into a look of surprise.

'Stella?'

Fred leapt to his feet and pulled on his lead to get to her, his tail wagging so hard it was making his whole body wiggle.

'This is Stella?' Zara said, her eyebrows hitched in interest, an amused smile on her lips.

'Alex, I'm so glad I've seen you,' Stella said, panting, rain dripping down her face, her hair plastered to her head. She bent, absently giving Fred an ear tickle.

'You are?' Alex said. The look in his eyes telling her he wasn't convinced.

'Yes, I am,' she said, trying to catch her breath. 'I've been calling you. I need to talk to you. Need to apologise.' She wiped the rain from her face, not caring that she would look like a drowned rat; she *had* to tell him. 'I know you didn't take my underwear. I'm really sorry I accused you.'

A snort of stifled laughter came from Zara's direction, earning her a stern look from her brother. 'Sorry,' she said, pressing her fingers to her lips and looking anything but.

'That's what I was trying to tell you when you threw it at me.'

More sniggers from Zara, earning her another reprimanding look and a frustrated huff.

'I know that now, and I...' Her words tailed off, her eyes growing wide as her gaze was drawn to a tall figure with a now-familiar swagger who was making his way to the ticket office behind.

'What's the matter?' Alex asked, turning and following her line of sight.

'It's Johan de Groote. I need to stop him,' she said urgently. 'I think he's stolen my mum's purse.'

'He's *what?*'

'Sorry, I have to go, but I still need to speak to you, Alex,' Stella called over her shoulder as she ran towards the ticket office.

Inside, she looked around frantically, but there was no sign of her father.

'*Arghh!*' Frustrated, Stella pushed her fingers into her saturated hair. A second later, gripped by a feeling of urgency, she rushed out of the ticket office and checked the waiting room. Finding no trace of him there, she headed out onto the platform which was empty but for a handful of youths on bikes apparently oblivious to the weather. Turning on her heel, she sprinted to the subway that led to the second platform, her feet echoing around her as she raced on, calling out apologies as she barged her way through.

She'd just alighted on the platform when she heard the low

rumble of a train as it snaked its way down the track towards the station. Glancing through the crowd of people, her attention was taken by raised voices over by the small waiting room. Her eyes widened in surprise as she saw Alex and Zara blocking the doorway to an enraged Johan de Groote.

THIRTY-NINE

'Get out of my way!' Johan's voiced boomed around the old station, bouncing off the cast iron rafters, turning heads and sending pigeons scattering. 'I need to get my train!'

Stella rushed over to them, her heart still racing, the acrid smell of diesel fumes permeating the air. Behind her came the screech of brakes as the train ground slowly to a halt.

'Stella needs to talk to you. Until she's done, I won't be moving an inch.' Alex squared up to Johan, his shoulders appearing broader than ever.

'Same here.' Zara's smile had been replaced by a surprisingly fierce expression.

'That's my train, I need to get it.' Johan looked distinctly agitated, his eyes shifty.

'You're not going anywhere until you hand over my mother's purse. We know you took it,' said Stella, her voice confident and strong.

'I have no idea what you're talking about. Now move, I need to board my train. I have a ferry to catch.' He went to push through them but Alex stood firm.

'Move,' said Johan, baring his teeth.

'If I were you, I'd hand over the purse before I call for that rather surly police officer who was standing by the entrance to come and give us some assistance.' Alex locked eyes with Johan, his gaze unwavering. 'I doubt very much you'd like to explain to him what it's doing in your possession,' said Alex. Johan wasn't to know he was bluffing, that there was no police officer.

Maintaining eye contact, Johan didn't budge. 'If you don't let me through I'll tell the police officer you've been harassing me.'

'Fair enough,' said Zara, 'I'll go and get him now; he can decide who's in the wrong here.' She turned to walk away.

'Wait!' Johan dropped his holdall to the floor, where he unzipped it and began rummaging around its contents, cursing under his breath. The flash of a shiny, dark object caught Stella's eye, sending a spike of recognition through her, but the item was hurriedly nudged out of view as Johan delved deeper into his bag.

Standing upright, he said, 'Here. Have it.' He pushed the purse roughly at her before scooping up his holdall and barging through them. 'Now get out of my way.'

They watched as he ran across the platform and jumped onto the train just before it started to pull away, its whistle tooting shrilly as it went.

'Wow! Is it always like this in Micklewick Bay?' asked Zara.

'No.' Stella shook her head, her mind reeling. 'It's usually a quiet little seaside town where nothing much happens.'

'You okay, Stella?' Pulling her gaze away from the disappearing train, she turned to see Alex looking at her, his eyes loaded with concern.

'Yeah, I'm fine, thanks, especially now I've got my mum's purse back. Thanks for your help, both of you. I wouldn't have caught him if it wasn't for you.' She gave a weak smile.

'You look drained.' Alex rested his hand on her shoulder, warmth from his touch radiating through her, igniting the spark that had been slumbering in his absence. 'I can imagine you're keen to get your mum's purse back to her, but why don't we meet back at my apartment in, say, an hour from now, then we can continue the conversation we were having before the drama kicked in?' He smiled at her, a hint of mischief in his eyes.

That Alex was open to talking about their misunderstanding – or rather, *her* misunderstanding – with the underwear filled Stella's heart with hope. 'I'd like that, thanks.' Despite the situation, she couldn't help but smile back at him. 'I'll give my mum a call, tell her we've got it and that Johan de Groote has left town; not sure which she'll be pleased to hear most.'

'I think I do.' He gave her a smile.

'Yeah, me too.'

By the time she'd returned home, Stella's skin was covered in goosebumps and she was shivering from the cold. She flicked the heating on, peeled off her wet clothes and treated herself to a tinglingly hot shower which helped warm her through. With her hair tied back in a plait, she pulled on her favourite loungewear, the urge to feel snuggly overriding her usual need to look smart and groomed.

Her mood felt suddenly lighter.

Armed with a bottle of wine, she knocked on Alex's apartment door, her heart lifting at the prospect of repairing their fledgeling relationship. She heard Fred give a cursory bark in the background.

'Hi, come in.' Zara greeted her with a warm smile, Fred pushing his nose through, the sound of his wagging tail hitting the wall. 'Alex is just in the kitchen.'

'Hi.' Stella smiled back, struck by just how much Zara looked like her brother, something that had completely escaped her attention the first time she'd set eyes on her at the Jolly. 'Hi, Fred.' She stooped to ruffle the Labrador's ears.

'Peace offering.' Stella headed towards Alex, waving the bottle of wine at him. She'd selected it from her rack; it was one she'd picked up at an exclusive wine shop to save for a special occasion.

'I'm shocked that you think I could be won over by a bottle of wine,' he said, adopting a faux offended tone as he took bottle from her. Glancing at the label, his eyebrows lifted. 'Actually, scrap that, this is a goodie. Apology well and truly accepted.' He gave a wide smile, his eyes crinkling appealingly at the corners.

'Phew!' Stella mimed wiping sweat from her brow. 'That's a relief.'

'Right, I'm going to take myself off for a soak in the bath, give you two a chance to talk,' said Zara.

'Okay, sis, enjoy.'

'I will, I've got this.' She held up a crumpled-looking paperback and smiled. 'I could be gone some time.'

Stella caught a glimpse of the cover. 'Ooh, yes, there's quite a buzz about that book. I've been meaning to read it myself.'

'I'll pass it on to you when I'm done.'

'Thanks, Zara.' Stella beamed at her, taken by her friendliness.

They watched Zara head in the direction of the bathroom. 'Coffee?' Alex asked.

'Sounds good.' Stella nodded, a thrill rushing through her at being in his company again.

Conversation was light-hearted while Alex attended to the coffee making. Stella learnt he'd been to visit his parents over the last few days, as had Zara. She'd been relieved to hear he'd been looking in the estate agent's window on behalf of his sister who was keen to get away from city living and relocate to Micklewick Bay. It was the reason she was staying with her brother, while she attended interviews at nearby hospitals.

With the small talk over and done with, Alex slipped into the seat opposite Stella at the island. She lifted her gaze from her cup, her eyes meeting his, a frisson of attraction sparking between them. It didn't make what she was about to say any easier. She swallowed, carefully marshalling her words.

'I want you to know how desperately sorry I am for accusing you of stealing my underwear. It's a terrible thing to do and I should have listened to you when you tried to explain, instead of storming on, bulldozing your words.' She paused, inhaling deeply, conscious of Alex's eyes on her. 'I'm ashamed to say I let the barrister in me override the real me – something I always said I'd never do – and it was unforgivable. It's actually been a real wake-up call; the last thing I want is to make a habit of it. I really am very sorry. And I hope with all my heart you can forgive me.' She was reluctant to explain how fear of the strength of her feelings for him had more than likely contributed to her explosive reaction. She didn't want him to think she was high maintenance, but the depth of her feelings for him, and the fact that they'd appeared so suddenly, had taken some getting used to.

Alex sat quietly for a moment. He steepled his fingers, resting his chin on the tips, his eyes searching her face.

Stella held her breath, it seemed like an age before he spoke.

'From what you've just said, I don't think I need to tell you how shocked – and hurt – I was that you'd think I was the sort of man who goes around stealing women's underwear for some kind of sick gratification.'

Stella winced. *Take it on the chin, girl.*

'But what I also found difficult was the fact, like you mentioned yourself, that you didn't give me the opportunity to explain. Instead, you just raised your voice and spoke over the top of me, then stormed out. It was hardly a fair battle, but you already know that.'

She nodded, remorse gnawing at her insides. 'I do. I'd give anything to turn the clock back.'

'I can honestly say, hand on heart,' he pressed his hand to his chest, 'that I have no idea how the underwear got in here. The first I knew of it was when Fred was running around with a pair of lacy knickers in his mouth.'

A bubble of laughter rose up inside Stella as she recalled the image of Fred with a pair of her knickers on his head. 'I know how they got here.'

'You do?'

'I do.' Stella nodded, recounting what Brooke had told her. 'So Fred's the phantom knicker-nicker.'

Alex's eyes went to the Labrador who was stretched out on the rug in front of the fire, snoring contentedly. 'The little ratbag!' He shook his head in disbelief. 'All that trouble he caused me, almost ruining my reputation. There'll be no treats for him for a week.'

At the mention of the word "treat" Fred scrambled to his feet and ran across the room. Parking himself beside Alex, he looked up hopefully, his tail swishing across the floor.'

Stella couldn't help but giggle. 'How can you resist that face?'

'Very easily after hearing that.' The affectionate look in Alex's eyes belied his serious tone.

When Fred had returned to his place in front of the fire – only after being given a treat! – Stella said, 'So, can you forgive me? Do you think we can start again, without my barrister sass?'

Alex looked directly at her, his expression turning serious. 'Of course I can forgive you, but...' He paused, inhaling deeply.

There's a but? Stella's stomach started churning, dreading what he was about to say.

'I really like you, Stella, more than like you.' He rubbed his fingertips over his brow. 'I've never been drawn to a woman in the same way I'm drawn to you, never had such strong feelings.'

'But?' she said, bracing herself for disappointment.

'The way you reacted to the underwear situation isn't the first time you've gone flouncy and huffy on me. When you mistook Zara for my girlfriend that night at the Jolly is another example. I could have got you completely wrong here, but the impression I have of you is that you seem to jump to conclusions without hearing an explanation, or waiting to find out if you've got it right.' He gave her an apologetic look. 'Much as I have these strong feelings for you, I'm not sure that's something I can live with, I'd find it too unsettling, wondering what was going to happen next.' He picked up his mug of coffee and took a sip. From the expression on his face, he wasn't finding this easy.

Stella sat quietly for a moment, processing his words, her whole body aching. She'd blown it.

FORTY

Compelled by the urge to fight for their relationship, Stella took a fortifying breath; she wasn't prepared to let it slip through her fingers. 'I totally understand why you feel that way, and much as I don't like the version of me you've just described, I get why you wouldn't want to take things further. But I can honestly say, that was totally out of character. Yes, I can be sassy, straight-talking and maybe even a bit blunt at times – well, maybe a lot blunt – but I'm not the person you've just described. I value the people in my life, and respect their feelings one-hundred per cent. All I can say in my defence is that I'd had a rotten week dealing with a slippery defendant and an even more slippery opponent. Plus, for some unfathomable reason, I'd got suddenly preoccupied with finding my father.' Stella didn't like to add how concern about her mum's recent health scare had been preying on her mind. She dipped her chin, looking him in the eye. 'If you have any doubts about my personality, just ask my friends; they wouldn't give me the time of day if I behaved like that as the norm. I'd have had my backside kicked right out of that friendship group, and deservedly so.'

'Yeah, I get the feeling you're right there,' he said with a chuckle.

'So does this mean we get a second chance?' She was struggling to rein in the hope that was rising like a tidal wave in her chest, her heart hammering.

Before she knew what was happening, Alex reached across, put his hand at the back of her neck and pulled her to him. In the next moment, his lips were on hers, warm and tender. Stella released a groan, her whole body suddenly on fire.

'Oops! Sorry.'

They finally pulled apart to see Zara dressed in a fleecy onesie, a towel wrapped around her head, the floral scent of her bubble bath infusing the air.

'Hey, no worries.' Stella felt the warmth of a blush creep over her face.

'Anyone ever tell you your timing's pants, sis?'

'Heaps of times.' Zara grinned at him. 'And for what it's worth, I'm chuffed to bits you two are back on track, you look kinda cute together.'

'That's just as well,' Alex said.

'Oh really?' Stella gave him a flirtatious smile.

'Don't suppose you fancy staying for dinner?' His eyes twinkled at her.

'I'd love to.' She beamed at him, her heart soaring with happiness.

'Steak, chunky chips and salad do you?'

'Mmm. Perfect.'

'You won't be disappointed, Alex is an amazing cook,' said Zara. 'His peppercorn sauce is awesome.' She padded over to them, her battered novel in her hand.

'Ooh, I can't wait to try it.' A thrill zinged its way through Stella's body, it felt good to be back on track with Alex. Though the spectre of her father's ill-fated visit lurked at the back of her mind, she was determined he wasn't going to spoil her evening with him – and Zara; she'd address that tomorrow. But for now, Johan de Groote had taken up more than enough of her thoughts for one day.

She glanced across at Alex, the smile he flashed melting her heart and sending butterflies dancing wildly in her stomach. She was determined not to allow any doubts to sneak in and spoil her enjoyment of this delicious feeling.

Her mum and Rhys popped into her mind. It hadn't gone unnoticed by Stella how attentive and considerate Rhys had been with her mum earlier that day. How his quiet reassurance had soothed and comforted her. Indisputable love had shone in her mum's eyes when she'd looked at him – it had been returned in equal measure by Rhys – and it had been heartwarming to see. They were a good fit, complemented one another – she hoped Rhys's children could see it too. Her mum had finally found love and was happy and content in a way Stella had never seen her before; she, more than anyone, deserved it. And if that was what being in love did for you, then Stella was happy to welcome it in with both hands.

* * *

'I wish you could've seen it,' Stella said, giggle-snorting. 'It was hilarious. Your brother's face was a picture.'

'Stop! I'm in serious danger of wetting myself if you make me laugh any harder.' Zara was bent double, she'd been howling with laughter as Stella had described how she'd flung her knickers at Alex and they'd landed on his head. Stella knew how to tell a good story, her comic timing honed to perfection.

'I'm glad you find it entertaining, sis.' Alex shook his head, the corners of his mouth twitching with a smile. 'It's poor Fred I feel sorry for, he sat there for ages with a pair of silky knickers hooked over his lugs, wondering what the heck was going on.' Alex couldn't help but chuckle at that.

'I'm just relieved you two have sorted yourselves out.' Zara was sitting on the sofa next to Stella, Alex in the seat opposite. 'Honest, Stells, he was as miserable as a wet weekend when he landed at our parents' place. Nothing would cheer him up.' She tucked her feet underneath her, eyeing her brother intently.

'I don't think I was that bad.'

'Oh, trust me, you were.'

The day after Stella had confronted Alex about her missing underwear, he'd hot-footed it to their parents' house, keen to lie low and lick his wounds. Whilst he was there, he'd poured his heart out to his sister, telling her how he felt about Stella and how devastated he'd been by her accusation and the fact that she'd refused to listen. He'd struggled to comprehend how she could see the funny side of it, put out that she'd sat and giggled.

'Honestly, Al, you'll be telling everyone about it at your silver wedding celebrations, making everyone laugh their socks off.'

'What? Even if I'm married to someone else?' he'd said, his face straight.

Zara had pulled a face at him. 'You'll see.'

Zara leant into Stella. 'Did I ever tell you about the time Al was, very briefly, in a boy band?'

'Ooh, no, do tell.' Grinning, Stella rubbed her hands together.

Alex clamped his hand to his forehead and released a loud groan. 'Zar, please!'

Stella and Zara looked at one another and fell into a fit of the giggles. 'You've *got* to tell me now,' said Stella.

'I so do. They'd called themselves "Studs" and Al here was on lead guitar – even though he couldn't play a note and is completely tone deaf.' Zara could barely get her words out for laughing.

'Studs?' Stella threw her head back, snorting with laughter. 'I love it!'

'This is so unfair, you two are ganging up on me.' Alex shook his head, unable to stop himself from laughing. 'We were fifteen at the time,' he said by way of explanation.

'Hah! That's no excuse! Got any photos, Zar?' asked Stella.

'I've got some at my place, I'll bring them up, show you them next time I'm here. I think you'll be very impressed by Al's floppy boy-band fringe and curling top lip.'

'Get knotted, Zar,' Alex said good-naturedly, making the two women laugh even harder.

* * *

The three of them chatted and laughed for the next few hours. Reluctantly, Stella realised it was probably time to head back to her apartment; she still had some prep she needed to attend to for tomorrow's trial and didn't want to be burning the midnight oil. Plus, after the earlier events of the day, tiredness had suddenly crept up on her.

'If you're still here on Friday, you're very welcome to join me and my pals down at the Jolly,' she said to Zara as she unfurled her long legs from beneath her on the sofa.

'Thanks.' Zara beamed at her. 'I might just do that, if Al can put up with me for that long.'

'After tonight, I'd say that's looking doubtful,' he said, his expression deadpan, making Stella and Zara giggle.

'We can walk down to the pub together,' Stella said. 'It's always a good night, we put the world to rights over fish and chips and a couple of bottles of wine.'

'In that case, you can definitely count me in,' said Zara, 'as long as your friends won't mind.'

'Oh, they won't mind; you'll fit right in.' Stella gave a warm smile. 'Right then, it's been fab getting to know you, but I'd really better go. I'll see you later.'

'Yeah, it's been fab getting to know you too.' Zara beamed.

'I'm wondering whether I should be worried about you two getting on so well, I've got a feeling I'm going to be outnumbered,' Alex said, clearly not worried about it at all, instead he seemed happy his sister and Stella had clicked.

'I reckon you should. What do you think, Stells?'

'I think he definitely should.' Stella adopted a faux serious expression before giving a playful lift of her eyebrows.

Alex walked her to the door, sliding his arms around her waist and pulling her close. 'I've enjoyed this afternoon with you, been good to have got things sorted out between us.'

'It has, I've enjoyed it too.' Smiling, Stella looped her arms around his neck, savouring the solid feel of him pressed against her.

He pulled her closer, his lips finding hers, the gentle graze of his stubble brushing over her skin. She closed her eyes and with a sigh, melted into him.

FORTY-ONE

It wasn't until Tuesday evening on her return from work that Stella noticed the hand carved stone bowl had gone from the coffee table, the empty space it had once occupied glaring back at her. She'd stopped in her tracks, her gaze sweeping the room. Her first thought had been that Andrea had moved it when she'd been cleaning that morning – owing to the Bank Holiday, Stella's cleaning day had been pushed back to Tuesday. It was only when she'd been unable to find any trace of the bowl – or broken bits of it in the bin, if that had been its fate – that it suddenly hit her, her mind rushing back to the confrontation with Johan de Groote the previous day, the flash of a dark stone-like object that had caught her eye as he'd rummaged through his holdall. It had been her bowl! The memory of him declaring it to be expensive followed next. 'The cheek!' She planted her hands onto her hips. He must have pilfered it when she'd gone to get his coat from the hallway, but how the heck had she not noticed? It's not as if it was a tiny thing. Then again, she recalled the shirt he'd been wearing had been loose-fitting and roomy, if he was skilled at stealing things, it would have been no problem for him to smuggle it out.

In the conversation she'd had with her mum when she'd called in on her way back from chambers, Stella had learnt that not only had the purse been emptied of cash, but the bank had been in touch the previous day. Before Alice had had the opportunity of cancelling her bank cards, a rash of unusual activity had been detected, prompting the bank to contact her. One of her cards had been swallowed at the local ATM as a result of numerous incorrect attempts at guessing the PIN. The others, including the ones relating to her business, had all been frozen. And now her mother was having to contend with the hassle of them being cancelled and having to await replacements.

Stella's already low opinion of her father plummeted lower still.

'At least he's gone, lovey,' her mum had said pragmatically. 'He could've caused a load more grief if what Pim told you is anything to go by.'

Stella hadn't been able to argue with that.

She'd spoken to Pim on the phone before she'd left chambers for Micklewick Bay, taking advantage of the quiet hours before The Cellar opened. He'd gone on to elaborate about the details of the text he'd sent the previous day. It turned out that Johan had stolen some jewellery from his mother. It had belonged to her grandmother and been passed down to her on her own mother's death, so the pieces weren't just valuable, they had enormous sentimental value too. 'He must've been snooping in her room to have found them,' Pim had said. 'My mother's devastated but she's told the police so I expect they'll be waiting for him when he lands back in The Netherlands.'

He'd also told her that his mother had been contacted by another woman, asking if she knew of Johan de Groote's whereabouts. Apparently, he'd disappeared with her purse and small painting that was worth a considerable amount.

'It would seem he has quite a lot of women chasing him,' Pim had said.

'But for all the wrong reasons,' Stella had added.

Ending the call, she'd sat in quiet contemplation, the letter she'd found in the back of the photo in her mother's bedroom finding its way into her mind. It served no purpose now, and in retrospect, Stella could see how difficult it must have been for her mother to write it. Hiding it away in the back of a photograph was less easy to get her head around; her mum clearly hadn't wanted it to be found just yet. In fact, Stella hadn't worked out quite when her mum had wanted her to find it.

Tears crowded her eyes as she recalled the words.

14th December 2018

My darling Stella,

I want to start by telling you I love you more than anything in this world and whatever I've done, I've always had your best interests at heart, and have always wanted to protect you from any unnecessary hurt.

I know you've always struggled to understand why I've never spoken of your father, or given you any details of him, but my reason was because I lived in fear of him hurting you the way he hurt me when he walked away that day and never returned. I never wanted you to experience that awful pain and I hope you can find it in your heart to forgive me.

As you grew older, I battled with myself, wondering if I should tell you his name so you could find him, but the thought of the disruption I know him to be capable of continued to prevent me from doing so.

But now is the time for me to share the information you've been so desperate to have. You can decide for yourself if you want to

act on it, all I ask is that you tread carefully and be the wise and sensible young woman I know you to be. If you have any doubts, however small, don't ignore them.
Your father's name is Johan de Groote and he was from a place called Harderwijk in Holland. I'm afraid that's all I know of him but if you're keen to find him, I'm sure the internet will lead you to him.
Be happy my beautiful girl. You've filled my world with joy and more happiness than I ever thought possible.

Mum xxxx

There was no need for the note now, and there was definitely no need for Stella to bring it to her mum's attention. In fact, much as she'd prefer to confess about snooping around her bedroom, Stella thought doing so would risk reopening the rift that had gaped when she'd last enquired about her father. It wasn't worth that; she'd just have to suffer it on her conscience as best she could.

If one good thing came out of the whole sorry situation, it was the realisation that her mum had been proved right about her father.

FORTY-TWO

The first Saturday in September arrived in a blast of joyous sunshine. Stella glanced over at Alex through the shade of her designer sunglasses. He briefly took his eyes away from the narrow, twisting-turning lanes of the moors he was negotiating and shared a smile with her. Stella felt her heart melt a little bit more.

'Not much further now,' he said, tucking into a pull-in place, allowing a tractor to pass. The farmer waved in acknowledgement as he went by. 'I'm just so relieved the weather improved so we could do this, I know you're going to love it.'

Happiness bloomed in her chest as she looked out at the stunning view before her. Undulating moorland stretched out for miles, still swathed in the remnants of its summer finery of purple, though now a little faded. The heather offered a vibrant contrast to the verdant patchwork of green fields, divided up by ancient dry-stone walls, that lined the swooping valleys where cosy farmsteads nestled. The plaintive bleating of the free-roaming sheep wafted in through the car's open window as they drove along.

Slowing at a junction, Alex took the right turn, which Stella noted from the old black and white road sign led to Great Stangdale. It was a road she'd travelled many times before on her way to the beautician's at Danskelfe, but she still couldn't imagine where Alex was taking her. He'd given her no clues, simply telling her to wear practical clothing and flat shoes. She'd been intrigued.

Fred gazed out of the side window in the back, his ears pricked in interest, his seat belt keeping him from jumping about excitedly.

After following a road that had a worryingly vertiginous drop down to a river, Alex took them along a bumpy track before coming to a halt. 'Here we are,' he said, pulling the handbrake on. Stella climbed out of the car and headed over to a wooden seat, a gentle breeze lifting her hair, the sun warm on her face. She couldn't help but gasp as her gaze roamed over the magnificent panorama. She turned to Alex as he let Fred out, and threw him a smile. 'It's stunning! I've never seen the dale from this view point before.'

'Thought you'd like it.' He ambled his way over to her, an easy smile on his face, Fred sniffing the ground around them, his tail swishing happily.

To the right the battle-scarred walls of Danskelfe Castle were visible through the trees, its flag fluttering idly atop the highest tower. The precipitous rigg of Great Stangdale swept right around as if protecting the villages and hamlets that nestled within its vast embrace.

The cackle of a pheasant caught her attention as it skimmed over the gorse bushes, resplendent in their vivid yellow blooms, its cries scattering a handful of rabbits, their white tails bobbing as they scampered away. Fred stopped in his tracks, striking a pose, one paw raised from the ground, making Stella and Alex laugh.

'I hope you're hungry,' said Alex, throwing his arm around her.

'I'm starving,' she said, wondering where he'd planned for them to eat.

'That's what I like to hear.' He pressed a kiss to her cheek and headed back to the car where he flung the boot open. She watched as he shook out a rug, laying it on the flattest area of ground. That done, he hefted a huge wicker picnic hamper and set it on the rug, Fred looking on with interest.

'Is there anything I can do?' Stella asked heading towards him, her hands in the back pockets of her jeans.

'You can help set this lot out, if you like, but keep an eye on Fred or he'll have everything devoured before we get a taste of anything.' He nodded to the hamper that was brimming with an array of foodie treats. 'I've brought him some of his own food.'

'Oh, wow! This looks like a pretty special picnic,' she said, kneeling down and taking the lobster rolls he handed her.

'Much as I'd like to take credit for it, I ordered the food from the deli back home.' He set two plates out, topping them with linen napkins and a mix of cutlery.

'Well it looks fantastic. I can't wait to tuck in; I'm starving,' she said, her mouth watering as she spotted the bowl of spiced chicken salad garnished with vibrant coriander leaves. 'And it's so kind of you to organise it.'

'Hey, we had to mark your good news somehow.'

* * *

Alex, with whom Stella had eventually shared her concerns about being followed, and told him of the threatening note she'd received, had suggested the picnic by way of celebrating the fact that the police had discovered the identity of Stella's stalker. DC Stephens had called her and confirmed that it was Vaughan Elliott who had been captured on CCTV entering her apartment building and posting the note in her pigeonhole. The car the barrister had been driving to follow and intimidate her had been traced and was found to have been borrowed from his brother – he didn't want to run the risk of anyone recognising his BMW.

'I can't tell you what a relief it is to know I can walk back from the Jolly without the feeling that I'm being followed,' Stella had said when she'd shared the news with Alex. 'I was starting to get paranoid every time I heard footsteps behind me.'

'I'm not surprised. It must've been horrible for you,' he'd said, wrapping his arms around her protectively. 'Though I have to admit, I'm struggling to get my head around the fact that it was a barrister who was behind it all.'

'Hmph. I'm not, Vaughan Elliott has always had dubious morals, always thought he could worm his way out of any dodgy situation. Only this time his mis-placed confidence made him sloppy: showing up at the apartment building and not stopping to think there might be cameras about.' She'd shaken her head and given a laugh of disbelief.

'So what'll happen to him now? He's broken the law, surely that means he can no longer practice as a barrister.'

'He's been suspended. Not only that, he's been kicked out of his chambers and he's been reported to the Bar Council, who'll wait for the report from the police until they decide what course of action to take with him, but I'd be amazed if he wasn't disbarred. He'll be prosecuted for it too.'

Alex had given a low whistle. 'And all because he took exception to something you'd said.'

'Hard to believe, but true.'

'Well, you need to put him behind you now and focus on the future.' He'd bent his head to kiss her. 'A future involving you and me.'

A nearby whimper, accompanied by a dull thudding sound, had made them both turn to see Fred looking up at them expectantly, his tail wagging hard against the floor.

'Don't worry, fella, the future includes you too,' Alex had

said with a chuckle as the Labrador trotted over, pushing himself between them.

'Of course it does! It wouldn't be the same without you, Fred,' Stella had said, smiling down at him.

* * *

With the remains of the picnic cleared away and placed in the boot of the car, out of the glare of the sun, Stella rested back on her elbows, stretching her legs out on the rug, Alex beside her. Fred sat in the cool of the shadow cast by the car. The heat of the sun was tempered by the light breeze that was brushing over the heather and wafting the faint scent of honey their way. She soon found herself getting lost in her thoughts, the cries of a buzzard circling overhead barely registering.

She couldn't deny, the last few weeks had been challenging, from the hassle she'd had with the Dixon trial to finally getting to meet her father and everything that had entailed. Though the experience had been less than pleasant, her curiosity about him had at least been satisfied. Her only regret was that he'd managed to unsettle her mum. She consoled herself that it had only been for a brief amount of time and it had, bizarrely, appeared to have strengthened her mother's relationship with Rhys. It was something Stella found herself being glad of. The more she got to know him, the more she realised what a thoroughly decent man he was, and how good he was for her mum. Seeing her mum glowing with happiness warmed Stella's heart. Her mother and Rhys were flying out to Tuscany today and were very excited by all accounts. Stella wondered if there'd be some kind of announcement on their return.

Her thoughts segued to her relationship with Alex, how he'd stirred feelings inside her she'd never thought possible to feel. And though she'd fought them at the start, she'd now submitted to them wholeheartedly and allowed her heart to experience love. She couldn't deny it, it was heady, all-consuming stuff.

She stole a look at him, taking in his handsome profile. Butterflies performed their now familiar dance in her stomach. He smiled, the glow of sunlight on his face.

'Perfect day for a picnic,' he said.

'Perfect day full stop.' She sighed contentedly, resting her head on his shoulder, inhaling his comforting aroma.

'It is.' Sitting back, he placed his finger under her chin and tilted her face towards him, drinking in her features before kissing her deeply.

Stella wiggled her toes as a wave of love washed over her.

A LETTER FROM THE AUTHOR

Huge thanks for choosing to pick up *Finding Love in Micklewick Bay*. I hope you were hooked on Stella's journey. If you'd like to join other readers in hearing all about my new releases and bonus content, you can sign up for my newsletter!

www.stormpublishing.co/eliza-j-scott

If you enjoyed this book and could spare a few moments to leave a review that would be hugely appreciated. It doesn't have to be long, just a few words would do, but for us authors it can make all the difference in encouraging a reader to discover our books for the first time. Thank you so much. If you click on the link below it will take you right there.

It's been fun getting to know Stella a little better for her story, *Finding Love in Micklewick Bay,* and getting to understand what makes her tick. I knew it wasn't going to be easy to crack through that tough exterior of hers, but I'm so glad Alex finally achieved what so many had failed to do! It's been nice to get a glimpse of her softer side. Who knew Stella Hutton would entertain the notion of falling in love? Her mum too! I do hope you've enjoyed their journey.

I should point out that I've taken liberties with the description of the lockers in the robing room of York Crown Court. I'm reliably informed that they're not, in fact, of the characterful, old wooden variety but are, instead, modern and made of metal which didn't go with the aesthetic I wanted to create for the room.

Once more, I thoroughly enjoyed researching another book in this series, and having the opportunity to venture back to the beautiful towns and villages that line the North Yorkshire Coast – as I mentioned in the earlier books, my fictional town of Micklewick Bay is actually an amalgamation of these places. Starting with the Victorian seaside town of Saltburn-by-the-Sea, with its grand houses that boast panoramic views of the beach and the sea, not forgetting the magnificent Huntcliff. It's thanks to this lovely town that Micklewick Bay has its pier and funicular, and if any of you are familiar with Saltburn, you've probably guessed Huntcliffe is the inspiration for my Thorncliffe. The quaint little fishing villages of Staithes, Runswick Bay and Robin Hood's Bay are the places I had in mind when writing about Old Micklewick, with their characterful houses that just ooze charm. I've spent many happy hours wandering their cobbled streets, ice cream in hand, keeping a watchful eye for those pesky seagulls! The bustling harbour town of Whitby must also get a mention, not least because of its delicious fish and chips – many portions of which were consumed in the name of research!

If you'd like to find out more about what I get up to in my little corner of North Yorkshire, or if you'd like to get in touch – I always love hearing from my readers!

KEEP IN TOUCH WITH THE AUTHOR

www.elizajscott.com

Bluesky: @elizajscott.bsky.social

facebook.com/elizajscottauthor

x.com/ElizaJScott1

instagram.com/elizajscott

bookbub.com/authors/eliza-j-scott

ACKNOWLEDGEMENTS

So, here we are at the part where I get the opportunity to thank everyone who has helped in the process of bringing this book together for publication. I have to start by saying a great big thank you to my wonderful editor Kate Gilby Smith. Kate's positivity and enthusiasm has continued right from the first book in the series which has been so heartwarming. It has been an utter joy to work with her on the Welcome to Micklewick Bay series, and I've particularly enjoyed our video chats where we've bounced ideas around. Her edits are insightful – and always kind! – and have helped polish Stella's story so it's the best it can be. Thank you, Kate!

I must also say a great big thank you to editorial operations director Alex Holmes who has worked tirelessly and patiently getting this book (and the others in the series) ready for publication. I really am very grateful for all you've done, Alex. I also owe a thank you to editorial assistant Naomi Knox for role in prepping Stella's story. Thank you to Storm's head of digital marketing, Elke Desanghere and publicity manager Anna McKerrow for helping my books on their journey. Thanks also to copy editor Shirley Khan and proofreader Charlotte Fry. Melanie Crawley also deserves a heartfelt thank you for her wonderful narration of *The Little Bookshop by the Sea*, *Summer Days at Clifftop Cottage* and *Finding Love in Micklewick Bay*. Her voice is just perfect for telling the stories of the lasses of Micklewick Bay!

I need to thank my lawyer friend for their advice that was

given so patiently while I was quizzing them about all things legal relating to Stella's story. Any errors are entirely my own.

As ever, I have to say a great big thank you to my lovely author friends Jessica Redland and Sharon Booth who are always so kind and supportive. I look forward to our get togethers over scones and cake enormously! You're both absolute stars!

The uber-organised Rachel Gilbey of Rachel's Random Resources deserves a thank you for organising another of her fabulous blog tours. I'm green with envy of her organisational skills. I don't know how you do it, Rachel! Thank you! Thanks also to the wonderful band of dedicated book bloggers who so generously give up their time to read and write a blog post about my books. I'm hugely grateful to you all.

Next up, I owe a warm thank you to the beautiful places I've named above for providing me with so much inspiration, not forgetting the residents for their friendly welcome.

My final thanks go to you, the reader, for taking the trouble to pick up my book and read it. Thank you so much for being a part of this journey with me, I really am truly humbled and grateful. I hope you'll stay in touch and follow the further adventures of the friends in Micklewick Bay.

Happy reading!

Lots of love,

Eliza xxx

Printed in Great Britain
by Amazon